The Forgotten Life of Connie Harris

THE
FORGOTTEN
LIFE
OF
Connie Harris

CARRYL CHURCH

Choc Lit
A JOFFE BOOKS COMPANY

Choc Lit
A Joffe Books company
www.choc-lit.com

First published in Great Britain in 2024

Cover art by Jarmila Takač

ISBN: 978-1781897997

For Mum and Dad — gone but forever in my heart.

AUTHOR'S NOTE

This novel was inspired by my childhood love of cinema, in particular the films of Humphry Bogart and especially Casablanca. My career as a Film Archivist taught me about nitrate film which features in the story. While I have included real locations and institutions, the entire novel is a work of fiction and has no bearing on those institutions in real life. The only element of fact was the fire at the Tivoli Cinema.

PROLOGUE

The body was sprawled at his feet, as if it were nothing to do with him. He flexed his fingers, studying their tremor with mild curiosity. He'd experienced it before, the adrenaline that accompanies taking a life, but not like this.

He snaked one arm under the curve of her delicate spine, the other under her legs, stumbling against the banister as he lifted.

Outside, the street slumbered beneath an anthracite sky. He loaded his cargo into the van and returned to the house. The half-empty bottle of whisky was waiting on the stairs where he'd abandoned it. The burning liquid slid down his throat — an elixir to numb the guilt.

A dog's bark ricocheted along the huddled terraces as he climbed into the van. He froze. No twitching curtains, no lights. *Nobody cares.*

With the crunch of gears, he pulled onto the road. The whisky bottle rolled across the front seat, then back as he rounded a bend.

Driving north away from Tiverton, houses gave way to vast emptiness, trees and bushes loomed out of the inky night. The road hugged the river, at the mercy of its bewildering contours. With each passing minute his thirst grew until it threatened to roar like the river beside him. The whisky bottle continued its game. Back and forth. Back and forth. Taunting him.

He pressed on, struggling to focus. The beam from his lights contorted like a kaleidoscope, menacing shadows subverted his vision. A deer skittered before his headlights. He swerved — the bottle fell to the floor with a thud.

At a field gate, he pulled in and cut the engine. Searching the floor for the bottle, he lifted it to his parched lips. The world stilled.

Dank air moistened his face as he stepped from the van. Nothing to see but barren moor, not a sound except for the rustle of trees and his own jagged breath.

He dragged his cargo from the back of the vehicle and launched it over the gate, then followed himself. He heaved the body onto his shoulder, as heavy and cumbersome as his kit bag.

The rough terrain disorientated every step. The ground swelled, then fell away without warning. They landed in a ditch, her body beneath his.

With earth-smeared fingers, he smoothed the hair from her brow.

Here in her shallow grave, the tears came.

He staggered away. The van choked to life. The whisky bottle rolled. The road wound on. He opened the window. Salt air whipped his cheeks.

His eyes grew heavy, the lids snapped shut.

He was flying, and then he wasn't.

PART ONE

April 1951

CHAPTER 1

Connie leaned against her locker, re-reading Michael's letter informing her he'd joined the Navy. She could sense her brother's guilt through the thin, crisp paper. He'd abandoned her and now he was putting himself out of reach.

'I can't deal with him, Con,' Michael had said to her at their mother's wake when the few relatives who'd come to pick over the fragments of her life shuffled off home and their father had drunk the house dry. 'I only stayed for Ma, but now she's gone . . .' He didn't look at her while he spoke. Guilt, she supposed, and shame. Connie studied the shine she'd achieved on Michael's scruffy old boots that morning while her eyes swam with tears.

'You need to leave too.' This time he met her gaze with a brief, earnest look. She had turned away then, turned away from those eyes, so like her own. It was easy for him; she didn't have anywhere to go.

Connie folded the letter and slipped it in her jacket pocket. She retrieved her pillbox hat from her locker and fixed it in place with a wince. Her arm smarted from the previous evening when her father twisted it because she'd forgotten to iron his shirt. He

4

was careful to leave no trace of his temper. He'd practised on her mother long enough.

The hat was her favourite part of her uniform. The forest-green material offset her eyes and the red trim complimented her hair. Connie brushed away a piece of lint that settled on one of her epaulettes and straightened her back, admiring the transformation in the mirror. She wasn't Frank Harris's daughter here.

In the foyer, Viv was waiting by the kiosk. Another Tivoli electric goddess in forest green. Her grin at Connie's approach fell away at the sight of the cinema manager, Mr Reynolds. They stood to attention.

He cast an appraising eye over each of his employees. Connie's focus settled on the slick combover which clung to his shiny scalp. He pulled himself up to his full height, the buttons on his waistcoat keening over his stomach. 'You'll do, ladies.'

Viv rolled her eyes as he moved on to his office at the front of the building.

'*You'll do*? The cheek of the man. He wouldn't enjoy it if we made him stand like a prize canary while we inspected his suit.'

Connie threw Viv a smile in solidarity and filled her tray with ice creams from the kiosk. 'He wouldn't earn *you'll do* from me. More like *you don't*.'

'You don't what?'

She spun around to find Charlie Smith looking at her with his ebullient brown eyes.

'I'm off.' Viv nudged her arm. 'Don't get too distracted.' She headed for the auditorium.

Connie's fingers closed around a choc ice, hoping it would cool the heat racing to her cheeks.

'Not sure you can sell that one.' Charlie gestured to the ice cream.

She looked at it, dismayed. He was right: she'd mangled it. Reynolds would have a fit.

5

Charlie fished out a ration coupon from his jacket pocket. She relinquished the choc ice into his long fingers, grateful he'd covered the cost and saved her from Reynolds' wrath.

'Blimey, Con, you've got a strong grip.' He winked and sauntered away with his spoils. She stared after him. His lithe frame disappeared through the side door, up to the projection room.

'Daydreaming, Constance?' Mr Reynolds eyeballed her.

She gathered up the rest of her ice creams and hastened to the double doors. Viv was waiting for her just inside.

'Did Charlie ask you?'

'Not this again,' Connie whispered.

Viv shook her head. 'You two have been sizing each other up for months. If he doesn't ask you out soon, I'll do it for him.'

Connie's lips spread into a smile and for once she was grateful for the gloom of the auditorium.

'We're up.' Viv ventured down the aisle, carrying her tray loaded with cigarettes.

Connie followed her to the front of the screen, self-conscious under the gaze of the projection light, knowing Charlie was the one in control of its beam.

She stood her ground as customers divested them of the contents of their trays. With the last item sold, Viv returned to the foyer to restock the kiosk. Connie ushered stragglers to their seats and turned her attention to the film. The feature was *The Daughter of Rosie O'Grady*, a musical in technicolour with, as far as Connie was concerned, too many gushing women.

As the whispers and coughs from the audience slowly ebbed away, she leaned against the wall, slipped her left foot free of her court shoe and rubbed her aching heel. Mr Reynolds chose that moment to poke his head through the door. A frown touched his face. Connie slid into her shoe and straightened.

Bored by a film she'd seen six times already, she allowed herself to drift back to her conversation with Viv. It was true, she and Charlie had been skirting around an inexplicable something for months. Charlie made a point of smiling at her whenever he walked past, seeking her out to share a joke. These small attentions he paid her, when she gathered them up, formed a whole big thing in her head. If Viv noticed too, what was holding him back?

A shriek from the depths of the auditorium snatched her attention. A wave of disgruntled shushing followed. It was always the same, some couple getting carried away in the back row, causing insult to their neighbours. Connie made her way up the steps, flashing her torch over the seating until the offenders shrank from the bright light. She stayed there for the rest of the film, a puritanical presence, and tried not to think about Charlie or her aching arm.

Two hours later, a sigh escaped her lips as the credits rolled. Connie took up her position at the door to wave the clientele through.

As the lights came up and the last straggler walked out into the remains of a sunny afternoon, she set about picking up discarded ice cream wrappers and sweeping up dropped cigarette ends trodden into the floor, ready for the evening's screening.

There was something disconcerting about the silence of an auditorium abruptly abandoned by the hundreds of bodies that only moments before had been transfixed by what played out on screen. The curtains hung thick and heavy across the stage. Dust motes gathered in the shafts of overhead lighting as if acclimatising to the now empty space. A haze of cigarette smoke clung to the stale air. But it was hers for a few precious moments and she found it pleasingly tranquil.

Connie glanced at the projection room window.

As if she'd conjured him, Charlie ambled in. She straightened, matching his height in her heels as he drew up in front of her. His face was textured with stubble and his eyes sparked with animation beneath his dark lashes. But it was his smile which always caught her attention. Charlie's dimples could stop traffic. His cheek muscles were working up to that smile right now.

He stooped to pick up an escaped ice cream wrapper.

'Thanks.' She took the wrapper, and his fingers grazed hers. 'How was the choc ice?'

'Perfect, despite its imperfections.' That smile again.

Connie laughed. 'That's a contradiction if ever I heard one.'

His smile faltered. 'Listen, I was thinking . . .'

The door to the auditorium opened with a clunk. 'Charlie, a brief word, if I may?' Reynolds crooked his finger. Charlie's shoulders slumped. He threw her a nod and walked back up the aisle.

Connie returned to her cleaning, more self-conscious than ever as the two men conversed in low tones. Sensing she wasn't about to find out what Charlie was *thinking* anytime soon, she let herself out of the back of the auditorium and dumped her rubbish in the bins behind the building. A stray black cat coiled himself between her legs. When she returned inside, Charlie was alone waiting for her.

'You've made a friend.' He gestured to the cat, crouching to stroke his matted fur.

'So have you.'

'Me and Tommy go way back, don't we, Tom?' The cat yawned, settling himself at Charlie's feet and fixing them with an expectant gaze. 'Sorry about Reynolds interrupting.'

'Serves you right for venturing outside your projection room.'

Viv walked in to collect their trays. Charlie sucked in a breath.

'Don't mind me.' She tipped Connie a wink and sauntered past. 'Spit it out, Charlie Smith, Connie hasn't got all day.'

Connie shot Viv a murderous look and returned her attention to Charlie, whose face matched the red kick pleat on her skirt.

'I envy you,' she said, trying to ease things along. 'Hiding away up there in your projection room, watching the films free from the huddled masses.'

His face lit up. 'Would you like to see it? The projection room, I mean. I could show you how it all works and . . .' He trailed off and coloured again. 'Not like that, I mean. I'm not trying to lure you into my den of iniquity, although . . .' That infernal dimpled smile spread once more.

She laughed. 'I'd love to.'

* * *

In the foyer, Connie checked for Viv and Reynolds, wishing to further incur neither her friend's teasing nor Reynolds' displeasure. This job was her lifeline, the thing that got her through each day with a smile on her face. Charlie held open the door to the projection room. 'Mind the stairs, they're steep.'

The wooden steps amounted to little more than a ladder. The door swung shut behind her, leaving them trapped in close proximity. 'I'm not going up first. If I fall, I might land on your head.'

Charlie chuckled. 'Fair enough.' He mounted the stairs, offering Connie his hand at the top. His fingers were warm as they enveloped hers. 'It's a bit cramped up here.' He shrugged in apology and squeezed past. She caught a hint of soap mixed with nicotine. They all smelled of cigarettes — the auditorium was like a giant ash tray.

'It's cosy.' She took in every detail of the room, which was dominated by two giant projectors standing side by side like a pair of canons.

'Gaumont-Kalee 21.' Charlie gave the nearest projector a pat, a hint of pride in his voice.

Her gaze drifted past the leather armchair, which sat next to the hatch-like window, to a small alcove containing a workbench with two large plates.

'What's this for?' Her fingers glided over the worn wooden top.

'Rewinding the film.'

9

A shelf above housed all sorts of equipment.

'This is a splicer for joining the films together.' Charlie offered her a metal contraption. 'And this—' he held up a glass bottle — 'is film cement. It sticks one reel of film to another.'

Connie studied the items, fascinated by the complexity of running film when downstairs in the auditorium it all appeared smooth and effortless.

A film poster next to the winding bench caught her eye.

'*Casablanca*.' Charlie's breath alighted on her neck as he stood behind her.

She glanced at him over her shoulder. 'One of my favourite films.'

'What do you like about it?'

'I don't have a crush on Bogart, if that's what you're thinking.'

Charlie grinned, dimples in full effect. 'I wouldn't suggest you were that shallow.'

Connie laughed. 'Oh, I can be.' Regarding the poster, she felt the weight of her need to show him film really mattered to her, she wasn't one of those girls taken in by the perceived glamour. 'Bogart has presence. I like the way the characters interact. They're all trying to survive in a complex world. I like how Rick outwits them but shows his vulnerability too, and I like the ending. He might lose the girl, but he gains a friend. Life doesn't always come wrapped in a bow.'

'You're a pragmatist.'

Connie shrugged. 'I'm not sure there's any other way to be.' She moved to the chair, overwhelmed by his closeness. Charlie cleared off the spools and gestured for her to sit. She sank into the leather, crossing her legs. 'What's your favourite film?'

'That's a tough one.' He rubbed his chin. She could tell he wanted to impress her too. They were working each other out, peeling away their layers. 'I'll tell you on Wednesday,' he said with a sheepish grin.

'Why Wednesday?'

'It's my night off. I checked the rota, seems you're off then too.'

'Interesting.' The anticipation was unbearable.

'I thought so.' He studied his shoes. She'd never seen Charlie Smith so tongue-tied. Eventually his eyes met hers and she was struck by their vulnerability. 'I could tell you over dinner?'

'Love to.' Connie glanced at the clock above the projection window to avert attention from her demented smile. Time had got away from them. 'I'd better get back. I haven't filled up for the evening yet.'

'I'll see you out.' He backed into the projector. It appeared Charlie was experiencing the same state of nerves she was.

At the top of the stairs, Connie pulled her torch from her pocket, although the glow in her cheeks could light the way. 'Thanks for the tour.'

With a last glance at his dimpled smile, she navigated the stairs, and then she was through the door, thrust back into the hubbub of the evening customers and Viv's quizzical eyes. Connie took a breath before joining her friend at the kiosk, attempting to keep her face serene.

She had a date with Charlie Smith, and no one was going to ruin it for her. Not Viv, not Reynolds and especially not her dad.

11

CHAPTER 2

Connie applied a slick of crimson lipstick, her stomach fizzing with excitement for the evening ahead. Her day off had dragged like a child's feet on the way to school as she'd gone about her chores. Even a walk into town to gaze at the shops failed to encourage time to quicken its pace. But all of a sudden it was 5 p.m. and she was rushing to wash, put on clean undergarments and transform herself into a woman Charlie would find hard to resist.

She sat on the bed and slid on her best stockings, the fine silk unruly between her fingers, then reached for her dress, pressed and hanging on the front of the wardrobe. The crepe de chine was cool against her skin. Fixing the belt, she slipped on her shoes and made for the door.

At the top of the stairs, her stomach rearranged itself into a knot as the back door slammed with such force the house shook. Her father was home from his shift at the Heathcoat factory or the White Ball pub, depending on how he'd chosen to spend the day.

Connie scolded herself for lingering over her make-up and tiptoed downstairs, grasping a slither of hope she could slip out unseen. The knot tightened as he appeared in the entrance hall.

Her father considered her through red-rimmed eyes, running a meaty hand over what was left of his ginger hair. 'Where are you going in that get-up?'

'I'm meeting some of the girls from work.' Attempting to keep her tone neutral, she pulled back her shoulders and descended the final steps.

He caught her arm at the bottom. 'My daughter doesn't dress like a cheap tart.'

'It's a dress and some lipstick, Dad.'

His grip tightened. Connie cursed her inability to placate him.

'Don't sass me, young lady.' His stale breath told her he'd been in the pub.

Holding her ground, Connie waited, hoping if she kept quiet, he'd relinquish his grip.

He brought his face closer to hers, his eyes glittering with ice. 'Where's a man to get his dinner?'

'There's a pie in the pantry.'

Distracted by feeding his belly, Frank released her, his broad back disappearing into the kitchen.

Connie snatched her mac from the peg by the door and left.

Her heels clipped away from the oppressive house in the shadow of the Heathcoat factory. It wasn't until she reached the bridge over the River Exe and the relative safety of the town centre beckoned that her breath ceased its stagger. She slowed her pace, her shoulders relaxed. A few more steps then the fear of retribution abated and the flutter of excitement returned for the evening ahead.

As Connie made her way along Fore Street, her eye was drawn to the neon sign for the Tivoli. Charlie was standing under it, smoking. He dropped his cigarette and straightened his tie. He'd put on a suit and his curly black hair had been Brylcreemed into submission.

'Evening, Con. That's quite a dress you're wearing.'

Connie laughed. 'Is that your idea of a compliment?'

'Doesn't it measure up?'

'We'll see.'

Charlie grinned, taking her arm, where only minutes before her father gripped her. What a different sensation his touch elicited from the same piece of anatomy.

The evening was mild, the sun slow to make its descent, casting shadows of the buildings in the soft light. Connie raised an eyebrow when they stopped outside the Palmerston Hotel. An establishment far smarter than she'd ever set foot in. She regretted her mac, especially since the weather showed no hint of rain. Her nerves returned. Charlie opened the restaurant door and gestured for her to go inside.

The décor was like a warm hug, from the dark oak panelling which ran around the perimeter to the deep red of the seating and the crisp white tablecloths. A waiter directed them to a window table, where candlelight flickered in anticipation of nightfall.

Taking the seat he'd solicitously pulled out for her, Connie studied Charlie from across the table.

'Is this all right?' Charlie asked. His eyes betrayed a hint of anxiety.

'It's lovely.'

His features relaxed, a twinkle returning to his gaze. 'You really do look . . .' The waiter appeared with menus, snatching the moment.

'You were saying?' Connie asked when he'd left them to make their choices.

Charlie coloured. 'I was saying you look lovely.'

'You don't scrub up so bad yourself.' She studied the menu to hide her embarrassment, attempting to decipher the names of the dishes into something she could recognise. She wasn't used to dining out. Apart from the occasional Sunday roast at the local pub when her mum was alive, she'd never been to a restaurant. Connie glanced at Charlie, who was frowning at the menu too, a flicker of uncertainty returning to his eyes. She wondered if he wasn't used to restaurants either, if she'd been taken in by his confidence.

When the waiter returned, warmth flushed Charlie's face. 'Could we have a few more minutes, please?' With a curt nod, the waiter moved on to his more discerning customers.

Connie took a sip of table water and surveyed the restaurant for a second time, now noticing the older clientele, the staid elegance, the empty tables, the air of snobbery. She realised how she and Charlie appeared to the rest of the room — a couple of kids playing at being sophisticated grown-ups.

'Charlie.'

He glanced up from his menu, his brow still knitted.

'There's a great chippy up the road. It's a lovely evening . . .'

A smile tugged at his lips and there was relief in his eyes.

Charlie took her hand. Without glancing back, they marched through the restaurant door, collapsing in a fit of giggles as soon as they were safely across the street.

'I'm sorry, Charlie, I couldn't understand a thing on that menu,' Connie said, recovering her composure.

'Me neither.'

'Really? Then why did you take us there?'

He offered a sheepish smile. 'I wanted to impress you.'

'Why?'

'Isn't that obvious?'

Connie's head spun as his arms slipped around her back. 'You're out of my league, Connie Harris.'

His lips came dangerously close to hers. She pulled back. 'Aren't you supposed to wait until the end of the date to kiss me?'

Charlie shrugged. 'We did just leave a restaurant.'

'Cheek.' She pressed her mouth against his, not caring she'd made a bold move.

'Blimey,' he whispered when she pulled away. 'Where's this chip shop?'

* * *

15

With their dinner wrapped in the previous day's headlines and tucked under Charlie's arm, they sauntered along the riverbank littered with towering reeds swaying in the gentle breeze.

They stopped at a bench. Charlie sat beside her, unwrapping their meal. Her eyes grew wide as he handed her the cod and chips she'd ordered. 'I'll never eat all this.'

'I'd like to see you try.'

'Is that a challenge?'

Charlie smirked. 'Do you accept?'

Connie answered by stuffing a chip into his mouth.

As their laughter faded, she sat back, picking at her food. Charlie would win the challenge; her appetite lived in a state of flux too in tune with the acute anxiety over what awaited her at home. She attempted to immerse herself in the tranquil scene before her. Water lilies floated on the surface of the river, graceful swans glided past, ducks skittered into the water leaving whirlpools in their wake. Charlie's warm thigh pressed against hers.

'You don't like the food?' Charlie noticed her untouched supper.

'It's not that.' She shook her head, embarrassed. How could she explain? 'I'm nervous.'

'What have you got to be nervous about?'

She shrugged, finding herself ridiculous.

'If it helps, I've got way more riding on this than you have.'

'How do you figure that?'

'I want a second date. If I can't persuade you to go out with me again, that's the last six months plucking up the courage to ask you down the drain.'

Connie shook her head and smiled. 'You are daft.'

He reached for one of his chips and offered it to her. 'So, what's it to be, Connie Harris? Are you at least going to eat one single chip to give a man a bit of hope?'

Connie leaned forwards, biting the chip from his fingers, and followed with a kiss on his lips.

* * *

'I'd better walk you home,' Charlie whispered. They attempted to disentangle themselves. Connie bit her lip, swollen from spending much of the past two hours kissing Charlie. With reluctance she hauled herself from his lap, the chill night air finding her limbs. Charlie stood too, brushing down his crumpled suit. Gathering up the remnants of their chip supper, he dumped the contents in a bin and took her hand.

Connie hunched into her mac as they made their way along the towpath in the shadow of darkness. Yanked from the warm cocoon of Charlie's kisses, the reality of what she might find when she returned home soon crept back into her mind. But then Charlie slid his arm around her shoulder and the fear retreated. She nestled into him, glad not to think about what might await her for a little while longer.

As they passed a large Victorian house, she paused under one of the trees edging the vast lawns. The air was heavy with the scent of the blossom hanging from above.

'This is my favourite house in Tiverton.'

Charlie regarded her dream home and raised his eyebrow. 'You aim high, Miss Harris.'

'Me and Mum used to love our evening walks. We'd look in at the houses when the curtains were still open and they were lit up inside, wondering at what sort of lives those people were living. This was Mum's favourite too. She used to say nothing bad could ever happen in a house like that.' She dipped her head, fighting the lingering grief for her mum.

When she glanced up, Charlie was studying her intently. 'Used to?'

'She died last year.'

He squeezed her shoulder. 'I'm sorry.'

'Thanks.' Connie felt bad for lowering the mood.

'I'll buy it for you.' He winked, sending her back into a happy state.

'Are you a secret millionaire or do you intend to rob a bank?'

Charlie's expression was grave. 'Don't think I plan on running films at the Tivoli for ever. One day I'm going to own my own cinema and you're going to live in that house.'

Connie grinned — she couldn't help it. 'If you say so, Charlie Smith.'

* * *

Diffused light spilled in at the edges of her curtains. Propping herself on her elbows, Connie's gaze roamed around her bedroom, settling on the dress she'd discarded over the wooden chair next to her dressing table. A smile crept across her lips. She licked them, remembering the heady joys of the previous evening. Charlie was a very good kisser, not that she had a wealth of experience, but he topped the modest list.

She froze at the sound of a chair clattering to the floor in the kitchen below. She'd found her dad passed out there when she'd returned, his bulk slumped like a beached whale across the table. Judging by the opening and slamming of cupboards followed by the jangle of pans, her father was awake, hungry and searching for something to ease his hangover. She rose from the bed and pulled on her dressing gown.

Connie opened her bedroom door, wincing at its creak. The cacophony coming from the kitchen fell into an eerie silence. She hesitated, before stepping onto the landing.

Her father's heavy tread in the hallway caused the familiar knot to form in her stomach.

'Constance!' he hollered, a rasp in his voice.

A liquid sensation travelled through her limbs as she descended the stairs. Her father continued to bellow her name like a raging bull.

Frank stood red-eyed at the bottom in a vest, work trousers and braces, his wiry hair wild with neglect.

'There's nothing for breakfast.' His breath, thick with the previous evening's drink, filled the small space.

Connie tried not to recoil. 'There was bread in the bin when I checked yesterday.'

18

Frank brought his face so close to hers she could see the threads of red veins criss-crossing his cheeks. 'Are you calling me a liar, Constance?'

'Course not, I'll go and check.' Connie darted past him, holding her breath more out of fear than disgust.

Frank followed, making his way through the kitchen to the toilet in the backyard. The hiss of his pee against the porcelain travelled through the door. Lifting the lid on the bread bin, her heart sank. It was empty, not even a crust. A crumb-laden plate on the draining board indicated her father had eaten the last of the bread when he returned from the pub the previous evening.

Connie checked the clock above the stove. If she left now, she might make it to the bakery and back before her shift started.

Frank emerged, scratching his stomach.

'I'll go out for bread.' Connie didn't wait for the thank you that would never come.

Racing upstairs, she pulled on her discarded dress and slid into her work shoes. In the hallway she grabbed her mac, slinging it around her shoulders as she let herself out of the house.

The morning was crisp but sunny, a welcome relief after the stifling confines of her home. Conscious of time, Connie broke into a run, breathless and dismayed as she approached the bakery and saw the orderly queue snaking down the street. She joined at the back, frustrated by the slow progress of her neighbours, who seemed to have all the time in the world.

When she returned with a loaf, her dad was waiting for her in the kitchen, feet propped against the table, sucking on a cigarette. She placed the bread before him and made for the door.

'Where do you think you're going?'

'I have to get ready, Dad. I'll be late for work.'

Connie turned to leave when she was yanked backwards, her hair gripped in Frank's fist, her face forced down to the loaf. The rich aroma of freshly baked bread filled her nose as her scalp seared with pain.

19

'Your work is here.'

He let go with a shove and returned to his seat, folding his arms across his belly. Connie steadied herself against the table before reaching for the breadknife and slicing him a generous doorstep, which she spread with a thin layer of butter. The urge to smash the slice into his face died before it had fully formed. She handed him his breakfast and walked out of the room.

In her bedroom, Connie stripped out of her clothes and hung the dress with care. She filled the basin and ran a flannel over her face, gulping down tears. With tremulous fingers, she reached for her hand mirror so she might examine her hair where he'd grabbed it. How many times had she watched her mother's tearstained face as she carried out the same inspection?

Her stomach rumbled, an incongruous concoction of fear and hunger, but there'd be no breakfast for her. She'd have to run most of the way to have a hope of being on time. Reynolds took tardiness very seriously and she couldn't afford to lose this job.

As she raced into town, Connie allowed herself to indulge the fantasy future Charlie had painted the previous evening. The big house where nothing bad could ever happen.

With the neon Tivoli sign in her sights, she slowed her pace along Fore Street. Her shallow breathing found its depth. By the time Connie joined Viv at the kiosk, she looked the picture of serenity, ready for Mr Reynolds' appraising eye.

CHAPTER 3

'Should we be doing this?' Connie glanced around apprehensively as Charlie unlocked the door at the back of the Tivoli and let them in.

'No one's going to be here at this time of night. If they are, I'll say I was worried Sam hadn't shut down the projectors properly. He's a trainee, after all.'

Connie stifled a laugh. 'Is that what this is about?'

Charlie took her hand, and they slipped inside. 'No,' he said when the door clicked shut. 'It's about not wanting this evening to end.'

They were standing in the darkness, bodies close, the only sound coming from their ragged breathing. She could just make out the outline of his face but little else.

'How many times have we been out now?' he asked.

'I dunno.' She did, it was seven, but she wasn't about to admit she'd been keeping count.

His hand came up to stroke her cheek before his lips found hers. Connie thought she might spontaneously combust, right there, like a reel of film.

In the projection room, she blinked as Charlie flicked the light on. He inspected the space, tutting at the careless way

Sam had left the lid off the film cement, a final reel hanging from the projector and on the winding bench, a half-drunk mug of cold tea which had already formed a skin. Tommy, curled up on the chair, regarded them before arching his frame into a languorous stretch and padding to the door.

'Sam treats this place like a doss house,' Charlie muttered as he set about bringing order to his domain.

Connie paused at the projector wanting to be the focus of his attention, but curious about the mechanics too. 'How does this work then?' She fingered the tail of the film which was trailing on the floor.

Charlie ceased tidying, his eyes alight. 'I can show you if you like?'

He freed the spool, lifting it to the top loader, then selected an empty spool from a pile next to the winding bench to take up the film at the bottom. His actions were swift and he spoke with clear instructions, not that she'd be able to take it in. Her eyes were mesmerised by the deft movement of his hands, his fingers lacing the film through the various sprocket drivers. Then he was finished and fixing her with a penetrating gaze. Connie fiddled with her necklace.

'Your turn.' Charlie gestured to the projector.

'I don't know what I'm doing, Charlie.'

'You were paying attention, weren't you?' There was a challenge in his voice, but his eyes were dancing.

'Course.'

'Well then.' He stood back, arms folded, no doubt enjoying the knowledge she'd found him more interesting to look at than the projector.

Not wishing to be humiliated, Connie took the leader and threaded it through in the most logical way, fixing the end into the take-up spool, all the while sensing Charlie's eyes on her.

He came closer to inspect her work. 'You were paying attention. Not bad for a first try, but you've made two mistakes.'

'Where?' Connie asked with feigned indignance.

'Here and here.' Charlie pointed out her errors.

Before Connie could move, his arms threaded under hers so he could direct her hands with his.

'It goes under rather than over this one, you see. Creates more tension.'

Connie turned to face him, lacing her arms around his neck. 'Tension, you say.'

'It's important to create the right amount of tension,' he whispered.

Connie slipped free before his lips found hers, ducking under his arms and moving around to the other side of the projector. She laughed as Charlie followed, backing her into a corner. Her body hummed with anticipation. She grabbed his tie and pulled him to her, willing to concede this time.

* * *

'Thanks for another lovely evening.' Connie stopped at the corner of Church Street, eyeing the road for signs of her father on his way home from the pub.

Charlie's arm came around her shoulder. 'Why don't you ever let me walk you to your door?' There was a smile on his lips, but his eyes were serious.

'We're practically at my door.' She gestured vaguely down the street.

'What are you scared of?'

Connie stiffened. 'Who says I'm scared?'

Charlie leaned his forehead against hers. 'I want to meet your dad, Con, and I want you to meet my parents too. I'm falling for you.'

She closed her eyes, revelling in the last part of his sentence while a fist of anxiety formed in her stomach at the first. 'I feel the same,' she whispered. His lips answered. She pulled away, fearful of being seen.

'First Sunday we're both free, you're having tea with my folks, and before long I'll have tea with your dad or whatever his equivalent of tea is. Okay?'

She forced herself to return his gaze, struck by the sincerity in his eyes.

'Okay.' She cupped his face. 'I have to go.' Connie planted a final kiss on his lips before racing up the road. When she was a couple of doors away from home, she glanced behind. Charlie was still at the corner, watching her. Hesitating outside her neighbours' house, she waved and ducked into the side alley. After a beat, she peeped out; he'd gone. Releasing a long breath, Connie walked on to the final terrace in the row and let herself in, apprehensive of what she'd find behind her front door.

In the entrance hall, she stood for a moment, her ears finely tuned to detect the presence of her father. The low rumble of his snores came from the sitting room. Connie slipped off her heels and followed the sound. Frank lay face down on the sofa in the kind of slumber only an evening in the pub could elicit. His arm hung to the floor; his hand had relinquished its grip on a bottle of stout. A foamy pool formed on the rug in the wake of its journey to the hearth, where it came to rest. Connie took the bottle to the kitchen and returned with a dishcloth. She soaked up the dregs of the spillage, and sat back on her haunches, regarding the sleeping bulk of her father.

How can I introduce Charlie to this?

CHAPTER 4

Charlie peered through the projection glass into the auditorium, where Connie was waiting in front of the stage. He dimmed the main lights and switched on the beam, illuminating the spot where she was standing. She shielded her eyes and squinted up at him. Chuckling, he returned to the record player and brought the needle gently down, then set the amplifier and raced for the stairs.

In the auditorium, Frank Sinatra crooned. Charlie drew up in front of Connie, pulling her into his arms and moving her across the floor. Her body was stiff against his and she kept glancing at her feet. He lifted her chin. 'Focus on me, not your feet. Let the music help you find a natural rhythm.'

'You're a good dancer, Charlie Smith. Have you had lessons?' Connie asked as he twirled her.

'Mum used to make me practise with her in the sitting room. She loved dancing and Dad was hopeless.'

Connie laughed. 'That's so sweet.'

'If you breathe a word . . .'

She rested her head on his shoulder, her body softening against his. 'Your secret is safe with me.'

They were finally melding with the music. She nuzzled into his neck.

Too soon the song came to an end. Charlie hummed the tune, keeping their dance going.

'I should probably get home.' Her voice lacked conviction.

'Stay.' He dipped his head to kiss her.

Sighing against his lips, she pulled back. 'You know I want to . . .'

Charlie searched out her lips again. His fingers edged through her soft curls. They backed into the front row of seats. He flipped one down, managing to edge himself onto the cushion. Connie was on his lap now, her lips still locked with his. His fingers glided up her legs. Reaching the top of her stockings, they lingered there. Connie pressed against him, her body answering his. It took all his strength to pull away, but the front row of a cinema was not going to be the location for their first time. Who knew what horrors the upholstery concealed.

'Blimey, Connie Harris,' he whispered. 'You'll be the death of me.'

They sat for a while, panting until they'd regained their equilibrium.

'I'd better go up and stop the record before the needle does its worst.'

Connie slid off his lap, and he stood, taking her hand. 'Come up with me? Then I'll see you home.'

She nodded — eyes bright in the beam of the projection light.

In the projection room, he lifted the needle from the spinning record, inspecting for damage, but all seemed well.

When he turned to face her, Connie was studying the projector.

'Do you want another lesson?'

Her eyes lit up. 'Are you trying to keep me here?'

He shrugged to mask his desperation. 'I might be.'

She grinned. 'Go on then. Just half an hour.'

Charlie lifted a can from a pile by the door and placed it in her hands. 'We're going to start at the beginning.' Sensing she was about to protest, he set his hand in the small of her back, gently moving her to the winding bench. He loved that Connie was so interested in his work. Over the last few weeks, he'd been giving her short lessons snatched between screenings. He treasured those minutes more than any other part of his day.

Half an hour later, she'd mastered the art of splicing film and had the first reel ready to go. Connie flashed him a triumphant smile as she loaded the spool onto the projector.

Tommy slipped in through the open window, dropping the remains of what was once a mouse at Charlie's feet. The cat leaped onto the leather armchair and promptly fell asleep.

'Charming.' Charlie rolled his eyes. Connie joined him to inspect Tommy's gift.

Pulling his hanky from his pocket, he scooped up the mangled creature and climbed out the window onto the roof. The cool air was a welcome relief from the stifling heat of the projection machinery. The weather had been too cold to bring Connie up here to his secret world, but tonight was perfect, still chilly but with clear skies revealing a blanket of stars. Setting the poor creature down in a corner, he called to her. Connie poked her head out the window. He offered his hand.

'Is it safe?'

He crouched before her. 'I'd never let a single hair on your head come to any harm.'

Her hand slid into his, warm from working with the film. He hauled her out, and led her around the parapet at the front of the cinema. They perched on the narrow wall which divided them from the roof.

Connie rested against him; her gaze focused on the twinkling stars. 'Wow, it's beautiful up here.'

'It is now.'

She laughed. 'If you feed me one more corny line, I'll . . .'

He threaded his arm around her back. 'You'll what?'

She leaned in, letting his lips find hers. Eventually, she pulled away with a shuddering breath, her face obscured in shadow.

'I have to go, Charlie, it's late.'

'We could sleep up here. Handy for work in the morning.' He was only half joking.

'You're daft. What if we rolled off?'

'What do I keep telling you?' He reached for her hand again, kissing her fingers. 'I'd never let anything bad happen to you.'

Her smile was almost mournful, tears filled her eyes, and she looked away.

Charlie cupped her chin. 'What is it?'

Shaking her head, she buried her face in his chest. 'I'm happy, that's all.'

He wrapped his arms around her. 'If this is happy, I'd hate to see you sad.'

Connie smiled up at him through shining eyes. He wanted to tell her he was in love with her, but she slipped from his grasp and stood, breaking the spell. He threw her a resigned smile. 'Okay, Connie Harris, I'll walk you home.'

CHAPTER 5

Michael's looping handwriting greeted her from the doormat. Connie snatched up the envelope, shoved it in her pocket and left to the distant growl of her sleeping father. A wave of guilt hit her as she marched along Fore Street; she hadn't replied to any of Michael's letters. And why should she? He knew what their father was capable of, and he left anyway. Left her at the mercy of a violent man. No. It wasn't for her to feel guilty, that was his burden alone.

At the Tivoli, Connie made for the cloakroom and drew the letter from her pocket, placing it inside her locker as if locking it away could make it disappear. Besides, what news did she have to share? Quite a lot actually. The job at the Tivoli for one, and Charlie . . .

She straightened her uniform and checked her reflection in the mirror. Charlie said she had the look of Rita Hayworth. The thought of him pushed her blues about Michael away.

'What are you smiling at, as if I didn't know?' Viv appeared behind. She leaned in, forcing Connie to move so she could fix her lipstick. If Connie was Rita Hayworth, Viv was Veronica Lake.

'Is that a new colour?' Connie asked as Viv painted her lips in lurid pillar-box red. 'Watch Reynolds doesn't have you for wearing too much make-up.'

'Stop changing the subject.' Viv slipped her lipstick in her bag. 'How's love's young dream?'

Connie's smile refused to be cast aside. 'He said he's falling for me.'

Viv rolled her eyes. 'Look at you, grinning like a demented clown.' Putting her bag in her locker, she closed the door and lit a cigarette. 'When you're married, don't you dare leave me here while you pop out a hundred kids.'

Connie laughed. 'You're getting way ahead of yourself.'

Viv's expression remained serious. 'I don't think I am. Charlie Smith has the look of a man who means business. Have you met his parents?'

'This Sunday.'

'See, he's gearing up to propose. A bloke only takes a girl home if he's planning on putting a ring on her finger.'

'It's only been a couple of months.'

'And how long did you two spend sizing each other up before he plucked up the courage to ask you out?'

Connie imagined a ring adorning her wedding finger. 'Do you really think so?'

'I'll make a small wager if you like?'

'Don't be daft, Viv.'

'Has he met your dad?'

Connie frowned. 'No. He's asked.'

Viv gave her a nudge. 'There'll be wedding bells this side of Christmas. I wonder what sort of ring he'll get you.'

Connie fiddled with the epaulettes on her jacket, avoiding Viv's shrewd gaze. Viv was right, Charlie was getting serious. She liked it, she wanted it, but her dad . . . 'We'd better get out there and face the masses.'

Viv drew on her cigarette before offering it over. Connie took a puff then stubbed it out in the overflowing ashtray on the table. They ventured into the foyer and stood side by side in their matching outfits like a pair of skittles, awaiting Reynolds' daily inspection.

* * *

Half an hour later, Connie eased herself into her flip-down seat, torch at the ready. The film blaring in the background was *The Miniver Story*, follow-up to the popular war film *Mrs Miniver*. Walter Pidgeon and Greer Garson returned to reprise their roles as the patriarch and matriarch overseeing a loving family in post-war Britain. The sugar-coated version of life irritated her. What about the men like her dad? The ones who returned forever changed. He'd had a promising career as a boxer before the war. Her mum would talk about how safe he made her feel, this big bear of a man who worshipped the ground she walked on. *Safe?* The notion seemed absurd now.

They noticed the change on his first leave after Dunkirk. He would become withdrawn like the moment of eerie stillness before a storm unleashed its fury. After the war, her mum never gave up trying to reach him, but he refused to be found. Having lost two fingers and a thumb to a mortar attack, his boxing career was over before it had begun. He turned to drink and found other things to do with his fists.

'Still okay for tomorrow?' Charlie whispered in her ear, dragging her out of her spiralling despair.

'What are you doing down here?'

'I've got Sam with me today.' He kissed her cheek before disappearing through the doors.

* * *

The following afternoon, Connie stood before a 1930s semi on a leafy street a little way from People's Park. The picket gate matched the colour of the red front door, and the well-tended garden was in full bloom. It was a far cry from the squat terraces that languished in the shadow of the Heathcoat

31

factory. She bit her lip and glanced down at her outfit. The dark green tea dress with cream flowers she'd spent the best part of a month's wages on no longer felt good enough for the likes of Charlie. Look at his house. It unnerved her.

Eyeing the street, Connie considered her options. Not a soul in sight on this sunny Sunday afternoon.

The moment to scarper evaporated as the front door drew open. Charlie was grinning at her from the doorstep. He walked along the garden path, hands in pockets, nonchalant in his swagger.

'Are you going to stand out here all day, Connie Harris?'

She realised her deliberations had been seen. Her mind raced, searching for a suitable comeback but then his lips were against hers and she forgot what she was doing. 'You look stunning,' he whispered, entwining her fingers with his.

He led her up the path past a laburnum tree, its vibrant yellow blossom billowing in the gentle breeze. A stained-glass window depicting a rainbow topped the red front door and a gold letterbox glinted in the sun. Charlie paused on the threshold and smiled. 'Relax.'

She offered him a tremulous smile in return as they stepped into the hall. The polish on the parquet floor could rival Mrs Bird, the cleaner at the Tivoli.

He ushered her into a sitting room which captured the best of the light with a large bay window overlooking the front garden and the pleasant street beyond. Connie attempted to rein in her gaze as she drank in every detail from the matching floral three-piece suite to the china dogs adorning the mantelpiece and the gramophone taking pride of place in the corner. Finally, her eyes settled on a middle-aged couple seated in armchairs either side of the hearth.

'Mum, Dad, this is Constance Harris.'

Mrs Smith was on her feet. She was a short woman with tight dark curls like Charlie. Her hand enveloped Connie's. 'Charlie doesn't stop talking about you. We're so excited to finally meet you, aren't we, Jim?'

Jim Smith was a broad man of about sixty with thick black-rimmed glasses and a warm smile.

Tea was laid out on the coffee table. 'We thought we'd be informal since you're practically part of the family.' Mrs Smith gestured for Connie and Charlie to sit on the sofa.

Charlie kept his hand in hers while his mother poured tea and offered around cake. Connie struggled to stay present in the moment. She glanced at Charlie's happy face. He was lovely, his parents were lovely, their home was lovely — too lovely for the likes of Frank Harris's daughter. She contrasted her surroundings with the cramped front room in her own house, the tired furniture, the cheap ornaments. Would Charlie still want her when he found out where she came from? Once he met her father and discovered he was a bitter drunk?

The room fell silent. Heat rushed to her cheeks as Connie realised she'd been asked a question. She lifted her gaze to Charlie, who squeezed her hand. 'Mum was asking about your dad.'

Connie forced a smile and addressed Mrs Smith. 'Sorry, I was too busy admiring your lovely home.'

The avoidance tactic worked like a charm. Margaret Smith, or Marge as she insisted Connie call her, was more than happy to talk about her flair for interior design.

* * *

'They loved you,' Charlie said when they reached the end of his street.

Afternoon tea had turned into supper. Once she'd relaxed, Connie revelled in the warmth of a loving family. Charlie's parents were a little fusty, but the affection that radiated from their home left her glowing.

'Your parents are so sweet.'

'You didn't find it weird, them being older?'

'Course not. They dote on you.'

Charlie shrugged. 'Mum calls me her miracle boy. They thought they couldn't have children, then I came along when they were about to give up.'

'No wonder you're the apple of her eye. Whoever you marry is going to have to make sure she wins your mum's approval.' She sucked in a breath, embarrassed by what she'd just said.

Charlie stopped walking and stood before her, an intensity in his gaze. 'I think she already has.'

Connie laughed and nudged him. 'You're the soppiest man I've ever met.'

'Only when I'm with you.' His arms slid around her waist. 'I'm in love with you. I want the world to know it.'

Her laughter died as warmth flooded her cheeks.

Charlie threw her a wry smile. 'I know you think I'm a clown but it's true. I need to know you feel the same, Con.'

Connie stroked a curl from his forehead. 'You know I do.'

His smile spread into a grin. 'Your turn next.'

She pulled back. 'What do you mean?'

'You've met my folks and cooed over photos of me in my pram, now it's my turn for revenge. I want to meet your dad and see your baby photos. I bet he's got some embarrassing stories about the young Connie Harris.'

Charlie's smile faded as she shook her head. 'There's not much to tell.'

'I find that hard to believe.'

Connie studied her shoes to hide the tears in her eyes.

'Are you ashamed of me?'

She met his gaze. 'You couldn't be more wrong.'

'So, what is it? You never talk about your dad. Don't think I didn't notice you dodge Mum's question back there. You've been dodging my questions since the day we met.'

'You wouldn't understand.'

'Try me.'

'Can't we enjoy this? Does it matter about families? Isn't it about us?' She brought her lips to his, relieved when he kissed her back.

'Fine.' He treated her to his dimpled smile, and she knew she was off the hook, for now at least.

They walked into the town past closed-up shops, past the neon Tivoli sign. At the bridge, they paused to watch the ebb and flow of the river beneath them. Charlie threaded his arms around her waist as she leaned against the railings, looking out. She could feel the vibration of his body against hers.

'I wish it could always be like this,' she whispered.

Charlie's lips brushed her ear. 'It can.'

Connie turned to face him. She didn't want to walk back to that house where she never knew what she was going to find behind the front door, she wanted to stay with him, frozen in time. Loved and blissfully happy.

CHAPTER 6

Connie's shoulder stiffened under his arm as they entered her road. Charlie still didn't know which house was hers. She insisted on saying goodbye at the corner. The thought barely registered before she stopped walking. He prepared for their usual routine.

Her kiss tasted of the raspberry trifle they'd eaten for pudding. He wouldn't push it today, not when things with his folks went so well.

As they parted, her furtive gaze slid to the end of the street. Charlie felt her unease in his stomach.

'I'd better go.' With a peck on his lips, Connie slipped from his arms.

She ducked down the side of a house near the end of the road. Maybe that was her home, and he was making too much of it. Charlie rounded the corner, but instinct made him pause. Unsure what he expected to see, he retraced his steps. The road remained empty before him, terraces huddled together, then the woman he loved slipped out of the shadows and let herself in to a house at the very end.

Unable to contain his curiosity, Charlie crossed over and walked along the road under cover of impending nightfall until he drew up opposite the small terrace Connie disappeared into. It was the shabbiest in the street. Her silhouette appeared behind a netted front window. She shut the curtains, snatching her from his sight. Charlie moved out of the shadows. The front door was rotten at the base, the paint around the windows blistered. Was this what troubled Connie — that her home wouldn't measure up? He released a breath, relieved her ambivalence about introducing him to her father had nothing to do with her feelings for himself.

Charlie lingered a moment longer, wanting to be near her. The house remained in darkness; he wondered where she was within its dank walls. Footsteps from further down the road roused him. Disquiet followed as he made his way home.

* * *

Enjoying a cigarette outside the cinema the following morning, Charlie waited for Connie. He'd lain awake last night thinking about the dilapidated state of her home, wondering about her father, seeing her situation with fresh eyes.

The chatter of female voices cut through the quiet of the enclosed space. Charlie dropped his cigarette, grinding it out with his heel. Connie and Viv walked down the alleyway towards him.

'I'll see you inside, Con.' Viv sauntered off.

He reached for Connie's hand. 'Morning.' He pulled her to him, breathing in the soft scent of her curls as his lips grazed her cheek.

'Morning.' She glanced up the alleyway, before pressing her lips against his.

When she pulled away, he studied her face, searching for signs of distress. What he expected to see, he didn't know. Charlie wanted to tell her he understood but he couldn't find a way to circumnavigate her pride.

'Are you okay?' His voice was low as he coiled whisps of her hair through his fingers.

'Course, why wouldn't I be?' Connie fixed him with a bemused expression.

He shrugged. 'There's nothing you can't tell me, Con.'

A frown touched her eyes. 'What are you talking about?'

'Nothing — just, you know, if there's anything worrying you, I hope you'd tell me.'

'Why should anything be worrying me?'

'I'm not saying it would . . .'

Connie sprang from his arms as Reynolds emerged from the street. She offered Charlie a puzzled smile before disappearing through the double doors into the cinema.

'Charlie.' Reynolds beckoned him over. He fell into step beside his boss. 'Your idea about a Bogart season to tie in with the release of *In a Lonely Place* — I think it's a good plan. He always draws a crowd.'

Charlie glanced across the foyer, relieved Connie was out of earshot. He wanted to keep it as a surprise. 'Great, Mr Reynolds. Leave it with me.'

Reynolds issued a curt nod before hastening to the kiosk, where Connie and Viv awaited their daily humiliation. Charlie watched, irritated as Reynolds' critical gaze travelled over his girlfriend. Connie threw him an eye roll. Relieved their awkward discussion outside appeared to be forgotten, he left them to it, heading for his projection room as an argument broke out between Reynolds and Viv over her bright red lipstick. Charlie mounted the steep staircase, his focus claimed by the prospect of a Bogart season. Connie would be out of that house soon — his plan was coming together.

CHAPTER 7

Reaching for one last packet of cigarettes, Connie added it to her tray and glanced up to find Viv studying her. 'What?' She lifted her hand to her cheek. 'Have I got something on my face?'

Viv shook her head. 'Make sure you enjoy the film tonight.'

'I intend to, so long as the audience behaves themselves.' The screening was *Casablanca*, and Connie couldn't wait to watch it again. The last time was with her mum and Michael during the war. The memory made her wince. Michael's letter remained unopened in her locker; another joined it the previous day.

'If you need backup, give me a shout.' Viv's expression was grave.

'What's got into you this evening?' Connie adjusted the strap on her tray.

'Nothing, now hurry up.' Her friend gently pushed her to the auditorium doors.

Two hours later, mesmerised by the film, Connie abandoned her post, choosing instead to lean against the back wall so she might see the full screen. It was rare for her to get the opportunity to watch a film in its entirety. Lifting her gaze to the projection window, Connie wished she was up there watching with Charlie — even better, running the film herself. She could now operate the projector unsupervised. Charlie joked she'd be after his job soon.

Viv appeared at her side.

'Shouldn't you be out there?' Connie whispered.

'Shh.' Viv gestured to the film. 'Concentrate.'

Connie returned her gaze to the screen; Viv was in a strange humour this evening. The thought evaporated as the final scene unfolded. Rick and Reynaud watching the plane leave with Ilsa on board. *Louis, I think this is the beginning of a beautiful friendship.* The best last line of any film as far as she was concerned.

As the screen faded to black, a title card flashed up. Connie blinked — she could have sworn it said her name. A gasp erupted from the audience as another title card appeared. *Will you marry me?*

Connie frowned, turning to Viv, who was beaming from ear to ear.

'Don't tell me you missed it?'

Members of the audience were on their feet looking around the auditorium, a hush of whispers growing to a crescendo. The full meaning struck her. *Connie Harris, will you marry me?*

Connie's gaze returned to the projection window.

'Go on.' Viv hurried her to the doors. 'Put him out of his misery.'

'You mean?'

'Yes.'

She bolted into the foyer.

Arriving at the projection room, breathless from hauling herself up the stairs, Connie found Charlie on one knee offering up a ring, a look of such vulnerable anticipation on his face she froze on the spot.

'Well, Connie Harris?'

'You daft man.' She ran into his arms; there was only one answer.

Charlie slid the ring on her finger. Connie held her hand up to the light, amazed by the glint of a single diamond.

Clapping and cheering drifted from the auditorium below. In a blissful daze, they peered through the projection window. He brought the lights up, illuminating Viv, who was on the stage, beckoning them to join her.

'Shall we?' Charlie asked.

Connie kissed him, wanting to savour this moment before the world crashed in. Eventually, they negotiated the steep stairs, wide grins on both their faces.

In the auditorium, Viv ran up the aisle, dragging them on stage to a cacophony of wolf-whistles and cheering from the audience. Never shy to exploit an opportunity, Reynolds joined them, making a speech about how the Tivoli was a family, most of which Connie failed to hear.

A journalist from the local newspaper happened to be in the crowd. He begged a photo and grilled them about their romance. Reynolds beamed from the sidelines. Connie couldn't share his enthusiasm, knowing her opportunity to tell her father was rapidly fading. She glanced at Charlie's happy face. She wouldn't allow Frank Harris to ruin it for her.

'When will the story appear in the paper?' she asked the journalist on his way out.

'Wednesday.'

Four days away. Connie hid her disquiet behind a bright smile.

* * *

As the last straggler was ushered out of the cinema, Charlie came to her side. 'Are you okay?'

'Course, I couldn't be happier.'

'You're not worried about your dad? I mean, you have told him about us?'

Charlie was so damned perceptive. 'I'm not worried,' she lied. 'I'm going to be Mrs Charlie Smith. How could I be?'

'I love you.' He leaned his head against hers. 'I do want to talk to your father. We need to get his blessing.'

'Can I trust you lovebirds to lock up?' Reynolds interrupted.

'Of course, Mr Reynolds.' Charlie opened the double doors for his boss to walk out.

'Wait.' Viv rushed through from the ladies. She stopped to engulf Connie in a hug.

'You knew, didn't you?' Connie threw her a wry smile.

Viv grinned as Charlie looked a little sheepish. 'Someone had to make sure you didn't wander off. Let me have another look at that ring.'

Connie lifted her hand.

'You did good, Charlie Smith.' Viv kissed her cheek and disappeared into the night.

Charlie locked the door. 'Alone at last.'

In the projection room, Connie brushed the cat hairs from Charlie's armchair before taking a seat and watching him tidy up. Tommy was conspicuous in his absence. Perhaps the cat sensed this was an evening for them to be alone. She enjoyed studying Charlie's face in serious repose as he focused on bringing order to the room ready for the following day. Was this impulse to organise his mother's doing? Her mind drifted to the Smiths' tidy home. Would she and Charlie live with his parents, or could they afford their own place? She hoped so. She wanted them to be alone.

'Leave it.' Connie stood, stopping Charlie before he could start rewinding the film.

'I don't like leaving nitrate out, that's all.' He placed the reel back in the can and sealed the lid.

'How did you get the title cards into the film?' Connie asked.

'I spliced them in.'

'Won't that get you in trouble?'

'I'll put it right in the morning. I think it's unlikely any-one will notice and if they do, it would be worth it.' His lips searched out hers.

Wrapping her arms around his neck, her body vibrated with expectation, a decision made as his hands glided down her back and over her buttocks, sending a jolt between her legs. The kiss grew deeper, a life of its own. Connie backed Charlie into the chair; he sat heavily, taking her with him. She unbuttoned her jacket, pulling it from her back and dropping it on the floor. Next her fingers worked the fastening of her skirt. His face was now the picture of concentration as her blouse followed the other garments. He ran his hand up her stockinged leg as she lifted her camisole over her head then returned to his lap, unbuckling his belt and drawing him out.

'Are you sure?' he whispered.

CHAPTER 8

'I wish I could take you home.' Charlie belted his trousers and reached for his tie.

Connie buttoned her blouse, then lifted her hand to his cheek. 'Me too.'

He caught her hand, entwining her fingers with his. 'I'd marry you here and now if I could find a vicar.'

'Not much chance at midnight on a Saturday.'

'Tomorrow then.'

Connie smiled. 'Okay.'

'I would, you know, but I want to give you a proper wedding. A white dress, the works.'

'White might no longer be appropriate.'

Charlie chuckled as she hoisted up her skirt. He sat on the chair watching her put the finishing touches to her uniform. Connie joined him, sitting on his lap, wishing they could stay as they were, coiled into each other. She'd have to tell her dad first thing. Maybe she'd make him a cooked breakfast, butter him up a little. He must realise she'd leave home sometime.

'What's going on in that head of yours?' Charlie asked, rousing her from her dilemma.

She shrugged. 'Sorry.'

'Don't be sorry, tell me what's wrong. I didn't hurt you, did I? I mean when we were . . .'

'I'm fine.'

'Con, I can tell when you're not being honest. You get a crease between your eyes.'

'I don't.' Connie stood, unable to navigate this conversation. 'I'd better go.'

'Hey.' He reached for her hand.

Connie's eyes filled with tears. Charlie stood too, enveloping her in his arms. 'Don't shut me out.'

She leaned her head against his shoulder, cursing herself for ruining what had been the most romantic, magical night of her life.

Charlie let go of her, reaching for his jacket. 'I'll walk you home.'

Connie slid into her shoes, searching for words to rescue her blunder. 'Charlie.'

He pulled on his jacket and turned to face her, a wound in his eyes as they met hers.

'I . . . I can't wait to marry you.'

His features relaxed. 'Neither can I.'

'Can it be soon? I don't care about a big wedding. I just want to be with you.'

'I'm not sure Mum will agree. She'll be beside herself with excitement. There's so much to organise and our families will have to meet. No excuses.'

Connie nodded. Charlie lifted her chin. 'Is that what's worrying you? That your dad won't approve of me?'

'How could it be that? You're perfect, Charlie Smith.'

'So, tomorrow?'

Connie dipped her head, studying her ring. 'Tomorrow. Meet us in the White Ball at 1 p.m.'

Charlie grinned. 'I'll be there.'

* * *

Connie unlocked the front door and crept into the entrance hall. Slipping off her shoes, she tiptoed to the stairs, listening for her father but all she could hear was her own jagged breath. It would be all right, she reassured herself as she fiddled with her ring. She'd take it off in the morning, until after she'd talked to her dad. Tonight, she wanted to sleep with it on, feel it around her finger. *Charlie's ring.*

Reaching the stairs, she froze as her foot scaled the bottom step. The hallway light flicked on. Her father stood at the entrance to the sitting room in his vest and braces, a half-drunk bottle of whisky in his hand.

His gaze dropped to her engagement ring. Connie's insides turned liquid. He grabbed her wrist. The ring sparkled in the light from the naked hallway bulb.

'Dad.' The plea in her voice irritated her. 'I was going to explain . . .'

Frank rounded on her, slamming the whisky bottle on the carpeted stairs with a thud. Yanking the ring from her finger, he dropped her limp wrist. Connie made to move away but he grabbed her hair, shoving her into the wall. His hand came under her chin as he pressed against her throat with his palm. Connie fought to breathe. His eyes met hers without a flicker of emotion. He threw the ring to the floor.

'Think you can leave me? You're like your mother, an ungrateful bitch.' The slap came sharp and hot against her cheek.

Connie tried to shake her head, but protestation was futile. Frank continued to press on her throat. Suddenly he let go. She struggled to keep her footing. Holding her throat, she gasped for air, then the sting of a fist met her jaw with a crack. Reeling backwards, another swipe came against her head and all went black.

PART TWO

May 1996

CHAPTER 9

Diffused light fell in pools across the auditorium, imbuing the chilly, empty space with a warm glow. Eddie snaked along the aisle, the floor tacky beneath his feet with years of spilled drinks and confections. He picked a seat in the centre. The threadbare velour fabric strained as he flipped it down, and the aged springs groaned under his weight. He closed his eyes, inhaling the whiff of dewy neglect. In the silence, his mind filled with possibilities. A packed auditorium, the caramel aroma of popcorn, the boom of a film playing on the screen.

A car backfiring on the street outside broke through his reverie. Eddie checked his watch — he couldn't put off meeting his staff any longer.

In the foyer, two workmen chiselled layers of paint from the Art Deco cornicing to the innocuous drone of daytime radio. At the kiosk the three remaining staff huddled in a circle.

Eddie cleared his throat; all eyes turned in his direction. 'Hello.' He raised his hand in an awkward wave, too aware of his mechanical movements. 'Thank you for coming.'

A woman with heavy eye make-up and a shock of cropped bleached hair folded her arms across her chest. She was wearing a T-shirt with the words *Girl Power* emblazoned on the front.

Unnerved, Eddie pressed on. 'Maybe we could all introduce ourselves: I'm Eddie, the new Tivoli manager.' He glanced at the woman and threw her a smile which she didn't return. If anything, she looked bored. 'And you are . . .' he encouraged.

'Linda.'

'Pleased to meet you, Linda.' The smile remained stuck to his face while he turned his attention to the other two staff. 'So, this must be Ben and Hayley?'

Hayley fiddled with one of her large hoop earrings while Ben shifted a dreadlock out of his face.

Eddie unglued the smile and continued. 'We should only be closed for a couple of months.' He noticed the decorators look at each other and smirk. 'Maybe three.'

'Will we lose our pay?' Linda asked.

Eddie met her kohled gaze. 'You'll be paid as usual.'

She nodded and dropped her arms to her side.

Buoyed by this small victory, he returned his attention to Ben and Hayley. 'Any questions?'

'Who's going to run the films when we reopen?' Ben asked.

'Me,' Eddie replied.

Linda shook her head and folded her arms again. Eddie was puzzled: why the hostility?

'So, if you're sure you haven't any more questions . . .'

Ben shrugged, Hayley continued to fiddle with her earing and Linda kept her arms plastered across her chest.

'Okay, I've got your contact details. I'll keep you updated.' He gave them the thumbs-up and wondered why he was behaving like an overzealous holiday camp rep.

They trooped through the glass-panelled front doors, squeezing past the skip, soon to be filled with woodchip and plasterboard as the workmen peeled away the layers of neglect. Eddie watched their progress up the alleyway that set the Tivoli back from the bustle of Fore Street. He hovered in the foyer, feeling like a spare part in what was now his cinema. He should have been more confident about the timescale, especially in the presence of the workmen, but looking at the challenge ahead, two months was optimistic.

In an attempt to reassert his authority, Eddie threw the decorators a stern glance and opened the projection room door. The stairs rose like a ladder onto a narrow landing. In all his years working in cinemas he'd never encountered a projection room with such stifling proportions. The box-like main space housed two Gaumont-Kalee 21 projectors standing side by side. They'd need replacing. Carbon arcs were rare these days and time-consuming to run, especially solo. He wondered how the previous projectionist coped.

An alcove to the side housed a winding bench and various outdated bits of equipment — spools, cores and splicers. He opened the single window and stuck out his head; the vaulted roof of the cinema spread out before him.

Next to the window was a battered old leather armchair, so tattered its sprung interior was visible through tears in the seat. Scratches on the sides suggested a cat once used it to sharpen its claws. Eddie perched on the arm, trying to reignite the spark that compelled him to use his redundancy money to lease a run-down old cinema. When he'd first set eyes on the place, it seemed bursting with romantic potential, now it felt more like a money pit. Sarah said it was a midlife crisis. *Does she have a point?*

He stood, agitated by the spectre of his ex-wife. In the corner of the room, his gaze settled on a single can of film sitting on top of the winding bench, conspicuous in the otherwise ordered space. A Post-it note was stuck to the top with the words *I'm sorry* scrawled in a cursive hand. Frowning, Eddie picked up the can. It was a little rusty. He tried prising off the lid, but it wouldn't budge. Searching around for something to aid his quest, he fumbled in his pocket for his keys and used one to inch up the lip.

It gave in a puff of noxious fumes. Inside was a reel of 35 mm film, no more than 400 feet. The film was a little warped and brittle to touch, and a fine layer of red dust speckled the base of the can.

Before he could investigate further, a shout from one of the workmen downstairs diverted his attention. Eddie resealed the lid, placed the can back on the winding bench and turned to go when he again caught sight of the Post-it note, which had floated to the floor. *I'm sorry.* Who was sorry and why?

He picked up the can again, shoved it under his arm and headed back into the gloom of the stairs.

* * *

It was still under his arm as Eddie walked through Tiverton that evening. The note piqued his curiosity enough for him to take the film home with the intention of resuming his investigation. Not that he thought of his flat on St Peter Street as home exactly. More a bolthole. A place to exist when he wasn't at work. Exeter would always be home. Sarah still lived in their house on Pennsylvania Road with their cat, Maude, and a man called Ian. Eddie hoped Maude was treating Ian to the full force of her mercurial personality.

Teenagers loitered smoking around the large wooden planters on Fore Street, subverting the council's attempt to bring a little green to the area. Two men worse the wear for a day on the drink regaled passers-by with their philosophical take on the world. Eddie made his way down Angel Hill, resisting the temptation to grab a Chinese takeaway, and peeled off to the right. The sun disappeared behind the tall Georgian terraces huddled together on either side of the road.

Inside his flat, Eddie set the film on the kitchen worktop, battling the loneliness he had yet to grow into after his divorce. He distracted himself by surveying the contents of his fridge as he considered his options for dinner. A slice of leftover pizza, a Ginsters pasty and a four-pack of beer. He couldn't fulfil the cliché of a divorced, middle-aged man better if he tried. Perhaps he should have picked up a takeaway after all.

Retrieving the pizza, he moved to the cupboard, pulled out a solitary tin of baked beans and set about assembling his unappetising meal. After the staff meeting that morning, his worries had begun to stack up. He shouldn't have promised to keep them on full pay when he didn't know how long they'd be closed. The cinema had been run into the ground. There was the rewiring to finish, the decorating, the new projection equipment to install, not to mention the number of seats that needed replacing or reupholstering.

But it's mine.

The thought was like a shot of adrenaline. Wasn't that the point? No more bowing to an increasingly disengaged management who swooped in with their calculators, raised havoc and left with furrowed brows, muttering about the prospect of DVDs. No more soulless multiplexes. The Tivoli needed work, but behind its crumbling Art Deco facade there was heart.

The microwave pinged, announcing dinner was ready. He pulled a beer from the fridge and carried his meal to the sofa. One of the things he loved about living alone was being king of the remote, but it was also one of the things he hated — how much mindless crap he watched now. Finding nothing on that interested him, he took a swig of beer and reached for *Cinema Paradiso* from his exhaustive selection of VHS tapes. It never ceased to bring a lump to his throat. Maybe it was finding the old film making him nostalgic. He'd felt a kindred spirit with Toto, having been about five years old himself when he'd discovered the heady delights of cinema. As the VHS player whirred into action, Eddie settled back on the sofa.

Two hours later, after indulging his love for cinema in the most elegiac way, he returned to the kitchen to take another look at the film. Using the bottle opener to prize off the lid, Eddie held the reel up to the naked kitchen bulb. There was a stickiness as he uncoiled it. From what he could gather, the actors were Humphrey Bogart and Claude Rains — *the final scene from Casablanca?* He frowned, hardly worth keeping. *What was there to be sorry about?*

As he uncoiled further, the image started to peel away from the film base. Eddie stopped, fearing he'd cause more damage. He coiled the reel up and returned it to the can.

His telephone chirruped to life, its ring shrill and jarring in the otherwise silent room. He picked up the receiver.

'Hey, Mum.'

'How did you know it was me?'

'You're the only person who calls me these days.'

There was an audible pause at the other end. He shook his head, regretting his bitterness. 'Anyway,' he rushed on, eager to ease her burden, 'what can I do for you?'

'How's the cinema going?' she asked, ignoring his attempt to make the call about her instead of him.

'There's a lot to do, but the decorators have started.'

'Are the staff nice?'

'They seem okay.' Eddie pulled over a kitchen chair and sat down. He didn't want to get into the whole situation with the cinema.

'You don't sound too certain.'

He glanced at the view of the River Exe from his kitchen window — one of the things which attracted him to the flat in the first place. There was something relaxing about a body of water.

'So, how are you?' he asked, eager for a change of subject.

'The book research is keeping me busy, but I miss my students.'

His gaze drifted to the can of film again. 'Do they look at old film reels at the uni, by any chance?'

'Possibly. One of the PhD students has some film archive experience. In fact, she's the daughter of an old friend, but I haven't managed to touch base with her since I've been on sabbatical. Might be worth an ask. Why?'

'A can of old film was left in the projection room at the Tivoli. It's probably junk.' He leaned back in the chair, coiling the phone wire through his fingers.

'Her name is Anna James, and her supervisor is Dr Graham Baker.' The smile in her voice suggested she was pleased to be of use. 'Telephone the postgrad office and they should track her down.'

'Great, thanks.'

'Are we still on for the Odeon, Thursday evening?'

'Sure, see you then.'

Eddie hung up. In some of their more bitter arguments, Sarah would accuse him of being a mummy's boy, but she never did appreciate what he and his mother survived.

His gaze was drawn to the film can once more, the fading evening sun from the kitchen window burnishing the rusted surface. If he wanted to find out why whoever left the film was sorry, he was either going to have to talk to his staff or get a professional to help him view it. As he sloped off to bed, Eddie recalled the disgruntled faces of his team and decided to take the path of least resistance. He resolved to phone Anna James in the morning.

CHAPTER 10

Light drizzle misted his windscreen as Eddie did his third circuit of the university visitor car park with increasing desperation. His need to get to the Tivoli and keep the workmen on track was a constant in his mind. Why he was letting the mystery film take up valuable time, he had no idea. Something about it captured his imagination and offered a distraction from his renovation woes.

Eddie spied a woman walking towards a row of parked cars with purpose and tailed her, feeling like a gumshoe from one of his favourite noirs. His patience paid off. The woman backed out of the space, and with a sense of triumph, he nabbed it, just before a red hatchback.

Anna James was seated at a desk surrounded by papers when he knocked on the open door of the postgraduate office. 'Come in.' Her voice had an American twang he hadn't noticed when they'd spoken on the phone the previous day. 'Take a seat.' She gestured to a chair occupied by a box of old photographs.

Eddie shoved the can of film under his arm and moved the box to an empty spot on the floor.

Anna flashed him a smile and came out from behind her desk. He'd guess she was a few years younger than him. Her teeth were impeccably straight. 'Anna.'

'Eddie,' he blustered, offering up the can of film. 'Thanks for helping with this.'

Anna searched around her desk, eventually finding a pair of round tortoiseshell glasses. The frames complimented the hint of copper in her dark brown hair.

She slid on a pair of white cotton gloves before she accepted the cannister and eased the lid free. Her nose wrinkled at the unpleasant smell.

'It's a bit sticky,' he said as she lifted the reel to the light.

Anna didn't comment. Instead, she unspooled the first few feet of film. 'Nitrate.' She regarded him with a frown. 'For future reference, if you see this spark symbol along the edge of a film, it's likely to be nitrate.' She spooled up the reel and placed it back in its can.

Eddie coloured. He should have known. Hadn't he watched *Cinema Paradiso* only the other evening? He recalled the scene where Toto rescued Alfredo from the burning wreckage of his projection room; the fire had started when a reel of nitrate film got caught in the projector.

Anna handed the can back to him and returned to her desk, tugging off the gloves. 'Where did you say you found this?'

'It was left in the projection room at the Tivoli cinema in Tiverton with a note which said *I'm sorry*.' Eddie felt a little foolish mentioning it.

'Whoever left it should be sorry. You're lucky they didn't burn the cinema to the ground. I hope you're insured. Nitrate film is highly flammable, which is why they stopped using it in the early fifties. As it decomposes, it has the ability to spontaneously combust. It needs to be kept in cool conditions.'

Eddie's eyes widened, remembering his stupidity leaving the film sunning itself on his kitchen worktop. As tempting as the insurance money would be, he had no desire to burn his cinema to the ground. 'What can I do with it?'

'Your best bet is to contact the fire brigade. They can dispose of it safely.'

Eddie tried to contain his alarm. 'Seriously?'

She removed her glasses and fixed him with a grave expression. 'Seriously.'

He scratched his head. 'Shame not to be able to view it though. I'd like to check what's on there.'

'If it's just scenes from *Casablanca*, it won't be of any value. It's probably part of an old show print. I can't advise running it through your projector. Like I said, it's a fire risk.'

'What about here?'

Anna's bobbed hair swished from side to side as she shook her head. 'Sorry, more than my life's worth to run it on one of our viewing machines. You can't mix students with combustible items.'

'I see.' He hovered, hoping she'd change her mind, but her attention had been reclaimed by the papers on her desk.

'Okay, well, thanks.'

She glanced up, briefly from her notes. 'Good luck.'

Eddie returned to his car with the can of film under his arm, which now felt less like a curious relic and more like a live grenade. He drove along the A396 to Tiverton, through picturesque villages and over ancient bridges. Every so often he'd glance at the film on the passenger seat as if he expected it to suddenly engulf him in a ball of flames.

He pulled up at the back of the Tivoli, still mulling over what to do. He couldn't help wondering over the note. What if this film meant something, like the reel of kisses at the end of *Cinema Paradiso*? What if Toto never played that reel? He made the decision then. He wouldn't dispose of the film with the fire brigade. It survived this long without spontaneously combusting. He'd hang onto it. Anna James was right about one thing though: he couldn't take it back to the Tivoli. He'd have to keep it at his flat.

CHAPTER 11

A file slid from the desk, sending papers scattering to the floor. Anna scrambled to collect them up. Maybe she should have been a bit more helpful, especially since their mothers apparently knew each other, but she didn't have the headspace to take on another problem. So long as the guy took the film to the fire brigade it would all be fine, and if he didn't, well, she'd warned him of the risks.

'Have you got a minute?' Graham walked in and, with a furtive glance, closed the door. 'How's it going?' His fingers grazed her arm, causing the hairs to electrify. The small room filled with the woody scent of his aftershave.

They sprang apart at a knock on the door. Pip, the post-graduate secretary, stuck her head around. 'Sorry, I didn't realise you were in a meeting. There's a phone call for you, Dr Baker. Shall I take a message?'

'Thanks, Pip.' He threw Anna a smirk. 'I'm almost finished here.'

Alone again, Anna folded her arms. 'Do you think she suspected anything? Sometimes I wonder if I should change supervisors.'

Graham frowned. 'You won't find anyone in the department with more expertise on early Gothic cinema than me.

Besides, wouldn't that draw more attention to us? What excuse would you give?'

She sighed. Perhaps he was right. 'I don't want to risk my PhD. I've worked too damned hard for this.'

'I admire your passion. Save it for this evening,' he whispered.

Anna was irritated to find herself smiling. She kept her voice low. 'What time?'

'I'll be over at seven once Deborah leaves for her yoga class, not that she cares what I'm up to these days. She and the girls are going for dinner afterwards, probably won't be back until the pubs close.' He pressed a quick kiss to her lips and left.

'See you then,' Anna said to the closing door. The slight frown Graham wore when he'd mentioned Deborah's disinterest hadn't escaped her attention, yet he insisted the marriage was over. Why then did he feel the need to tell her what his wife would be doing during their precious time together? As if she didn't already feel guilty enough. She let out a long breath and returned to her research documents. The remnants of his aftershave clung to the air, and she knew for the rest of the day her mind would hum with anticipation.

* * *

That evening, Anna marched down Sidwell Street towards her flat, clutching a bag containing a Marks & Spencer ready meal for one. Deborah's yoga teacher had sprained her ankle — that was the end of Thursday evenings for the next few weeks. She knew when she'd entered into the affair with Graham there would be times like this. Days when he cancelled their plans at the last minute due to events beyond his control. She'd always come last, and she'd accepted that. *Almost.* What a cliché she'd become and how like her mother.

'Anna?'

Anna paused her furious stomp and turned in the direction of the voice. It took her a moment to place him. It was the man with the nitrate film reel.

'Hello again.' A hint of colour flushed his cheeks. He offered her an uncertain smile and she noticed for the first time his slight dimples and brown eyes beneath a mop of dark hair.

Anna rallied. 'Hello.' She must have looked bewildered because he felt the need to qualify who he was.

'Eddie, the man who tried to burn down your office earlier.'

'I remember. I hope you got rid of the film?'

'I left it on a radiator inside the Tivoli. We could use the insurance.'

Anna blinked, regarding him until his smile spread into a grin. *Ugh, I'm not in the mood for jokes.*

'Sorry.' He shook his head as if reading her thoughts. 'Off anywhere nice?'

For inspiration, she glanced down Sidwell Street with its numerous takeaways and bars and realised she didn't have the energy to come up with an exciting destination. 'Heading home. Belmont Park.'

Eddie nodded. 'I'm waiting for my mum. She's late.' He rubbed the back of his neck. 'We go to the cinema every week, but she always arrives as the trailers are about to roll.'

It was then Anna realised they were standing outside the Odeon. At one time it must have been a striking building. Now, its 1930s facade had seen better days. 'Smart woman, dodge the adverts.'

Eddie's smile was thin. 'I suppose so.' He stared down the street.

Anna searched for a way to bring their awkward meeting to an end. 'Well . . .'

'I was about to go into the cinema for a drink, would you be willing to keep me company? Stop me looking like a loser.'

All she wanted to do was go home, eat her sad ready meal and drown her sorrows with the bottle of wine chilling in her fridge, the wine she'd bought to share with Graham. The thought of him gave her pause. Why should she spend an evening alone when he was at home with his wife? She nodded. 'Sure.'

They climbed the steps into the Odeon cinema with its bright foyer and display of every kind of food Anna tried to avoid even though Graham loved her voluptuous figure and made her feel sexy. The sickly sweet smell of popcorn assaulted her nose, sending a jolt of hunger to her stomach.

'What can I get you?' Eddie hovered at the food counter.

'A diet coke, thanks.'

He ordered her drink and the same for himself. They wandered to a set of seats with a clear view of the ticket booth so Eddie could spot his mother when she arrived. Anna wasn't sure whether it was sweet he went to the cinema with his mother every week or a little Norman Bates. He looked like a fairly sane, regular man, not that she was the best judge. As his gaze drifted to hers, she averted her eyes, glancing around. She rarely went to the cinema these days, which was odd for a film studies PhD student. She was too busy with research or waiting in for Graham.

'Don't you work in a cinema?' she asked, recalling Eddie having mentioned the Tivoli.

He winced. 'Yeah. Well, actually I own it. I know what you're thinking, a bit weird watching a film on your night off, but it's kind of a family tradition.'

'I can't imagine my mom wanting to hang out with me every week and the feeling is mutual.'

'It's a bit . . . I don't know . . .' He seemed embarrassed as he searched for the words.

'It's nice.'

Eddie smiled, clearly relieved, and sipped his drink.

'Which film are you seeing?'

'*Trainspotting*.' He glanced at the ticket booth again then met her gaze, perhaps noticing her surprise. 'Mum's pretty open-minded.'

Anna nodded and sipped her drink too. The coke fizzed in her empty stomach. An awkward silence settled on them.

She searched for a way to fill it, puzzled as to why she was trying so hard when she didn't need to. 'What's your favourite film?' She screamed inwardly at the lame question.

Eddie didn't seem to notice but offered up a grin. 'I have a film I tell people is my favourite and I have a true favourite. Which do you want?'

Anna laughed. 'Both.'

'Okay, so my fake favourite is *Rocky*, which I do genuinely think is a good film.'

Unable to suppress her eye roll, she followed it up with a bemused smile.

Eddie defended his choice. 'It's a sensitive portrayal of heroism and realising your potential against all the odds.'

'Did you read that off the back of the VHS?'

He looked wounded. Anna felt a little guilty. She hadn't even seen it. She was aware she could be a bit of a film snob.

'So, your real favourite?'

Eddie sat forward as if he was going to share some earth-shattering secret. '*Cinema Paradiso*.'

'But that's a much better film to admit to than *Rocky*.'

He shrugged. 'Depends on your audience.'

'I suppose.'

'What about you?'

Anna took a moment to consider the question. 'Do I have to pick just one?'

'You can have a fake favourite too if you like.'

'For my PhD I'm researching femme fatales in early Gothic cinema, so maybe *Rebecca*.'

He sat up, alert. 'I assume you mean the 1940 adaptation? Judith Anderson made a menacing Mrs Danvers.'

'You've seen it?'

'What self-respecting film nut hasn't?'

Anna hid her surprise behind a smile. He was challenging all her carefully constructed academic prejudices.

'And the real favourite?'

'*Cinema Paradiso*.'

Eddie raised his eyebrows. 'Really?'

'Come on, what other film better encapsulates the joy of cinema in such an expressive and moving way?'

His gaze held hers for a beat before he looked away and shifted in his seat. 'I couldn't have put it better myself.'

Anna sipped her drink, taking a sideways glance at Eddie. He was using the straw to mix the ice around his cup with a furrowed brow. There was something about him, like he carried a secret. His sad eyes put her in mind of Bogart, although that was where their similarities ended.

'They're going in.' She gestured to the queue moving up the stairs to screen one.

Eddie cast around. 'And yet my mother is nowhere to be seen.' He smiled in a resigned way. 'Listen . . . about that film I found, is there any way you'd consider letting me view it? I know I'm asking a lot, but I can't stop thinking about the significance of the note. I'd love to look at the film for no other reason than to satisfy my curiosity.'

Anna suppressed a sigh. *Why do men always want something?* She was about to reinforce her position when he stood. A tall, willowy woman entered the foyer and waved at Eddie. Anna recognised her as one of the film department's doctors who had gone on sabbatical as she started her PhD. She glanced at Eddie, finding him a little more intriguing. His mum was also hard to miss. An upright elegant frame, artfully dishevelled silver curls and beautifully dressed in jeans and a soft pale-blue jumper, she had the kind of grace Anna dreamed about possessing.

His mum beamed as she drew up in front of them. 'Anna, what a lovely surprise. I knew your mum many years ago. I've been meaning to get in touch ever since she wrote to say you were doing your PhD at Exeter.'

Surprised Dr Humphries had any connection with her cynical mother, Anna smiled. 'I was keeping Eddie company while he waited for you.'

'I know he hates my tardiness, but the adverts are such a bore.' She winked at her son before turning her attention back to Anna. 'Will you join us?'

It was a nice offer, but after her disappointment over Graham, the lure of the wine in her fridge remained strong and Anna knew she wanted to be alone after all. 'That's kind but I must be going.' She lifted her shopping by way of excuse. 'It was lovely to meet you.' Anna addressed Eddie. 'Thanks for the drink.'

'Thanks for keeping me company.'

She hesitated. 'About that reel, I can't have you burning down the cinema. Call me tomorrow when I'm in the office. I'll book you a viewing slot, but you'll have to let me run it.'

Eddie's face lit up. 'Thank you, I really appreciate it.'

Before she could change her mind, Anna headed for the exit, feeling strangely bereft. At the doors, she paused to see Eddie and his mother walking arm in arm to the auditorium.

CHAPTER 12

'Don't go getting excited, Mum.' Eddie could sense his mother thought she'd caught the whiff of potential romance in the foyer. There was a buzz emanating from her as they entered screen one.

He scanned the rows of seats in the gloom while the trailers flashed behind. The darkness concealed his embarrassment as she asked patrons to allow them to shuffle past.

'I didn't say a word,' she whispered when they were finally seated.

Eddie focused on the screen. The Tivoli couldn't hope to attract a film like *Trainspotting* for a while. Small-town cinemas couldn't compete with the multiplexes. Still, it was nice to get a preview. Perhaps if they could get the place finished in good time, it could be the Tivoli's opening film. Wouldn't that be something? Or what about *Cinema Paradiso*? What was it Anna said? *Encapsulates the joy of cinema in a moving and expressive way.* Something like that. He liked it.

It was fun to chat about film with someone other than his mum, who always knew more than him, although his nerves had compelled him to crack too many lame jokes. His regret was the discomfort he caused by putting Anna on the spot about viewing the nitrate film. Eddie cringed. It was true though, he wanted to see what was on that reel and why someone left the note. He'd quite enjoy seeing Anna again too. The thought struck him as interesting, but then, on screen, Renton came hurtling towards them and for a while he forgot everything else.

* * *

Eddie opened the fridge to assess what breakfast options might be available. The can of film on the top shelf surprised him. *Did I put it there?* He must have, no doubt some ingenious plan to keep it cool after the beers he'd sunk the previous evening when he'd returned from the cinema. *Did Sarah have a point? Maybe I am drinking too much.* He shook his head, not wanting to exist in a world where his wife — correction, ex-wife — was right about anything. Finding nothing appealing for breakfast, he picked up his rucksack and headed to work.

In Fore Street he stopped for a bacon roll and a takeaway coffee — Sarah's head was exploding somewhere right now — and ventured down the graffitied alleyway to the Tivoli.

The foyer was cloaked in gloom and the cinema eerily silent. The workmen would arrive soon with their daytime radio and easy banter.

In the small corner office, little more than a cupboard, he tucked into his roll, thinking about the previous evening. His mum had been very restrained not to go on about Anna. She'd said the same thing she'd been saying his whole life with that whimsical look in her eyes. 'I just want you to be happy, Ed.'

The thought led him to pick up the phone. Hopefully Anna would remember her agreement to let him view the film. He wondered what had changed her mind.

The nice lady in the postgrad office quickly tracked her down. Anna came on the line.

'Hi, it's Eddie, from last night.' His cheeks flushed. That sounded like they'd had some sordid one-night stand.

'Ah, Mr *Cinema Paradiso*.'

He relaxed, she sounded pleased to hear from him. 'The very one.'

'You wanted me to commit a felony by letting you view nitrate film on university premises?'

'Indeed.'

The rustle of papers filled the line. She must be checking her diary. 'How about early Sunday? Fewer eyes to ask questions.'

'Sounds good.' That way he could put in a full day at the Tivoli, free of the workmen.

'Shall we say 8.30 a.m.? Come straight to the postgrad office.'

'Great. I really appreciate this.'

'Hmm, that's what I'll tell my supervisor if we burn the place to the ground.'

Eddie chuckled. 'Thanks, Anna.' He hung up.

Raised voices outside told him the workmen had arrived. He ventured to the foyer to let them in.

An hour later, he'd retreated to the projection room. The sense he was intruding settled on Eddie each time he crossed its threshold as if the space retained ghosts unwilling or unable to move on to the next realm. It only added to his curiosity about the film and whose shoes he was stepping into. He sensed they were big and not easy to fill, but he wasn't sure where that feeling came from. He should just ask Linda about the previous projectionist, but the sneering reaction it might instigate made him shrink from the idea. Whatever offence he'd unintentionally committed, he was hardly going to solve it by avoiding the woman. He resolved to make Linda his friend. Eddie turned his attention to the room and what he could achieve in order to get it ready.

He opened the window and climbed out onto the roof. There was a narrow flat section behind the parapet which hung over the front of the cinema. A small wall divided it from the rest of the vaulted roof, providing a seat. He took a moment in the sun, imagining countless projectionists before him sneaking out here for a cheeky cigarette.

Back inside, Eddie regarded the battered old armchair. There was something about it which lent a cosiness to the space, but it was taking up valuable room. He'd add it to the list of things to throw out.

With a burst of enthusiasm, he set about organising the area. There wasn't much room for improvement, but a few well-placed hooks might keep some of the spools off the floor. A couple of new shelves would help with storing cans before they were returned to the distributer. Eddie searched around for a sheet of paper and a pen; he needed to make another list.

Two hours later, hunger drove him back to the foyer. He'd noticed a solitary chocolate bar in the kiosk earlier, he couldn't recall which brand. As he entered, he was pleased to see the main walls being plastered — progress at last — and surprised to find Linda in situ behind the kiosk, flicking through a magazine. It wasn't as if there was anything for her to do. She glanced up as he approached, her hair freshly bleached with an added streak of scarlet, eyes thick with kohl.

'Morning, Linda.'

'Afternoon.' Linda's face remained expressionless as she checked the clock behind.

'Is it already? How time flies when you're having fun.' He swallowed, thinking of ways to sound like less of a prick. He wanted his staff to like him, but sensed Linda could smell his desperation. 'Everything okay? Was there something you wanted?'

It may have been his paranoia, but he could have sworn she threw him the smallest of eye rolls. With that much make-up it was hard to tell. Nails painted in pink to match her hair thumbed through magazine pages adorned by celebrities.

'Just checking in.' Linda closed her magazine, her black-painted lips spreading into a thin smile. 'Can't hang around here all day.'

She picked up the last chocolate bar in the kiosk and left. He noticed it was a *Turkish Delight*. No matter, it wasn't his concern anymore.

CHAPTER 13

Anna set down the telephone and checked her watch. She was teaching a seminar in half an hour. As much as she loved interacting with undergrad students, the nerves still got to her. She started packing up her things with the intention of getting a few minutes fresh air to calm the liquid sensation in her stomach, when Graham entered the office with his familiar furtive glance and closed the door.

'Am I in trouble?' Graham's voice lacked its usual confidence.

Anna wasn't in the mood to talk about him standing her up the previous evening.

Graham didn't wait for her answer. 'Can I make it up to you tomorrow? I can stay over. Deborah's going to her sisters for the weekend. I've said I'm doing a work thing, which is sort of true because I hope to be doing you.' He followed up with an unbearably sexy grin.

Anna shoved her lesson plan into her bag, feeling a frisson of excitement mixed with intense irritation. A concoction only Graham seemed to conjure. 'Okay, oh damn, hang on.' She'd agreed to meet Eddie. 'I have a thing Sunday morning, early, a breakfast thing at the uni.'

'Can't you get out of it?'

Anna hesitated. She didn't want to back out on Dr Humphries' son. 'Sorry, I can't, but it shouldn't take long, then we'll have the rest of the day together.'

'Just the morning, I'm afraid. Debs is back at one.'

Anna stared at the wall. She hated it when he called his wife Debs. 'Sure, no problem, I'll be back for brunch.'

* * *

The following morning, Anna stood at her sitting room window, annoyed with herself for having nothing better to do than watch for the first glimpse of Graham's car on the street below. She hadn't considered herself the type of woman who would become a mistress; it was a betrayal of the sisterhood. Acclimatising to a new country made her just about lonely enough for her principles to go flying out of the window, or maybe that was a convenient excuse.

Before she could spiral into an existential crisis, Anna spied his Mondeo pulling into a space on the opposite side of the road which ran along the edge of leafy Belmont Park. This couldn't go on for much longer. Graham was brought in to cover Dr Humphries' sabbatical. In a few months she'd return, and he might be forced to move to another institution. Then where would they be?

Anna couldn't help admiring Dr Humphries. Her work on the femme fatale was ground-breaking. Now she was writing a book on the portrayal of women in film noir. Perhaps she'd be willing to be Anna's new supervisor . . . what would that be like? Her thoughts cartwheeled to Eddie. Is that why she'd agreed to run his film, because she had an academic crush on his mother? *Oh God, am I that pathetic?*

Graham lifted something from the back seat, distracting her from the question. A dozen red roses. His eyes made a sweep of the street. In a few moments he'd be at her front door. She moved to the intercom, anticipating his ring.

* * *

Anna was pulled from the fog of sleep by a car honking its horn in the street outside. She leaned across Graham, straining to see the time on her digital alarm clock: 8.18 a.m.

'Shit.' She sprang from the bed and searched for clothes, regretting the two bottles of wine they'd sunk the previous evening.

Graham stirred too. 'What's going on?'

'I have a breakfast appointment, remember?' She yanked up her jeans.

'Surely you're not going into the university on a Sunday?'

'It's the only time he could meet me.'

'He?'

'Yes, Graham, a man. Quite a few of them populate this planet, you know.'

'Who is he?'

Anna grabbed her hoodie, gave it a quick sniff and pulled it on, enjoying his jealousy.

Graham propped himself up. 'Is this about last night?'

She winced at his reaction. Fuelled by wine, Anna broached the thorny subject of their future. What would happen at the end of his contract? Graham dodged her questions and a stony silence ensued until Anna suggested Dr Humphries would make a better supervisor anyway.

Graham reached for his boxer shorts where he'd discarded them on the floor. 'I know you're worried about the future.'

'It's fine, I'm not annoyed, but I have to keep this appointment.'

'What about breakfast?'

'There's bread and cereal in the kitchen.'

He pulled on his shorts. 'You know that's not what I meant.'

Anna shrugged. 'I'm just trying to live my life. I made these plans before we arranged last night. I can't organise everything around when you're free.'

Graham looked downcast but he met her gaze. 'I know. I love you, Anna. This is hard for me too.'

She leaned across the bed to stroke his face. 'I love you.'

'What if I was free?'

Anna sat on the bed and pulled on her trainers. Despite assurances his marriage was over, Graham had never come this close to validating their relationship. 'What are you saying?'

'Last night, you made me realise we need to talk about the future. *Our* future.'

This was the conversation she'd been longing for, but his timing was terrible. 'Hold that thought, I have to go.'

And she forced herself out the door.

CHAPTER 14

Eddie pulled into the university car park, gratified to find it almost empty. Cutting the engine, he glanced at the film can, wrapped in a towel on the passenger seat beside him. After it's time in the fridge, a certain amount of condensation had collected. He vaguely remembered something about old film needing to acclimatise to warmer temperatures and hoped he wasn't causing further damage.

A cool wind whipped at his face as he made his way across campus. A security guard hovered by the door to the postgrad building. Not wishing to incur questioning without Anna, Eddie threw him a nod and sat on a bench outside.

The campus was practically deserted. Too early for students at the weekend, he supposed, not that he had ever been one himself. After his mum showed him how to work a projector at the age of five, his path was set. By the time he should have been studying for an undergraduate degree, she was embarking on one herself as a mature student, but she never pressured him to take an academic route. He appreciated her sanguine attitude about the choices he made. *I just want you to be happy, Ed.*

Eddie was dragged from his reminiscing by the sound of footsteps and laboured breathing. Anna appeared, looking like she'd just got out of bed. Perhaps she had. The thought of Anna in bed distracted him in a way he couldn't articulate.

'Morning, sorry I'm late.' She pushed open the door and rummaged through her bag, eventually pulling out her staff ID, which she showed the security guard. He let them through.

Eddie followed her down long corridors and up a flight of stairs before stopping at a row of doors.

'These rooms are normally used by film students on their final projects.' Anna tried the first door. Finding it locked, she tried a second, which was open.

Eddie blinked as she switched on the light. The window-less room was about the size of a large cupboard and contained at the centre a machine for viewing film called a Steenbeck. He'd only used one once, when he'd visited a film-processing lab in London. It was a bit like a bulky table in the middle of which was a viewing screen the size of a computer monitor. In front of the screen were four large discs or plates, one to hold the film picture and the other for a separate soundtrack. Between the sets of discs were various drivers. Two plastic chairs were placed in front of the Steenbeck and to the right was a winding bench.

Anna gestured to the film and smirked. 'What's with the towel, did it take a shower?'

Eddie grimaced. 'I stored it in the fridge. Was that a terrible idea? I was trying to help it acclimatise.'

'It's not ideal. You can freeze old film under controlled conditions, but domestic fridges won't really help.'

'I hope I haven't caused any damage.'

Anna took the can and handed him back the towel. 'Let's find out.'

Eddie offered his car key as she struggled with the rusty lid. They both recoiled at the smell.

Donning her glasses, Anna set the film on the winding bench. 'I'll need to put it on a core so we can attempt to view it, that's if it isn't so shrunk it won't run.'

'Shrunk?' Eddie peered over her shoulder.

'Film stock shrinks with age, nitrate especially, and that aroma is a heady cocktail of nitric oxide and nitrogen dioxide.'

The film made a sucking sound like shoes on a tacky surface as Anna wound it onto a core.

'It's not seriously sticky yet, but it's getting that way. The emulsion side starts to come away from the base side, causing the picture to disappear.' Towards the end of the reel, a splice fell apart. 'Dried out. Can you pass me the splicer, please?'

Eddie retrieved the familiar bulky metal contraption from a shelf to the side of the bench and passed it to Anna. 'How do you know so much about old film?'

'Back in New York, I did an internship with the film archive at the Museum of Modern Art. In the end, I decided it wasn't the career for me.'

'Wow.' Impressed, Eddie watched her lay the two pieces of film along the metal sprockets of the splicer and run the tape across.

She brought the leaver down, puncturing the perforations. 'It's a shame to use tape but I don't think we'll be keeping this reel once we've viewed it.'

With the film on its core, she carried it to the Steenbeck and placed it on the plate closest to the screen. With deft hands she threaded the film through the various drivers.

'Yikes, this is going to be painful.' Anna flicked the lights off and sat in one of the plastic chairs. Eddie took the other. He was acutely aware of their breathing in the confined space.

The film bowed and rolled on the screen and the optical soundtrack emitted a pained howl. He recognised the final scene from Casablanca through a haze of scratches. Rick and Renault watching the plane carrying Ilsa and her husband take off, escaping the Nazis. Their voices were distorted, but it wasn't the dialogue that interested him.

As the final iconic words were spoken by Bogart, the film faded to black. Anna turned to face him as something flashed on screen.

Eddie sat forward. 'Did you see that?'

She frowned and returned her attention to the Steenbeck. 'Can you go back?'

'Not easily.' She eased the film backwards, the perforations straining to jump off their sprockets. A title card with the words *Connie Harris* materialised on screen.

'Now go forwards.'

Another title card came into view.

Will you marry me?

Then the film went to black and ran off its leader.

Eddie sat back, astonished. 'A wedding proposal?' He was more intrigued than ever.

Anna pulled off her glasses. 'What a beautiful way to propose. Who is she?'

He shook his head. 'I have no idea.'

Anna regarded him. 'Well, whoever Connie Harris is, I hope she said yes.'

PART THREE

July 1951

CHAPTER 15

A broad smile spread across Charlie's lips when he walked into the kitchen the following morning and was met with two sets of expectant eyes. The mouth-watering aroma of a cooked breakfast filled the room.

'Well?' His mum approached, oven gloves in her hands.

'Would I be grinning like this if she'd said no?'

She dropped the oven gloves, engulfing him in a clamorous hug. His father offered his hand, which Charlie shook once he'd been released from his mother's grip.

'I've made a fry-up. I thought it would work for both celebration and commiseration.' She returned to the stove.

'Glad you had faith in me.' Charlie pulled out a chair.

'Connie must come for tea. We need to make plans.' His mother placed a plate of bacon and eggs in front of him.

Charlie's father sipped his coffee. 'Steady on, Marge, you don't want to ambush the poor girl.'

Charlie threw him a grateful look.

'Nonsense, what bride-to-be doesn't want to discuss her wedding? With her mum having died, she'll appreciate some maternal input.' Another plate of breakfast arrived in front of his dad.

Marge set a rack of toast on the table and took a seat, a cup of coffee in her hands.

'Aren't you joining us?' Charlie cut into the fried egg, satisfied by the ooze of the yolk melding with the bacon. Breakfasts like this remained a rarity under rationing. He appreciated the trouble his mum had gone to.

She beamed. 'I'm watching my figure. There's a wedding in my future.'

'Maybe I'll bring Con over this evening. I'm meeting her dad at the White Ball this afternoon.'

'Lovely. Why don't you invite her dad for tea too? We'd like to meet him, wouldn't we, Jim?'

'We'll see, Mum.' Charlie reached for a slice of toast. He wasn't convinced Mr Harris was the type of man who appreciated afternoon tea. He had no idea what to expect from his future father-in-law.

* * *

Charlie arrived at the pub ten minutes early, the fry-up still leaden in his stomach. He'd passed a slow morning helping his dad mend a hole in the fence where foxes were getting into the back garden.

'Don't mind your mother's fussing,' his dad said as Charlie cut down a piece of wood. 'Her only son is getting married, it's a landmark moment in a mother's life.'

'I don't mind.'

'Nervous about meeting Connie's dad?'

Charlie carried the wood over to the hole. It was a little too long. 'I am a bit. Connie never talks about him. I get the sense things aren't . . . I don't know. It must be hard, losing her mum last year.'

He caught his dad glancing at the house, where his mum was reading a book on a sun lounger by the back door. 'It must.'

It was these little gestures that made Charlie realise how happy his parents were.

Located on Bridge Street next to the river, the pub was packed with factory families. A former coaching inn, there was a long saloon bar and beamed ceiling. A painting of John Heathcoat, the factory founder, hung over an inglenook fireplace. Charlie ordered a pint and took a seat on a bar stool, hoping a table might become available before Connie arrived.

Twenty minutes passed as Charlie sipped his beer wishing he had a newspaper or book to pass the time. With one eye on the door, he tried to relax, absorbing himself in the conversations around him. The chief topic of gossip was a break-in at the factory yard overnight. One of the delivery vans had gone missing. Various names were bandied around, Frank Harris among them. Charlie listened to a none-too-flattering description of his future father-in-law. The beer joined the fry-up in his knotted stomach.

'Can I get you another?' The barman reached for his glass.

Charlie checked the clock above the bar: 1.28 p.m. 'No thanks, I'll be off.' He slid from the stool and made for the door.

Outside, he hesitated. It wasn't like Connie to be so late. Fearing he'd misunderstood their arrangement, he headed in the direction of her house.

Church Street was quiet as he made his way along the terraces. Outside Connie's home, he was struck again by its shabby appearance, emphasised in the bright light of day. He knocked, hoping in vain to hear footsteps. No answer. He peered at the front window, curtains closed against the world.

Anxiety led him back to the White Ball in the hope they'd turned up in his absence. With lunch over, the pub had emptied out. A quick scan but no sign of Connie.

'Changed your mind about that pint?' The barman held up a glass.

'I'm looking for someone. Connie Harris. I was supposed to meet her here with her dad, Frank. Have they been in?'

The barman rolled his eyes. 'You're a brave lad, getting embroiled with that family. Frank was in last night, drank himself stupid. I chucked him out myself. I've not seen hide nor hair of him today. Have you tried the house?'

Charlie frowned, dispirited at this news. 'No answer.'

'Anyone seen Frank Harris?' the barman called to the vicinity.

His question was met with head shaking or laughs of derision.

'He's most likely sleeping it off. As to the daughter, I couldn't say. Pretty girl, shame she's got him for a father.'

Charlie nodded. 'If you see her, tell her Charlie was here.'

'Aye, I'll do that, lad.'

* * *

Charlie called at the house one last time then headed home, unease roiling in his stomach. For the first time, he realised the love of his life could be hiding something much darker than the state of her home.

He paced his parents' garden until his dad offered to accompany him back into town to look for Connie. The Sunday streets were desolate as they passed through the centre. Everyone was at home, tucking into ham sandwiches and squares of sponge cake.

'Try not to worry. Maybe there's been a family emergency and she's been called away.'

'I don't think she's got any family.' Charlie winced. How little he knew about the woman he wanted to spend his life with.

At the house, he watched his dad assessing the building before them. 'Blimey,' he muttered.

'I know.' Charlie knocked, sensing the silence within. He glanced at his dad.

'I'll knock on a couple of neighbours' doors. Someone must know where they are.'

Charlie followed, grateful for his dad's calm, practical nature. The house next door was empty but the one after was answered by a short woman in her fifties, her hair pinned in curlers under a scarf.

'Not seen them for a couple of days. Police were round here earlier asking about him though. Doesn't surprise me, the way he carries on.'

The neighbour opposite, a willowy woman with a face set in permanent repose, repeated a similar story. 'They keep themselves to themselves. Her mum was a saint for putting up with Frank Harris. Still, you make your bed. I'm sure the police will have him. Maybe she's down the station bailing him out.'

Charlie turned to his dad. 'I hadn't thought of that.'

They retraced their steps, Jim jabbering reassurances at his side. His dad's musings did little to counter the terror building in his head. Whatever happened to Frank Harris, Connie needed him.

Walking with purpose up Canal Hill, they found the double-fronted Victorian police station closed. Charlie banged on the door, his frustration growing with every passing second. With no answer, he hammered again until his dad rested a placating hand on his shoulder. But as they turned to go, footsteps from within reached their ears. An officer of about his dad's age peered at them over half-moon spectacles from the crack in the door.

'We're closed.' He pointed to the opening hours on a plaque.

'Please, this is urgent. My fiancée is missing. Her father is Frank Harris.'

The door drew open. 'Frank Harris?' The officer stood to one side. 'You'd better come in.'

They followed him into a room at the front of the building. Another officer sat with his feet up on a desk.

'They're looking for Frank Harris.'

The officer behind the desk straightened. 'So are we. What have you got to tell us, son?' He gestured to a seat.

'My fiancée, Connie Harris, was supposed to meet me at the White Ball with her dad this afternoon, but they didn't

82

show up. I've been back a couple of times and to the house too. A neighbour said you were looking for Frank.'

'I don't envy you, having him for a father-in-law.' The officer chuckled.

'I haven't met him.' Charlie felt his face flush.

'You might want to meet the father before popping the question. Happen you've had a lucky escape.'

A surge of rage so hot it burned his retinas pulsed through Charlie. He stood up. 'I need to know Connie is safe.'

'All right, son.' His dad's hand came around his arm.

The officer pulled out a pad and pen. 'When did you last see her?'

'Last night. I proposed at the Tivoli where we both work. I'm the projectionist and Con's an usherette.'

'What time was this?'

'We left the Tivoli soon after midnight.'

The older officer regarded him over his spectacles. 'Bit late to be at the cinema?'

'Our boss, Mr Reynolds, asked us to lock up.'

The other officer raised an eyebrow before returning to his notes. 'You were there alone?'

Charlie nodded, feeling like he was the one being interrogated.

'I see.' The officer scribbled something on his pad. 'What happened after you left?'

'I walked Connie home, then returned home myself.'

'Anyone vouch for that?'

'I can,' Jim piped up. 'I heard my son come in shortly after twelve thirty. I remember because I went to the bathroom, and he was coming up the stairs.'

Charlie glanced at his dad, grateful for his lie. He had been home, there was nothing to hide.

'So, when you said goodbye to Connie, did you see Frank Harris then?'

'No, like I said, I haven't met him. Connie never lets me see her into the house. We always say goodbye on the corner of the street.'

The officer frowned. 'That didn't strike you as odd?'

'At first, but when I saw the state of her home, I thought maybe she was ashamed, and I didn't want to push it. I'm going to take her away from all that, give her a better life.'

The officer exchanged a look with his colleague. 'We have put a call out for Frank Harris. A van has gone missing from Heathcoat's. As a foreman, he would have access to the keys. Can you give us a description of Connie?'

Charlie conjured her face. 'She's about my height with auburn hair, like Rita Hayworth, and green eyes and . . .' He trailed off.

The officer scribbled in his notebook. 'Any friends she might have gone to?'

Viv came to mind. 'Yes,' Charlie ventured, hoping Connie would turn up for work tomorrow full of explanations. 'Her friend Viv Anderson, but I don't know where she lives.'

'We'll look her up. Give us your contact details and we'll keep you informed.'

Charlie gave his address and pushed back his chair. 'There must be something more I can do?'

'The best thing you can do, lad, is go home and wait for her to get in touch.'

Outside, Charlie pulled up his collar, chilled despite the warm evening, and followed his dad down the road, disquiet accompanying every step.

'Can we check the house one more time, Dad?'

'Course we can.'

'Thanks.' Charlie thrust his hands in his pockets, his limbs numb with fear. With no idea where Viv lived, there was nothing to do now but sit tight until morning and see what the Tivoli revealed.

CHAPTER 16

Something cold and wet explored her cheek, stale breath warmed her ear. She forced open her eyes. Pain lanced through the lids, it hurt to blink.

'Here, Bear.' A voice, male and earthy, punctured the fog coalescing in her brain.

Bear emitted a low bark somewhere close to her head. The noise resonated so hard her lids flicked open again. Above, gossamer clouds floated across azure blue skies. She stared, mesmerised by their languid movement, but the pain was too much. It hurt to look, it hurt not to.

Her gaze attached itself to a black tail moving through the undergrowth away from her. A tangy mix of earth and metallic blood tinged the air. She could taste it. Her fingers searched the ground. She was lying on something soft and damp. Moss or grass?

The dog was back with a bristled tongue against her cheek. A shadow stole the sun and a shape loomed above.

'You all right, miss?'

A man with a whisp of white hair stood over her, the furrows in his brow so deep as to make rivulets across his forehead as if he existed in a permanent state of anxiety. A black-and-white dog wagged its tail at his side and continued its investigations of her body with its inquisitive nose.

'I don't think she can understand me, Joe.'

A young, roughhewn face with hazel eyes and a slightly crooked mouth appeared above. He wore a flat cap over a shock of ginger hair.

'Hello?'

She tried to answer but her head throbbed and the arid feel in her throat prevented her from making an audible sound.

'Grab that horse blanket from the cart, Dad. She's shivering.'

It was true, her limbs appeared to be moving of their own volition.

She could hear the deep tones of Joe's voice, see the shapes of the words as his lips moved, but the pulsing in her ears broke the sound into shattered bursts.

His father returned, handing Joe the blanket. 'She's taken one hell of a battering. What if she's broken something?'

'We can't leave her lying in the damp earth, she'll catch a chill. Can you wiggle your toes, miss?'

She did as she was asked, but the exertion required seemed at odds with the task. Joe gave a nod of satisfaction at her efforts.

A blanket was placed across her body, giving off the scent of hay. Its comfort was undermined by the heft pressing against her ribs, as if someone had laid an anvil on her chest.

'I'm going to lift you now, miss.' She cried out as rough hands slipped under her back and legs. Her head lolled back, the horizon tilted. Then shadows and oblivion.

She awoke to the clip of hooves, every jolt of the cart pulsing in her head. Gnarled trees entwined above. Fractured sunlight warmed the sore muscles in her face. Her body felt restricted, swaddled like an Egyptian mummy. She glanced down at herself. She was lying in a cart, wrapped in a blanket; her stockinged feet, grass-stained and muddy, poked out at one end. The dog lay curled asleep in the corner. The silhouettes of Joe and his father sat aloft at the front, their voices low and troubled.

The cart ground to a halt, the men climbed down and the dog jumped out. Their footsteps died away. Minutes passed, her lids grew heavy, sleep invited her to surrender.

'Hello, there.' A woman's voice at her side caused another agonising jolt. She shifted her gaze and found herself looking into a pair of concerned hazel eyes framed by vibrant ginger curls. 'Who have we got 'ere?'

Words remained out of reach, unable to circumnavigate the pain lodged in her head and throat.

'What's your name, maid?'

Panic spread across her chest, causing her jagged breath to catch. She tore her eyes from the woman's expectant gaze.

She didn't know.

CHAPTER 17

After their third visit to the squat house on Church Street the previous evening yielded nothing, Charlie was back there again at the break of dawn. His desperate knocks on the door elicited only a bark from a neighbouring dog.

He made his way to the Tivoli, more convinced than ever something was seriously wrong.

The first to arrive, he tore through the building looking in vain for Connie. The place was eerily empty apart from Tommy, who accompanied him on his search, another pair of eyes. In the projection room he busied himself by cleaning down the projector. The end of their evening replayed in his mind. Connie in his arms, their bodies locked together on the chair.

An interminable hour later, Charlie was waiting in the foyer, where he'd spent the last half an hour watching the alleyway for a glimpse of forest green. Viv rushed in.

'Is there any news?' She gripped his arm.

Charlie's heart sank. 'The police told you?'

'They came round late last night. Oh, Charlie, where can she be?'

His eyes filled with tears.

Viv took his arm. 'Come on, we'll talk upstairs.'

* * *

Viv perched at the open window and drew on her cigarette, offering it to Charlie. He shook his head. His stomach was so sick with worry he couldn't face a smoke.

'Did she talk to you about her dad?' he asked, searching for clues.

'Nothing specific. I got the sense he was a difficult man. I mean, he has a bit of a reputation in certain circles.' Viv blew out a billow of smoke. 'I knew she was nervous about introducing him to you.'

Charlie was sitting on the projection room floor with his back against the wall. He buried his face in his hands. 'Why didn't she tell me? I would have understood.'

'She was scared of losing you.'

He shook his head. 'I love her, how could she think that?'

Viv shrugged. 'I don't think Con's had much unconditional love in her life before now.'

'What if something terrible has happened? I can't stand it.'

'Don't think like that. There has to be an explanation.' Viv checked the clock. 'We'd better talk to Reynolds. He'll be here soon.'

* * *

To his credit, Reynolds proved sympathetic when Charlie and Viv stood before him ten minutes later. Pitching his hands together, he sat behind his desk, genuine concern furrowing his brow.

'I like to think we're family here at the Tivoli. Family look out for each other. If you need to take time off, Charlie, I can enlist Sam or even run the films myself. Did the police give you any idea how extensive their search is?'

Charlie shook his head. 'I telephoned this morning, there was no news.'

'Right.'

'I'd like to keep working in case she comes here. I think I'll go mad waiting at home.'

Reynolds nodded. 'I agree, better to keep busy. Viv, you'll have to double up today until I can rearrange a few shifts.'

'Yes, Mr Reynolds.'

Outside the office, Charlie scanned the foyer, half expecting to see Connie at the kiosk loading her tray. He glanced at Viv; her gaze was drawn in the same direction.

'I'll see you later,' Charlie mumbled. Viv nodded goodbye. There was nothing they could do now but wait.

* * *

Charlie set about preparing for the afternoon screening. Going through the technical checks gave him a focus and kept his hands busy, but every time he allowed his mind to wonder, his stomach plummeted. He couldn't recall another time in his life when he'd felt this scared.

The film was *All About Eve* starring Bette Davis. Connie had been looking forward to it. The thought made his fingers shake as he tried to lace the reel through the projector. He'd just finished when Reynolds stepped into the room.

'The police are in my office.'

'There's news?'

Reynolds expression was grim. 'I'll take care of things here. Better not keep them waiting.'

Charlie's blood ran cold as he raced down the stairs. Viv met him in the foyer.

Two constables were standing at Reynolds' desk when they walked in, one of which he recognised from the previous evening. A large brown paper bag was placed before them.

Charlie looked from the bag to their faces.

'I understand you're Constance Harris's fiancé?'

'That's right.' His voice didn't sound like his own.

'You'd better take a seat.' He gestured to a chair. Charlie gripped the back as Viv clutched his arm.

'We found Frank Harris's body near Countisbury on the north Exmoor coast. He'd stolen a van from Heathcoat's factory in the early hours of Sunday morning. We believe he lost control and drove over the cliff.'

Charlie's insides turned liquid. 'Connie?' he whispered.

'We haven't found her body, only this.' The officer glanced at his colleague, who opened the paper bag and pulled out her forest-green usherette hat. 'It was floating in the sea, not far from where the van hit the rocks.'

Charlie stared at Connie's pillbox hat as if he could stare it out of existence. Viv at his side buried her face against his shoulder, shaking with tears.

'You recognise the hat?'

He nodded. 'It's part of the uniform. Connie was wearing it on . . .' Words failed him.

'We're very sorry.'

He cast around, searching for a way out of this nightmare. 'But you haven't found a body? She might . . .'

'The area is prone to strong rip currents. If she got caught in one, she'd have been washed out to sea. The Bristol Channel runs along that part of the coast. The lifeboats are searching, but you should prepare yourselves.'

Charlie's features crumpled.

'We'll give you some time.' The officers left the room.

He closed his eyes, struggling to remain upright while Viv shook against him. He clung to her as the walls closed in, crushing his dreams in their wake.

CHAPTER 18

The first thing she noticed was the light forcing her lids open. A beam from a window to the right of the bed fell across her legs, illuminating the pattern of climbing roses on the eiderdown. She tried to sit up, but pain pulsed in her head, creating waves of pressure. Her arm swung out, upsetting a glass of water on the bedside table. It clattered to the floor, spilling its contents across a threadbare rug.

The noise roused someone from within the house. A heavy tread on the stairs, the creek of a floorboard and the door moved open.

She lifted her arm to shield her face as if expecting an attack. But a voice like warm treacle quelled her nerves. It was the woman with the red curls.

'We was wondering when you'd wake up. I said to George, if the maid isn't awake by tomorrow, we'll have to do something, and 'ere you are.'

With hands on hips, the woman's gaze was drawn to the upset glass.

'I'm sorry,' she croaked. The sound surprised her.

'You've found your voice at last. No need to be sorry. I'm Agnes. I don't expect you remember our meeting yesterday afternoon?' Agnes stooped to pick up the glass. Her red curls were tied back in a long plait, spun with streaks of silver. She wore a plain dress in calico and a floral apron with large pockets. 'You gave us all a fright. Still, you're awake now. Remembered your name yet, love?'

There was kindness in Agnes's gaze as she waited for her reply, but the answer remained out of reach. A pitying smile spread across her lips. 'Not to worry, it'll come. I'll fetch you a dish of tea.'

With Agnes gone, she took a moment to study her surroundings. The bedroom was narrow with a vaulted ceiling. A large timber beam ran through the centre and the stone walls were whitewashed. An attic perhaps? Opposite the brass bed in which she was lying was a dressing table with an oval mirror, but the mirror had been covered with a sheet. Next to this was a stand with a washbowl and jug.

Exhausted by these observations, she sank back into the soft pillows and traced the pattern of climbing roses along the eiderdown with her finger.

As her lids grew heavy, Agnes returned with a steaming mug of tea, placing it on the bedside table. 'How are you feeling?'

She lifted her hand to touch her brow, noticing her arms. They were livid with purple bruises. Her palms were grazed as if she'd fallen and tried to stop herself.

'Lord knows what happened to you,' Agnes continued. 'Do you recall anything?'

She shook her head. Pain surged at her temples.

Agnes patted her knee beneath the eiderdown. 'Is there anyone who might be missing you? We're isolated out here but if you can recall where home is, I'm sure when you're up to it we can get you there.'

A tear slid down her cheek. She could offer nothing in answer to these questions.

Another pitying smile from Agnes. 'Well, we'll have to call you something until you get your memory back.' Casting around as if for inspiration, her gaze settled on the eiderdown. 'How about Rose?'

She gave a small nod.

'Rose it is.'

Male voices drifted up the stairs. 'That'll be my boys back for their tea. I'd best go down to see to them. Drink up, Rose.' Agnes gestured to the mug and made for the door.

'Rose,' she whispered as Agnes's footsteps died away.

* * *

Rose struggled to sit up and reach for her cup, a roughhewn stoneware affair. She took a tremulous sip, the tea tepid on her lips and sore in her throat. She searched for the answers to Agnes's questions. No clue as to who she was or how she came to be in this place filtered to the surface. Panic gripped her then receded into the haze of her mind. Placing the cup back on the bedside table, Rose ran her fingers over her face, her skin swollen and tender to touch. Her hands came to rest in her lap. The nails were dirty, she didn't like it.

Agnes returned, clutching a chamber pot. 'Thought you might be in desperate need.'

Rose blanched.

'Give over, maid, you need to use the pot. Let me help you up then I'll wait outside.'

As Rose stepped from the bed, pain lanced through every limb. Stumbling, Agnes's strong arms steadied her progress until she was standing above the pot, shivering in her thin nightie. Lowering herself, need overcame decorum. The smell of her piss was repellent in the close air. Agnes returned, helped her back into bed and took the pot. 'I'll bring you some soup, I expect you're famished.'

Thick tiredness dragged at her limbs and pulled at her eyelids. Without so much as a whisper, sleep reclaimed her. But Agnes soon returned carrying a tray.

'Best keep you awake for a bit, love. Here.' Agnes waited for Rose to sit up before placing the tray with a bowl of soup and a crust of bread before her. The smell woke her stomach. Rose picked up the spoon, taking a careful sip. The soup was thin and a little salty but warm. It slid down her throat like a trail of fire, burning her empty insides. Glancing up from her bowl, she noticed Agnes studying her, satisfaction in her eyes.

'Where am I?' Rose asked, as much because she wanted to know as to divert Agnes's curious attention.

'Exmoor. North of Simonsbath.'

Tears filled her eyes and Rose averted her gaze to the soup. The names meant nothing to her. Was Exmoor where she was from? Why didn't she know?

CHAPTER 19

Days passed, and the colour palette of bruising on her arms gradually changed from purples to greens and yellows. The rest of her body appeared unharmed apart from a long scratch on her leg as if she'd been caught on a gate or fence. It was her head that told a different story. A relentless throbbing not only around her temples but her jaw and throat. Agnes applied a daily mixture of compresses and various homemade rubs with strange smells. Something was working, Agnes reassured in her singsong voice. Time would set things right.

'Will I see a doctor?' Rose asked when Agnes presented her with a pile of clothes so she might venture beyond her room.

Lifting a pair of dark corduroy trousers, Agnes appeared not to have heard the question. 'You're as tall as a giraffe and skinny like one too. These belong to our Joe, but you can roll them up. My things will drown you.'

Rose stepped self-consciously from between the covers to wash at the large china bowl. She thought to ask about the doctor again, but Agnes laid out her undergarments, which she'd laundered.

'These are fancy,' Agnes said, fingering the delicate lace trim of the camisole. 'Hark at you, maid. Get yeself dressed and I'll see you downstairs.'

Rose plunged her hands into the lukewarm water, took the soap and worked it between her fingers, taking care to clean her nails first. Examining their shining moons, her spirits lifted then sank again as she tried to wash her face. The skin was tight, the scars and bruising too fragile to touch.

Once she'd finished, she patted herself dry and slid into her undergarments. They felt supple against her body but not familiar in the way she hoped. She tugged on Joe's trousers and rolled them to her ankles, then Agnes's voluminous blouse, which she tucked in and secured with a string belt. A woollen cardigan and a pair of knitted socks completed the outfit.

Rose eyed the mirror under its sheet. She lifted the cloth gingerly and recoiled at her own reflection. It wasn't just the swelling across her right eye, the livid bruising to her cheek and throat, it was the shock of her own reflection. The woman staring back at her was a stranger. Her hand shook as her fingers grazed her cheek, to make certain it was real, that she was real. A rush of tears sprang from her eyes. Rose took a step back, unable to stand the sight of this apparition.

A shout from outside lured her away from the glass. She moved to the window and peered out. Joe was in the yard with his father trying to capture a sheep which had made a bid for freedom. Bear circled the animal too, alert to his master's whistles. The men attempted to corner the sheep while it ran around them. It was the first time she'd laid eyes on the other occupants of the house since they'd found her on the moor. She'd heard them, of course, but only Agnes visited her room. Now she found herself momentarily distracted from her worries. The sheep barrelled in Joe's direction, knocking him off his long legs. Agnes hadn't exaggerated when she said her son was tall. He'd inherited her ginger curls, which sat above a square-jawed face. His father was stockier as he stared down the errant sheep on bowed legs. Eventually the entertainment was over. They corralled the runaway back into the field, Bear snapping at its heels.

Moments later, their exuberant voices drifted up the stairs.

Drawn out by their high spirits, Rose ventured to her door. At the top of the oak staircase she hesitated, before gripping the banister and allowing her feet to lead her into the hallway.

The hall was an oblong room with a quarry-tiled floor and a long bench running down one side where an array of coats hung above and boots in various sizes stood beneath. The front door had been left open, inviting in a warm breeze and the tweet of birdsong, the bleating of sheep and the rustle of trees, the only sounds she'd heard over the last few days.

Three doors led off from the hallway. She drew closer to the one from where she could hear laughter. It was ajar. Rose peered through the gap into the long, stone room.

Father and son sat at a worn pine table, with a mug of tea in front of each of them. Gauzy puffs of smoke drifted from the older man's pipe. Agnes's voice carried but she remained out of view. Encouraged by Agnes's presence, Rose took a deep breath and pushed open the door. The creak of tired hinges alerted the room to her presence.

Joe looked up, failing to hide his surprise. Noticing his son's changed expression, the older man turned in her direction. Only Agnes chatted on, unaware of Rose's presence. Bear approached, wagging his tail.

Joe's father struggled to his feet. 'Away, Bear.'

Agnes glanced up from her place at the stove, her face breaking into a warm smile. 'How lovely.' She approached, taking Rose's hands and giving them a squeeze. 'Come on, Joe, get the girl a chair. Out of the way, Bear.'

Joe's complexion matched his hair as he stood to offer his own, almost upsetting his chair in the process.

Rose sat on the proffered seat, sensing the eyes of the room on her. Agnes set down a teacup and filled it from a large brown betty pot at the centre of the table. Rose's gaze was drawn to the pot. It seemed familiar but no sooner did the thought arrive than it evaporated. She tore her gaze away and concentrated on picking up her cup. As she did so, she caught

Joe's hazel eyes studying her from the seat opposite. Instinct made her touch her scar. He looked away as if embarrassed by her injury.

'It's lovely to see you up and about.' Agnes joined them, pouring herself a tea. Bear returned to his bed in front of the Aga. 'You remember Joe and George who found you on the moor.'

Suddenly shy, Rose nodded, but regretted it immediately as pain surged through her head. An awkward silence settled around the table. The easy chatter and laughter from before she entered had vanished. Rose felt guilty her presence had so obviously punctured the camaraderie of the family. She should have kept to her room.

Joe downed what was left in his mug and stood. 'I'd best get on.'

George stood too and followed his son out of the room.

'Don't mind them.' Agnes took a noisy slurp. 'They're not used to company, 'tis all.'

Rose sipped her tea, her mind returning to the stranger in the mirror. She couldn't blame Joe for his disgust. She looked like she'd been pounded with a meat tenderiser. Perhaps it was better she couldn't recall who she was, what she'd looked like before or why someone had seen fit to destroy her face.

CHAPTER 20

Charlie forced himself down the stairs to the front door past framed family photos. His parents' wedding, his dad looking proud in his RAF uniform, Charlie's childish face grinning from behind a bucket and spade on their last seaside holiday before the war. Connie had studied them all when she visited for afternoon tea, her bright eyes delighting in every detail while he stood behind, arms threaded around her waist, confident they'd have a similar wall of memories themselves one day. *Their memories.*

In the hall, his mother intercepted him. 'Are you sure this is wise, love?'

'I need to see it.'

'Countisbury is a long drive.'

The newspaper landed on the mat with a thud. Charlie made to pick it up, but his mother swooped in as she'd done with every paper over the last week.

'I can't avoid it, Mum.'

Marge handed the paper to him with evident reluctance. Connie had made the front page again. *Here's Looking at You, Kid* — *Tivoli Two* — *Love's Young Dream Ends in Tragedy.*

There was a photo of him and Connie grinning in front of the screen the night he'd proposed. Just ten days ago.

Beneath was a photo of Frank Harris. Last week she'd been missing, now the tone changed to tragedy. Unable to face the article after all, Charlie handed the paper back to his mum and walked through the door.

His dad was waiting in the car parked on the opposite side of the road. Charlie stepped out, the newspaper article still dominating his senses. A passing truck honked its horn, a near miss. His escape brought him no comfort.

'Steady on there, son,' his dad said when he climbed in next to him.

Charlie nodded, unable to speak for the tremor in his voice.

They set out in silence, driving north away from the town. Within minutes they were surrounded by countryside. Fields dotted with hedgerows, the winding road following the sparkling river, an indomitable influence forcing man to yield to its flow. For a while he tried to lose himself in the scenery, but the pull of the newspaper article was far stronger than the palette of greens outside the window. *Love's young dream* — more like a nightmare, one that started in vibrant technicolour and quickly faded to black and white.

Charlie had learned many things about his love in the past few days. Aside from the fact she'd been living with a sadistic father, Connie had a brother, Michael, who'd seen fit to waltz off and join the Navy, leaving his defenceless sister with their lone brutal parent. The police had discovered the letters when they'd searched Connie's locker. Charlie couldn't wrap his head around the secrets Connie kept.

Michael had been interviewed by the Navy. The police subsequently ruled out the possibility Connie would have left in search of her brother. She hadn't even opened his last two letters. Viv took it upon herself to write to Michael. Charlie wasn't capable of finding the words, though he knew he would have to meet him.

He glanced at his dad, his eyes locked with the road. This was tough on his parents, having a son who could barely function. Sleep evaded him, but when it did catch him in its

101

snare, memories of Connie danced through his dreams and broke him in the morning when he woke to his new reality.

His gaze returned to the window on their approach to Dulverton, a small town of huddled cottages, a gateway to the moor. Glimpses of life flickered past, then they were climbing, up and up, the car straining in first gear against the gradient of the road. At the top, the moor opened up on all sides. Vast swathes of bracken, heather and gorse covered hills sitting under immense skies, an unending horizon.

Another half an hour and they skirted the small village of Simonsbath. A church perched on a hill, its gravestones leaning into the elements, a handful of cottages, then the road forked right and climbed north again putting the moor back in charge. He wound down the window, aghast at how remote this land was. Both ruggedly beautiful and treacherous in equal measure. Nausea pitched in his stomach. As if sensing his state of turmoil, his dad patted his knee. 'It's all right, son. Not much further.'

Tears pricked Charlie's eyes. His dad had been his rock over the last few days, understanding by instinct what he needed. When Charlie came to him, asking to make this pilgrimage, he'd merely nodded as if he'd been expecting it. His mum, on the other hand, was dead set against the idea. He knew she wanted to protect him from the pain. What she failed to understand was that with each passing day he was unable to cauterise his wounds before fresh ones were inflicted.

The road curved sharply as they reached the coast. It made Charlie dizzy. The vast blanket of browns and greens of the moorland came to an abrupt halt. Ahead, the sea stretched out, metallic against skies of slate, a miasma of greys. It was as if they'd reached the end of the world. In a way, they had. His dad held the car steady navigating the tree-lined route, then trees gave way to bracken and they were on the edge. The cliffs of the granite moor, some of the highest in the country, tumbling into the sea below.

His dad stopped the car. Charlie stepped out and leaned against the bonnet, unable to look over the edge of the cliff without his world tilting. No wonder the police concluded Connie had drowned. No one would survive a fall like that. The realisation was like a sharp kick to his stomach. He staggered back and threw up on the side of the road, then he was crouching, tears cascading down his cheeks. The last thing he remembered was his dad holding him against his shoulder with only the sea, the moor and the wind to hear his pain.

CHAPTER 21

'Where did you find me?' Rose asked as they settled to a meal of stewed lamb. She studied her plate, wanting to save the family the embarrassment of looking directly into her scarred face. It was hard enough to bear it herself, let alone see the discomfort it caused others. She'd noticed over the previous days as she spent more time downstairs that Joe in particular struggled to meet her gaze.

George slurped a mouthful of stew then cleared his throat. ''Twer on the moor, not far from the road into Simonsbath.'

Rose threw him a furtive glance, then frowned into her stew.

''Twer lucky we had Bear with us. You were buried in a ditch.'

She nodded. This was not welcome news. Her attacker could still be out there somewhere. 'Should we inform the police?'

Rose glanced up to see father and son exchange a look she couldn't identify.

'Did you fix the fence?' George addressed Joe, following his question with another noisy slurp.

'Aye, there'll be no more escapees this summer.'

'I've almost finished your dress, Rose,' Agnes ventured. 'Should be ready this evening. It's one of mine I've cut down, but it will be an improvement on that baggy old shirt.'

'Thanks, Agnes.' She set down her spoon. Had they not heard her question? A thought occurred. 'My clothes, the ones I was in when you found me . . .'

'The blouse was ripped but I'm sure we can do something with it. The skirt was ruined, I'm afraid.'

'Could I see them, please? It might help me remember.' She felt daft asking, but it was worth a try.

'Course, love. We'll have a look after dinner. Eat up now.' Agnes patted Rose's hand.

Rose picked up her spoon. Sensing eyes on her, she glanced up to find herself the subject of Joe's intense gaze. He returned to his stew and the rest of the meal passed in silence.

* * *

Rose looked in dismay at the mud-smeared pile of clothes Agnes laid out before her, searching as much for a clue as to who she was as to ascertain their condition. The dark skirt was stained with grass and mud, and a long tear ran up the seam. It matched the scratch on her leg. The blouse was stained too, which was a shame because it looked like it had once been lovely. There was another tear to the shoulder.

'Anything come to mind?' Agnes lifted the blouse to the light. 'I'll give it a good soak, see if we can't get them stains out.'

Rose shook her head, the action causing the dull ache to tighten its grip.

'Never mind, it'll come.' Agnes lifted the skirt out of the way, taking it to the scullery, and returned to her chair where she'd been working on Rose's dress all day. 'Nip upstairs and try this on. I want to see how it fits.'

Before the mirror in her bedroom, Rose slid down the trousers and unbuttoned Agnes's blouse. She stood for a moment in her undergarments, running her fingers over the scar on her leg. It was already fading. Each day her wounds got a little better, but there was something melancholy about the process, as if losing the scars meant she was losing connection with how she'd come to be there.

Rose returned her attention to the dress. She pulled it over her head, the light-blue cotton coarse against her skin. She fastened the buttons which ran down the front and admired the full effect. Agnes was a skilled seamstress. The style was practical with large pockets sewn to each side. The skirt fell away to just below her knee. She swished before the mirror, inspecting it from all angles. As she turned away, a flash of something clouded her vision. Rose saw herself wearing dark green in front of a mirror doing as she was doing now. As quickly as it came, it was gone.

She reached for the bed and sat, taking a steadying breath as she tried to recapture the image, but a fog obscured the vision. Maybe this was the start of her memories emerging. It had to be a good sign.

Invigorated by this thread of hope, Rose returned downstairs. In the kitchen Joe was seated at the table, whittling a piece of wood with a penknife, and George had retired to his chair in front of the Aga. Agnes glanced in her direction and clapped her hands with glee.

'Well, look at you.' George gave an appreciative nod. Joe stared for a beat, before returning his focus to the wood.

Rose blushed as Agnes came to her side, turning her one way and then the other. 'It fits better than I could have dreamed. Mind you, you've the easiest figure to work with. There's not an ounce to spare. Not like me.'

'Leave the maid alone.' George drew on his pipe.

Rose hovered, deciding not to mention the flash of something she'd seen upstairs in front of the mirror. It had been so fleeting, she questioned if it happened at all. As the family went about their evening routines, she made her way outside to the yard and leaned against the stone wall, appreciating the sun on her face, feeling it ease her aching muscles.

The fresh air felt good against her skin. She lifted her arms, studying the thin web of veins that criss-crossed along to her wrists. Touching two fingers to her neck, she found her pulse and marvelled at the robust beat of her body when her mind was so thin and insubstantial.

Agnes appeared at the door, breaking into her thoughts. She offered up a pair of old boots, their soles worn but serviceable. 'These are mine, see if they fit. I don't go out much these days.'

Rose took the proffered boots. She wondered about Agnes's confinement to the house. The woman never ventured beyond the barn in the yard, her slipper-shod feet taking her there to feed the chickens. 'Thanks, Agnes.'

Bending caused the pain in her head to intensify but she managed to pull on the boots and tie the laces. The world tilted momentarily as she stood. The boots were a little unyielding, but the fit wasn't too bad and at least they didn't pinch.

Agnes smiled. 'Make sure you don't wander too far. There's nothing but moor for miles. We don't want to lose you.' With that she went back inside.

Rose stood for a moment staring at the house with its crooked stone body and dark windows glinting in the sun. Then she walked to the gate at the side of the yard and looked out across the moor. A thin haze lingered over the valley. The landscape stretched as far as the eye could see, a mismatch of grassy fields, trees, gorse and heathers. Sheep and birds were the only sign of life. Overwhelmed by its vastness, Rose had no wish to lose herself within its inhospitable wilds. She stayed where she was, leaning against the gate, chasing fragmented thoughts.

After a while, she found herself drawn to the farm track, the track along which she'd been brought to this place. The trees knitted overhead, allowing shafts of fractured light to fall in between. She recalled how she'd seen them from the cart on her arrival. It felt like a lifetime ago. Days stretched into weeks, the rising and sinking of the sun the only markers of time in this isolated land.

After about a mile, the track forked to the right and the dense trees cleared, opening up the moorland. Rose paused to look back at the farm, but it was completely obscured, enfolded by the valley like a pimple hiding within a deep crease in a weatherworn face.

As she continued further down the track, the beauty of the moor, starkly rugged, frightened her in a way Rose couldn't articulate. Her eyes searched the horizon for any signs of human inhabitation. Something glimmered in the far distance then disappeared, swallowed by the endless landscape. To her right she could make out the sparkle of the river, the destination of the tributary that ran near the farm.

Rose felt her insignificance in this strange, barren land. An acute loneliness settled on her. Who was she? Was someone missing her? In whose thoughts did she linger, and would they ever find her here?

CHAPTER 22

Charlie sat on his bed, turning the engagement ring over and over between his fingers. The police had discovered it at the bottom of the stairs in Connie's house. Dwelling on how it ended up there sent him into a dark pit of despair.

Today, Reynolds was holding a small memorial for Connie at the Tivoli. Something to mark her passing. It felt like giving up, like accepting his darling girl was dead in the sea. Three weeks and there was still no body, but the police found her usherette jacket snagged on a rock at low tide. Another damning piece of evidence to add weight to the narrative.

It was the sad story of a young woman returning home with an engagement ring on her finger to face her father's alcohol-fuelled rage. Frank had been seen in the White Ball that evening. He'd drunk so much the landlord threw him out with a bottle of whisky to ease his progress. Frank returned home and sunk that whisky before turning his fists on his daughter. The police had found blood on the stair banister. *Connie's blood.* Charlie gripped the ring so tight the diamond cut into his finger.

A neighbour recalled hearing an engine at around 1 a.m. The police believed Frank stole the van from Heathcoat, loaded a battered Connie inside, then headed for Exmoor and drove them both off the cliff. Whether Connie was already dead by this point, the police couldn't say. The back doors of the van were thrown open on impact with the rocks, leaving Connie's body at the mercy of the sea as the vehicle sank. Frank's substantial girth had been wedged in place by the steering wheel.

A light knock on the door dragged him into the present.

'Charlie, love.' His mum came to his side. 'Viv's downstairs. She wants to know if you're going to the memorial.'

'I can't, Mum.'

'Your suit's all pressed and ready. Come on, for Connie. It will help. Her brother will be there, you should meet him.'

Facing Michael gave Charlie the impetus he needed, if for no other reason than to have someone on which to unleash his rage. He stood. 'Give me ten minutes to sort myself out.'

* * *

Viv looked as bad as he imagined he did, her skin pallid under her pillbox hat. It was Reynold's idea that the usherettes wear their uniform as a mark of respect to one of their own. Charlie allowed his mum to straighten his tie. The suit was the one he'd worn on his first date with Connie when he'd tried to impress her with posh cuisine, and she'd opted for fish and chips by the river. He could still taste her lips, speckled with salt and vinegar.

Viv kissed his cheek. 'Ready?'

Charlie followed her out of his parents' home. 'We'll be here,' his mum called as they walked through the gate.

'Your mum's lovely,' Viv said. 'Connie thought your folks were wonderful.'

Charlie couldn't speak. He didn't want to hear it.

Sensing his need for silence, Viv fell quiet until the Tivoli sign came into view on Fore Street. 'Michael's coming.'

Charlie nodded. 'Mum said.'

'It will be nice to meet him.'

He stopped walking. 'Will it?'

'I know you're angry. I'm angry too, but it's not Michael's fault.'

'He left her with that brute.'

Viv didn't challenge him, and they moved on. The stone lying on his chest since Connie's disappearance grew heavier. Reynolds and all the staff were waiting for them outside the cinema. A poster behind advertised *In a Lonely Place*. Bogart's melancholic face stared out from the wall.

A tall man with Connie's auburn curls stepped forwards. Michael was wearing his Navy uniform. It lent a certain authority although he was about Charlie's age. His eyes were Connie's too and a similarity in the shape of their mouths made Michael hard to look at. He offered his hand.

Charlie ignored it. He knew this man was trying to build a bridge, but he couldn't cross the gaping hole Connie left. 'Did you know?'

Michael looked askance.

'Did you know what your father was capable of when you left her with him?'

'Charlie.' Viv's placating hand rested on his arm.

'It's okay.' Michael glanced at Viv before returning his attention to Charlie. 'I told Connie she needed to leave too. I hoped she'd listen.'

'Hoped?' Charlie clenched his fists. 'You hoped? What good was that to Connie?'

Michael held his gaze. 'I'm truly sorry.'

Seeing the woman he loved reflected in Michael's pleading eyes, the fight drained from Charlie's body. He glanced at the people behind, remembering where he was and the purpose for this gathering. He'd let it go, for Connie.

* * *

The memorial passed in a blur. As the other staff dispersed, Charlie hung back with Viv. Michael hovered in the alleyway, pulling on a cigarette, his discomfort evident.

Viv checked over her shoulder. 'We should talk to him.' She fished out a cigarette, offering Charlie one.

He shook his head. 'And say what?'

'I dunno, he must be a bit lost.'

'You go over if you want, I've got nothing else to say.'

She lit up. 'Come on, Charlie, Con wouldn't have wanted this.'

Charlie threw Viv a sharp look. He knew she was right, but the fist of anger was too clenched to shift. 'I'm sorry, Viv, I can't.'

She gave a small nod and walked away to Michael, whose features relaxed on her approach. Charlie wished he'd taken a cigarette after all. He leaned against the wall with his arms folded, emotions ricocheting between devastation and blind rage.

After a few minutes, Viv returned. 'Michael asked if we'd like to see Connie's room at the house before he hands it back to the factory, in case there's anything of hers we'd like to keep.'

Michael was watching them, apprehension clouding his face. His expression reminded Charlie so much of Connie at the end of an evening about to return to her home, tears pricked his eyes. He gave a small nod.

In a daze, he followed Viv and Michael along Fore Street, the route he'd taken with Connie so many times. The low hum of their conversation melded with the voices in his head. Viv occasionally glanced back to check he was still there. On Bridge Street, Charlie paused to look at the iridescent water of the River Exe, unable to fathom a few weeks before, Connie and he had leaned against the railings wrapped in each other's arms, thinking about their future. He should have understood then — the day Connie met his parents. He knew something was wrong, the way her eyes dimmed whenever he mentioned meeting her dad. How could he have been so blind?

Viv took his arm, and Charlie flinched. It wasn't Viv, it was anyone who touched him. He only wanted Connie's touch, Connie's arms, Connie's hands.

Viv stayed by his side, shepherding him the rest of the way to Church Street, Michael a few steps ahead. At the house, he unlocked the door and gestured for them to go in. 'Take as long as you need, I'll wait here.'

Inside, Charlie's eyes roamed over the enclosed hall. Dark, gloomy, the faint musk of mould. He couldn't associate his vibrant, beautiful Connie with this place. The self-recriminations he'd tried to suppress broke free. *You should have done something. Why did you let her stay here?*

He followed Viv into a small sitting room at the front, sparsely furnished with a sunken fraying chesterfield before the hearth. A few dusty ornaments littered the mantelpiece, a framed photo depicting a family group. Connie was almost unrecognisable with long plaited hair and missing teeth, Michael at her side, a few inches taller, the same willowy frame and corkscrew curls.

They ventured through to the kitchen, another pitiful space with rotten worktops and a stone sink. The back revealed an outside toilet and bricked-in yard.

The stairs creaked underfoot as they made their way to the bedrooms. A double at the front appeared untouched. Floral wallpaper peeled at the edges, mould climbed the wall beneath the window and a lamp with a dusty pink shade sat tipsily at the side of the bed. Grey nets hung from the windows. Viv peered inside an oak wardrobe, recoiling at the smell of mothballs. Men's clothes hung in the ample space — a few shirts, a jacket. The other side was empty.

Charlie returned to the landing, staring down the final door. It had to be Connie's room. He couldn't stand that this was her home, that he'd let it be her home. Tears pooled before his eyes as he recalled the house she'd shown him on their first date, the one where nothing bad could ever happen. What he'd give to see her in that house now.

Viv came to his side, linking her arm through his. 'Come on.' She pushed at the door.

Charlie froze on the threshold. In contrast to the rest of the house, this room was a sanctuary. It encapsulated Connie. It smelled of Connie. He walked in, studying every detail through misted eyes. Either side of a window which overlooked the backyards criss-crossing the terraces were twin iron beds. One neatly made, unused — Michael's — the other with the covers rumpled. He pictured Connie, late for work, flinging the quilt over her sheets. The dress she'd worn to meet his parents hung on the wardrobe door. The dressing table held some of her jewellery, a brush with strands of her hair.

'Do you want anything?' he asked Viv, a splinter in his voice.

Viv cast around. 'I dunno, Charlie. I think you should choose first, don't worry about me. Do you want to be alone?'

He nodded. 'Thanks, Viv.'

'I'll wait downstairs.'

He stood for a moment with his eyes closed, picturing Connie moving about the room — her refuge. Slumping on her bed, he buried his face in his hands. Nothing he chose would make up for what he'd lost, for the physical presence of Connie in his arms. He lay his head against her pillow, breathing in the faintest tang of her scent and letting the tears fall. Taking a hanky from his pocket, he attempted to stem their flow. His gaze alighted on a book on the bedside table. A book of poems. He hadn't known Connie liked poetry. At the back, two photos tumbled out. One was of him. He'd given it to her a few weeks before when she'd asked for a picture. He was standing in his parents' garden, a little self-consciously under the camera's gaze. Connie said she liked it because it captured his true smile. Slipping the photo in his pocket, he studied the second image. It was a woman with Connie's eyes and mouth, but her hair was straight. She was standing outside the front of this very house, but it didn't look shabby. In fact, it looked well cared for and the window boxes were in full bloom. He turned the image over. In Connie's handwriting it said, *Mum, 24 July 1945*.

Returning the book to the bedside table, he stood, roaming around the small space, letting his fingers glide over her things. Things Connie had held, touched, worn. Things she would never touch again.

CHAPTER 23

'I'm getting used to having you around, Rose,' Agnes said after dinner as they sat side by side in the barn, skirting the last of the fleeces.

Rose smiled but it was thin. She was losing track of time and with each passing day, her frustration grew. The farm received no visitors, and the family were so busy with shearing season, they showed little interest in helping her find where she belonged as if the world beyond the farm made no impact on them and they on it. They wore their isolation with stubborn pride.

Agnes paused her work to study her face. 'Your bruises are healing well. How's the headache?'

'It comes and goes,' Rose replied. It was true, the headaches had lost their intensity over the last few days, but her memory continued to evade her. 'Should I see a doctor?' she ventured. It was the third time she'd asked this question.

'There's no doctor out here.' Agnes pulled a burr from her fleece. 'I don't know what I'd have done this week without your help.'

Rose nodded, focusing on freeing a thorn from the fleece she was working on. It was always the same oblique answer

— no doctor available. But surely these moorland farmers were occasionally in need of medical help, or perhaps they relied on the land to heal their ails like Agnes with her compresses and potions. Rose finished her fleece and added it to the pile.

Agnes stood, hands on hips, surveying their work. 'That's enough for today, let's go in.'

At the house, George dozed in his chair by the Aga. An occasional puff of smoke from his pipe was all that told them he was awake. Joe sat at the table, whittling the same piece of wood, which was transforming into a cooking spoon.

Rose followed Agnes, taking a seat by the hearth. 'What about in Simonsbath?' she asked, not willing to drop her quest just yet.

'Simonsbath? You'll not find a doctor there.' Agnes took up her sewing, another dress she'd started for Rose.

Exasperated, Rose stood. 'I could do with some fresh air.'

In the hallway she paused, hearing George's voice drift through the door she hadn't fully closed. 'The maid is right; she should see a doctor.'

Returning to the gap, Rose peered into the room. The only person in her line of vision was Joe at the table, his attention focused on the wood in his hands.

'I don't see why. My compresses have done the job on them bruises,' Agnes protested.

Joe paused his whittling. 'I agree with Mother. It's risky. What if the brute who put her in this mess is looking for her? What if by telling folk where she is, we're putting her in danger?'

Rose sucked in a breath. Did Joe have a point?

'It's not our business,' George replied. 'We need to let folk know the maid is here. Someone will be looking for her. People don't fall out of the sky.'

'Aye, but Dad, do you not think it's dangerous with the state she was left in?'

'What's the alternative, have her live here with us? We can barely feed ourselves, let alone another mouth. A doctor should check her over what with her memory loss.'

Joe leaned forward in his chair. 'That makes me uneasy too. What if they ask questions about how she came to be here? What if they think it was us that put her in that state?'

'Why should they think we had anything to do with it? We only found the maid, offered her shelter.' There was a warning in George's tone.

Joe set down his penknife and wood. 'We didn't tell any-one straight away and . . . folk have long memories.'

There was a pause. Rose could sense the tension through the thick stone walls.

'It's shearing season. We'd too much work on to lose a day gallivanting about for a doctor. Folk will understand, it's our livelihood. You can make enquiries when you take the fleece to the market tomorrow. I'm certain she's a towny maid — them delicate hands haven't seen a day's hard labour,' George replied.

Joe nodded. 'If I make enquiries I'll have to tread with care, 'tis all.'

'Aye, lad, fair enough.'

The room fell silent. Joe pushed back his chair. 'Happen I'll take a walk meself.'

Rose slipped out, racing across the yard and through the gate. The jolt from her limbs caused the pounding in her head to intensify. She slowed her pace once she was sufficiently away from the farm not to invite suspicion.

The sun burnished hues of orange across the moor. There was a nip to the air as it made its languorous decline, a welcome respite from the stifling confines of the farmhouse and the conversation that had taken an unsettling turn. She breathed in the scent of honeysuckle and grass, casting her eye over the infinite landscape.

At the river, she stared into the water, studying her reflection in the soft ripples. She crouched, letting her finger disrupt the surface, Joe's words replaying in her head. *What if the brute who put her in this mess is looking for her?* The prospect had occurred to her too, but surely a doctor would be discreet?

Rose couldn't fathom why Agnes was so against her seeking medical help, unless it was pride in her herbal remedies.

Heavy footsteps yanked her from considering this further. Joe stood a few feet away, Bear panting at his side. The dog ran to her and she stroked behind his ears.

Joe followed. 'Sorry, we didn't mean to creep up on you.'

She tilted her face towards him, the sun in her eyeline causing her to squint. 'It's fine.'

'Would you like to be alone?'

She considered the unending moor and found herself in need of company. 'I don't think so.'

Rose fell into step beside him, trying to match his long stride. They followed the river, accompanied by the rustle of Bear searching for pheasants and rabbits in the undergrowth.

'Do you like walking?' Joe asked.

'I don't know what I like. I don't know if this—' she lifted her arms, gesturing to the wild landscape — 'is familiar to me or foreign.'

He shook his head. 'I can't imagine how hard it must be for you to feel so . . .'

'Lost?'

'Aye, I suppose.'

'Your family are very kind. If I'm going to be lost, there are worse places to be found.' Did she believe that? Yes, she mustn't lose sight of Agnes's care, or how they'd taken her in when food was short. She threw him a smile, finding herself shy under his gaze.

'We don't get many visitors — any visitors.'

'That must be hard for you, here alone with your parents.'

Joe's expression darkened; his eyes drifted to the horizon. 'It wasn't always just me.' He hunched his shoulders as if cocooning himself. 'I had a brother, a few years older. He were in the war. It terrified him. Came home on his first leave and begged Dad to hide him. Dad said he couldn't. We found him, the morning he was due to go back. He'd taken the hunting rifle and turned it on himself.' Joe's words tumbled out in a torrent as if he'd been carrying their burden so long, he couldn't hold them in a second more.

She stopped walking and met his gaze, unflinching. *So that's what he'd meant. Folk have long memories. That's why Agnes didn't want to involve the police or a doctor. It's shame.*

He shrugged. 'I'm all they have now.'

'Joe, I'm . . . That's awful.'

Rose felt his loss and understood he was desperately lonely. She could see it in his eyes and recognised that pain in herself. This land was all they had, and he'd be expected to take it on, just him. There was no escape.

They walked under the weight of a heavy silence. *War*— it sounded recent. She must have lived through it herself. Her head filled with questions but now was not the time to press him on the subject. Rose searched for something to lighten the mood. 'How old do you think I am?'

Joe shrugged. 'That's a terrible question for a maid to ask a man.' There was relief in his eyes. 'Maybe a year or two younger than me.'

She laughed. 'That's not terribly helpful if I don't know how old you are.'

Joe smiled too. 'I'm twenty.'

'Twenty. Gosh.'

Joe's smile spread into a grin. 'Gosh?'

Rose giggled. 'I don't know where that came from. Is it a funny thing to say?'

'Fancy talk, 'tis all.'

'*Gosh*,' Rose repeated. For a split second, their laughter freed her from the burden of her situation. Maybe it freed him too. 'Perhaps I'm from somewhere fancy.' She lifted her hand to her bruise, a reminder of her precarious circumstances.

'Does it hurt, to laugh?' he asked.

'A little.'

Bear emerged from the bushes then dived in again, tail wagging. His presence seemed to have stolen the moment. They'd reached the next stile as the orange sun sank lower in the sky.

They stood side by side in contemplative silence, but it didn't feel heavy anymore. She took pleasure in the shadows cast by the sinking sun across the gleaming land of pinks and greens. An idea took shape in her mind. 'Would you take me to the place where you found me?'

A shadow fell across Joe's face. 'It's too far to go now, we won't make it before sunset, maybe during the day . . .'

'Tomorrow?'

'I've the market tomorrow.'

'How about the day after?' she persisted. It felt important. Could seeing the place offer her a clue as to who she was? She kept the ridiculous notion to herself and waited for Joe's reply.

Eventually he nodded, then gestured to the sinking sun. 'We'd best head back.'

They retraced their steps, Rose grateful for the silence to nurture the flickering flame of hope. Tomorrow Joe would make enquiries at the market, and the day after she'd see the place where she was found.

CHAPTER 24

Rose woke to the familiar dull ache lancing through her head, intensified by the clip of horse's hooves in the yard. Throwing back her covers, she kneeled on her bed and pulled the curtain to one side. Joe was leading Scotty, the old shire horse, around to the front of the cart, which was loaded with fleeces for the market. His face was closed in concentration as he secured the tack then, in one deft move, hauled himself up to the driver's seat. Agnes ran from the house, thrusting a food parcel into his hands. Joe smiled at his mother. Rose thought about his brother and the sad secret that hung over the farm. Joe took the reins, and the cart heaved forwards.

Turning away from the window, she surveyed the room which had provided her refuge for the past month. At the mirror, she swept her hair to one side. The bruising continued to retreat; the scar across her cheek too had lost its ghoulish quality. Soon, that faded scar would be the only evidence of her injuries.

In the kitchen, Agnes stood before the Aga stirring a pot of porridge for their breakfast. Rose lifted the kettle to fill in the scullery.

'You're part of the family now, Rose.' Agnes smiled as she set the kettle on the stovetop.

'I'm grateful for all you've done to welcome me into your home.'

'We shan't want you to leave.'

'Do you really think Joe might find something out?'

Agnes patted her hand, but her eyes dimmed. 'He'll do his best.'

Rose smiled, half excited for news, half nervous to learn what her origins might be. The shadow of her attacker lingered in her mind.

George walked into the kitchen and eased his stocky frame onto his chair at the head of the table. Agnes served him porridge while Rose warmed the brown betty pot for tea. It flummoxed her that she knew the names of inanimate objects but not the details of her own life. The pot in her hands elicited a familiarity, but she couldn't surmise what it meant.

How did she know how to make tea, dress, eat, drink, even read and write, but she didn't know her own name or how she'd come to be in this place? Anxiety pitched in her stomach. Glancing at George and Agnes going about their morning, she pushed the feelings away. Joe would come home with answers, she was certain, and if he didn't, well, maybe her memories would resurface soon.

The flash in the mirror, the teapot, were surely both parts of the puzzle, she just needed to wait for the full picture to reveal itself.

* * *

The day passed slowly. Helping Agnes where she could, Rose spent her free time roaming the farm, reluctant to venture beyond its confines to the indomitable skies of the moor. How did Joe find enough to sustain him within these wilds? She recalled his whittling the previous evening, the skill of his large hands, the careful way he handled the wood. Joe found his joys in simple pleasures — there was much to admire in that.

It was almost dusk when the clatter of hooves alerted them to his return. Eager for news, Rose left her inhibitions at the door and rushed from the house to greet him. He looked weary but rallied at the sight of her. Rose offered him a smile, shy at the intensity of his steady gaze.

Joe jumped down from the cart as George appeared from the house. 'You get in, lad, you must be famished. I'll see to the horse.'

'Thanks, Dad.' Joe followed Rose inside. In the hall he sat on the bench and pulled off his boots.

Rose's shyness returned, preventing her from asking the questions that had been on the tip of her tongue all day. Instead, she waited until he'd settled himself at the table with his dinner and a glass of cider. But it was Agnes who asked the question before she'd summoned the courage.

'Did you find out anything for Rose?'

'I'm sorry.' He glanced briefly in her direction. 'I asked around, but no one seems to know of a missing girl.'

Rose's eyes filled with tears. Agnes's warm hand squeezed her shoulder. 'There now, love, don't go upsetting yourself.'

Drying her eyes on her sleeve, Rose stood. 'Thanks for trying.' Before they could offer further condolences, she ran from the room, almost colliding with George as he returned from the stables.

In the barn, Rose found her voice. The volume of her disappointment surprised even her. She wailed uncontrollably, shocked by the depth of her pain. There was no one to claim her, no one waiting for her to return. After a few minutes, the crunch of boots on gravel told her she was no longer alone. Joe stood in the doorway, shadow obscuring his face.

Rose filled her lungs with air, battling to regain her composure. Her ragged breathing eventually slowed to a stagger. 'You must think I've lost my mind.' She laughed at the irony in her statement before releasing more tears. His arms came around her. She leaned against him, letting her body vent its pain. 'I'm alone,' she whispered.

Joe stroked her hair, his lips grazing the top of her head as he spoke. 'You'll never be alone, not if I have anything to do with it.'

She lifted her face to his, then his lips were against hers, rough and hard, filled with need. She kissed him back, sinking further into him, his fingers entwined in her hair.

A fragment of memory surfaced. She was kissing another man in another time and place. She wanted to keep hold of it until she could see him, but Joe pulled away, and the memory drifted out of reach.

Panting, they regained their breath. Rose touched her lips, blistered against his rough stubble. Joe stepped back, unable or unwilling to meet her eye, then he was gone. She leaned against the cold stone wall, listening until his footsteps died away. When she returned to the house, he'd taken up his wood and penknife.

'There she is.' Agnes gestured to the seat by the hearth. Rose let herself be talked to, keeping her focus on Agnes's animated face. When she found the courage to glance in his direction, Joe's eyes never left the wood in his hands.

* * *

'Was there really no news for the maid at the market? Nothing in the local paper?' George asked his son the following morning.

Rose hesitated at the threshold of the open door. Eavesdropping was becoming a habit.

Joe didn't look up from his bowl. 'Like I said, no one knew of a missing maid and the paper didn't mention it either.'

'Did you buy a copy? I'd like to have a gander.'

'I used it on the fire.' Joe gestured to the Aga.

His father clicked his tongue. 'You might 'ave checked first.'

'Poor girl, she were broken-hearted,' Agnes added.

Joe pushed away his bowl.

'You all right, love? It's not like you to be off your food.' Agnes moved into view, resting her palm across her son's forehead.

'Give over, Mother. I'm fine.' Joe stood too fast, sending his seat crashing to the floor. He righted his chair and made for the door.

'Happen he's lovesick.' His father's voice carried as Joe hurtled into the hall. Rose moved out of his way.

'Mornin',' he muttered, propelling himself to the front door.

'Joe.'

His shoulders slumped.

'Are we still going today?' she asked.

Joe frowned.

'To the place, where you found me?'

He shook his head, staring past her. 'I've a lot on.'

'If I helped . . .'

'It's not anything you could help with.' He turned on his heel and was gone.

Rose swallowed her disappointment. Was Joe angry because he'd kissed her or because he'd failed to bring her good news?

George left next, nodding to Rose in greeting before following his son across the yard.

In the kitchen, Agnes's eyes lit up when she entered. 'Morning, Rose, love. I've fixed your blouse.' She held the cream garment up to the light from the window.

Rose could hardly see where the tear had been. She marvelled at Agnes's skill. 'You're a magician.' The fabric fell softly between her fingers.

Agnes smiled, taking pleasure in the compliment. 'I enjoy sewing. I might see what else I can repurpose for you. Shame I'm not a cobbler though, nothing I can do about them boots.'

Rose followed Agnes's gaze to the rough old boots on her feet. They were practical for the farm but that was about all. 'I'm grateful for anything, you know that.'

'Aye, love, it's not as if we ever get visitors.'

'Do you never get lonely?' Rose ventured, thinking about Agnes's loss.

'My boys are company enough. It's lovely having you around though, makes me feel less outnumbered.' She squeezed Rose's arm. 'Go up and try it on, I'll see to them chickens.'

Rose climbed the stairs in a quandary. Did she want to become a permanent fixture? Was this a life she could live? Where had she been before? Did it matter? *It must*.

As much as she was making a home here, she shouldn't get comfortable. Somewhere out there, her real life was waiting for her.

She mustn't lose sight of that.

In her bedroom, Rose pulled off her dress and slid on the blouse. Goosebumps scattered along her arms, that sense of familiarity — the blouse, the texture against her skin, the insubstantiality of the feeling, the same as when she kissed Joe. She turned to study herself in the mirror, leaned in to examine her fading bruise. A flicker of something in her peripheral vision, a face behind, red lips, blonde waves, then it was gone. Rose stared at her reflection, willing it to come back. Nothing.

Unfastening the buttons with care, Rose took a hanger from the back of the door and hung the blouse so she could see it from the bed. It was just a blouse, but it was also a connection with her past, part of her true identity. A reminder 'Rose' wasn't real.

When she returned to the hall, Joe came in from the yard, a sheepish expression on his face. 'I was after Mother.'

'She's feeding the chickens.' Rose tucked a stray curl behind her ear, finding the confines of the hallway suffocating as if whatever hung between them was taking up too much space.

He cleared his throat. 'We'll leave directly after lunch.'

Her eyes filled with grateful tears. 'Thank you.'

* * *

True to his word, Joe waited for her in the yard as soon as their plates were cleared. They set out following the contours of the river, Bear at his master's heel. Slate skies parried with hints of blue. The air was warm, thick with the humidity of late summer. Rose sensed a coming storm and wondered where that knowledge came from. Joe seemed disinclined to conversation, and she was grateful for the time to let her mind roam. He made no mention of what passed between them in the barn. She was grateful for that too.

Leaving the river behind, they headed east. At a stile, Joe offered his hand.

'It's not too much further,' he said, as if with their hands connecting he felt the need to break the silence.

Rose nodded. 'You had the cart with you that day?'

'Aye, you remember that much.'

'I remember the pain of the bumpy drive.'

Joe grimaced. 'Sorry.'

Rose shook her head. 'You saved my life.'

Her eyes met his and she smiled.

'We'd stopped to look at prospects for moving the flock to the furthest field on our way back from the market. Couldn't believe it when Bear discovered you.'

'Ah, yes, it's Bear I owe my life to.'

'Aye, happen it is.'

Silence found them again as they followed the rough ground further south. Rose stumbled and tripped on the uneven clods of earth, self-conscious of her clumsy long limbs. Joe reached out to steady her. She clung to him, appreciating the solidity of his arm.

A breeze gained force as the ground fell away towards the road. Joe stopped walking. 'Here we are.' He pointed at the ditch. 'Doesn't look like much.'

Rose crouched along the ridge. The ditch was empty, the grass parched from harsh winds and sun. She ran her hands over the earth, her brow furrowed. Joe stepped away as if he sensed her need to be alone.

After a few moments she stood back too. Tears crested her lashes as she stared at the ground. It was a ditch, nothing more. His hand rested on her shoulder.

'I don't know what I expected to find here. I thought I might have left something behind. Something that would bring a memory or a clue as to who I am, but there's nothing.' Tears filled her eyes. 'I'm sorry, I've wasted your afternoon.'

He cupped her cheek, wiping fresh tears away with his thumb. 'Time spent with you is never wasted.' His mouth came down to hers with that same urgency. They fell to their knees, then they were in the long grass, bodies entwined. There he was — the man, fragmented, an apparition.

She yielded to Joe's kiss, but he pulled away. 'We have to stop.'

The man was gone. In panic she reached for Joe again, desperate to reconnect to whatever brought on the vision.

Joe's voice broke through her reverie. 'Rose, not like this. I want you, but not here, not like this.'

His words pulled her from the trance. Scrambling to her feet, humiliation burned her cheeks. Rose straightened her dress and stalked off in the direction they'd come, flailing across the uneven ground.

Joe grabbed her hand. She snatched it away, breaking into a run.

'Rose, for pity's sake.' The thud of his footsteps followed, then he caught her around the waist, their bodies fell back to the earth, his lips found hers and the man appeared again.

CHAPTER 25

Charlie pushed open the door to the projection room with trepidation. It was as chaotic as he'd feared. For the last few weeks, Sam and Mr Reynolds had managed the screenings between them while he was at home treading water against a tide of grief. His parents had been killing him with kindness until he'd been compelled to return to work, to free them from the burden of his pain. But the Tivoli was so littered with memories, there was nowhere to hide.

Forcing himself above the prevailing tide, he attempted to focus on bringing order to the space. All the while, the Connie whose voice chatted in his head watched from the leather armchair in the corner, her lips lifted in a half smile, eyes dancing with amusement.

Tommy circled his legs, and Charlie crouched to stroke him. 'Did you miss me, Tom?'

He watched as the cat made his way to the chair, leaping to settle himself across the top. Charlie tried not to indulge the sense Tommy was leaving the seat clear out of respect for Connie.

Picking up two cold cups of tea, he poured them down the sink. If Sam didn't want tea, why did he insist on making it? His brown betty teapot was slick with old leaves. He emptied them into the bin.

The workbench was a mess. The final reel of the previous evening's film had yet to be rewound. He cranked it back, then searched for the can.

Once he'd made a stack by the door, he cast around for any other films that appeared out of place. His gaze settled on a single can on the shelf above the winding bench. *Casablanca*. It was the reel he'd tampered with for his proposal to Connie. The memory stilled him. Taking a deep breath to ride the crest of pain, he glanced to the empty chair.

'You liked my proposal, didn't you, Con?'

Charlie shook his head. He needed to stop talking to her. His heart might be broken but he hadn't lost his mind — not yet.

He reached for the can and took out the reel with the intention of removing his title cards, but he couldn't face it, not today. Instead, he searched around for the rest of the film and realised it was missing. Sam must have sent back an incomplete film to the distributer. Charlie returned the reel to its can and looked for somewhere to stow it out of his sight until he had the courage to put it right. The bottom drawer of the small filing cabinet beneath the winding bench would do. He pulled it open, removed a couple of old files and placed the film inside.

An hour later, the room felt more like home. Charlie lifted the first reel of the day, *The Browning Version*, onto the projector and threaded it through, trying to block the memories that flooded his every task. Connie's long fingers lacing the projector under his guidance, the realisation he was in love with her. Connie talking about why she liked *Casablanca*. He never answered her question, *What's your favourite film?*

He ran the reel, checking the first few frames, grateful it wasn't vibrant technicolour to hurt his eyes, but black and white. The sombre story better suited his current mood. In truth it didn't matter what the film was, he just needed to get through it. A knock on the door and Viv stepped into the room. The sight of the uniform sent another spike of pain.

'Morning, Charlie.' Her voice was overly bright.

He offered up what he hoped was an encouraging smile. 'You look . . .' Viv faltered.

'Awful?' This time his smile was genuine.

Viv let out a strangled laugh. 'I was going to say well, but that seemed like a stupid thing to say.'

Charlie chuckled. 'Yeah, not great, Viv. *Charlie, your fiancée might be dead, but you look very well on it.*'

Viv's smile faded.

'Too much?'

'A bit.'

'Connie liked my jokes.'

'She did.' Viv squeezed his arm. 'We've missed you.'

'Thanks.'

A heavy silence settled between them. Viv fidgeted with her sleeve.

'You'd best get off or Reynolds will be on the warpath.' Charlie wanted to save them both.

Viv rallied. 'The new girl's starting today.'

Her words winded him. All Charlie could do was nod.

She turned to go. At the door she paused. 'Promise me you won't stay up here getting maudlin all day.'

'I promise.'

'I'll pop up later.'

'You don't need to, Viv, I'll be fine.'

Viv's eyes pooled with tears. 'You're not fine, Charlie Smith, and neither am I.'

Charlie listened to the clip of her heels on the stairs, then he was alone with the silence and the dust motes.

CHAPTER 26

Rose scattered corn for the chickens. They pecked at her boots, impatient with her slow progress.

Agnes's voice roused her from a daze. 'Any eggs? Breakfast won't make itself.'

She stared at the corn in her hand. 'Sorry, I got distracted.'

Agnes shook her head. 'I don't know what's got into you lately, love.' She chuckled and went inside.

Scattering the rest of the corn, Rose checked the hen house for eggs, gathered them in her arms and made for the door.

Joe and his father were seated at the table. Rose sensed Joe's eyes on her as she moved around the kitchen helping Agnes prepare breakfast. This was how it had been for the past two weeks. Long days waiting for Joe. Waiting for him to finish his farm work, waiting for him to suggest an evening walk, waiting for his lips against hers, waiting, always waiting.

Each day they danced the same steps. Snatched moments, frantic kissing, then they'd return to the house and go to their beds, frustrated.

After breakfast she went to the barn, her heart thudding against her chest so loud she was sure all of Exmoor could hear it. No more than a minute passed before he was there, pushing her against the wall. She sank into his kiss and the visions came again. She wanted to see him, this man who invaded her time with Joe, but he stayed in the shadows, and when Joe's lips left hers, he slipped away too. Each time she promised herself she'd really look, that she'd focus on her mind and not the physical sensations of her body, but Joe's ardent kisses won. Did she want Joe or the man his kisses conjured? Rose had no idea.

'I'll try and finish early today.' He nuzzled her neck.

Rose sought out his lips again. He groaned and pulled away, running his finger lightly over her bruise. 'When we're wed, we'll make love everywhere.'

A spike of unease ran through her, the sense she'd done this before. 'Wed?'

Joe nodded.

They sprang apart at George's tuneless whistle outside.

'I'll see you later.' Joe pecked her lips before venturing to the barn door.

Rose peeled herself from the wall but lingered a while, needing to settle her nerves before she went back indoors.

* * *

The following week, Rose stood at the gate at sunrise looking over the moor waiting for a wave of nausea to pass. The last of the swallows flew in formation, leaving the chill of late September skies for the heat of African suns. She studied their flight, feeling neither a longing to be with them nor a desire to stay. She was suspended in a void, her existence real yet make-believe.

Rose took in deep breaths and made her way back to the house. She wasn't sure what ailed her, but each morning for the last few days a heaving would rise in her stomach with the break of dawn then retreat as if her body were in rhythm with the sun. Was she homesick? How could she yearn for a home

133

or people she couldn't remember? Did her body know while her mind remained shrouded in fog?

*　*　*

Three days later the heaving in her stomach found its freedom. Rose shoved Joe from her arms, running for the house, only making it as far as the yard.

Joe failed to hide his disgust as she reached for the steadying solidity of the wall. Agnes appeared in the doorway.

Rose bowed her head in shame. 'I'm sorry.'

Agnes's arm came around her shoulder. 'No harm done. Joe, don't stand there gawking, get the maid some water.'

Joe ducked into the house, clearly relieved to have a purpose that took him away from her vomit. Failing to meet her eye, he handed Rose the water. She took careful sips, her cheeks burning with humiliation.

*　*　*

George returned alone for lunch claiming Joe wanted to finish chopping up a tree that came down in high winds the previous week. Rose sought him out before dinner as he made his way through the yard, an axe slung over his shoulder.

'You'd best keep your distance.' He walked past her into the barn.

Stung, Rose pulled her cardigan tightly around her, watching his retreating back. Unable to face company, she made for the river.

Trees hung low over the water, their branches heavy with summer growth, leaves burnished, ready for the changing season yet to come. The river would soon hide under a blanket of red and gold. For now, a few leaves rested on the surface. Crouching at the edge, she caught sight of her reflection, mesmerised by the changes the last two months wrought. A fading scar across her cheek gave outward voice to her physical injuries. Although she was still plagued by occasional headaches, all her other bruises were gone. Her auburn curls grew wild and unruly about her slim face, her skin glowed, weathered from hours outdoors, and her body felt stronger, fuller. Her breasts strained at the buttons on the dress which had hung loose only two months ago.

Hearing footsteps, she stood quickly, reaching out a hand to steady herself as a cacophony of colours momentarily danced before her eyes. Hoping it was Joe come to say sorry, Rose was surprised to see George amble in her direction.

'You all right now, maid?'

Rose smiled — he handled illness better than his son. 'I'm well now, thank you.'

'Joe thinks you've caught something, but I don't see how, you've seen no one but us . . .'

She shrugged, unsure what to add.

Eyeing her stomach, he put his pipe in his mouth. 'Time will tell.' He went on his way.

Puzzled, Rose watched his silhouette disappear over the ridge, then stalked back to the house.

Agnes was seated by the Aga, sewing. 'You're looking well, Rose, you're glowing.'

'I feel fine now. I don't know what was wrong this morning, perhaps something I ate.' She pulled up a chair.

Agnes set down her mending and checked behind as if making sure they were alone. 'Have you had your monthlies while you've been here?'

'Monthlies?'

'You know, when you bleed.'

Rose felt colour rise in her cheeks. She hadn't. What with the shock of this new reality, the thought hadn't occurred to her. She shook her head.

'You and Joe have grown close.'

Rose studied her hands, the implication slowly dawned. She looked up. 'Oh no, we haven't . . .'

Agnes frowned. 'Are you sure, love? Our Joe will marry you. Don't have any fears there. We're all liable to get carried away.' She leaned forward to share a confidence Rose wasn't sure she wanted to hear. 'George and I weren't exactly innocent of the ways of the flesh when we got married.'

Desperate to be away from this conversation, Rose stood. Undeterred, Agnes warmed to her subject. 'There's no need to worry, we've noticed the way our Joe looks at you. Does my heart good to see him happy. It's not been easy for him these last few years.'

'Sorry, Agnes, I need some fresh air.' She rushed from the room despite Agnes's protestations and made for the track.

* * *

Rose had no idea where she was going or how long she'd been walking when she heard the distant clatter of hooves. Dusk descended, casting shadows across the landscape. She'd gone beyond the confines of the farm and out onto the moor, following the river as it wound its way between dark hills, hoping to reconcile her mind with the truth of her body. She was pregnant by a man she had no memory of.

Joe drew up on Scotty. 'Rose.'

She heard him dismount, the clop of the horse falling into step beside him. Rose surveyed the dark shapes across the moor. If she scrambled up one of the banks, they couldn't easily follow.

'You're not talking to me now, maid?'

'Don't call me maid, I'm not your daughter.'

'I hope not.'

Irritated by the laughter in his voice, she straightened her features and stopped walking. 'Make sure you don't get too close.' Her tone was mocking.

Joe took her hand. 'I'm sorry, I'm not great with sickness, but Mother says it's women's stuff.'

So, Agnes hadn't told him. It would only be a matter of time and then he'd know she was carrying another man's child. They'd all know.

'Will you come home, Rose? Please?'

Home? It wouldn't be, not for much longer. She nodded, casting around at the darkening, inhospitable landscape. What choice did she have?

Joe smiled, threading his arms around her back. Rose shuddered, unsure if it was the chill of the evening air or the ghost of her past catching up with her.

'Are you cold?'

'A little.'

He mounted Scotty and offered his hand. Rose gripped it, putting her foot in the stirrup and allowing him to pull her onto the horse's back. She nestled in front of him, feeling the warmth of his body behind — solid, cocooning, safe.

Scotty walked at a languorous pace back along the river. Stars twinkled above like pearls in a blanket of deep blue and Joe whispered his favourite promises in her ear, the ones about their marriage, their children, the farm and their future. Promises she knew she wouldn't let him keep.

CHAPTER 27

When Rose came down to breakfast the following morning it was clear something had changed. Joe barged passed her as she entered the kitchen. At the Aga, Agnes couldn't meet her eye. Rose understood then, she'd told him.

In the hallway she found Joe pulling on his boots.

'Leave me be, Rose.'

'You know?'

'Aye, I know.' He didn't bother to conceal his disgust.

'I had no idea I was pregnant. How could I?' She hated her pleading tone.

He pulled his cap on and walked outside.

Unable to face Agnes, Rose returned to her room. She perched on the bed at the window, watching Joe push a bicycle into the yard and pump its tyres.

His father drew up at his side. 'Where are you off to, lad? There's work to do.'

'I'll be back tonight.' Joe mounted the bike and cycled away.

George shook his head and returned to the house. She heard Agnes's voice, fretful in the hallway, and George's soothing tones. Rose kept to her room, too ashamed to face them, too aware her fate was in their hands.

She passed the morning pacing the narrow space, occasionally stopping at the blouse hanging on the door to feel the soft fabric between her fingers as she'd done almost daily since Agnes mended it for her. No memory came, only a sense of the familiar. Rose lay on her bed with the blouse in her eyeline, the sole item she could say was truly hers. She had no money and no idea where to go. The world outside the farm was as alien as the moor and those rugged lands lay between her and the rest of humanity.

When she didn't materialise for lunch, a gentle knock came against her door. Agnes entered carrying a tray which she set on the bed. It reminded Rose of her early days on the farm. Agnes sat beside her and took her hand, her skin rough but warm.

Rose blinked away tears. 'I had no idea,' she whispered.

Agnes's arm came around her shoulder. 'You don't know who the father is?'

She shook her head.

'Our Joe will come round. I've never seen him so happy as you've made him in the last few weeks. You're a gift to us all, Rose.'

A tear slid down her cheek. Agnes's words offered no comfort. How could she stay, how could she leave?

Agnes gave her shoulder a squeeze and stood, waiting for her to pick up the spoon. 'Your soup will get cold. Eat up now, love.' Rose wasn't hungry but she obliged.

Satisfied, Agnes made for the door. 'Laundry day. I'll strip Joe's bed. Bring your tray down when you've finished.'

Rose nodded and threw Agnes a tremulous smile.

Half an hour later she carried the tray to the kitchen. Agnes was seated by the Aga in her rocking chair, her head dipped, absorbed by something in her lap, the bedding abandoned on the flagstone floor at her feet. Rose set down the tray with a clunk, and Agnes's head shot up. Her fingers closed around a scrap of newspaper which she balled into her fist. 'The rubbish our Joe keeps in his room.' She tutted, tucking the ball of paper in her apron pocket. 'Best get these sheets seen to.'

* * *

Rose spent the afternoon helping Agnes with the laundry, her hands plunged in soapy water for so long her skin tightened and her fingers wrinkled at their tips. All the while she listened for Joe. Bear appeared restless too without his master. He fussed around her skirts while Rose pegged out the sheets then scampered off to chase a bird or his own tail. Back in her room, she waited. The screech of bicycle breaks alerted her to Joe's return as dusk stretched its shadowy arms around the farm. She could just make out his silhouette as he wheeled the pushbike into the barn then his tread echoed in the hallway below.

'Joe, is that you?' Agnes's voice travelled up the stairs.

'Aye, I'm famished.'

He sounded himself. Rose took a breath before leaving her room; she couldn't avoid him for ever.

In the kitchen, Joe's tall frame dwarfed his mother. They stood side by side at the table with their backs to the door, deep in whispered conversation. Rose hesitated on the threshold, curious as to what they were discussing in hushed tones, when George came up behind, startling her, Bear in his wake. She forced a smile and stroked Bear's ears. 'Evening, Rose.' George fixed her with his astute gaze.

At the sound of her name, Agnes and Joe turned in their direction, a shadow passing over their faces like naughty children caught in a misdemeanour. Agnes moved to the Aga and opened the door. Something slipped from her hand into the fire.

CHAPTER 28

His cheeks ached with the effort of maintaining the smile he wore, but Charlie was determined not to let it slip. Viv held her hand aloft for the small gathering to admire the diamond ring sparkling on her wedding finger. Mrs Bird cooed in delight. Even Reynolds mustered a modicum of enthusiasm before muttering something about staff turnover and retreating to his office. Charlie studied his shoes, desperate to keep his features in check. He was happy for Viv and Michael, of course he was, but he couldn't help indulging in a moment of grief. It should have been him and Connie.

He cast around the foyer; patrons were starting to trickle in for the matinee. A tall man with a shock of ginger hair under a flat cap caught his eye, not only because his farm clothes made him conspicuous among their usual clientele but because he was staring at Charlie with a furious scowl. Perturbed, Charlie returned his attention to Viv.

'I'd best get the film ready.' He gestured to his watch. 'Congratulations, Viv.' He kissed her cheek and made for the projection room before she could protest. Glancing over his shoulder at the queue snaking from the entrance doors to the kiosk, he noticed the man with the ginger hair pushing a bike back up the alleyway. Charlie frowned; he evidently wasn't keen on seeing a film after all.

In the projection room, he let the smile slide off his face. All too soon his eyes filled with tears. Charlie wiped them away with his sleeve and focused his misty gaze on the projector.

The knock on the door didn't surprise him. It was bound to be Viv, checking he was all right. He straightened his tie and ran his fingers through his hair then let her in.

Viv stood before him, anxiety furrowing her usually smooth brow. Connie once told him Viv liked to be economical with her facial features to stave off wrinkles. He had no idea why he was thinking about that now. A lit cigarette sat between her fingers. She offered it to him.

Charlie shook his head. 'I'm fine.' He wanted to fence off her sympathy before he dragged them both down. 'Enjoy this. I couldn't be happier for you and Michael.'

Viv's blue eyes regarded him. 'I know you are, Charlie, but I'm not stupid. It must hurt like hell.'

Charlie thrust his hands in his pockets and studied the floor. 'Everything hurts like hell.'

'Michael wants you to know he's sorry he left Connie behind. He was young and selfish — he hates himself for it.'

Charlie shook his head. 'What's done is done. Con would be happy something good came out of this. Who would have known you meeting Michael at her memorial would lead to the fastest wedding in history? She'd have got a kick out of that.'

Viv squeezed his arm. 'You're a good man, Charlie Smith. One day you'll—'

'Don't, Viv. You of all people know that's not what I want to hear right now.'

She dipped her head. 'You're right, I wasn't thinking.'

Charlie wanted her to leave. He was too miserable to be around her happiness. He didn't like himself for it. Rallying, he forced a smile. 'Be happy. If the past few months have taught me anything, you have to grab it.'

Viv met his gaze and nodded. 'See you later.'

Charlie closed the door and walked to the chair, lifted Tommy and set him on his lap, stroking his soft fur. 'Everyone is so sure they know what Connie would have wanted, Tom. Connie wouldn't want you to be sad, Connie would want you to carry on with your life, Connie would have hated you being alone, Connie this, Connie that. I know they're trying to help . . .'

He sighed, regarding the pile of film cans next to the projector ready for the screening. *The Mating Season*. Of all the bloody films to have to sit through.

Tommy stretched and lowered himself to the floor, then circled the cans of film and sat regarding Charlie with his amber eyes.

'Fine, I'll stop moping, but I'm not doing it for you, I'm doing it for Connie.' He moved to the projector and lifted the first reel from the can. He didn't know how he was supposed to carry on, but somehow, one day turned into another. Life. It went on regardless of how much you chose to engage with it.

CHAPTER 29

Rose sat cross-legged in the coarse grass staring at the ditch. She considered lying in it, as if by re-enacting her position when she was found, she might discover a portal to take her back to where she belonged. *Do I want to go back?* Glancing at the barren moorland all around, she thought about Joe's kisses, the sense of the other man she'd had while Joe's lips were against hers. The sensation was warm, happy. She'd felt loved, but was that about Joe? She hadn't known him well then, she wasn't sure she knew him any better now.

After an awkward dinner the previous evening, Rose retired to bed unable to sit with the family in stultifying silence while Joe threw her mystifying looks from across the room.

Lightly touching her belly, not yet showing but there all the same, Rose contemplated her options. Joe may forgive her in time but somewhere out there, the man who fathered her child might be missing her, maybe even looking for her, or worse, believing her dead. She owed it to her unborn child to find him, she owed it to herself, whoever she was. Joe's voice whispered in her mind . . . What if that man was the one who left her for dead in a ditch? Either way, she needed to know the truth.

A distant bark stilled her thoughts. Rose stood to see Bear racing towards her, Joe striding in his wake. The dog came to her side, wagging his tail, sniffing for affection. Rose stroked him, letting Bear hold her focus.

Before long, Joe drew up, brow furrowed, gaze trained on the grass. Eventually, he looked up, eyes filled with uncertainty. Rose waited, unable or unwilling to help him.

'I'm sorry I was short with you before. It was a shock, realising you'd been with another man. I thought . . .' He pulled off his cap and raked his fingers through his hair. He didn't seem to know what he thought.

'I didn't deceive you, Joe. This is as much a shock to me as it is to you. More so. I'm carrying a child and I have no recollection of how it came to be.'

Joe looked away.

'I should go.' She walked past him.

He caught her arm. 'Rose, I want to marry you.'

She shook her head, saddened at the wound she was about to inflict. 'I have to find my baby's father. I have to know the truth.'

'You don't.' He kneeled before her. 'The truth is here, us.'

Rose stared at her stomach again. How quickly she'd come to thinking of a presence there. 'The truth is, I'm going to have a baby that isn't yours. A baby who will be a part of me for the rest of my life. How will you handle it?'

'There will be more babies.' He reached for her hand, threading his fingers through hers. 'Our babies.'

'What if there aren't? What if for some reason I can't give you a child?'

Joe frowned. 'Why should we not have more?'

'I'm not saying we won't, but we can never be certain. If this situation has taught me something, it's just that. There is no certainty, there is only now.' Rose walked away, leaving him with her words and her ditch and with no idea how any of this was going to end.

* * *

145

That evening Rose tried to absorb her mind in chores, helping Agnes prepare the dinner, all the while her stomach churning with her precarious situation. She had to leave. But with no money and no knowledge about the world beyond the confines of the farm, she didn't know what to do.

'You all right, love?' Agnes patted her hand. Rose had been staring into the pot of stew.

She lifted her gaze to Agnes's — her warm eyes undid her resolve. 'I'm fine.'

'Has our Joe spoken to you?' The hopeful expression on Agnes's face pierced Rose's heart.

She managed a nod, grateful when George walked into the room. 'Joe says he's going to stay and finish the fencing. Can you keep something hot for him? He won't be back until sundown.'

'Course.' Agnes regarded Rose again before spooning the stew onto waiting plates.

Another meal passed in uncomfortable silence. Rose was thankful not to have to meet Joe's eye across the table, but aware his parents were exchanging curious looks. His decision to avoid her suggested he'd taken heed of her words and decided to withdraw his proposal. She didn't know whether to feel disappointed or relieved.

Rose offered to wash up, glad to have the scullery to herself. Tears blurred her vision as she plunged her hands in the warm soapy water. She set the last dish to drain, when George walked in.

'You're leaving?'

She dried her hands on a dish towel and glanced at George, his expression passive.

Rose nodded, the decision finally made in the moment. 'It's for the best.'

'Aye.' George struck a match against the stone wall and lit his pipe. 'Happens I agree with you there. How will you travel?'

Rose shrugged. It was all she'd been thinking about and still she had no idea.

'I'll take you to Dulverton, you can catch a train south from there.' He reached into his shirt pocket for his wallet, pulled out a few notes and offered them to her.

'I can't . . .' She knew he couldn't afford it.

George shook his head. 'You must.'

Rose wiped a stray tear away with her sleeve and took the notes, sequestering them inside her dress pocket. 'Thank you.'

He drew on his pipe, releasing a plume of smoke. 'Better not say goodbye. I'll tell them I'm going to the smithy in the morn. Meet me on the lane at sunrise.'

Rose nodded, struggling to maintain her composure.

George turned to go. At the door he paused, his crooked silhouette dark against the fading light. 'Rose . . . don't ever come back.'

She watched the shadows swallow him whole.

No. She wouldn't come back.

PART FOUR

June 1996

CHAPTER 30

The distant thunder of a drill intensified Eddie's headache. They'd started work in the auditorium, pulling out the worst of the seating and replacing the floor. He returned his gaze to the note: *I'm sorry.* Why he'd kept it, stuck to the noticeboard in the office like a memento, Eddie couldn't say beyond the fact it intrigued him. Anna insisted he get rid of the film. Her face had been so stern, he'd followed her instructions and contacted the fire brigade. The film was no more, extinguished in a ball of flames, but its contents had become implanted in his mind over the last month. His curiosity about it grew.

The drilling stopped, replaced by laughter, an even more unlikely sound. Eddie ventured into the foyer, where the smell of fresh paint lingered from the newly decorated walls. His mum was leaning against the kiosk counter chatting to Linda, who didn't seem to be able to keep away from the place. Perhaps most startling of all, Linda was smiling. He hadn't realised she possessed the necessary facial muscles. The workmen had downed tools and drifted to the kiosk too.

Eddie cleared his throat and the camaraderie evaporated instantly, making him feel like a teacher calling an end to playtime.

'Ed.' His mum waved. The workmen shuffled back to their tools and Linda, who was seated behind the kiosk, threw him a scowl.

Eddie addressed his mum. 'What brings you here?'

'It's about time you gave me the tour.' She took his arm. 'Linda and I were talking about *Trainspotting*. She's a fan of Ewan McGregor. I see big things for that young man.'

Linda beamed.

'Right, well, great.' Eddie steered her gently to the projection room.

'See you later, Linda,' his mum threw over her shoulder as they departed.

At the bottom of the stairs, Eddie paused. 'Go careful, they're steep.'

His mum rolled her eyes at the suggestion her sixty-plus years might be an obstacle.

'I'm only warning you.'

In the projection room, Eddie cleared off the old armchair, which he still hadn't thrown out, for his mum to sit. When he turned to face her, she was staring at it, transfixed.

'Are you okay, Mum?'

'There's something strange about this place.'

Eddie shrugged, perhaps she sensed the ghosts too. 'One cinema is much the same as another.'

She dragged her gaze in his direction and shook her head as if she were shaking something off. 'That's not true, Ed. They all have their unique quirks. You should know that.'

'How did you get so matey with Linda? She won't give me the time of day.'

'You have to find out what makes people tick. Linda's wearing a T-shirt with *Choose Life* emblazoned across the front. I remembered it from *Trainspotting*, so I commented on it and that was that.'

Eddie smiled as his mum joined him at the projector with a twinkle in her eye.

'A Gaumont-Kalee 21. I haven't had my hands on one of these for at least ten years.'

He watched, amused while she circled the machine. 'What happened to the reel of film you found? Did Anna help you?'

'Yeah, it was the final frames of *Casablanca* with a marriage proposal at the end. Anna insisted I have the film destroyed because it was nitrate.'

'A marriage proposal, how romantic.'

Eddie raked his fingers through his hair. 'The note left with it has me puzzled. It said, *I'm sorry.*'

'Strange. Do you know anything about the last projectionist?'

'He left before I took over the lease, which was just as well, I couldn't have afforded another wage. I guess I put him out of a job.' Eddie couldn't help feeling there was more to the story.

'Without you, the cinema might not have had a future. Stop being so hard on yourself. This is a tough business, especially now.' She always knew how to make him feel better.

He noticed her gaze settled on the projector again. 'Do you want to try it out?'

A guarded smile spread across her lips. 'I thought you'd never ask.'

* * *

Later that afternoon after his mum left for home, Eddie was puzzling over a calculator, trying to pin down a budget for the new equipment he'd need. He'd secured a couple of xenon projectors from a cinema in Plymouth that was upgrading. Linda stepped through the open office door, disturbing him. *Doesn't she have a home to go to?*

Eddie leaned back in his chair, attempting to convey a relaxed, friendly manner. 'How can I help?'

'What's that?' She pointed to the note pinned to the board.

'It was left on the winding bench with an old can of film,' he said. 'The film turned out to be nitrate, a highly flammable stock. I had to dispose of it. Leaving a flammable film on the premises wasn't exactly . . .' He trailed off as Linda folded her arms.

'Anyway,' Eddie rushed on, 'I don't suppose you know anything about it.'

She blinked as if expelling the question, then shrugged.

Sensing he wasn't going to get anywhere, Eddie suppressed a sigh. 'Was there something you wanted, Linda?'

'Only to let you know I'm off and there's mouse droppings under the kiosk.'

'Oh right, thanks.'

Linda paused at the door. 'She's dead nice, your mum.' With that, she left.

Eddie grabbed a pen and added calling pest control to his long list of things that still needed completing. He stared at the note again.

'*I'm sorry,*' he whispered and he was. Sorry he couldn't get on with his staff, sorry he didn't possess his mum's ability to charm. Sorry he'd leased this cinema because he'd thought it might fill the void after his divorce and deliver him safely home.

CHAPTER 31

Anna sat at the back of the crowded lecture theatre, mesmerised by Graham standing behind the lectern in front of a rapt audience of undergraduate film studies students. She loved watching him in action. That ability to be intellectually stimulating while oozing charm and dry wit. Her thoughts turned to Dr Humphries. She'd attended one of her lectures just before she embarked on her PhD and found her similarly enthralling. More so, if Anna were honest. She could even recall her outfit. Dark grey wide-leg trousers with a crisp white T-shirt beneath a cashmere cardigan and Converse on her feet. It was odd to think she was friends with her mother — what could they have in common? From Dr Humphries, her mind meandered to Eddie. She should give him a call to check he'd disposed of the film and find out if he was any closer to discovering its origins. The proposal was so intriguing. She couldn't imagine anyone giving her such a romantic gesture.

The lights coming up and students filing out of the theatre pulled her back to the present. Anna stayed where she was, watching a couple of female undergrads linger to ask Graham questions. A nugget of jealousy worked its way through her system as they all threw back their heads in laughter, but then

Graham's gaze flickered to her, where it stayed for a second too long. Anna felt her cheeks flush and the jealousy retreated.

Ten minutes later they were making their way to the postgrad office.

They paused outside his door. 'I've got a spare half an hour if you'd like to go over your research progress?' Graham said in a voice that sounded inflated and fake.

Anna cast around. No one was paying them attention apart from Pip, who threw her an absent wave. She actually did want to go over her research, something Graham rarely made time for these days. 'Sure.'

His office had been Dr Humphries' before she went on sabbatical and hints of its former occupant remained. Shelves weighed down with books on film theory lined one wall, although Anna noticed the section on film noir — Dr Humphries' specialism — relegated to the bottom. Various houseplants adorned the window ledge, some clearly suffering from neglect under Graham's stewardship — not that she was any better at keeping plants alive. A framed still from the 1922 film *Nosferatu* hung above the desk. That was definitely a Graham addition. The ghostly outline of a larger picture marked the magnolia paint, and she wondered what occupied the space before.

'So—' Graham gestured for her to sit — 'I have some bad news.'

Anna remained standing. As if sitting ever made unpleasant news more palatable. 'What kind of bad news?'

He leaned against his desk in an awkward pose. 'You know my contract is coming to an end. It seems the university won't be able to offer anything further. Dr Humphries will be back for the autumn term.'

Anna cast her eyes downwards, conflicted. The thought of Dr Humphries returning sent a flutter of excitement to her stomach, but if that meant losing Graham . . .

'I've been offered a lectureship at Bristol. Debs isn't impressed, but there we are.'

Her head shot back up. 'Hang on. Bristol? Debs is going with you? What happened to the promises you made last month about being together full-time? What about my PhD?' Anna's eyes grew hot with anger.

Graham appeared to shrink. 'If you want to blame someone, blame your precious Dr Humphries. The woman must be in her sixties. If she'd do the decent thing and retire, let a younger man step into the breech, I wouldn't be forced into this situation.'

Anna's retort was cut short by the trill of the telephone on Graham's desk. He snatched it up, no doubt relieved to have a way out of this conversation. She threw him a derisory look.

Graham offered the phone. 'Pip says there's a call for you.'

Anna took the receiver. 'Hello, Anna James?'

'Anna?'

Her heart sank. *How did she even get this number?* 'Hi, Mom, you shouldn't be phoning me at uni.' Anna couldn't decide which was worse, continuing her fight with Graham or a conversation with her mom when her emotions were already in turmoil. Graham waved and disappeared through the door.

'Now, darling, don't go being rude, you know the time difference has me confused. Anyway, I'm ringing with good news, and I won't let you ruin it.'

Anna tried to shake off her bad mood. 'Go on, what's your news?'

'I'm coming to England.'

'When?' This was a surprise.

'A few weeks. I was hoping I could visit. I've met someone and I want to introduce you.'

Anna sucked in a breath. 'Again? Jeez, Mom, what happened to being independent? Spending time with yourself? Let me guess, you're getting married?'

'We're not getting married. And for the record, I've got to know myself and this time . . . it's different.'

'Different how?'

'Let me tell you about—'

Anna realised she didn't want to hear it. 'I can't talk right now. I'm in a supervision meeting. Congratulations, I hope you'll be very happy.'

Her mom's voice wavered. 'Anna, I wish you'd say it like you mean it.'

She stared at Nosferatu, his bat ears and vampiric teeth holding her gaze while her mom's rebuke hung between them. Her vision clouded.

'Anyway, I'll call you when we land, and we'll take it from there.'

Anna bit her lip. 'Sure, but call me at home, it's not okay to phone the uni.'

'I'll try to remember. Bye, darling.'

Hanging up the phone, Anna realised in the heat of their strained conversation, she'd forgotten to ask her mom how she knew Dr Humphries. She snatched up a pencil from the desk, intending to leave Graham a note on his open desk diary. An entry for the following week caught her eye.

1 p.m. Viewing: 25 Park Road, Tiverton.

The lined paper danced before her eyes, tears blurring her vision. *If he's moving to Bristol, why is he viewing a house in Tiverton?*

CHAPTER 32

The slight breeze coming in through the open window brought welcome relief as Eddie surveyed the bits of projector spread across the available floor space. The Kalees were gone and his old but new Westrex Westar 35 mm projectors with xenon lamps had been lugged up the narrow stairs in pieces by two burley men and himself. It would take the best part of the day to get them assembled. He peered through the small square glass into the auditorium, and was pleased to see the replacement flooring being laid and the electrician installing the new sound system. A smile worked its way across his lips. Maybe, just maybe, it was coming together.

'Eddie?' Anna's voice surprised him. He dusted down his jeans and went to the top of the stairs. She was standing at the bottom with the door to the foyer propped open clutching two Styrofoam cups. He hoped it was coffee, he needed the fuel. 'One of your workmen let me in.'

'I'll come down.' At the bottom they did an awkward shuffle in the cramped space while he took the cups from her, so she didn't have to climb the narrow stairs with her hands full. It *was* coffee — the smell was heaven. 'This is a nice surprise.'

She followed him up to the projection room. 'I was in the area and thought I'd check out the Tivoli to make sure you didn't burn it down with that reel of nitrate.'

Eddie chuckled. 'As you can see, the Tivoli is still standing, and the film went up in flames under the supervision of the fire brigade.'

'Glad to hear it.' Anna gestured to the coffee he was holding. 'Can I have one of those?'

'Of course,' Eddie blustered, handing her a cup. 'Thanks for the coffee.'

'Mom taught me never to turn up empty-handed. It was about the only piece of advice from her I ever listened to.' Anna surveyed the room. 'What's going on here?'

Eddie cleared off the leather armchair and gestured for her to sit. She lowered herself carefully.

'I finally got my projectors. The problem is now I have to assemble them.'

'Need some help? I'm not sure what use I'll be.'

'That would be great.' Eddie kneeled beside the various parts, self-conscious as he tried to work out where to begin. He attempted to focus his attention away from the fluttering in his gut that Anna sought him out, brought him coffee and was now offering to hang out with him while he put bits of projector together.

'Does this thing have a manual?' Anna asked, putting her glasses on.

Eddie fished it out from under various tools and passed it to her, grateful to have help deciphering the complex instructions.

For the next hour he worked on fixing the base to the pedestal, while Anna chatted in the background and offered occasional directions.

'So, this is where you found the mystery film?' she asked, draining her cup.

'On the winding bench.' Eddie pointed.

Anna stood. 'Huh.' She stepped over to the bench and looked around. 'What about the note, did you keep it?'

Eddie nodded. 'It's downstairs in the office, pinned to the noticeboard.'

'And no one here can tell you anything?'

'Linda, the box office manager, might know something, but when I asked, she wasn't forthcoming.' Eddie sat back on his haunches. 'I get the sense she's mad at me, but I've no idea why. I leased this place as the doors were about to close. Without me, they'd have been out of a job.'

'But the projectionist didn't stay?'

'Retired, as far as I know. I wouldn't have been able to keep him on, in any case. I intend to run the films myself.' Eddie stood to lift the lamp house into place.

Anna checked her watch.

She was bored. He couldn't blame her. 'Do you want to get lunch?' he blurted, not wanting her to leave when she was such good company.

She offered up an uncertain smile. 'Sure, I guess I could stick around.'

'I'm buying,' he offered to squash any doubts. 'You brought me coffee and deciphered those instructions, it's the least I can do.'

'When you put it like that, how can I refuse?'

* * *

In the foyer, Linda was positioned behind the kiosk, this time with a novel. *Is she checking up on me?* He didn't expect her to work her hours when there was nothing to do. She raised a sculpted eyebrow as Anna emerged from the projection room.

'Hello, Linda.'

She threw him a nod and returned to her book.

Eddie glanced at Anna, who smirked and thrust a hand in Linda's direction. 'Hey, I'm Anna, pleasure to meet you.'

Clearly taken aback, Linda rearranged her scowl into a wary smile and shook Anna's hand. 'Linda.'

'Are you looking forward to the cinema reopening?' Anna asked, leaning a casual arm against the counter.

Linda set down her book and shrugged. 'If it gets that far.'

'Why wouldn't it? Eddie's installing the new projectors.'

'Have you seen the progress in the auditorium?' Eddie ventured, buoyed by Anna's presence.

'We'll see.' Linda returned to her book, Irvine Welsh's *Trainspotting*. Ewan McGregor's Renton shuddered with withdrawal on the cover.

'Wow,' Anna mouthed as Eddie marched her outside. 'You've got your work cut out there.'

'Tell me about it.' His thoughts were dragged back to the immediate issue of where to take Anna for lunch. Despite living in the town, Eddie had no idea what the best eating options might be. On Fore Street, he spied the bakery, who he already knew did a great bacon roll. He was about to suggest a takeaway when Anna beat him to it.

'Fancy grabbing lunch here and eating outside?'

It was like she was telepathic. 'Great idea.'

Fifteen minutes later they were heading for a bench in the People's Park, at Anna's suggestion. She seemed to have a pretty good sense of Tiverton despite not living there.

Clutching warm bacon rolls and more fresh coffee, Eddie breathed in the sweet scent of freshly cut grass infusing the soft sunshine. It was good to put distance between himself and the Tivoli. As they took a seat, Anna put on sunglasses.

'Thanks again for your help today,' he said to distract himself from gazing at her. He handed her a roll from the brown paper bag.

'You're welcome. I can see what you're up against with Linda.'

'When Mum visited, she had Linda eating out of her hand in minutes.' He shook his head. 'She won't give me the time of day.'

'I wish my mom was like yours instead of . . .' She trailed off. 'Do you know how they became friends?'

Eddie shrugged. 'No idea. I take it you're not close?'

'She rang me last week from New York to tell me she's met someone new. Three divorces and she hasn't learned a thing.' Anna took a bite of her sandwich.

Eddie sank his teeth into his lunch too, appreciating the salty tang of bacon and brown sauce oozing from the warm bread while he searched for an appropriate response. 'I've only been married once. I couldn't begin to imagine putting myself through three divorces and having the faith to keep going. She must be an eternal optimist.'

'If they have a big enough bank account, her glass is half full.' Anna dipped her head. 'Maybe I'm being unfair,' she muttered.

'Which number is your dad?'

'I've never met him. As far as I know, they didn't make it down the aisle.'

Eddie took a sip of his coffee. 'I'm sorry. For what it's worth, I've never met my dad either.'

Anna's raised eyebrows peeked over the top of her sunglasses. 'I'm intrigued.'

'It's a long story and not really mine to tell.'

'You're very protective of your mom.'

Eddie shrugged. 'My ex saw that as a character fault.'

Anna laughed. He noticed a smudge of ketchup on her lip. 'Ah, I see. So there must be something wrong with your mom. Was she always visiting?'

'Quite the opposite. Mum's life was far too full for her to spend her spare time hanging out with Sarah and me. Nah, Sarah didn't like that I could talk to my mum. She said I was emotionally immature.'

Anna removed her sunglasses. 'I had noticed that about you.'

Eddie looked at her, detecting a twinkle in her eyes. Self-conscious, he grinned. 'I'll have to work on that.'

'You should.' She licked the sauce from her lip.

Tearing his gaze from hers, he popped the last bit of roll into his mouth and swilled it down with the dregs of his coffee.

'Oh God.' Anna shoved her sunglasses on again and grabbed him by the arm, attempting to conceal herself behind his shoulder. He lost his grip on his coffee cup, sending it hurtling to the grass. Reaching to retrieve it, Eddie looked up to see a man with a trim grey beard and arty glasses walking with a woman swathed in a chiffon scarf. They appeared to be arguing about something before the man's gaze settled on Eddie and Anna. At first Eddie thought it was the falling coffee cup that caught the man's interest, but when he glanced at Anna, he could tell something was very wrong.

'Eddie, can we leave?' Her voice hit a shrill note.

He frowned, watching the couple move away, the man glancing over his shoulder. 'What is it?'

Anna was already on her feet when the man stalked back in their direction. Arriving at the bench, he cleared his throat. 'Anna, this is a surprise.'

She went pink. 'Graham, I mean Dr Baker, what brings you to Tiverton?' There was a hard edge to her voice Eddie hadn't heard before.

Graham narrowed his eyes and threw Eddie a glance. 'I think you already know.'

Eddie wondered if he should introduce himself since Anna clearly didn't plan to.

He was about to speak when Graham addressed Anna again. 'Might we have a minute?'

No one moved. Realising they were waiting for him to leave, Eddie walked away to the park entrance.

The sun retreated behind thick cloud. It was appropriate, given the way the day had started to turn. Puzzled as to what was happening, Eddie scrunched up the takeaway bag and searched around for a bin. *Why the weird tension?* He glanced across at them. Although he was too far away to hear what they were saying, their discussion appeared impassioned, all arms gesticulating. It slowly dawned on him. He'd assumed Anna was single, but now he sensed her relationship with the doctor wasn't strictly that of supervisor and student. Dumping their rubbish in the bin, he thrust his hands in his pockets, feeling foolish. It was almost a relief to know she was attached.

Anna returned, red-faced and blotchy.

'Everything okay?' Eddie cocked his head towards Graham's retreating back.

'Yeah, fine. A disagreement over my research.'

Eddie nodded. People didn't generally get that worked up over research in the middle of a park, or maybe they did.

'We're involved,' Anna relented. 'I guess it's fairly obvious, although Graham would freak out if he thought you knew.'

Eddie frowned. 'Why should he freak out?'

'That was his wife, so . . .'

'Right.' Eddie stared across the park, a tight sensation clawing at the bacon roll in his stomach. 'I should probably get back. Those projectors aren't going to build themselves.' He set out with grim determination, not bothering to check if Anna was following.

'Hey, Eddie . . .' She caught up with him. 'Did I say something wrong?'

'I didn't realise how late it was, that's all.' He walked on, aware he was being rude and brattish, but for some reason he couldn't stop. Her trainers padded behind.

The streets seemed littered with people. They blurred into hazy shapes, blocking his path and adding to his irritation. Old women out shopping, bored teenagers loitering with a cigarette, tramps swigging from a can of warm beer. And Anna's presence taking up too much space in his mind as they reached the alleyway leading to the cinema.

'I'm going to head home.'

Eddie forced himself to look at her. 'Sure, it's no fun being indoors on a day like this.' Droplets of rain pelted his head, contradicting his statement.

Anna nodded — her expression inscrutable behind her dark lenses. 'See you around, Eddie. Thanks for lunch.'

He watched her go, weaving her way along Gold Street, wondering what her visit had really been about and whether they would have reason to cross paths again.

CHAPTER 33

Eddie let himself into the Tivoli and went straight up to the projection room, barely acknowledging Linda, who remained exactly where he'd left her. Frustrated by the lack of space to pace out his anger, it slowly ebbed into guilt about the way he'd treated Anna.

He slumped on the chair too heavily, feeling the bite of a spring in his posterior. Judgemental wasn't a look he liked to wear, but having been on the receiving end of infidelity, the wound still ran deep. Sarah's affair had blindsided him. Sure, he worked long hours, but she'd known what the life of a cinema projectionist involved when they'd got married. It was a mutual friend who had gently opened his eyes to his wife's extracurricular activities. They'd tried to make a go of things for a while, but the trust was gone. In the end, he was the one who did them both a favour and walked away.

His attention returned to the partially assembled projectors. For the next three hours, Eddie set about finishing the job, relieved to have a focus. The workmen had downed tools and Linda was gone too by the time he emerged into the foyer, hot and tired.

The sun was making a leisurely exit, bathing the front of the cinema in soft light which pooled across the steps into the foyer. He stood for a moment, taking in the progress of the last month. The freshly painted walls gleamed in the evening rays. The kiosk had a new ticketing system, and on closer inspection, the shelves were free of dust — so Linda had been doing something with her time. He pushed his way through the doors into the auditorium. Wiring hung from the walls where the new speakers were being installed, rows of usable chairs were stacked at one end and the floor was half finished, but still, it was progress. His dream might come true, so why did he feel so flat?

Rather than face an evening alone with his morose thoughts, Eddie let himself out of the back of the cinema and climbed into his car, heading for Exeter. *Running home to Mummy?* Sarah's words still stung. Who else but his mother could he really trust?

Fractured light dappled the road as he drove along the treelined route. Ruby cows grazed in the fields either side of Stoke Canon bridge, at home among the trickling tributary of the River Exe. The landscape dotted with trees, fields and electricity pylons gave a sense of modernity to the pastoral scene.

Twenty minutes later, he pulled up outside his mum's flat, which covered the top floor of a Victorian conversion in Heavitree. Eddie loved it here despite the painful associations it held of the aftermath of his divorce. If his mother hadn't gently asserted her need for independence, he might have become a permanent fixture.

Giving the buzzer a courteous ring, he pulled out his key, let himself in and climbed the five flights of stairs. His mum was fiercely protective of her private life, and he respected her boundaries. She'd always maintained if there was a man in her life worth meeting, Eddie would be the first to know. He was still waiting.

She was in her bright sitting room overlooking the gardens in a tree pose, yoga mat rolled out in front of her. 'Hello, darling, this is a lovely surprise.' She rolled into a downward dog, before folding herself into a child's pose and gracefully rising to her feet. Rolling up her mat, she planted a kiss on his cheek. 'Tea, or something stronger?'

'Tea's good, thanks, Mum.' Eddie followed her through to her galley kitchen, where tumbling houseplants hung from the ceiling and colourful china adorned the shelves. He filled the kettle while his mum selected mugs. They moved around each other in a familiar routine.

With a mug of tea each, green for her and builder's for him, they returned to the sitting room. His mum curled up on her favourite armchair like her cat, Atticus, who was sleeping on the sofa. Eddie sat at the other end. Atticus opened one eye then jumped down, stretching his long grey body and leaping into his mistress's lap.

'What brings you here?' She sipped her tea and threw him a quizzical look as she stroked Atticus under his chin to the hum of his purr.

Eddie shrugged, unsure where to begin. She was incapable of small talk and seemed to read him at fifty metres. 'I assembled the new projectors today.' His gaze shifted to the window, where trees swayed in the fading evening light. 'Anna helped me for a while.'

Like a magnet, he glanced back, searching for a reaction. She leaned forwards, eyes burning with interest. 'Anna helped you?'

'Yeah, it would have been a lot harder without her.' It was true. A twinge of guilt resurfaced. He'd have to phone and apologise.

'How's her research going?'

Eddie winced at the memory of Graham. 'She's having some issues with her supervisor.'

'Really?' That animation again. 'What kind of issues?'

Eddie stopped himself saying more. It wasn't fair to drag his mum into Anna's mess with Graham, not when she'd be returning to the university herself soon. 'She didn't divulge details.'

'I hope she can sort something out. That Graham is a bit . . . obsequious.'

'In what way?'

Her expression closed. 'I shouldn't gossip. How's the Tivoli? Have you found any common ground with Linda?'

Eddie didn't want to think about work. 'Not really.' He took a sip of his tea, hoping for a change of subject.

'Have you considered what you'll do for the opening? It might be a great opportunity to bring the staff together.'

'Like what?'

'I don't know. You need to think about it, Ed.'

She was right. He'd been too distracted, and surely getting the Tivoli finished and open was the whole point?

'Why don't you get the staff together and ask them for their opinions?'

Eddie studied the patterns on the surface of his tea. 'Maybe.' It wasn't a terrible idea. He nodded. 'Got any biscuits?'

'I made sugar-free blueberry muffins. They're in the tin on the kitchen counter.'

'Sugar-free muffins? They sound delicious.' Eddie chuckled and made for the door.

'Don't knock them until you've tried them.' His mum's eyes shone with laughter. 'And when you come back, I want to hear more about Anna.'

CHAPTER 34

Anna joined the queue of students at the library desk, a stack of books in her arms, one in particular she'd been waiting to take out for months. It was a collection of essays on women in film noir, including one by Dr Humphries.

She was in the midst of shoving the books in her rucksack when she almost collided with Graham, who was hovering by the door. They'd barely exchanged a civil word since the previous week when she'd run into him at the park. The memory was not one she wanted to dwell on. She'd used her visit to Eddie as a foil to spy on Graham and his house viewing, destroying their burgeoning friendship and her integrity in one decisive swoop.

'Anna, might I have a word?' Graham peered at her over his glasses.

She took off her own and slid them into her bag. 'I'm on my way to . . .' Nowhere came to mind.

His eyes pleaded.

She sighed. 'Fine.'

In his office, Anna dumped her rucksack on the floor and took a seat. Graham pulled out his chair. 'You're still mad at me?'

'What do you expect? One minute you're telling me we're going to be together, the next you're leaving for Bristol, then you're house-hunting in Tiverton. What am I supposed to think? And with no mention of helping find a new supervisor for my PhD.'

'You're right, I'm sorry.' He wheeled his chair closer, so their knees were almost touching. 'The house-hunting was Debs's idea. She wants to stay in the area while I get a flat in Bristol and come home at weekends, which means giving up our place in Exeter and going for a cheaper option so we can afford two homes.'

Anna folded her arms. She didn't particularly want to hear the details of Graham's property portfolio.

'It strikes me as the perfect solution,' he continued. 'I'll be alone in Bristol all week . . .'

Anna unfolded her arms and fiddled with a piece of cotton which had come free from her jumper sleeve, waiting to hear how them being in different cities provided any sort of a solution.

His warm hand closed around hers, stilling her fingers. 'Transfer your PhD to Bristol, that way I can continue as your supervisor.'

She glanced up. 'That's one hell of a commute, Graham.'

His thumb stroked her wrist. 'Move there too.'

Anna forced her eyes to meet his. Had she understood him correctly?

'We could carry on as we have been.'

She snatched back her hand, riding the wave of anger until it crashed to shore in a flurry of furious words. 'Move to Bristol so I can carry on being your fucking mistress?'

'For God's sake, Anna, keep your voice down. You'll get us both suspended.'

'You're fucking incredible. I'm changing supervisors effective immediately.' She stormed from his office in a blur of tears.

* * *

Half an hour later, Anna flung open the door to her flat. Numbness settled on her on the drive home. All she could think about was how stupid she'd been, how naive. In New York, her friends prioritised dating over their careers. Her own mother seemed unable to exist without the support of a man. Anna, determined to be different, had ploughed on through her academic career. Coming to England to do her PhD was supposed to be the pinnacle, but in truth she'd never been so lonely.

In the bathroom, she stepped into the shower, appreciating the way the hot water soothed her body and stifled her sobs. Ten minutes later, she dressed in jeans and a blouse, grabbed her keys and left, eager to be away from the flat where she'd spent so much time with Graham.

Outside, the evening was sultry, the sky azure blue, the trees green and lush. She walked past Belmont Park in the direction of town, with no particular plan other than to walk off her malaise.

On Sidwell Street, Anna paused outside the Odeon cinema. It had been ages since she'd spontaneously watched a film. She scanned the available options. *Fargo* was due to begin in ten minutes.

In the foyer, she stopped in her tracks. Eddie had just stepped away from the box office, two tickets in his hand. Of course, his weekly film outing with his mom. She contemplated slipping away but he'd already seen her. He offered up a smile that didn't quite reach his eyes.

'Hey,' Anna walked over to meet him. 'Waiting for your mom?'

Eddie's gaze flickered to the doors. 'Aren't I always?'

'What are you watching?'

'*Fargo*.'

'Me too.' She uttered the words without thinking.

'You'd better be quick, they've almost sold out.'

'Right.' Anna hurried to the ticket office. She checked behind in time to see Eddie engulfing his mom in a hug. Dr

Humphries was wearing a long spaghetti-strap dress with a delicate floral pattern over a T-shirt and white tennis shoes, somehow managing to epitomise summer and upstage most of the cinema's younger clientele. They exchanged a few words then looked in Anna's direction. She offered a wave.

Dr Humphries approached. 'Anna, it's lovely to see you again. I was explaining to Ed, something's come up and I can't make this evening. Would you consider taking my ticket? It's supposed to be a fabulous film.'

Anna glanced at Eddie, who appeared unable to meet her gaze.

'Are you sure?'

'Absolutely. The ticket will only go to waste.' Dr Humphries' eyes burned into hers. 'You'd better go in. See you soon, Ed.' She planted a kiss on her son's cheek and was gone.

Eddie handed Anna her ticket. 'You don't mind, do you?'

'A free ticket? Of course not. What was the emergency?'

He stared after his mother. 'I have no idea.'

CHAPTER 35

The auditorium was packed. It took them a while to locate two seats together. He glanced at Anna as they settled themselves. This evening had taken quite the unexpected turn, and he wasn't sure how he felt about it yet, but he couldn't help smiling at his mum's lack of subtlety.

He wrestled open the bag of Revels he'd purchased earlier and offered them to Anna. In the gloom, her white teeth gleamed as she smiled and took a handful. The fresh hint of tangy shampoo lifted off her hair. Pushing the notion to one side, Eddie focused on the barren snowscape cut to ominous music of the opening scene.

Two hours later, they emerged with smiles on their faces.

'That was incredible,' Anna said. They made their way down the stairs into the foyer, their fellow audience members buzzing around them. 'Do you want to grab a drink?'

'Sure,' Eddie agreed, half gratified she'd suggested it, half annoyed he was so eager to spend more time in her company.

A blanket of darkness cut against the bright lights of Sidwell Street preparing to welcome late-night revellers to its multitude of takeaways. Eddie self-consciously thrust his hands in his jean pockets, uncomfortable in his own skin. He tried to listen to Anna's enthusing about the film, but the tension from their last meeting was hard to shake off.

They headed along the high street. Anna stopped outside a pub near Cathedral Green.

'What can I get you?' she asked him at the bar.

'You don't have to buy me a drink.'

'Sure I do, you paid for my ticket.'

'That's true. Okay, a pint of Old Speckled Hen, please.'

She ordered the same for herself and they returned outside, finding a table under an awning. The garden was busy with students enjoying an end-of-term drink.

Anna took a deep breath and released a sigh. 'It's good to be out.' She lifted her glass. 'To friends and excellent movies.'

Eddie returned her toast. 'You're in a good mood this evening.'

'I shouldn't be. Graham and I are finished.'

'Oh.' He frowned into his pint to mask a surge of happiness. 'Sorry.'

Anna shrugged. 'Hey, were you mad at me? I got this sense last week I'd pissed you off.'

Eddie coloured, grateful for the gloom of the low-lit garden. 'Not mad exactly. When you mentioned Graham was married, it hit a wound. My ex, Sarah, she cheated on me, so . . .'

'Shit, Eddie, you must think I'm a bitch.'

'Don't be ridiculous. I recognise it's never that simple.'

Anna shook her head. 'I am a bitch. I didn't consider his wife's feelings.'

Eddie sipped his pint, unsure how to respond. 'Maybe that's his responsibility.'

'Don't be nice to me. I don't deserve it.'

He was dismayed to see tears in her eyes. 'Anna.'

She pulled out a tissue and blew her nose. 'Fuck,' she whispered.

Eddie hesitated, searching for words to ease her burden.

'Anyway . . .' She recovered her composure, overcompensating with a bright smile. 'We're done and I have good news.'

'What's your good news?'

'I'm not sure it's good exactly,' she faltered, 'but I need a new supervisor. I wondered if your mom would be willing to take me on. My research falls within her expertise. What do you think?'

'I can't speak for Mum, but I'm sure she'd be interested,' Eddie replied, glad to be on safer territory.

'Maybe I should have raised it when I saw her earlier.'

'Do you want me to pass the message on?'

Anna smiled. 'Thanks.'

The table full of students next to them was getting a little rowdy. Eddie felt his age as he found himself disgruntled. As if reading his mind, Anna glanced in their direction then threw him a small eye roll. He couldn't help grinning back, relieved the tension had cleared.

'How's work?' she asked.

The grin slid off his face. 'Okay. The Tivoli is actually getting pretty close to completion.'

'Congratulations, Eddie, that's great news. What do you have in mind for the grand opening?'

Eddie grimaced. 'That's the problem, I don't know. Mum suggested I get the team involved, a sort of bonding exercise.'

'Not a bad idea. Are you any closer to making friends with Linda?'

'No, I'll need something spectacular to get through that wall of ice.' Maybe he was being a bit mean.

'Why don't you start by discussing what the opening film should be?'

'I've already set my heart on *Cinema Paradiso*.' He threw her a sheepish smile.

'An excellent choice, I'd love to see it on the big screen again.'

'Will you come? I'd appreciate a friendly face.' It was true, he didn't have many people in his life he could rely on. He'd lost half his friends in the divorce.

'Count me in, but I do think you should ask the team's opinion too.'

'I know, you're right.'

'You've got to get Linda onside. How else will you find out about the note, the film reel and the projectionist?'

Eddie smirked. 'Sounds like the title of a murder mystery.'

'Who knows? It could just be.'

* * *

Two more pints later they left the pub. Anna clung to his arm as they retraced their steps along the high street.

'Wow, that'll teach me to drink on an empty stomach. Those Revels in the cinema are all I've eaten since lunchtime. My breakup with Graham stole my appetite but now I'm starving.'

Eddie tried to ignore the mention of Graham, he was having a great time. 'We can stop for chips, if you like? I've got the munchies too.'

Anna halted and looked at him, her face serious. 'An excellent plan, lead on.'

Finding themselves back on Sidwell Street, they joined a queue of mostly students at one of the takeaways. The chips were a little soggy under too much vinegar, but Eddie hardly noticed. As they strolled, Anna regaled him with stories about her mother, who did sound like an outrageous woman.

Anna ground to an abrupt halt at the end of the road. 'You don't have to walk me home.'

'I think I do. I won't sleep tonight worrying if I don't see you safely to your door.'

'You're sweet, Eddie, did anyone ever say that about you?'

'Once or twice.' They carried on walking.

'Hey,' she stopped again. 'How are you going to get home?'

It was a good question. He'd driven in and hadn't planned on sinking three pints. 'I'll stay at Mum's.'

'Don't forget to ask her about being my supervisor.'

'I'll do it the moment I step through the door.'

Anna grinned and moved on. Skirting Belmont Park, she came to a stop outside a pretty Georgian building. 'This is me, first floor.' She pointed skywards then turned to face him. 'Thanks, you turned a shitty evening into a pretty great one.'

Eddie smiled. 'Any time. I'm always here for nights out on the rebound.'

'You're becoming a good friend, Eddie.'

He inwardly sighed. *Friend.* 'You too.'

Before he had time to react, she leaned in, grabbing his collar and pulling his mouth down to hers. Her lips tasted salty, balancing out the vinegary chips.

After a beat, she pulled away. Their eyes locked and Eddie leaned in to kiss her again, but she stepped back.

Embarrassed, he studied the paving stones beneath their feet.

'Sorry, not sure where that came from. It's been an emotional day.' Her face was obscured in shadow. Maybe that was for the best, he didn't want to see the regret in her eyes.

'It's fine. No harm done.'

'This isn't going to be weird, is it?'

He averted her gaze. 'Course not. I'll see you around.'

'Bye, Eddie, I'll call you.'

Eddie hurried away, his feet unable to keep up with his need to put distance between Anna and him.

CHAPTER 36

Anna eyed the phone on the console table in her flat, her fingers twitching to pick it up. She'd spent the last three weeks torturing herself about Eddie, trying to avoid Graham and muddling through the mess of finding a new supervisor. Dr Humphries wasn't due back for another week and since Anna had wrecked the evening with Eddie, he was unlikely to put in a good word with his mom. *Why the kiss? Emotional turmoil after Graham? Because we'd had a fun evening? Because I wanted to?* Perhaps a little of all three. Anna sighed, searching for a reason to call him. In truth, she'd left it far too long.

Checking her watch, she gathered up her research notes and shoved them in her rucksack. The university library had emailed the previous day asking if she could catalogue a set of glass negatives, part of a substantial donation. Anna was happy to oblige, making use of her archivist training and earning her a little extra money too.

The first person Anna saw as she entered the library was Graham.

'Hi.' He ran his fingers over his beard. 'How's it going?'

Anna gestured to her packed rucksack. 'As you can see, it's going.'

'Might we have a word?' The furtive glance, so familiar, sent a jolt to her chest.

'I'm on my way to special collections.'

'I'll walk you.' He fell into step beside her, his voice a low murmur. 'I've been offered a permanent contract at Bristol. I'm leaving a little earlier than expected but the dean knows your situation and will set up a meeting about your PhD supervision.'

'Thanks.' Anna forced a smile. 'Congratulations.' One of them needed to take the higher road.

'Debs is staying behind. We put in an offer on the house in Tiverton.'

'Okay.'

'We'll see how it goes with weekends.'

They reached the door to the special collections room. Anna offered her hand. He looked a little wounded. 'I'll see you around.'

'Sure.' His hand lingered as she gently extracted herself from the handshake.

'Good luck, Graham.'

With a sigh of relief, she approached the desk and gave her details. While the librarian went to retrieve the negatives, Anna studied the hand held by Graham's moments before. Loneliness enveloped her. She rallied as the librarian returned with a box. Work would see her through.

In a booth, Anna took a seat, put on her glasses and donned a pair of white gloves. She set about unwrapping each negative with care. It was methodical work and just absorbing enough to stop her mind straying into dangerous territory.

Each negative was wrapped in faded newspaper. Anna found herself distracted by the occasional article or adverts for exotic things like carbolic soap. The negatives themselves were less interesting but she persevered, reminding herself the extra cash would come in handy.

She was about to take a break when a newspaper headline mentioning the Tivoli caught her attention. Anna freed the newspaper from the negative and smoothed it out on the desk.

The full headline read: *Here's Looking at You, Kid — Tivoli Two — Love's Young Dream Ends in Tragedy.* Beneath the headline there was a picture of a man and a woman smiling for the camera in front of the cinema screen. She peered at the image.

Pulling off her gloves, Anna returned to the collections desk and asked to use their phone. He answered on the second ring.

'Eddie, it's Anna.'

'Anna. Long time, no speak.' His voice held a note of hesitation.

She decided to be direct. 'Look, I know I should have called sooner, and things are a bit weird between us, but can we meet up this evening? I think I've solved your mystery.'

CHAPTER 37

Eddie dumped his bag on the kitchen table, opened the window and surveyed the contents of his fridge. *I really should throw out that Ginsters pasty.* Closing the door, he checked the clock. Anna would be here in ten minutes. He could either have a shower or nip to the corner shop to see what he could rustle up for dinner. He opted for the shower. Better to be clean with disappointing food options than a sweaty mess with a fully stocked fridge. If she wanted to eat, he'd order in. He practically had a hotline to the local Chinese anyway. It might cheer them up to hear him ordering for two for a change.

He'd just pulled on clean jeans and a T-shirt when the doorbell chimed. He buzzed her in then opened his front door and waited. Anna appeared in the stairwell dressed in a long summer dress and denim jacket. Her hair had grown in the month since they'd last laid eyes on each other. It suited her. 'Hey.'

For a second he stared until he remembered himself. 'Sorry, you'd better come in.'

'Thanks.' She followed him into the kitchen, which he decided was the tidiest room if she could overlook his neglected breakfast things piled in the sink.

'Drink? I've got tea, coffee or beer.' He cast around for inspiration. 'Water?'

'Water would be good, thanks, I'm driving.'

He opened the cupboard and retrieved a couple of glasses. 'I'll join you, it's so hot out.' Filling the two glasses from the tap, he gestured to the small kitchen table. Anna pulled out a chair. He handed her a glass and leaned self-consciously against the kitchen counter. 'So . . .'

Anna took a sip and set down her glass, meeting his gaze. 'Before we get to why I'm here, I wanted to apologise about that night and then not calling . . . My life's been a bit chaotic lately.'

'It's fine, don't worry about it. I knew you were in a weird place that night. We all do messed-up things when we're feeling sad.'

Her shoulders slumped in relief, and she flashed him her perfect teeth. 'Thanks.'

Eddie sipped his water. Her relief brought him no comfort but at least they'd cleared the air. 'I mentioned to Mum about becoming your supervisor. She's keen if you still are?'

Anna grinned. 'Definitely, I appreciate it.'

Lost for further conversation, he studied the diamond patterns on the linoleum floor.

'How's things at the Tivoli? Is Linda any friendlier?'

Eddie set down his glass and suppressed a sigh. 'Not really. The cinema is pretty much ready apart from some last-minute snags, but I've decided to wait until September to reopen. Summer is never a good time of year for cinemas.'

'Did you sort out some ideas for opening night?'

Eddie grimaced. He'd tried with Linda only that morning. When he'd suggested *Cinema Paradiso*, she'd studied him with those kohled eyes until he'd mumbled something about putting ideas in a hat. 'I'm going to have a meeting with the staff next week, see if we can pin it down.'

'Great. Well, I'll be at the opening with bells on.' Anna reached for her rucksack. 'So, Connie Harris . . .'

Eddie had all but forgotten the reason for her visit. 'Ah yes, I'm intrigued.'

Anna nodded. There was a strange look on her face, and she seemed hesitant like she was reluctant to tell him.

'Is something wrong?'

'No, it's . . .' Anna pulled out a manila envelope. She extracted a newspaper cutting, unfolding it with care. The paper had faded to sepia. 'I found this when I was going through a box of glass negatives at uni. Each one was wrapped in newspaper from years ago. The headline mentioning the Tivoli and the photo of the couple caught my eye.' Anna glanced up at him. 'You'd better sit down.'

Eddie frowned, pulling out a chair. Anna pushed the newspaper cutting across the table. He picked it up and studied the photo. His jaw dropped.

'Am I right?'

PART FIVE

April 1956

CHAPTER 38

She wrapped her fingers around the china cup, trying to eke out the last of the tea's warmth while her eyes scanned the newspaper. An advertisement for local deliveries from Exe Valley Butchers caught her attention. An image of a sheep adorned the side of the van. Grace couldn't see sheep without thinking about Joe and the farm.

It had been a harsh shock when she'd stepped off the train from Dulverton. Changing her name from Rose was George's idea. 'In case our Joe gets it into his head to search for you, maid. A clean break is what the lad needs.' She'd readily agreed, but there were days when she'd give anything to see Joe's face. It had been an innocent time, a prelude to the shock of the last five years. The farm seemed like another world, another life, as if it existed in its own dimension.

Eddie on the chair beside her tapped the table with her teaspoon, his short legs swinging back and forth. Disgruntled patrons glanced in their direction.

'Stop it, Ed.'

'I'm bored.' He reached for the newspaper, pulling it towards him, almost sending her saucer crashing to the floor.

'Eddie, no.' She smoothed the paper left on the table by the previous occupant and glanced across the tearoom at the windows flecked with droplets of rain. As her gaze swept back, Grace noticed an elegant woman with pearlescent skin and dark brown hair regarding them from beneath heavily made-up lashes. As Grace met her eye, the woman stood, moving her voluptuous frame in their direction. Grace returned her attention to the paper, hoping she'd pass them by. This was the third time she'd seen her in the tearooms over the last couple of weeks. Her inquisitive eyes made Grace uneasy.

Sensing a presence at her side, she looked up. The woman was wearing an usherette uniform she recognised from the Odeon. Perhaps she'd seen Grace scuttle away with her mop and bucket into the shadows of the imposing cinema.

Grace batted Eddie's hand as he reached for the teaspoon again. Involuntarily, she shivered. They'd come in to escape a downpour which had soaked them both to the skin.

'You're cold.' The woman turned to the waitress, catching her attention immediately. 'Another pot of tea and two buttered crumpets, please.'

Grace marvelled at how this woman occupied the world with such ease and authority.

She returned her attention to Grace, offering her hand. 'Beatrice, Bea.'

Her hand was enveloped by cool, manicured fingers. 'Grace.'

'May I?' Bea gestured to the vacant seat at the table and draped herself without waiting for a reply. 'How old is he?'

Grace glanced at her son. 'Four.'

'You're raising him alone?'

'How did you know that?' Grace struggled to keep the incredulity from her voice.

'You aren't wearing a ring.'

She'd considered buying one to avoid this kind of prying, but it wouldn't have been money well spent when their bellies were empty and their limbs cold.

When she didn't answer, Bea continued her interrogation. 'Does the father help?'

Grace was stunned by the impertinence of the question. How could she explain her memories were an unfinished patchwork quilt, the last five years the only squares. It would make her sound mad or worse, like one of the women who walked the streets after nightfall. She hadn't come to that — not yet.

Sensing this conversation was somehow significant though, Grace shook her head.

The tea and crumpets arrived. Bea gestured for the waitress to place them in front of Grace and Eddie.

Too hungry for pride, Grace offered the crumpet to her son and watched, relieved and grateful, as he took it between his fingers. She ate the other crumpet herself, slowly, lingering over the buttery taste.

Bea lit a cigarette, regarding them eating, a look of intense pleasure in her eyes. 'Has anyone told you you're a striking woman?'

Grace returned a baffled expression and set down her crumpet, self-conscious under Bea's concentrated gaze.

'How tall are you? Five foot eight or nine? You have the figure of a model and a sharp, intelligent face.' Bea reached out a long finger, lightly lifting Grace's chin.

Grace tried not to flinch under her touch, amazed this woman believed she had the right to manhandle a stranger.

Bea sat back, dropping her cigarette ash into the tray on the table. 'You clean at the Odeon. I've seen you leaving as I arrive for my shift.'

Grace nodded.

'Have you met the manager, Mr Sanders?'

'I work for Mrs Arnold.'

Bea shrugged as if the name of the head cleaner meant nothing to her. 'He's looking for new girls, usherettes. It's a coveted job.'

Grace envied the usherettes milling around in their lovely matching uniforms like goddesses from another realm.

Bea checked her watch. It looked expensive, hanging off her wrist like a beautiful gold bracelet. 'I have to go.' She stubbed out her cigarette. Grace couldn't help thinking it was a waste, she'd only smoked half of it. 'Meet me at the foyer this evening at five. I'll introduce you to Sanders.' Bea glanced at Eddie then swept from the tearoom, pausing at the counter to settle the bill.

Grace turned back to Eddie, who appeared as stunned as she. His butter-smeared face broke into a grin. She kissed his curly black hair, unsettled by the enigmatic Bea and the thread of hope their fortunes might finally be about to change.

* * *

An hour later when the waitress's frosty looks and her long empty teacup compelled her to venture back into the rain, Grace walked home wondering how she would keep her appointment with destiny.

Gripping Eddie's hand, they hurried across Sidwell Street under the gaze of the ostentatious cinema. Grace couldn't explain what first attracted her to the Odeon. She'd happened upon it one chilly autumn afternoon during her first week in Exeter. Furnished with a new name, Grace had walked the streets for hours searching for work, lost, frightened, regretting leaving the farm, thinking about Joe and his kisses, thinking about her baby growing inside.

The cinema called to her, a fellow survivor rising from the barren landscape devastated by bombs which had wiped out the buildings opposite. She loved the stark lines of its Art Deco exterior. It was shouty and proud. Drawn in by its bright lights, and the opportunity to be a little closer to something glamorous, she'd marvelled at the grand foyer with its fluted columns and bas-relief panels. An advertisement for a cleaner completed the circle. The cinema would enable her survival in this stark new world.

The rain had eased to a fine drizzle by the time they turned into their road. Eddie dragged his feet. She lifted him onto her hip and glanced up at the shabby terrace where they occupied an attic room. The building was full of girls like her — a single room, no questions asked. Grace was one of the house's longest occupants. She'd watched other girls come and go, some on to better lives with husbands and homes of their own, others — well, she didn't like to dwell on the others. Now Grace didn't bother to make friends. No one stayed around long enough.

Letting themselves in to the gloomy entrance hall, she hurried past Mrs Blythe's door, wanting to avoid the audible weeping that occasionally drifted through the paper-thin walls. Grace mounted the narrow stairs, so accustomed to the musty smell her nose no longer reacted. Mrs Blythe turned a blind eye to those forced to live in the shadows as long as you paid your rent on time and didn't ask questions about what went on in her parlour. She watched Eddie too when Grace was in desperate need. If the old widow hadn't taken her in, she dreaded to think where she would have ended up.

Straining under the weight of her now slumbering son, Grace gripped the banister, passing door after door, paint blistered on the damp walls. At the top she unlocked their room. With relief in her aching limbs, she lay Eddie on the iron bed they shared, easing him out of his coat. He curled in a ball, peaceful in his slumber.

Grace pulled off her mac too and slung it over the back of her only chair to dry. Opening the narrow oak wardrobe, she cast over the modest selection of clothes. She needed to look her best. The blouse Agnes had mended for her and a dark red skirt she'd been given by one of the girls who'd moved on to a better life were the finest garments she owned.

Eddie sneezed, causing him to stir. Grace feared he was getting a cold. She stroked his black curls until he settled again.

It never occurred to her to utilise Mrs Blythe's services to make her pregnancy disappear, although the old lady suggested it. Grace clung to the baby growing inside, someone to love and to love her in return, a part of herself when the rest remained a mystery, one that she'd so far failed to solve.

The police in Exeter had no record of a missing girl and her precarious situation made her shrink from pressing them further. An unmarried woman raising a child in a boarding house where her landlady performed illegal abortions? With no ring on her finger, they'd draw their conclusions — she wouldn't risk them taking Eddie away.

Grace tugged off her damp clothes and slid into the blouse. It still sent goosebumps scattering along her arms, but the room was cold, and she'd learned her fleeting memories brought her no closer to finding her truth. After Eddie was born, she'd plucked up the courage to see a doctor, knowing he was under oath. He diagnosed retrograde amnesia. A condition which affected only her memories and not her skills and abilities. It explained why she knew how to do everyday things like read, write or make tea but had no recollection of when she'd learned those things in the first place. He'd warned her that her memories may continue to prove elusive. Flashbacks were sporadic, their secrets as insubstantial as a diaphanous cloud.

Pulling on the skirt, Grace fastened the buttons, a little looser than last time she'd worn it. Eddie shuddered beside her. She smoothed his brow and kissed his soft cheek.

'Mummy has to go out later.' Her voice was bright, but her chest contracted with guilt the moment the words left her lips. She hated leaving Eddie with Mrs Blythe. 'Mummy might be able to get a better job. That would be good, wouldn't it, sweetheart?'

Eddie sneezed again. Grace pulled a hanky from her sleeve and held it to his nose. Mrs Blythe's smoky flat wouldn't do him any good.

Half an hour later they were venturing downstairs, anxiety forming in her stomach as she patiently waited for her son to navigate the steep steps with his hand in hers. When they eventually made it to Mrs Blythe's door, the anxiety weighed like a stone.

Mrs Blythe was seated in front of her electric fire, a cigarette butt dangling between her lips, grey hair pinned into curlers and covered with a scarf. She regarded Grace from behind thick-framed spectacles as she set down her knitting.

'What is it now? I had him yesterday morning. We can't keep on like this.'

Grace's back stiffened. 'I've got an interview at 5 p.m. I shouldn't be more than an hour. It's for a better job, more money, but if I don't go today, I'll miss my chance.' She flinched at her pleading tone.

Mrs Blythe clicked her tongue and stubbed out her cigarette in an overflowing tray. 'One hour.'

Grace's shoulders slumped. 'Thank you.'

* * *

Walking away from the house, Grace tried not to think about Eddie's snotty face or red-rimmed eyes when she kissed him goodbye, handing him into her landlady's care.

She shivered, pulling her mac tightly around her as her heels clicked along the high street.

Bea was talking to another usherette in the foyer when Grace walked in. She hovered inside the glass-fronted doors with one eye on their conversation. Then Bea was walking towards her, the full skirt of her uniform swishing as she moved.

'Come with me.' She beckoned Grace to follow. It was fascinating to see the cinema come alive. Grace was used to operating in the shadows, cleaning up after the previous day's fun in the grey silence of the early morning. Distracted, she struggled to keep up with Bea's stride.

They walked up a flight of stairs to a mezzanine where a restaurant overlooked the main foyer. The chairs and tables had been cleared to one side to make room for girls who were parading up and down at the far end. A man with dark hair greying at the temples and a sharp roman nose smoked a cigar as he watched the display from behind a table, a bored look on his face. Bea walked to his side, whispering in his ear in a way that suggested their relationship went beyond manager and subordinate. The man — Sanders, Grace assumed — let his gaze fall in her direction before addressing the room.

'That's enough, ladies, we'll be in touch.'

Grace watched, fascinated as the girls paraded out of the restaurant, hips swaying to full effect.

Bea beckoned her over. 'What do you think, Mr Sanders?' She circled Grace, pushing down her shoulders and flicking out her hair.

Mr Sanders regarded her through a haze of cigar smoke. 'Without the mac.'

Bea tugged the mac from Grace's back and gently pushed her forwards. Grace stood as tall and proud as she could, chest out, shoulders back.

Sanders' gaze glided down the length of her body, lingering over her legs before climbing back up to study her face.

'Try her out this evening. If she looks good in the uniform and can carry a tray, she'll do.'

Without giving her another glance, he walked away.

Bea took her arm. 'Let's get you into a uniform. You can shadow me this evening.'

Panic gripped her as Grace caught up with what was happening. 'I can't tonight, I told my landlady I'd be back in an hour . . . she's looking after Eddie for me.'

'Honey, you heard the man. He wants you to start right away.'

Grace tried to keep up with Bea's fast pace as she led her up another flight of stairs to a cloakroom. A uniform was thrust into her hands. Grace could scarcely take any of it in before she was manhandled out of her remaining clothes. Five minutes later she stared at herself in the mirror. The uniform was a crimson-red dress with epaulettes on each shoulder, gold buttons down the front and a belt to cinch the waist. The full skirt fell to her knee. It felt wonderful and oddly familiar. She never wanted to take it off.

Bea stood behind. 'I knew it. You were made for this.'

Dragging her gaze from her reflection, Grace's thoughts returned to Eddie. 'I can't do this evening, Bea, my little boy. I can't leave him so late, not without more notice.'

Bea sighed. 'All right. Stay until the interval, then sneak out. Sanders will have gone home by then, but sort something quickly. You saw the queue of girls. If you want this job, you'll be expected to start tomorrow.'

It was too good an opportunity to miss. Grace knew Mrs Blythe wouldn't abandon Eddie if she was late, but she'd tear several strips off her.

With her mind made up, she followed Bea back down the stairs and into the foyer. A woman wearing navy-blue cat-eye spectacles and a matching blue dress clipped across the concourse, throwing Bea a wave.

'That's Mary, Mr Sanders' secretary.'

Before Grace could respond, Bea reached into her pocket and handed her a small metal torch. 'You'll need this. Come on, there's no time to waste.' She led her to the kiosk, where they loaded up trays with chocolates and cigarettes. Bea took ice creams on hers. Grace followed her through the double doors into the auditorium, concentrating on mimicking Bea's every move, but before long, instinct led her too. She withstood the barrage of customers, never feeling more herself.

Grace's gaze swept over the auditorium as if she were viewing it through fresh eyes. As a cleaner she hadn't appreciated the scale of the space when it was lit up and ready for an evening screening. Ribbed plasterwork inclined along the ceiling to the top of the proscenium then fell away on each side, surmounted by shallow figures above the stalls. The film was *The Ladykillers* but there was little time to pay attention. Just being in that space with the film flickering behind, the hush of the audience and the audio booming filled her with a sense of home she couldn't articulate.

When the interval finally came, Grace tore up the stairs to the small cloakroom. She pulled off her uniform, throwing it into a bag, and tugged on her old clothes. Then she ran all the way home.

Mrs Blythe was waiting for her on the threshold of her flat, hands on hips, fag end hanging from her thin lips, which were pulled into a scowl.

'I'm sorry.'

'You said an hour.'

'I know. The interview went on longer than expected, but I got—'

Mrs Blythe held up a calloused hand. 'I've done you more favours than I've had hot dinners, young lady. I thought you were a bit smarter but you're like the rest. Getting yourself in the family way then expecting others to pick up the pieces. Well, it has to stop.'

Grace nodded. It wasn't the first time she'd been party to this particular lecture. 'How is he?' She peered past Mrs Blythe into the flat.

'Asleep. He's got a cold. I gave him a nip of whisky.'

Grace frowned.

'Don't like my methods, don't leave him with me.'

Blythe stood to one side. Grace slipped into the room and scooped Eddie into her arms from where he slept on the settee, the same sofa on which he'd come into the world.

'Thank you,' she mouthed as she walked through the door.

In her room, Grace settled Eddie on the bed, then carefully removed the uniform from the bag and hung it on the front of her wardrobe. She undressed herself, washed at the small corner sink and slipped into bed beside her son, coiling around his warm, slumbering body. She lay in the dark thinking about the uniform with its glinting gold buttons, comforted by its presence in the room. It wasn't only the way the uniform caressed her skin. When she was wearing it, she felt herself, a connection. It was as if the uniform was hers and the clothes she was wearing were borrowed. She couldn't explain it, but Grace sensed this job might change her fortunes. She must find a way to make it work.

CHAPTER 39

Charlie watched his girlfriend settle on his mother's floral sofa. Jane was wearing a pale-blue dress with a daisy pattern. The combination of sofa and dress gave the impression she was being consumed by a garden. A frown touched her face as he took the chair opposite. He knew she wanted him to sit next to her, to take her hand, but he'd lost the ability to be demonstrative for the same reason he'd failed with all his girlfriends since . . . he wouldn't ever have that kind of blind faith again. *You like this one.* It was true, he did. Jane was sweet and she laughed at his jokes even when it was obvious she hadn't understood.

His shoulders relaxed when his mother entered the room with a tea tray.

'I wish you'd let me help, Marge.' Jane smiled.

'It's no bother, I like someone to fuss over.' His mum set the tray on the coffee table, her gaze flickering briefly to his dad's empty chair.

Charlie's dad had died suddenly the previous year, leaving a gigantic hole in their lives. One minute he was watering the roses, the next he was flat on his back. With Charlie still at home, his mum put a brave face on it. He dreaded to think what she'd do when he moved out. Maybe this was it, for him too.

He met Jane at the funeral directors which was run by her parents. He and his mum were charmed with the quiet way she organised things around their grief. Jane was compassionate, and if his dad's death taught him anything, it was not to keep hesitating over life, but to grab it with both hands. So, he'd grabbed Jane — not literally, Jane was very proper, but he'd grabbed the opportunity. Now time was passing, and his mother was dropping hints about weddings with all the subtlety of a brass band.

Jane poured the tea, gripping the floral pot in her small, neat hands, brown ponytail bouncing as she passed a cup to his mother, then him, before finally serving herself. The epitome of the perfect daughter-in-law, *the perfect wife.*

She reached into her handbag and pulled out a woman's magazine. 'There's a dress I want to show you, Marge.'

His mother lifted her glasses to her face. The pair of them looked content as they pored over the glossy pages.

'I might take mine outside.' Charlie stood, tea in his hand. Neither of them protested. He knew what they wanted to talk about.

The air was easier to breathe out in the garden. He strode across to his father's favourite bench and took a seat, staring back at the house. Today was five years since his first date with Connie. It was ridiculous to keep the anniversary, but once a date like that embedded itself in your head, it wasn't easy to shift. The intervening years might have faded his memory, but the feelings hadn't gone away. Perhaps it was unique to them, the way Connie made him feel. He hadn't captured it with anyone, not even Jane.

A shout from the back of the house halted his downward trajectory. A smile spread across his lips at the sight of his godson, Johnny, hurtling towards him.

'Uncle Charlie, look.' Johnny offered up a red matchbox car. 'It's like Dad's.'

'That's amazing, Johnny. Where's your mum?'

'Inside.'

Moments later, Viv walked towards them carrying Abigail on her hip.

'This is a lovely surprise.' Charlie stood to kiss her cheek. Viv set Abigail on the grass and heaved her heavily pregnant frame onto the bench.

'Johnny wanted to show you his car, I hope you don't mind. I got the sense in there I was interrupting something.' Viv gestured to the house.

'Don't mind them, they're planning my future, that's all.'

She flashed him a bemused smile. 'How are you?'

Charlie shrugged.

'I know today is hard.'

'Thanks.'

Viv sat back and rubbed her stomach. 'Are they really planning your future?'

'Probably.'

'Shouldn't you be involved?' When he didn't answer, Viv found his hand and squeezed it. 'It's just today.'

Charlie nodded. 'How's Michael?'

Viv rolled her eyes. 'Working. That's all he ever does these days.'

Michael had left the Navy the previous year and bought a garage.

'He's found his passion.'

'His passion used to be me.'

'You're eight months pregnant, Viv. I don't think he's lacking in passion in that department.'

She grinned. 'He smells of engine oil though. Can't get it out of his clothes for love nor money. How's the Tiv? I miss it.'

'It's not the same without you, but we're muddling along.'

Viv nudged him. 'Liar.'

'Do you think you'll come back this time?'

'Not likely after Reynolds made me leave the minute he sniffed out another pregnancy. Cheeky old bastard calling my belly unsightly. Besides, Michael's got me doing the accounts for the garage and someone has to look after this lot.' Johnny and Abigail glanced up from where they were playing on the lawn at their feet.

'You love it.'

A smile tugged at her lips. 'I suppose I do.'

* * *

An hour later, with Viv and the kids gone, Charlie walked Jane back into town. He was on the late shift at the Tivoli. Her parents lived on Wellbrook Street in a flat above the funeral directors. It gave him the creeps. On his last visit, a range of caskets were on display in the large front window, sitting on pedestals draped in silver cloth. Fake floral arrangements adorned the wall behind. It all felt so claustrophobic, he didn't know how Jane could stand it.

As they approached Bridge Street and the crossing over the River Exe, a familiar tightness spread across Charlie's chest. Jane would sometimes pause to look at the river in the exact spot Connie had. He knew Jane wanted him to join her, but he always hung back. She was starting to suspect he was scared of water.

'Did you have a good chat with Mum?' Charlie asked in a bid to divert his attention.

'It was pleasant. Shame you weren't there though. I'd have preferred to be with you.'

His brow furrowed; it hadn't occurred to him Jane wanted him to stay. 'Sorry, I thought you were going to chat about clothes.'

'We do sometimes, but it's nicer if you're there too,' she said, linking her arm through his.

'I'll remember next time.'

She rested her head briefly against his shoulder. 'How's Viv?'

'Yeah, good. You know Viv.'

'Not really. She doesn't like me.'

'What makes you think that?'

'I tried to be friendly, but she wanted to see you.'

Charlie shrugged. 'Viv's helped me through a lot.'

'I know, but you've got me now. You can talk to me.'

Except he couldn't.

Charlie found he was holding his breath, a reflex that happened almost without him noticing between the bridge and Wellbrook Street where it intersected with Church Street. He hadn't been down that road for years.

They stopped outside the funeral directors. The window dressing had been changed to a pale wooden coffin with a bouquet of red and white carnations on top in the shape of a heart. He wondered if it was Jane's care and attention which had gone into the display.

She turned to face him. 'Are you coming in to say hello to my folks?'

He checked his watch. 'Not today, I've got to get to work.' He noticed tears pooling in her eyes. 'Hey, what's wrong?'

'You do love me, don't you, Charlie?'

'Course.' He forced the word from his lips.

Jane's smile seemed overbright. She stood on tiptoe and kissed him. He pulled her close, suddenly needy for her love. 'I'll call you tomorrow.'

She nodded. Charlie walked away, knowing her eyes were following him as he rounded the corner.

Tommy was waiting for him at the back of the Tivoli when he let himself in. He'd started to look mangy, skeletal under his matted hair. Charlie stooped to stroke his ear, hearing Tommy's low purr.

In the projection room he poured Tommy a saucer of milk. The cat sniffed at it, then sloped to the chair and curled himself at its centre. It was beginning to look tatty, a bit like Tommy himself. The arms were a little scuffed and torn.

Charlie turned his attention to the projectors, hoping to restore his equilibrium.

'Am I being unfair, Tom?' He carried the first reel of *All That Heaven Allows*, a melodrama with Rock Hudson and Jane Wyman, over to the winding bench. The previous year the Tivoli upgraded its projectors to run VistaVision and a Cinemascope screen, which meant the films now showed in widescreen. Connie would have loved it. He glanced at Tommy, who regarded him with his amber eyes as if he were saying: *You think about her too much.* Charlie sighed. Connie shared his passion for film, Jane didn't. It shouldn't matter, they had other things to talk about, but somehow it did.

He'd brought Jane to the Tivoli once, eager to share his world. She'd made polite noises but never mentioned wanting to return. When he'd asked her what her favourite film was, she'd said she didn't much care for films. There was nothing wrong with not liking films — except, why date a projectionist? *Why date a funeral director's daughter?* He supposed everyone was interested in death, given they'd all go through it someday; film on the other hand was purely optional. Still, he couldn't fathom why an attractive girl like Jane would want to hitch her cart to a man so clearly broken. Or maybe that was the attraction. Grief was her parents' business, she'd been dealing with it her whole life.

Loading the spool onto the projector, he selected the next can. Charlie was starting to find himself irritating. What had he achieved in the last five years? He was still living at home, trapped more than ever by a sense of duty to his mum; he was still working at the Tivoli, despite his big plans to have his own cinema. Five years ago to the day, he believed his dreams were within reach, there for the taking. Connie, his cinema, the house where nothing bad could ever happen. In a blink, it all turned to dust. He shook his head. He dwelled on the past too much. Jane was a lovely girl, nice to be around, kind, pretty. *What are you waiting for?* Tommy might have asked if he hadn't dropped off to sleep.

CHAPTER 40

Staring down Mrs Blythe's door the following morning, Grace couldn't believe she was back here again asking more favours, but she'd realised there was no alternative. If Mrs Blythe refused to help, at least to start with, Grace had no hope of keeping the job.

The old woman opened the door, regarding Grace as if she'd been expecting her. 'What now?'

Grace swallowed what little reserves of pride she retained and launched into her rehearsed speech, hitting all the top notes about making a better life for her son, how much she could pay once she'd got her first paycheque.

Mrs Blythe folded her arms, letting Grace's words hang between them for longer than was strictly necessary. Eventually, she gave Grace a curt nod. 'I can have him this week, but you'll have to sort something out after that. I can't be up till all hours waiting for you to come home.'

She considered hugging Mrs Blythe but settled for a heartfelt thank you and raced up the stairs before the old woman could change her mind.

* * *

As Grace walked into the Odeon that afternoon, elated to be back in her usherette uniform, the first person she met was Mrs Arnold.

'You might have had the courtesy to tell me you weren't coming in today.' Mrs Arnold looked her up and down. 'I can see why now.' She took her mop and limped away.

'Sorry!' Grace called after her. In her rush to sort out childcare for Eddie, letting her old boss know she'd got a new job had slipped her mind. Filing the guilt away for now, she scanned the foyer for Bea.

She swept in moments later, her face pinched in a frown. As her eyes lifted to Grace, the frown gave way to a smile. Sanders appeared in her wake. Grace stood to attention while his dark gaze ran over her uniform, before moving briskly on, offering them both a curt nod. There was something familiar about the moment, as if she'd stood to attention for another pair of eyes in another time and place.

'Don't mind him.' Bea's eyes remained focused on his retreating back before she dragged her gaze to Grace. 'Ready to venture forth into the fray?'

Grace grinned. She wasn't just ready, she couldn't wait.

* * *

By the time she knocked on Mrs Blythe's door to collect Eddie that evening, Grace was buzzing, although her feet ached and her back too. The trays were heavy and standing for a two-hour matinee hard on her soles, but it was all worth it for the magic of watching happy faces mesmerised by the screen, collectively escaping whatever worries they carried in their daily lives.

When Mrs Blythe opened the door to her smoky domain, the sight of Eddie, snot-filled and tearful, sent her mood into freefall. How could she have been so selfish? Carrying Eddie upstairs, his head rested against her shoulder, Grace felt her heart might tear in two.

The week continued in much the same pattern. By day she was swept up in a whirlwind of escapism and chocolate bars, by evening she drowned in guilt as Eddie coughed his way through each night. By the end of the week, his cough had improved, but Grace was no closer to sorting out a better arrangement for his care.

'What's eating you?' Bea asked, sidling up to Grace as she was mulling this over while pinning up her hair in the cloakroom.

She studied Bea in the mirror. She'd been so kind; Grace couldn't fathom why.

'I'm worried about finding someone who can have Eddie while I'm here.'

Bea pulled a cigarette from her bag and offered her one; Grace shook her head. Mrs Blythe's chain-smoking put her off forming a habit.

'I thought your landlady was happy to have him?'

'I wouldn't say happy, and it's only for this week. She won't have him longer-term.'

Bea lit up. 'Leave it with me. You're not the first girl to have this problem. I'm sure we can figure something out.'

Grace hoped so. She couldn't face returning to cleaning after experiencing the heady delights of being an usherette. She gazed down at her uniform, never tiring of the way the fabric swished against her skin.

Bea followed her gaze. 'You do look splendid. Sanders has noticed, you know.'

Grace felt herself blush.

'There's no need to look coy. He's come to rely on me to help him find suitable girls. He commented the other day how I'd hit the jackpot with you.'

As flattered as she was, Grace felt a frisson of unease. There was something about Sanders' hard gaze that made her uncomfortable. She wondered again at what sort of relationship Bea was entangled in.

* * *

On Saturday evening, Bea caught Grace on her way out of the cinema. 'I've found you a sitter.'

'Already?' Grace was relieved, anything to get Eddie out of Mrs Blythe's toxic flat.

'Have you met Betty who runs the kiosk? Well, it's her daughter.' Bea drew closer as if she feared being overheard. 'She's in the family way and needs the extra money and the practice.'

Grace searched her mind, trying to locate Betty among the many new faces she'd met that week. She settled on a plump woman with tight blonde curls and a warm smile who couldn't be more than thirty-five. How did she have a daughter old enough to look after a child?

'How old is her daughter?'

Bea shrugged. 'Does that matter?'

'I can't leave Eddie with a minor.'

'Betty's got five kids, and this is her eldest. I think she's pretty well versed in childcare.'

Feeling only a little reassured, Grace nodded.

Bea frowned. 'Come on, Grace, at least try her out. Betty said you could bring Eddie round tomorrow afternoon to meet her brood. What have you got to lose?'

'I was going to treat Eddie to an afternoon at Northernhay Gardens. I feel like I've hardly seen him this week.'

'Popping round to Betty's doesn't need to take the whole afternoon.'

'Thanks, Bea, I am grateful. I feel so guilty leaving him, that's all.'

Bea covered Grace's hand with hers. 'God, you mothers. It's enough to put me off for life.'

* * *

The following afternoon, Grace and Eddie stood before a blue front door that would have benefitted from a lick of paint. The house was in one of the maze of streets behind the cinema. Grace couldn't deny how convenient it would be to have Eddie so close to where she worked. Betty answered the door, greeting her with the warm smile which served her so well behind the kiosk.

'Hello, Grace, and this must be Eddie.' Betty crouched to Eddie's level. He buried himself deep within Grace's skirts.

'He's a bit shy.'

'Not to worry. Come on in, I'll introduce you to Sally.'

They followed Betty past the stairs, where two pairs of eyes peeped at them through the banister, scurrying away as soon as Grace met their gaze. Betty led them into a sitting room overstuffed with a mismatch of furniture. She gestured for them to sit.

'Sally!' she hollered.

Footsteps from a room above moved at speed. Moments later, Sally appeared. In contrast to her mother, she was wiry, all limbs and no boobs. Sally greeted them with a shy smile, her bump hard to avoid under a too-tight dress.

Betty set a hand on her daughter's shoulder. 'This is our Sal.'

'Hello, Sally, this is Eddie.' Grace ruffled his hair.

'Nice to meet you, Eddie.' Sally offered her hand. Glancing at his mother for approval, Eddie shook it. Sally produced a boiled sweet from her dress pocket. 'Is he allowed?' she asked Grace.

Grace nodded. 'What do you say, Ed?'

Eddie whispered his thanks and the sweet was passed into his hand. His eyes grew round as if he'd never seen such treasure.

Grace relaxed. Sally couldn't be more than sixteen, but she seemed like a pleasant girl. It could hardly be worse than leaving him with Mrs Blythe.

* * *

'How would you like to spend a few days playing with Sally?' Grace asked when, an hour later, she and Eddie walked up the path leading to the war memorial in Northernhay Gardens.

'Will you be there?' Eddie looked up, hopeful.

'No, darling, Mummy has to work, but I'll be close by, and I'll pick you up each evening and take you home to bed.'

Eddie's brow furrowed as he considered this. 'Will there be more sweets?'

'I expect so.' She stopped walking and crouched in front of him. 'This job is going to mean we'll have more money for nice things, Ed. Won't that be good?'

He nodded.

'Good boy. Now, let's play hide-and-seek. You go first.'

Grace watched her son scamper off in the direction of the closest bush, flanked by what remained of the Roman city wall. It was moments like this she dwelled on his father, but what use was there missing someone who existed only as a fantasy in her head?

After the police, the city library provided her next thread of hope. Without a date or a location, Grace struggled to pinpoint what she was looking for. The back issues of the *Express & Echo* and the *Exeter & Plymouth Gazette* for 1951 told other people's stories and not her own. Wherever she belonged, her disappearance hadn't been newsworthy in Exeter.

Dark shadows pressed in, questions she'd carried around for the last five hard years. *What happened to Eddie's father? Was he the one who'd haunted her kisses with Joe?* She'd built an image of a good man, a wonderful man, but in truth she had no idea. Sometimes she fantasised she'd run into him by accident, their eyes meeting across a busy street — he'd recognise her, claim her. But what if he was the one who had left her for dead in a ditch?

Grace noticed Eddie peep out from behind the bush and pulled herself together. 'I'm coming!' she called. Eddie was her first priority, and for that reason the life she was making now with just the two of them was safest. All she really knew of her past was that someone had beaten her up. It was hardly a strong foundation. Somehow, she'd have to carry on being enough for them both.

CHAPTER 41

The noise persisted, a distant popping sound. Charlie forced his eyes open and was met with the gloom of his bedroom, soft morning light filtering in at the edges of his curtains. There it was again. He threw back the covers and rose from bed, drawing the curtains to one side. All appeared well as he cast his eye over the garden at the back of the house. There was a trail of smoke on the horizon, in the direction of town. Moments later, the whir of sirens. He checked his alarm clock: 5.45 a.m. Someone was having a bad start to their Wednesday morning.

Ten minutes later, Charlie stood before the bathroom mirror, assessing the state of his stubble. He was reaching for the razor when a knock on the bathroom door stalled him. 'I'm busy, Mum.'

'Josie next door says the Tivoli's on fire.'

Charlie flung open the door and was confronted by his mum's fluffy pink robe and curlers. 'What did you say?'

'A fire at the Tivoli.'

He pushed past her into his bedroom and threw on the previous day's discarded shirt and trousers. Before his mother could say another word, he'd raced down the stairs, pulled on his shoes and shot out the front door.

Charlie wasn't sure why he was running or who he expected to save. Surely no one would be in the building at this time of day? *Tommy.* That bloody cat often slept inside despite his best efforts to coax him out. Charlie felt sick; he'd left Tommy sleeping on Connie's chair the previous evening. Hadn't had the heart to wake him. *Connie's chair* — what if it had been destroyed?

Quickening his pace, Charlie was breathless and sweating when he turned into Fore Street. A crowd were gathered at the alleyway which led to the cinema, firemen ushering them back. His stomach plummeted as he drew up to see thick smoke rising from the back of the building. He spied Mr Reynolds at the front of the crowd.

Charlie pushed his way through.

'He's the projectionist,' Reynolds explained to a nearby fire officer who was about to ask him to move on.

'What's the damage?'

Reynolds sighed. 'Mainly the back end. They've got it under control but the cinemascope screen, the masking equipment, the amplification apparatus and much of the roof are destroyed. Fortunately, the foyer and projection room have escaped, but we'll be shut for months.'

A long breath escaped his lips. The projection room, Connie's chair — his memories were safe. 'When will we be allowed in?'

'Once the fire officers have dampened down the building.'

Charlie scanned the area of devastation. 'Anyone seen Tommy?'

Reynolds shrugged.

The next hour passed in a blur as they watched the officers get to work. Any attempts to help were rebuffed and Charlie's pleas for Tommy met with deaf ears.

Eventually he and Mr Reynolds were permitted down the alley to speak with the chief fire officer, who confirmed Reynolds' fears about the extent of the damage. A mewing drifted up from one of the adjacent gardens. Tommy jumped down from the wall and coiled himself around Charlie's legs. He'd never been so pleased to see the daft cat. Scooping Tommy into his arms, Charlie nuzzled his matted fur.

The cat fixed him with his steady gaze, then jumped from Charlie's arms and ambled off in the direction of Fore Street. Charlie watched him go, realising their destinies were no longer intertwined. Tommy paused at the top of the alley and turned to look at him, then carried on, in search of a new home.

Charlie felt a subtle change inside. If Tommy could start again without hesitation, why couldn't he? He glanced at the blackened Tivoli and then at Mr Reynolds. 'Is it okay if I get off, sir? I'll pop back in an hour.'

'You go, Charlie. There's nothing any of us can do until the building is secure.'

'Thanks.' He turned away from the Tivoli and walked home. There was something he needed to retrieve. Something he'd bought over a month ago but hadn't had the courage to see through.

Half an hour later, he was walking down Angel Hill past the Victorian town hall to the river.

Charlie pulled up short at the sight of Jane rounding the bend into Bridge Street. Her face broke into a relieved smile and she ran into his arms.

'I heard about the fire. Are you okay?'

Charlie took a deep breath. 'I'm fine. Better than fine.' He looked at the glistening water of the river bubbling in the sunshine then smiled at Jane and pulled the small jewellery box from his pocket.

The ghost of Connie lingered at the railings. Forcing her from his mind, he dropped to one knee and took a leap of faith into his future.

CHAPTER 42

'Good evening, Grace.'

Grace paused in loading her tray with confections to find Mr Sanders studying her. He was a handsome man for his age, although she wasn't sure how old he was. She guessed around fifty. He leaned against the counter, a plume of smoke drifting from the cigar between his fingers.

'Evening, Mr Sanders.'

When he didn't move on, she glanced at her tray, unsure whether she should carry on with her task or wait for him to speak.

'How are you enjoying working here?'

'I love it.' She blushed at her gushing tone, but it was true. The last month had transformed her life from one of grey struggle to something closer to vibrant technicolour.

His eyes crinkled with amusement. 'I'm pleased to hear it.'

Grace smiled, unsure how to respond.

'The uniform becomes you.' His gaze drifted to her legs. It seemed to take an eternity for it to travel back up to her face, where it settled with intense scrutiny.

'Thank you.' She looked longingly at the confections, hoping he'd leave her in peace.

'Well, good evening, Grace.' Before turning away, he paused and met her eyes. 'Try not to spend too much time watching the film tonight. It's come to my attention that you have a tendency to focus on the screen.' With that he walked off.

Her cheeks flamed. Bea had warned her twice not to get so engrossed in the film. *Sanders doesn't like it if we don't keep our eyes on the patrons rather than the screen.* It was hard not to when there was so much to see. Films, books, they all enriched her understanding of a past she couldn't recall.

As if she'd conjured her, Bea appeared at her side. 'What did Sanders want? Your cheeks match the colour of your dress.'

Grace blinked away tears of humiliation. She needed this job. 'He warned me about watching the films.'

Bea laughed. 'Is that all? It's his way of reinforcing his authority. Did he give you a compliment beforehand?'

'Well, yes. He said the uniform suited me.'

'I bet he did.' Bea looked in the direction Sanders had gone, then returned her attention to Grace. 'There you are then, darling. You're doing splendidly. If Sanders gives you any more trouble, come straight to me.'

Grace smiled. 'Thanks.'

Bea squeezed her arm. 'James Dean tonight. I know where my eyes will be, and it won't be on the patrons.'

* * *

The film was *Rebel Without a Cause* and focusing on anything but the screen was challenging, but Grace's determination to make a good impression outstripped her desire for James Dean. At 11 p.m. when the cinema doors were finally locked, she trudged wearily up the stairs to retrieve her coat. Helen, one of the other usherettes, came hurrying away from the staff cloakroom, tears streaming down her face.

'Helen, are you all right?'

Helen paused and wiped a tear from her cheek, smudging her eye make-up. Grace was about to offer her a handkerchief when Sanders emerged from the cloakroom. He threw them a dark look and disappeared in the direction of his office.

Grace touched Helen's arm. She flinched. 'I'm fine,' she snapped, and stalked away.

Hastening to the cloakroom, Grace grabbed her coat, curious about what she had or hadn't seen. But then she raced to the stairs, her focus reclaimed by the pressing need to collect her son.

* * *

Grace walked at speed along the pavement, the clip of her heels echoing in the chill night air. Her pulse hammered through her chest as she scanned the street for threat. Relief washed over her as she reached Betty's front door. Sally answered straight away.

'He's fallen asleep again.'

'Never mind, not much you can do about that, Sally. It's so late for him.' Grace stepped into the warmth of the house feeling a twinge of guilt. Eddie's broken sleep was becoming a problem. Walking him home in the cold night air wakened him more. By the time they climbed the stairs to their attic room he was buzzing. It could prove impossible to get him back to sleep and even harder to wake him in the morning.

She kneeled beside the sofa, where Eddie was in a deep slumber. Stroking his cheek, Grace attempted to coax him awake. Eventually he opened his eyes, taking a moment to understand where he was. 'Time to go home, sweetheart.'

Five minutes later, with Eddie's hand gripped in hers, they were back out in the dark, navigating the route home as quickly as they could, Eddie's short legs struggling to match his mother's long stride.

Having Sally care for Eddie was a godsend and liberated him from Mrs Blythe's smoke-filled flat, but the walk home left Grace vulnerable. And Sally's growing bump was a stark reminder that all of this was temporary. Nothing could be relied upon. Any life she tried to build would be transitory because like Rose, Grace wasn't real. She was playing make-believe and always would be. Her true life had yet to be found.

CHAPTER 43

Grace smoothed a curl from Eddie's sweaty brow and sat back, relieved he was finally sleeping. He woke her in the early morning complaining of a sore throat. A fever followed and now a headache. She checked the clock on the bedside table. There was nothing to be done, her afternoon shift had started twenty minutes ago. No doubt that would be the end of it. By tomorrow one of those preening girls would have her job. Staring at her uniform hanging on the front of the wardrobe, her heart sank. It had been a nice dream for a while.

In an attempt to divert her mind, Grace tried to read a novel Betty had loaned her, but her gaze drifted with persistence to the uniform. With each passing minute her disappointment became more acute. Two hours later, she was contemplating what to fix for supper when a knock on the door startled her. Blythe rarely took it upon herself to climb so many stairs.

She was shocked to find Bea glaring at her on the other side.

'Why the hell didn't you turn up this afternoon? Sanders is spitting fire.'

'You can't come in, Eddie's poorly.'

Bea swept into the room, giving Grace little option but to stand aside. 'I'll be fine.' She came to an abrupt halt.

Grace followed Bea's gaze over her humble dwellings — the corner above the sink where a mushroom grew from the black mould surrounding the pipe, the peeling wallpaper, the threadbare rug across floorboards so insubstantial beams of light came through the cracks from the room below. She turned to Grace, her features pinched into a frown.

'You can't live here.'

Eddie stirred as Grace fought down a frisson of irritation. She moved to the bed. His little fists rubbed the sleep from his eyes. 'What choice do I have?'

Bea rummaged inside her bag and retrieved a set of keys. 'Pack your belongings, you and Eddie are coming to stay with me.'

'That's very kind, but—'

'I have a spare room. It's modest but clean and dry. I had no idea you were living like this. Take the keys.' She shook them for emphasis.

Obediently, Grace opened her hand.

'Do you have paper and a pen? I'll write down the address.'

Grace found an old envelope in her chest of drawers and a coloured pencil discarded by Eddie and passed them to Bea, who scrawled out the address.

'Go there this evening. I'll square things with Sanders.'

'I can't thank you enough.'

Bea offered up one of her tight smiles. 'I'll be back late. Wait up and we'll talk.'

* * *

As Grace carried Eddie down the stairs, their few belongings dragging her down, Mrs Blythe stepped from her flat.

'So, it's true, you're leaving?'

'Just visiting a friend.'

215

'That's not how your friend explained the situation when she said you were moving out of, and I quote, "my grim little establishment".'

Grace coloured. 'Oh, I'm sure she didn't mean—'

'I know exactly what she meant.' Mrs Blythe folded her arms. 'Let me know either way by the end of the week.' She glanced at Eddie's snotty face. 'And for pity's sake, keep that child away from other people.' She turned back inside and slammed the door.

Outside, Grace checked the address Bea had written out for her. It was in Heavitree. With Eddie sick, she could hardly take him on the bus. Grace shifted him into a more comfortable position and prepared for a long walk.

Half an hour later, her back on the verge of giving up under the weight of Eddie and their belongings, they stopped outside a large Georgian house on a leafy street. A far cry from the scruffy terraces Mrs Blythe occupied. Grace marvelled at how Bea could afford such an address on her usherette's income. She took Eddie's hand as she set him down, and they made their way up the paved path to an imposing front door with black-and-white checked tiles under the porch. She fished out Bea's set of keys and inserted the mortice into the lock.

Inside was a tiled entrance hall and set of double doors. Grace ventured through. Bea's flat was number six, which suggested more stairs. Summoning the last of her strength, she dragged their belongings up two flights, Eddie in her wake. Number six was on the second floor. Grace unlocked the door and walked in.

The flat smelled clean with a hint of Bea's perfume. A small entrance hall gave way to a sitting room with a grate at one end and two sash windows overlooking the street. Eddie recovered something of his adventurous spirit as they explored the rest of the flat. A bedroom overlooking a bricked-in courtyard at the back was obviously Bea's. Strewn with clothes and the bed unmade, it had a lived-in yet glamorous feel, much like Bea herself. The second bedroom was smaller but luxurious to Grace's eyes. A double bed, a chest of drawers, a small fireplace and basin in the corner. The sash window overlooked the garden too.

'What do you think, Eddie?' Grace crouched before her son.

Despite his poorly state, his eyes shone. She touched her palm to his forehead; it was cooler. At least the fever had passed.

'Let's get you something to eat and tucked up in bed.'

Setting their bags on the floor, Grace changed Eddie into clean pyjamas. She left him in the sitting room with a favourite teddy and strict instructions not to touch anything and returned to the hall, off which was a narrow kitchen with a belling oven, sink and worktop. Grace searched the cupboards, finding an almost-finished bottle of gin and a crust of bread. Bea clearly didn't attend to her domestic needs. Taking the crust, she slathered it with butter from a dish on the counter. It would have to do until she could get supplies. In the sitting room, she handed Eddie the meagre offering, her stomach rumbling too. Watching him satisfy his hunger was almost as good as satisfying her own.

An hour later, Eddie fell asleep on the sofa. Grace searched out fresh linens and made up the bed, before tucking him between the clean sheets. She longed to join him herself but remembered Bea's words about wanting to talk, so she returned to the sitting room with her novel in the hope she wouldn't be kept up too late.

The next thing she knew, Bea was standing over her.

'Oh dear, look at you.' Bea shrugged off her coat as Grace sat up, rubbing the sleep from her eyes and retrieving her book from the floor.

'What time is it?'

'Midnight.' Bea grimaced. 'Sorry, I didn't mean to stay out this late.' She lit a cigarette and stood at the window overlooking the street as if she were checking for someone.

'I squared things with Sanders by the way, but you'll have to make sure you don't miss another shift. How's the patient?'

'A little better, the fever has passed. I'm hoping it's just a bad cold. Was Mr Sanders very angry?'

Bea took the seat opposite wearing a mercurial smile. 'Yes, but not about you. I'm sure you realise by now, I'm his mistress.'

Grace attempted to keep her facial features in check.

'Despite his sometimes hard exterior, he's good to me and there are certain advantages.' She gestured to the room. 'Are you scandalised?'

Grace studied her hands. 'It's none of my business.'

'You are, I can tell. Let's have a drink.' Bea leaped to her feet, making for the kitchen. Grace's empty stomach cowered at the thought.

Bea returned with the gin and two tumblers, sloshing a generous measure into each and passing one to Grace.

'To friends.' She raised her glass and knocked back the clear liquid. Grace could only manage a sip, feeling her stomach burn.

'I need to keep a clear head for Eddie,' she explained when Bea shot her a questioning look.

'You're a good mother, better than the one I had.' Bea went to pour herself another drink, but the bottle was empty.

'I try. It doesn't feel like it sometimes.'

'You're human, but you love him unreservedly. He'll remember that when he's grown.'

Grace set down her glass, forcing out the question which had played on her mind ever since Bea rescued her from Mrs Blythe's miserable lodgings. 'Why are you so kind to me? You got me a job, you've welcomed us into your home . . .'

Bea smiled. 'You want to know what I want in return?'

'I suppose so.' Recent experience hadn't made her accustomed to acts of unconditional kindness.

'I like you.'

'That's it?'

'Isn't it enough?'

Grace shrugged. 'I'm not used to it, that's all.'

'Are you going to finish your gin?' Bea gestured to Grace's glass.

'You have it.'

'Marvellous.' She joined Grace on the sofa and sipped the drink, studying her with a curious expression. 'Where did you get that scar?' Bea lifted her hand to touch the faint line across Grace's right eyelid and cheek.

Grace flinched, not because it hurt but because the scar reminded her of her lost life. She was careful to cover it up but clearly her make-up had worn off.

'Sorry, I don't mean to pry.'

'It's fine. In truth, I don't know how I got the scar. I lost my memory.' She glanced at her friend. Bea was regarding her, eyes wide with questions. She sighed. 'It's a long story.'

Bea drew her legs up beneath her. 'Good, I love a long story.'

Grace set about relaying what she knew of her life thus far. When she'd finished, Bea sat for a while in silence staring into her empty glass.

'Gosh, Grace, I can't imagine how hard that must feel. There are things in my life I'd gladly forget, but to have such important bits missing . . . I don't know what to say.'

'What can you say? Nothing will change it.'

Bea lifted her hand again, tracing the scar with her finger. 'I can't imagine anyone wanting to hurt this face.'

Grace felt colour bleed into her cheeks. Bea was looking at her with such intense yet tender affection. She searched for a way to deflect her attention. 'Did you make it up with Sanders?'

Bea let her hand drop to her side. 'We always make it up.'

'Won't I be in the way? Surely he keeps this place so you can be alone?'

'We'll work out a rota.'

'Honestly, I hate to think of walking in or putting you in an awkward situation. Sanders might . . .'

Grace's sentence was swallowed by Bea's lips pressing against hers. It was the most bizarre sensation, everything was somehow too soft. After a beat, Bea pulled away.

'Well, that was . . . interesting.' Bea stood, making for the door. 'Time to break into my emergency supply of gin.'

Grace appreciated the moment alone to gather her thoughts. Before she could assess them, Bea returned, pouring herself another drink and knocking it back. She regarded Grace from the safety of the opposite chair. A giggle erupted from her lips.

'How gauche of me to make a pass at you on your first evening here. Don't look so alarmed, I'm not going to eat you. When you shared your story, it got to me, I suppose. I take it you're not a girl with a grey area?'

Grace struggled to meet Bea's eye. 'I'm afraid not.'

'Shame, I rather enjoy a grey area.'

'Bea, if this is going to be awkward . . .'

'It only needs to be awkward if we make it so. I've had too much to drink after an emotional evening and felt terribly moved by your story. I thought I might indulge in a little fantasy. You don't share that fantasy, so that's the end of it. All's fair in love and war. Let's go to bed.' She threw back the rest of her drink. 'Separately, of course.' Bea giggled again and this time, Grace did too.

CHAPTER 44

Charlie hovered at the open back door, a bottle of warm beer in his hand. His mother, Jane's mother, Jane and her cousin Edith were laying out food on the trestle table he'd set up that morning ready for their engagement party. His gaze roamed over his parents' garden decorated with bunting sewn by his mother. *Charlie and Jane.* Balloons bobbed in the warm breeze.

He flinched as a heavy hand landed on his shoulder. 'You all right, Charlie?'

Charlie glanced at his soon-to-be father-in-law. Clive had a habit of creeping up on him. His job as a funeral director made him adept at hiding in the shadows. A quiet presence, there but not seen. 'I'm fine, thanks, Clive.'

He gave Charlie's shoulder a squeeze and ambled outside to join the women.

Charlie's mother seemed very much at home among their new family. It was a relief to see her happy again. Whenever he entertained doubts, he'd remind himself how happy his mum was.

I wish I didn't have doubts.

Jane turned in his direction and gave him a small wave. Charlie waved back and forced a smile across his lips. *Jane, his fiancée. Charlie and Jane. The happy couple.*

Dragging his gaze from the scene, Charlie ventured through to the front of the house. Guests would be arriving soon; he needed to get himself in a better frame of mind. He opened the front door and stood for a while leaning against the porch, sipping his beer.

She was standing in the street before him, anxiety etched into her face, looking one way and then the other, her green-and-white dress hugging her slender figure in the breeze. She turned in his direction and the anxiety left her features. Her eyes lit up as he approached. Charlie blinked the image away.

'Charlie, love.' His mum appeared at his side, rosy-faced as if she'd been at the sherry. 'What are you doing out here?'

'Nothing, Mum.'

His mother studied him. 'Jane's a lovely girl. I know her light might not shine as bright for you as . . .' Her sentence died.

Charlie offered up a reassuring smile. 'I'm fine.'

His mum kissed his cheek and went inside. Funny how, since he'd got engaged to Jane, no one could say Connie's name. Not even him. As if uttering it out loud would cause the thin thread holding this new life together to snap.

He was about to turn back inside when Viv arrived with Michael and their brood.

'We're early, I know, but I had to fit it around James's feeds.' She bustled through the gate, already back to her pre-baby size despite having given birth only three weeks before.

Charlie smiled at the slumbering James in Viv's arms. 'He's perfect.'

She grinned. 'I know.'

Michael offered his hand. Charlie shook it, trying not to think about how, if Connie were here, they would have been brothers-in-law.

Johnny tugged at his sleeve. 'Is there cake?'

'Yes, mate, there's cake in the back garden.' Johnny raced off with Abigail in tow.

'You'd better stop them demolishing the table,' Viv addressed her husband. Michael nodded and followed his kids into the house.

She regarded Charlie. 'So, how are you?'

Charlie hoped his smile masked his inner turmoil. 'I'm okay.'

Viv gestured to a bench hiding under a laburnum tree in the corner of the small front garden. Charlie wasn't sure if anyone ever used it. Viv was quiet for a moment as they took a seat. He was grateful for the silence.

'You don't have to go through with it, you know.' She uttered the words so softly he wasn't sure if it was to prevent them being overheard or because James had fallen asleep.

Charlie didn't say anything but shifted in his seat.

'I'm not suggesting you don't go through with it. But if you don't want to get married, then don't. The sky won't fall in, that's already happened.' She lifted her gaze to his. The unspoken inference made his stomach tighten.

'And if you could decide before I go to Exeter for a new dress, that would be helpful, although not essential.' Viv winked.

He smiled, relieved someone had said it. 'Thanks, Viv.'

* * *

An hour later, the party was in full swing. Charlie stood beside Jane, talking to one of her numerous friends. The conversations were always the same: *Where will you live? How many children do you want?* There were nudges, winks, warm smiles. He swigged his second beer, trying to stay in the moment, to control his mind from wandering into dangerous territory. *What would Connie have said? Done? Seen? Would she have wanted a party like this?* Occasionally he'd catch himself smiling, making up conversations in his head. Other times he wanted to scream for it to stop. *Five years.* Five goddam years.

A clink of glasses dragged him from his reverie. Clive was about to make a speech. Jane's small hand slid into his. Why did he have to differentiate? Jane's hand was small, Connie's hand . . . *Why can't I stop?*

Charlie forced his mind to focus on the speech. Clive must have made a joke at his expense because a titter of laughter spread through the gathering, all eyes were on him.

'Come on then, Charlie, what have you got to say for yourself?' Clive's voice contained a hint of uncertainty.

Charlie offered up a nervous laugh. He cast around the sea of faces, the expectant eyes. Jane came in to focus at his side. 'Charlie?' she whispered.

He dropped her hand, suddenly too clammy in his. The air thickened, he struggled for breath. Grabbing at his tie, he attempted to loosen it. 'I can't breathe,' he whispered, before dropping to the ground.

CHAPTER 45

'Is this normal?' Bea frowned as Eddie picked up his bowl and licked the remnants of his porridge.

Grace laughed. 'Quite normal.' She and Eddie were now a permanent fixture at Bea's flat, having finally told Mrs Blythe two weeks ago she no longer required her 'grimy room'. Bea hadn't made another pass at her, and Grace believed her when she'd put it down to drunken folly. Apart from seeing one another at the Odeon, Bea was often out. It was only on the rare occasion they both had a Saturday off that she'd rise like a phoenix and join them at breakfast with a cup of strong coffee.

Sanders' visits were generally scheduled in advance. Grace became fastidious about keeping their belongings to the bedroom and the door closed. She always made sure she and Eddie were out if she wasn't working, conscious everything rested on Bea's relationship with him. She had no idea if Sanders even knew she was staying there, and Bea was never forthcoming, which suited Grace. It wasn't her business.

'What are you doing today, Bea?' Grace took a cloth and wiped her son's hands.

Bea sipped her coffee. 'I might need the flat this afternoon.'

Grace nodded, her gaze directed at the window flecked with droplets.

'Sorry, I know it's beastly out.'

'It's fine, I need a new book. We can go to the library or find a café.'

* * *

That afternoon she and Eddie set out for town huddled together under an umbrella borrowed from Bea.

Despite ten years passing, post-war building work was still going on all over the city. Grace marvelled at the way the high street was taking shape. It engendered an air of renewal and hope.

The drizzle intensified as opaque clouds swept across the granite sky. Sensing the coming storm, Grace steered Eddie into Tinley's teashop on the edge of Cathedral Green. The earthy musk of petrichor gave way to the caramel aroma of baking. Settling at a table near the window, they shrugged off their damp coats. Grace picked up the menu and for the first time realised she could afford to buy whatever they wanted — within reason.

'What do you think, Ed, shall we treat ourselves?'

Eddie's smile matched hers, and his head bobbed up and down in an enthusiastic nod. The waitress appeared as they grinned like loons.

'What can I get you?'

'We'll have a cream tea for two, please.' Grace tried to contain her excitement.

While they waited, her eyes drifted to the window over-looking the cathedral. The rain was coming down now in swathes, lashing against the small panes of glass. A queue formed as tourists jostled for a table. She cast around the café, noticing a man a few years older than her seated at a single table on the other side of the room, watching them. Grace averted her gaze. When she inevitably looked back, he threw her a smile. Flushed, she returned her attention to Eddie, catching him contemplating emptying the contents of the salt pot all over the floor. She snatched it out of her son's hand. 'Stop it, Ed.'

Their cream teas arrived, a welcome distraction. Eddie's eyes grew as large as saucers. Grace cut a scone in two, spreading it liberally with cream and jam. She watched, elated as her son tucked in. Pouring the tea, she let her gaze lift to the man across the café. He was talking to the waitress. She looked away, focusing on cutting her scone. He was attractive, at least from a distance, with sandy hair and a wide smile. There was something open about his face. Grace seldom thought about dating anyone. The girls at the Odeon all had beaus in some form or another, then there was Bea and her clandestine activities with Sanders. Until that moment, Grace hadn't entertained the idea perhaps she was lonely. Her focus had been Eddie and their survival since the day he was born.

Absorbed by her musing, Grace didn't notice a presence at their table until Eddie tapped her arm. She dragged her gaze from his jam-smeared face to find the man smiling down at them.

'Do you mind if I join you for a moment? They needed my table but it's still rather wet outside.' He gestured to the rain-spotted windows.

Grace shrugged. 'Of course.'

'William.' He offered his hand.

'Grace.' She returned his handshake. He had big, soft hands, suggesting he didn't work in a trade.

'It's a pleasure to meet you, Grace. And this is . . . ?'

'I'm Eddie,' her son said with a confident grin.

'How do you like that scone, Eddie?'

'It's the best thing I've ever tasted.' Eddie's face was earnest as he licked his jammy fingers.

Grace offered up a nervous smile, finding she could no longer eat such messy food in front of this stranger. It was a pity because she'd been enjoying it. She took a sip of tea.

'Would you like some?' She proffered the pot.

'I don't want to deprive you.' William pulled out a chair and sat down.

'You aren't. There's far too much for one and Eddie thinks tea tastes like pond water.'

William laughed. It was a gentle chuckle. 'In that case, yes please.'

Relieved to have a purpose, Grace poured a second cup.

'Are you local?' William asked. Now he was up close, she could see his eyes were pale blue.

'Not far,' she said, purposefully vague.

'Sorry, that was too familiar. I was curious as to whether you were on holiday.'

Grace smiled. 'No, we're local.'

'Me too. Just moved here from Southampton.'

'How do you like it?'

'It's lovely. Southampton was so devasted in the Blitz there's not much of the old city left.'

Grace gestured outside. 'Exeter took its fair share too. The building work feels like it may never end.'

'I hope it doesn't. That's why I'm here. I'm an architect.'

'Won't Southampton miss you?'

William smiled but it seemed wistful. 'I don't think so.'

'Mummy, can I have yours?' Eddie cut in, eyeing her half-eaten scone. She pushed the plate towards him, grateful to have it finished but certain Eddie would be complaining of a tummy ache later.

'Does your husband work locally?'

Grace felt her face grow hot. 'There is no husband.' She looked at Eddie hoping he wouldn't announce he'd never met his father, but the scone commanded all his focus.

William had the good manners not to press her further. He sipped his tea and glanced at the window. Grace followed his gaze. The rain finally moved on, leaving a smattering of blue in its wake.

'Looks like it's brightening up,' she observed for something to say.

'I'll leave you in peace.' William stood, fishing for something in his coat pocket.

'I didn't mean to imply you should leave.'

He placed a business card on the table. 'I'd very much like to do this again. My number is on the card, home and work.'

Grace picked up the card and studied the embossed lettering. *William Banner, Architect.*

'Thanks for the tea.' He ruffled Eddie's hair and was gone.

Grace stared after him, feeling inexplicably bereft. She dragged her gaze to Eddie, whose checks were flushed and puffy. 'I don't think I can eat any more, Mummy.' He set the scone down with a groan.

Grace kissed his cheek. Catching the waitress's attention, she asked for the bill.

'It's been paid, the gentleman settled your bill.'

'Thank you.' Grace suppressed a slight wave of irritation. It was a lovely gesture, but this was the first time she'd been able to afford to take Eddie to tea and she'd wanted to pay for it herself. 'Please could we take the scone to go?'

'Of course, Miss.'

They left, the scone wrapped in a paper bag and Eddie clutching his stomach. She felt for William's card in her pocket. Maybe she would call him. Perhaps it was about time she considered her future.

CHAPTER 46

Grace knocked on Sally's front door, sweat blooming at her armpits. In contrast to the previous day, the sun beat down from an azure sky. Eddie's hand slipped from hers. He tugged off his cap to reveal black curls sticking to his forehead.

'I know, Ed, it's sweltering.' Grace searched for a handkerchief to mop his brow.

Knocking again, she wiped his face. Still no answer.

A neighbour emerged from the house next door. 'You'll not find them in. The girl went into labour, ankles like balloons. I told Betty last week she had pre-eclampsia. They're at the hospital.'

'Oh no, I hope she'll be okay.' But the woman had already walked away up the street. She cast around with no idea what to do. Her shift was due to start in ten minutes.

With no alternative, Grace led Eddie towards the Odeon, rehearsing what she might say to explain the presence of her son and wondering how she would manage to keep him entertained for the next few hours. As long as Sanders wasn't around, she might get away with it.

When they walked into the foyer — five minutes late, thanks to Eddie's slow pace — hope evaporated. She was confronted with Mr Sanders storming in her direction. His hard gaze took in the sight of Eddie.

'What's the meaning of this?'

Grace swallowed. 'I'm sorry, my sitter had to go to—'

'I'm not interested in your domestic arrangements. You can't bring a child into my cinema.'

'I know, I thought . . .' Grace had no idea what she thought.

Bea approached from the kiosk. 'Grace, why is Eddie here?'

'Sally's gone into early labour.'

'Oh Lord.'

'Enough.' Sanders raised his hand. 'I'm down a second projectionist, I can't have an usherette with a brat in tow.'

'I can do it.' Grace uttered the words without thinking.

'Do what?'

'I can run the film.'

Sanders' critical frown grew deeper as Bea's mouth fell open.

Grace surprised herself. She couldn't explain it, but she knew she could do it. 'I've done it before.'

'You have?' Bea looked flummoxed. 'When?'

Grace frowned. 'I don't know . . .' She started to lose her nerve under Sanders' oppressive gaze.

'Are you serious?' His tone matched his stare.

'I am.'

He turned on his heel. 'Let's try you out.'

Grace gripped Eddie's hand, aware several of her colleagues were following her progress as Mr Sanders marched her to the projection room. Inside, Fred, the main projectionist, was inserting the carbon into one of the arc lamps. His eyes betrayed his surprise when they gathered before him.

'Fred, Grace here claims she can run film.' Sanders' tone suggested he expected her to be proved wrong.

'Right.' Fred scratched his head and frowned. 'I've set the arc lamps on both machines. We need to prepare the first reel. Here, I'll show you . . .'

Sanders placed his hand on Fred's shoulder. 'If Grace says she knows what she's doing, there's no need to show her, Fred.' He folded his arms.

Grace understood he intended to stay and watch her lace the projector. Feeling a cold sweat break out across her spine, she eyed the machinery, surprised to find it familiar.

She set Eddie on a wooden chair in the corner and shot him the kind of look that said, *Don't you dare say a word.* Her son appeared as fascinated as everyone else.

Selecting the first reel, Grace checked there was enough leader and loaded the spool onto the top of the projector, taking her time, all the while aware of Sanders' eyes on her every move from across the room.

As Grace laced the film through the sprocket drivers, she sensed another pair of hands guiding her. As if by instinct, she followed. Feeling the lightest breath on her neck, she turned. And there, for a split second, it was him. Dark curls, dimpled smile. Grace blinked and he was gone.

Unsettled, she returned to the task in hand, cleaning the lamp so it was free of dust then checking the focus. She ran the first few feet of film down to the countdown leader. Grace stopped the machine and directed her gaze at Sanders.

He stepped out of the shadows to inspect her work, casting over the projector, then stood back. 'Fred, what do you think?'

Fred failed to meet her eye as he joined Sanders at the projector. After a few moments he scratched his head again. 'Looks fine to me, boss.'

Sanders didn't look pleased. If anything, he seemed irritated. He fixed Grace with one of his intimidating stares. 'I'd rather have those legs out front but your skills in the projection room may just have saved your job. You can work here with Fred for the rest of the day.'

'Thank you, Mr Sanders.'

He nodded and walked to the door, pausing at the exit. 'Grace.'

'Sir?'

'Don't ever bring your brat here again.' He threw Eddie a baleful look and was gone.

Grace glanced at her son, who returned her look of consternation.

'Mummy, I'm not a brat.'

She cupped his face in her hands and whispered. 'No, Ed, you're not a brat. He is.'

CHAPTER 47

Grace watched for Bea's signal while she and Eddie remained out of sight at the side of the cinema as they'd done every working day for the past two weeks. After a couple of minutes, Bea poked her head out and beckoned them in. She gripped her son's hand as they ducked through the doors and straight up the stairs, her heart hammering against her chest. Reaching the projection room, she propelled Eddie inside and shut the door, leaning against it to capture her breath.

'All right, Grace?' Fred checked over his shoulder from his place at the winding bench. Eddie let go of her hand and raced across the room to see what Fred was working on. 'Hello, Eddie. How's my favourite assistant today?'

Eddie flashed him a toothy grin.

Grace hung her bag on the peg by the door. 'What shall I start on?'

'Can you clean down the lamps?'

'Sure.' She moved to the projectors while Eddie took his place on the wooden chair to watch Fred wind the film.

'How's Sally doing?' Fred enquired, his gnarled hands pausing to mend a broken splice.

'She had a baby girl but they're likely to be in the hospital for a while yet.' Grace wondered how much longer they'd manage to continue this ruse. Sanders had reluctantly agreed she could keep working in the projection room but his position on Eddie remained unchanged. That Fred agreed to help hide Eddie was an absolute godsend, but she feared it was only a matter of time before their luck ran out and Sanders discovered them. She glanced at Fred, who reached the end of his reel and was easing his stooped frame off the stool.

Removing the arc mirror, Grace checked the lamp house was free of dust before giving the mirror a polish and fixing it back in place. Next, she checked the projector gate and used the special lint wipes to clean the lens. She lifted her gaze to Eddie, who was watching her hands as if transfixed.

'Do you fancy being a projectionist when you grow up, Ed?'

He gave her his sweet, dimpled smile. She thought again about the return of the flashbacks; the man who had haunted her kisses with Joe now haunted the projection room. She'd begun to wonder if he was actually dead, and it was a ghost she was seeing and not a fragment of memory. He seemed to appear when her mind was engaged in a task, as if he really were guiding her along. She knew it was fanciful, but she liked it. She liked him.

It made her think about other things too. How did she understand how to work a projector? It wasn't the sort of thing one happened to know — it was an acquired skill. Had she worked in a cinema? If so, which one? There were several in Exeter, not to mention further afield.

'I'm popping out for a smoke,' Fred said, derailing her train of thought.

Grace nodded. She fingered the small piece of card that had been in her cardigan pocket for the past fortnight. She hadn't yet called William Banner. He'd probably forgotten all about her and maybe that was for the best, but ever since their meeting, he'd lingered in her thoughts — or at least, the idea of him and what he represented.

A tap on the door yanked her from her musing. Grace glanced at Eddie, who was already on his feet moving to his hiding place behind the racking where they stored the film. Grace opened the door to find Bea on the other side.

'Sanders is on his way round with a couple of cinema managers. One from the Savoy and the other the Gaumont in Plymouth.'

Grace's stomach flipped. 'What am I going to do about Eddie?'

'Where is he?'

'You can come out, Ed.'

Eddie appeared from behind the racking. Bea offered her hand. 'Come with me, I've got the perfect hiding place.'

Grace set about lacing the previews ready for the afternoon screening, hoping Fred would hurry up and return. The thought of having to perform her duties in front of Sanders and his colleagues made her stomach tighten.

She was double-checking the focus when Sanders walked in with the two men in tow. He didn't look pleased it was Grace and not Fred on duty.

Ignoring her presence, he talked to the men about the projection equipment. One of them, a roundish man with a rosy face, met her eye and offered a warm smile. Grace smiled back, doing her best to melt into the shadows.

'Are you going to introduce us?' he enquired when Sanders reached the end of his monologue.

Sanders slid his gaze to Grace then back again. 'Of course. This is Grace, one of our usherettes who we're trying out as a projectionist.'

'Pleasure to meet you, Grace. I'm Alec Jenkins. We have a couple of lady projectionists in our Plymouth cinema. No reason why women shouldn't be able to do this kind of work, eh, Sanders?'

'Indeed.' He checked his watch. 'It's about time you ran those previews, Grace.'

She nodded and smiled as the gentlemen made their way out.

Moments later, Bea returned with Eddie. 'I can't stop, I should be out there. Betty said she'd cover for me.'

'Thanks, Bea, I owe you one.'

'By the way, I'm afraid Eddie's been seen. Helen was watching from the restaurant balcony when I ushered you through.'

'She won't tell, will she?'

Bea looked uncomfortable. 'She might. We've never seen eye to eye. Helen was involved with Sanders when I first arrived. I rather replaced her in his affections, and she's still, shall we say, feeling scorned.'

'That's why she was upset.'

'Sorry?'

Grace shook her head. 'Nothing.'

'Anyway, it might be worth you speaking to her since I won't do any good.'

'Thanks, Bea.' Grace couldn't help feeling disquieted by this news.

Fred returned as she dimmed the lights in the auditorium.

'What did I miss?' he enquired with his lopsided smile.

* * *

Once the main feature was running, Grace joined Fred, who was teaching Eddie how to splice film with a piece of discarded leader. Her attention returned to the mystery of where she'd learned her projectionist skills.

'Fred, are there any other lady projectionists in the area?'

Fred scratched his head, which he did in response to most questions. He reminded her of Stan Laurel. 'Not that I know of. You're a bit of an enigma.'

'Do you think you could find out? I'd like to know if any previous lady projectionists suddenly left in the last five years.'

He looked puzzled. 'I can ask around. Any reason in particular?'

Grace shrugged. 'Curiosity.' It was a vague answer but the best she had.

Fred nodded. 'How did you learn, out of interest?'

'Oh, just here and there.' She could hardly admit she didn't know.

The puzzled expression returned to his face, but he didn't press her further.

'Right.' Fred focused his attention on Eddie. 'Better get this splice finished.'

* * *

As the last spool ran off the projector, Grace packed away, hastily wanting to catch Helen before she got to Sanders. She glanced at Eddie slumped in the chair, eyelids decidedly heavy.

'Fred, could you keep an eye on Eddie for a few minutes?'

'No problem, take your time.'

Grace ran down the stairs, catching Helen as she stepped into the foyer.

Before Grace uttered a word, Helen held up her hand. 'I know what this is about. You shouldn't be bringing your child here.'

'I realise that, but I have no choice, my sitter just had a baby of her own and I haven't managed to find anyone else.'

Helen folded her arms. 'Where's his dad?'

Grace studied her shoes. 'He died,' she whispered. She hated the lie, but it was one she'd told so many times it tripped off her tongue.

A brief moment of sympathy flickered across Helen's face. 'Well, I suppose you can't help that.'

Grace waited, hoping she was winning her round.

Helen sighed. 'I won't tell for now, but you need to sort this out. Your friend Bea might think she has Mr Sanders wrapped around her little finger, but he won't appreciate being deceived.'

'Thank you, I'll do everything I can to find a solution.'

Helen nodded. She was about to move on, but something made her pause. 'Tell your friend not to get too comfortable with Sanders. He has a roving eye. Once he sees something shiny and new, he'll drop her without a second thought.'

Grace couldn't help fearing her words were probably true.

238

CHAPTER 48

'Are you sure you don't mind having Eddie?' Grace brushed down her dress while Bea assessed her outfit.

'It's all agreed, now stop trying to get out of it. I must say, you do look splendid. Green is your colour.'

Grace smiled. 'Thanks for lending me the dress.' She swished the full skirt one way then the other in front of the mirror. They were in Bea's bedroom, discarded clothes strewn across the bed.

'Where is he taking you?'

'It's a party at his boss's house. I've no idea where.' It had taken her another week to pluck up the courage to call William Banner.

Bea raised her eyebrows, impressed. 'I'm rather jealous. It's been ages since I went on a proper date.' She sat on the bed, her smile fading.

'Is everything okay?'

'Course it is. Ignore me.'

Grace sat beside her. 'I do so appreciate everything you've done for Eddie and me. I don't know where we'd be without you.'

'It's my pleasure.' Bea gripped her hand and kissed it. Her eyes lingered on Grace, then she stood up. 'Right, you'd better be on your way or you'll be unfashionably late.'

In the entrance hall, Grace gathered Eddie into her arms. 'Be good for Bea, Mummy will be back before you know it.'

'He'll be fine, we're going to get up to all sorts of mischief.' Bea ruffled his hair, but Eddie looked uncertain.

* * *

Five minutes later, Grace was waiting outside their front gate for William. She was surprised when he arrived on foot. He was taller than she remembered, although they'd spent most of their time sitting down. He wore a suit and his sandy hair appeared even blonder in the evening sun which fell across the street, casting elongated shadows of them both.

'Grace.' He offered up his wide smile.

'Hello, William.'

'I hope you don't mind walking? It's such a lovely evening and it's not far.'

'That's fine.' Grace didn't mind but she regretted borrowing Bea's heels, which pinched slightly at the toes.

They set out for the city centre before peeling off in the direction of St Leonards.

'Thank you for agreeing to come this evening.'

'Thank you for inviting me.' Grace cringed inwardly at their polite conversation. William seemed less confident than he had in the café. He linked his hands behind his back then changed his mind.

Grace tried to distract herself with their surroundings. Victorian terraces gave way to white stucco mansions set back from the road.

'Where's your little boy this evening?' William broke the silence.

'Eddie. He's at home being looked after by my friend Bea.'

'He didn't mind you leaving him?'

'I wouldn't say that exactly, but he's in good hands.' Grace wondered if that was true. Bea was hardly the maternal type.

'It must be hard, raising him alone.'

'It's all he's ever known, just me and him.'

'His father . . .'

'Died.'

'I'm sorry.' William glanced ahead. The road rose in a steep curve.

Grace felt the familiar twinge of guilt. She searched for something to ease the tension. 'How are you finding Exeter so far?'

A smile touched his lips as if he were relieved to venture into different territory too. 'I like it. Everything's here — the city, the shops, the river for escape and relaxation. I used to row back in Southampton, I miss it.'

Grace wasn't surprised, he had a rower's build. Broad-shouldered with big arms.

'Why don't you see if there's a club here?'

'I've been so busy with work there hasn't been much opportunity.'

'Ah yes, rebuilding the city.'

William looked gratified. 'You remembered?'

'It's on your card.'

Colour flushed his cheeks. 'Of course, how silly of me.'

Grace smiled. 'I did remember, as it happens.'

They stopped outside a substantial stucco house with arched windows over four floors and immaculate lawns bordering a gravel driveway. The lilt of laughter and conversation drifted from the building.

William paused at the gate. 'Before we go in, I want to apologise. I've started this evening all wrong. I meant to say when I arrived how lovely you look, but nerves got the better of me and I missed the opportunity. I'm not terribly practised at this, taking someone out. Work has claimed most of my time.' He ran his fingers through his hair and met her gaze. 'I kicked myself for not getting your number. When you called,

I was elated. I haven't stopped thinking about you since the day we met in the café.'

Grace fiddled with her bracelet, another loan from Bea as she tried to cool the flush rising from her neck up. 'I'm flattered, and for what it's worth, I'm not used to this either. With Eddie and me on our own, I haven't been on a date in, well . . . not since Eddie's father.' It was sort of true. Joe barely counted.

'We'll have to guide each other.' William opened the gate and smiled. 'Shall we?'

* * *

An hour later, Grace was midway through her second gin, standing next to William while they made strained conversation with his boss and his wife, who kept asking Grace questions she couldn't answer. *I hear you have a son, where is he educated? Have you put his name down for Exeter Cathedral School? I'm surprised you don't know how competitive it is.* She sipped her drink, wondering when they'd get fed, and took the opportunity to glance at the other guests while there was a lull in the interrogation. All the great and the good of Exeter were there: bankers, architects, business owners. Anyone with a vested interest in the future of the city as it emerged into this new era of post-war regeneration. As she made a sweep of the room, she was startled to see Sanders leaning against the opposite wall, smoking a cigar, persistent gaze directed at her. She gave a brief nod and returned her attention to William as his boss and his wife made their excuses and drifted away.

'Sorry about that,' William whispered. 'You've been an incredibly good sport putting up with all this boring talk.'

Grace smiled, somewhat relieved he was finding the conversation boring too. The presence of Sanders added another layer of tension she could do without.

'Looks like we're about to eat.' William gestured to the terrace, where a buffet had been laid out under an awning. Guests were already starting to congregate. 'You find us a table. What can I get you?'

'I don't mind.' She was so hungry, she didn't care. Her eyes searched for Sanders again, relieved there was no sign of him.

Outside, tables dressed in crisp white cloths were arranged across the lawn. Lights strung between trees twinkled in the warm breeze. She'd never attended anything so grand. Finding a table towards the back of the garden, Grace watched William enter the fray at the buffet, his tall body and long arms giving him the advantage of reach as guests vied for food. She was quite absorbed by the scene, when she sensed a presence at her side.

'Good evening, Grace.'

She stood. 'Hello, Mr Sanders.'

'I didn't know you moved in such salubrious circles.' His smirk told her he was mocking.

'I'm here on a date.' Not that it was any of his business.

'Lucky fellow.' His gaze drifted to her outfit. 'Isn't that one of Beatrice's dresses?'

Grace coloured. She'd forgotten she was wearing Bea's dress. Of course Sanders would recognise it, perhaps it had been a gift from him.

'She loaned it to me.'

He leaned in, intense eyes focused on hers, the hint of stale cigar on his breath. 'It looks much better on you.'

Grace had no idea how to respond. It was a ridiculous comment, Bea would look stunning in sackcloth. Fortunately, William appeared with their food. She'd never been so pleased to see his boyish grin.

Sanders lingered a moment too long before nodding his farewell.

William set down the plates stacked with exotic-looking food. 'Friend of yours?'

'My boss.'

'Oh dear, do you mind?'

Grace shook her head, determined not to let Sanders ruin the evening.

* * *

The food proved to be mediocre; what it lacked in taste it made up for in pretension. Vol-au-vents, cheese wheels and devilled eggs vied for space in her queasy stomach. Black Forest gateau and baked Alaska crowned the dessert menu. It didn't help that the exchange with Sanders thoroughly stole her appetite. Grace tried to feel grateful, aware a meal like this was an experience in itself, but she'd give anything for fish and chips. She thought about Eddie and how wide his eyes would be as William cut into his slice of baked Alaska.

Having been persuaded to try a sweet sherry with dessert, which she washed down with a final gin, Grace was thoroughly sozzled by the time William suggested they leave. He'd proved good company when they'd been alone, and Sanders kept his distance for the rest of the evening.

Grace swayed at the gate. William caught her arm to steady her. They made their way along the road, the clip of their shoes the only sound as the buzz of party music and voices faded into the night.

'I'm afraid I'm not much of a drinker,' Grace admitted. 'My friend Bea could drink me under the table. This is her dress.' She hiccupped. 'I'm not sure why I told you that.'

William chuckled. 'Well, it looks wonderful on you.'

'That's what Sanders said.'

'Who's Sanders?'

'My boss.'

His brow furrowed. 'I'm not sure that was appropriate.'

'Damn right it wasn't. He's sleeping with Bea.' Grace laughed at William's scandalised face. 'Sorry, I have no idea why I told you that either. That third gin must have loosened my tongue.'

'This Sanders fellow sounds like a rogue.'

'Don't worry, I can look after myself. I always have.'

The comment seemed to silence him, putting an end to their easy conversation. That hadn't been her intention. Grace searched for something to say, aware her arm was still linked through his. The fresh air was gradually returning her to a state of sobriety. Maybe it had that effect on William too.

244

They turned into her road. Grace noticed the light on in the flat; Bea was still up. No doubt she'd be keen to deconstruct the evening in microscopic detail. Grace wasn't sure what to tell her about Sanders other than to omit his comment regarding the dress.

William followed her up the path to the front door, his expression inscrutable.

She searched for her key in her handbag. 'Thank you for a lovely evening.'

He fiddled with the cuff on his jacket. 'I'm sorry for going quiet back there. Your last comment rather hit home. I admire your courage, Grace.' He met her gaze.

Grace gave a small shrug. 'I don't know that I'm terribly courageous.'

'I disagree.' He took her hand, his fingers warm as they entwined with hers. 'I'm sorry that party was so dreadful.'

She threw him a smile. 'It was an experience.'

He stepped forwards. 'Would it be okay if I kissed you?'

Without bothering to reply, Grace leaned in with the sense this was a new beginning. After so many years of struggle, she had a job she loved, a home for Eddie, friends, and now she'd met a lovely man.

As William Banner's lips met hers, Grace closed her eyes, luxuriating in the pleasure of being kissed without pressure or expectation. In the second before he pulled away, there was the man with the dark curls.

CHAPTER 49

A warm breeze teased the corners of the newspaper as Charlie scanned the situations vacant page. The Tivoli was likely to remain closed for several months. He'd visited the previous week. It was a devastating sight. At the screen end, scaffolding stabilised the roof, where daylight flooded through the remaining beams. Although much of the seating and flooring escaped, the fire had eaten around the fabric-lined walls, leaving a blackened husk. The culprit was believed to be a discarded smouldering cigarette. Still, the bits that mattered to him survived. The foyer, the projection room, its friendly ghosts intact. He knew those memories lived inside him, but if he'd lost his projection room it would have felt like losing bits of Connie all over again. His thoughts cartwheeled to the chair and then Tommy — had the daft cat found a new home?

Returning to the paper, he attempted to bring his mind back to the task in hand. His doctor advised he was in need of a focus since his 'episode' at the engagement party the previous month. He'd asked if there was anything bothering Charlie. There was plenty, most of which Charlie kept to himself. The source of his malady was a deep wound that seemed impossible to cauterise. Better to ignore it than allow it to fester in the open.

General conclusions were drawn that the fire at the Tivoli was the source of his stress. It was true that, without work, he'd had too much time on his hands to think lately and weddings weren't cheap — at least, not weddings organised by Jane and his mother.

Jane was trying to persuade him to join her family business, but he couldn't see himself in the funeral trade. The prospect of being confronted with a dead body made the hairs on the back of his neck stand to attention. That hardly made him a good candidate for the role.

He glanced up to see Jane regarding him with the same, slightly anxious expression she'd been wearing since the engagement party. Charlie threw her a reassuring smile and returned to his paper, hoping she'd leave him alone. Instead, she took a seat on the garden bench beside him, her face hovering in his periphery as she looked over his shoulder.

'Any luck?'

'Not so far.'

'Cup of tea?'

'Thanks.'

He watched her walk back to the house, appreciating the way her yellow summer dress swayed with her hips. Jane didn't know what to say to him. No one did, except maybe Viv, who had enough on her plate with her brood.

Charlie was about to give up with the job search when his gaze reached the final advert on the page. It was for a projectionist at the Odeon in Exeter. The closing date was the end of the week. He hastened to the house as Jane emerged with a tray.

'I've found a job to apply for.'

'What about the tea?' She followed him back inside.

'Can I take mine to go? I need to get this application in the post this afternoon or I'll miss the deadline.'

'What's it for?' Jane set the tray on the kitchen table.

'A projectionist at the Odeon in Exeter.'

'Oh.' She frowned. 'I thought you were going to consider working for Dad or at least getting something local.'

'Exeter's not far. I've got my dad's old car.'

Jane poured his tea, adding milk and one sugar. He couldn't deny she made the perfect cup of tea. 'Isn't it time you found something a bit more . . .'

'More what?'

'Serious.' She offered him a chocolate digestive biscuit from a plate she'd arranged on the tray lined with a paper doily. Jane paid attention to detail.

Charlie shook his head. 'Serious? What's not serious about being a projectionist?'

Jane stroked his arm, her touch as light as a feather. It was her way of communicating something difficult. There'd been a lot of arm stroking each time another wedding expense came to light. 'It's not exactly a career with prospects. Dad is keen to train you up, then we could take the business on when he retires.'

Charlie sighed. He couldn't think of anything worse, and he was wounded too. Being a projectionist might not be the most lucrative career, but he had plans, big plans. It made him think of Connie, their first date and his bravado as he shared his hopes for their future. He forced the memory away. 'It's only for a few months until the Tiv is back up and running.'

Jane nodded. 'I thought . . .'

'You thought what?'

'That you might not go back.'

He felt his chest contract. 'Why wouldn't I go back? I love it there.'

'Are you sure it's good for you?'

'Good for me?' Charlie sipped his tea. It was still too hot. He set down the cup, exasperated.

Jane shook her head. 'Forget I said anything. If you're happy then I'm happy.'

Charlie took her hand and pulled her to him. 'I'm fine.' He leaned down, kissing her lightly on the lips. When he pulled away, she was smiling. It made him feel better.

CHAPTER 50

Fred pulled on his coat as Grace laced the projector. He was taking a well-earned evening's leave. 'Right, I'm off. Both lamps are ready to go. Are you sure you'll manage?'

'Thanks, Fred, I'll be fine, and I've got Eddie here to assist.' Her son looked up from his comic and grinned.

Fred paused at the door. 'About your lady cinema projectionist's enquiry. I asked around, no luck I'm afraid. None in Exeter. I also checked with my mate in Crediton, and the Tivoli in Tiverton is closed due to a fire. There's a couple of lady projectionists in Plymouth, but none that have left suddenly.'

Grace considered this, but Plymouth seemed an unlikely place for her origins. It was at least two and a half hours away from the farm where she'd been found. 'Thanks anyway, Fred.'

'See you tomorrow.'

Grace turned back to her son, finding her eyes filled with tears. 'Stay here, Ed, I need to use the ladies. Remember, don't answer the door to anyone and don't touch a thing.'

Eddie nodded, still absorbed by the *Beano*.

In the bathroom, Grace splashed her face. She must have picked up her projectionist skills somewhere, but like all her efforts to discover the truth, it only ended in disappointment.

Perhaps it was time to stop trying. Life was good at the moment, why allow her missing past to blight her present?

She looked up to find Mary, Sanders' long-suffering secretary, beaming at her from behind her cat-eye spectacles. She matched them to her outfits. Today was pink to compliment the pink fluffy cardigan stretched across her generous bust. 'Evening, Grace, are you interviewing for the job tomorrow? I didn't see you on the list.'

'What job?' Grace reached for the towel.

'The projectionist job, it was in the paper last week. Quite a few applicants. I don't blame you though, I wouldn't fancy being shut away in the projection room. You'll be glad to get out front again, I'm sure.'

Grace backed away, stunned. 'Is Mr Sanders in his office?'

'I think so.' Mary pulled on a coat the colour of a flamingo. 'Have a lovely evening.'

'Thanks.' Grace ran to Sanders' office, self-righteous indignation fuelling every step. She hammered on the door then walked straight in uninvited.

Sanders was sitting behind his desk, smoking, studying a set of papers. He looked up, annoyed, and then amused.

'Grace, what brings you to my door, all red-faced and fuming?'

'Is it true? Are you replacing me?'

Sanders sat back. 'Surely you didn't think the job was yours?'

'That's exactly what I thought.'

He took a drag on his cigar, his lips spreading into a conceited smile. 'A shrewd businessman doesn't hide a woman like you where no one can see her. He puts her on display where his patrons can enjoy the sight of her as much as he does.'

Grace didn't know whether he expected her to be flattered or furious, but as blind rage surged through her veins it was clear she'd gone for the latter. 'Isn't my work good enough?'

'It's exemplary, but as I said, your considerable talents are required elsewhere.'

'I don't want to be out front standing around when I can be in the projection room running the film, making it all happen.'

Sanders eyes narrowed. 'Standing around? Are you suggesting that's all usherettes do?'

'I didn't mean it like that. I—'

'I understand. You're cursed with beauty and intelligence, but I'm afraid in this business the former wins the argument. I pride myself on having a team of usherettes who satisfy the desires of our male patrons while giving our female patrons glamour to aspire to. I'm hardly going to part with my prize jewel.'

Sanders stubbed out his cigar and stood, walking around the desk until he was directly in front of her. He smelled of nicotine and expensive cologne. 'Weren't you a cleaner when you started here?'

Grace studied her shoes. 'Yes, sir.'

'Surely becoming an usherette was a step up for you?'

Her palms grew damp with sweat. 'It was.'

'I remember when Beatrice brought you to me. Even in that scraggy old mac you were wearing, you outshone an entire room of preening girls.'

'I appreciated the opportunity.'

'But now you expect more?'

Grace steeled herself. 'I've been doing a good job as a projectionist. I don't think it's fair not to give me a chance.'

'You're right, Grace, it isn't fair, but there's also the matter of your son. I know everything that goes on in this cinema. No one so much as sneezes without my hearing about it. Did you really think you could keep sneaking the boy in behind my back?' His eyes glittered with triumph.

So, Helen had told him. Dismayed, Grace opened her mouth then shut it again. There was no viable excuse.

'I can see how much the job means to you. I admire your determination.' He sat on the edge of his desk regarding her. 'There is one way you could keep the projectionist job, if you really want it.'

251

'Anything.' Grace winced at her naked desperation.

A small, self-satisfied smile tugged at the corners of his mouth. He checked behind and stood to close the office door, which Grace had left wide open. When he met her gaze, his eyes danced with intrigue. 'You're aware of my arrangement with Beatrice?'

Grace didn't comment.

'Your discretion does you credit. Things have become a little, shall we say, tired in that department. I've expressed my admiration for you. Admiration that goes beyond the confines of this cinema. Seeing you the other evening on a date at that party — well, I was jealous. Extremely jealous.' He reached out to touch her hair, coiling a strand between his fingers. 'If you were interested in an arrangement of our own, I could see my way to making you our first female projectionist.'

Grace took a step back, cursing herself. Sanders had set a trap and she'd walked straight into it. She stood, frozen to the spot, humiliation burning her cheeks.

His smile fell away, the warmth in his eyes cooling into pools of ice water. He returned to his desk and pulled out the chair. 'I see my overtures are not welcome. Very well then, Grace. You can finish up this evening. Tomorrow, I look forward to seeing you in your usherette uniform. Shut the door on your way out.'

Stunned, Grace turned on her heel and walked out of the office. Letting herself into the projection room, she found Eddie just as she'd left him. Shock gave way to fury. 'Time to go, Ed.' Grace offered her hand.

Eddie slid down from his seat. 'What about the film?' He looked longingly at the projector.

'That's not my job anymore.' She blinked back tears.

With Eddie's hand gripped in hers, Grace marched back to Sanders' office, opening the door without knocking. Sanders was pulling on his coat. The self-assured smile he wore faded as he set his eyes on Eddie.

Grace stood before him, riding a wave of adrenaline to counteract the apprehension swirling in her stomach. 'You can stick your job.' She checked the clock on the wall behind. 'The next film is due to screen in ten minutes and there's a queue at the kiosk. Good luck finding someone who can run it.'

Without waiting for a response, Grace walked out of the office, Eddie's feet tripping over each other as she propelled them down the stairs.

* * *

On the walk home with Eddie trotting at her side, Grace's anger slowly receded into the shadows, replaced by a sadness which felt at once inevitable and familiar. Just as she'd found the prospect of a secure home tugged out from beneath her feet when she was Rose at the farm, the same was about to happen again. She'd have to tell Bea what transpired with Sanders. Their days together in the flat were surely numbered. How wrong she'd been the other evening with William to think her life was finally falling into place.

The flat was empty when she let them in. Grace helped Eddie into his pyjamas and together they brushed their teeth at the sink in their bedroom. *Was Bea with Sanders now? Was he breaking off their 'tired' arrangement?*

Grace fell into bed, too exhausted to wait up for Bea, too miserable to think about their future. She was still awake two hours later when she heard a key in the lock, the clunk of Bea kicking off her heels, the clink of the decanter as she filled a glass. This was the melody by which she'd fallen asleep every night for the last few months, but for how much longer?

CHAPTER 51

Charlie stood across the street from the Odeon awestruck by the imposing building, towering over a stark landscape. It could eat the Tivoli several times over. A hive of renewal was going on in the surrounding areas. Remnants of the Blitz could still be seen all over Exeter, but new buildings were springing up like daisies. He checked his watch and straightened his tie. Ten minutes. Taking a deep breath, he strode across the road.

Inside was just as grand. A sumptuous foyer spread out before him, a restaurant on the mezzanine above. His thoughts returned to the blackened husk of the Tivoli and his heart contracted. In contrast, this was the cinema of his dreams, a proper picture palace. A building fit for the purpose of elevating film.

At the ticket booth, he gave his details. A woman directed him to the mezzanine floor. 'Mr Sanders' secretary will fetch you shortly.'

Charlie mounted the stairs, drinking in the scenery on all sides. At the restaurant he found a table overlooking the foyer and waited, watching people come and go, the usherettes loading their trays, their crimson dresses swishing as they moved.

At exactly 2 p.m. a woman approached wearing green cat-eye spectacles and a matching green two-piece. She introduced herself as Mary and led him through a door to the side of the restaurant and down a small corridor. They came to a halt outside an office. She knocked and gestured for him to go through.

Mr Sanders was younger than he would have expected, having been accustomed to Mr Reynolds. His hair was greying at the temples, but his tight curls sat close to his head and framed a handsome face. Dressed in an expensive suit, his aftershave was noticeable in the air despite the window behind being open. Charlie felt rather unsophisticated in his department store suit. Sanders was scribbling something in a notebook, a cigar smoking in an ashtray at his side. A man not to be hurried. Eventually he looked up.

'Mr Smith.' Sanders fixed him with a gaze like plywood and offered his hand. His limp handshake failed to match his commanding exterior.

'Nice to meet you, sir. It's Charlie.'

Sanders gestured to the vacant chair opposite, casting his sharp eyes over Charlie's resumé. 'You have impressive credentials. Nine years working as a projectionist at the Tivoli.'

'That's right. I started as an apprentice when I was sixteen then had a gap when I did my National Service. During that time the main projectionist left, and I took over upon my return.'

'Sorry to hear about the fire. What a tragedy.'

'Thanks, they're hoping to open again in a few months.'

Sanders reached for his cigar and took a drag. 'I'm looking for someone reliable who'll stay the course. If this is a fill-in until the Tivoli reopens—'

'It's not,' Charlie cut in, alarmed. 'I'm keen to advance my career and working in a larger venue is the logical next step.' It was a good lie, but it might turn out to be true.

Sanders regarded him before inclining his head. 'As I said, I'm looking for someone reliable. I've been messed around lately. Our second projectionist left without notice and we've been making do with a woman, a former usherette.' He sat back. 'A real stunner.' He shot Charlie a conspiratorial smile that failed to reach his eyes. 'When I explained her talents were best served out front, she quit. I should never have given her a shot in the first place, but at the time there was no alternative.'

Charlie wasn't sure how to respond. He couldn't help feeling bad for this woman, whoever she was. Sanders' gaze rested somewhere in the distance as if he couldn't care less whether Charlie shared his indignation or not.

Abruptly, Sanders stubbed out his cigar and pushed back his chair. 'Let's show you the projection room and see how you get on with the equipment.'

The projection room was huge in comparison to what he was used to at the Tivoli. He and Connie would have had no need to dance in the auditorium, he could have twirled her around in here to his heart's content. Before he had time to study the thought, Sanders gestured to the projectors. They were British Thomson-Houston projectors, different to the Kalees he'd used at the Tivoli, but the set-up looked the same. The room was spotless and well organised. He couldn't have done a better job himself. Whoever this poor woman was, she clearly knew her stuff.

Sanders asked Charlie a few more questions and then pointed to a can of film. Charlie set about preparing the reel for screening. As he worked, he realised how much he'd missed it, the feel of film between his fingers, the skill required in lacing the projector, the attention to detail necessary for framing and focus. A sense of loss for the Tivoli punctured his enjoyment of the task.

Ten minutes later he had the film running. Sanders left him while he went into the auditorium to check the results. Charlie cast around. *Could I feel at home here?*

Before he could answer his own question, Sanders returned with a satisfied look on his face. 'We'll be in touch, Mr Smith.'

* * *

'How did it go?' His mother appeared in the entrance hall the moment Charlie walked through the front door.

'All right, I think, Mum.' He kissed her cheek.

'You're back later than expected.'

'I took my time, explored Exeter a bit.'

'Jane's been on the phone, wanting to know how it went.'

Charlie sighed. 'Right.'

'She's concerned for you, love.'

'I know. I wish she'd stop going on about me working for her dad. Being at the Odeon today made me realise how much I miss the Tivoli. I want to go back when it reopens.'

'But will you take the job at the Odeon if they offer it?'

'I'm not sure.' He took off his suit jacket and draped it over the stair banister. 'I didn't like the manager. He seemed . . . conceited and a bit shifty. He told me the previous projectionist was a woman and that he'd rather her talents were used out front.'

'A woman?'

'It's not that unusual. More women are training to be projectionists and why not? I taught Connie for fun and she took to it like a duck to water.' A wistful smile spread across his lips.

When she didn't comment, he glanced at his mum. She was wearing what he'd come to think of as the 'Connie' expression. Concern mixed with a hint of apprehension.

Charlie felt a prick of irritation. 'Give over, Mum, I'm allowed to talk about her. What's the problem?'

'It's been a long time, darling, and Jane, well, it's not fair on her to harp on about Connie all the time.'

'I don't.' He hesitated. 'Do I?'

Marge touched his arm. 'I'll make us a nice cup of tea. You must be parched.'

Charlie stood in the entrance hall, staring after his mother. She might not have answered his question, but her silence was loud and clear.

257

CHAPTER 52

Bea hadn't yet risen when Grace and Eddie headed off to the shops the following morning. Purchasing a newspaper, Grace treated Eddie to a teacake at Tinley's. Being back there reminded her of William.

She perused the situations vacant while Eddie munched his teacake. An advert for projectionists at the Gaumont in Plymouth caught her eye. Grace cast her mind back to the friendly man she'd met in the Odeon projection room. Alec Jenkins, wasn't he the manager? He'd admired her skills and hadn't minded the fact she was a woman. She was tempted to apply, but after telling Sanders what he could do with his job, Grace couldn't see him giving her a reference. Pushing that depressing thought to one side, she flicked through the rest of the paper.

When she was finished, Grace downed the dregs of her tea and glanced at her son, his face smeared with butter. She took a napkin and attempted to clean him up despite his protestations. It was a relief to see him like this, fed, his cheeks full of colour. Things were good for a while, and she had Bea to thank for that.

'Ready to head home?' Grace offered her hand. *How much longer will we have a home?*

Eddie's sticky fingers entwined with hers as they stepped outside. Grace couldn't help wanting to linger, to enjoy this life before it was taken away. They idled at the shops, looking in the windows of Boots, Marks & Spencer and Walton's department store.

On Paul Street, they were about to step off the pavement when a bus pulled up beside them. Grace snatched Eddie to safety.

'Mummy, that lady's staring at you.'

Grace cast around. 'Who's staring at me?'

'Look.' Eddie pointed at the bus. On the other side of the smeared glass, a woman of about her age with long blonde hair was studying Grace. As Grace's gaze met hers, she banged on the window as if she knew her. Grace checked behind and, finding no one there, realised Eddie was right. The woman was gesturing to her, lips moving in speech, a look of desperation on her face. Grace offered a nervous smile, trying to work out if she could place her. The woman started pushing her way through the crowded bus, but she had a pram with her and couldn't get past a large man who was blocking the exit. Before she could get any further the bell rang, and the doors swung shut. The woman returned to the window, a look of helpless devastation across her face. The bus sped her away.

'Who was the lady, Mummy?'

Grace stared after the bus, unsettled by the incident. Surely the woman had mistaken her for someone else?

She crouched to meet Eddie's concerned gaze. 'It doesn't matter, darling, I don't know who it was.'

They crossed the road, heading for the flat. Grace couldn't put the strange woman out of her mind. There was something about that face, the bright red lips, the swathe of gold hair.

When they entered their road, Grace's attention was claimed by the prospect of seeing Bea. She pulled out her keys and let them in, nerves playing havoc with the tea in her stomach.

Bea was in the sitting room, still in her robe, smoking. She offered up a weary smile when they entered.

'Hello, you two, what have you been up to?'

'Mummy took me for a teacake and then a weird lady tried to talk to us from a bus.'

Bea glanced at Grace with a baffled expression.

Grace smiled. 'It's true, I have no idea who she was.'

'Strange. I've had an odd day too — well, an odd night.' She patted the seat beside her.

'Eddie, why don't you do some colouring in our bedroom?' Grace pulled out a colouring book she'd brought at the newsagents.

Eddie snatched the book from her hands and disappeared through the door.

Dumping her bag, Grace took the offered seat. 'There's something I need to tell you too.'

'Oh, yes?' Bea sat back, expectant.

Grace suddenly wanted to stall for time. If only they could remain, suspended in this moment. 'Why was your night odd?'

'Oh, Sanders was in one of his moods.'

'He didn't say anything, did he?'

Bea stubbed out her cigarette. 'He said plenty, what are you worried about?'

Grace sighed. 'Yesterday I found out he's interviewing for a new projectionist, my job. I confronted him.'

'Swine, good for you.'

Grace swallowed, dreading the next bit. 'He said I could have the job if I . . .'

'If you what?'

'He made a pass at me.'

Bea laughed, but it quickly died when she noticed Grace's pained expression. 'You can't be serious. What did he say, exactly?'

Grace struggled to meet Bea's gaze. 'He suggested we have our own *arrangement*.'

'Are you certain?'

'I'm certain.'

Bea stood, pacing the length of the room before rounding on Grace, her eyes blazing. 'Why are you doing this?'

'I'm not doing anything. I turned him down and I quit.'

'You're jealous.'

'What?' Grace was genuinely shocked.

'Ever since you got the projectionist job you've been full of it. Going on and on about this film and that like you made the bloody things. You think you're a cut above the rest of us, but a few months ago you were scrubbing the floors. It was me who quite literally pulled you out of the gutter and for what? For you to try and steal what I have.'

Grace was stunned. She'd thought Bea would be upset, but she hadn't considered she might not believe her. 'Bea, I—'

'Leave. Go. I don't want you here.'

'Please, you're overreacting.'

Bea looked at her. The chill in her eyes made Grace shiver.

'If that's what you want?'

Bea nodded. 'I'm going to work. I'd like you gone by the time I wake up tomorrow.'

CHAPTER 53

Charlie sat at the kitchen table, studying the wedding seating arrangements Jane brought round as if he were trying to solve a complex puzzle. He'd promised to have it checked by the end of the day. His mum was better placed to have an opinion on this stuff. *If I'd taken the job at the Odeon, I wouldn't be stuck here looking at seating plans.* Sanders rang the previous day to offer him the position. Maybe he shouldn't have been so principled, but it didn't sit right, taking a job that belonged to someone else.

The chime of the doorbell brought welcome respite. Viv was on the other side, James in the crook of her arm, a look of utter turmoil on her face.

'What's happened?'

Viv moved past him into the house, her gaze darting around. 'Is your mum here?'

'She's out shopping, why?'

'Can we sit down?'

'Course, you can help me check the seating arrangements for the wedding. At this point, I don't care who sits where.' He chuckled, but Viv looked stricken. 'What's happened, Viv?'

'Let's sit outside.'

He followed her into the garden, taking a seat on his dad's bench.

Viv turned to him, her brow furrowed, eyes liquid with tears. Charlie's stomach dropped. 'What's wrong? Is it Michael or one of the kids?'

She shook her head and paced in front of him. 'Michael told me not to tell you. If he finds out I'm here, he'll string me up.'

'Tell me what? Viv, spit it out. You're scaring me.'

'I saw Connie.'

Charlie stood. 'What?'

'Oh God, Charlie, it was her, I know it was.' Viv sat down, leaving Charlie to pace. 'Yesterday, I was on the bus. I'd been shopping in Exeter, looking for a new dress for the wedding. No luck as it happens, the whole of Exeter and I couldn't find a single dress I liked.'

'Viv.'

'Sorry, anyway, so I'm on the bus. It was packed to the nines, standing room only. I'm squashed up against the window with some man's umbrella wedged in my back — at least, I hope it was his umbrella. Suddenly this woman is standing on the pavement, and, Charlie, I swear it was Con. She had exactly the same hair, the same face. She was staring at me too but like she didn't know who I was. I banged on the window, I was saying her name, but she just kept looking at me, baffled. There was a little boy with her, age about four or five. He had black curly hair, the same as yours. I tried to get off the bus, but I had James and the pram. I pushed and pushed but there were too many people blocking my path and before I could get past the bus pulled away. That's when I started screaming.'

'Screaming?'

'They thought I was crazy, but the driver pulled over and let me and James off at the next stop. I ran with the pram back to Paul Street but there was no sign of her. I must have walked up and down the road a dozen times. I'm sorry, Charlie, I lost her.'

Charlie couldn't take it all in, Viv was talking so fast. His mind swam with confusion. It wasn't possible.

Viv stood, guiding him back to the seat. He sat heavily and buried his face in his hands.

'Charlie?' She crouched in front of him.

Eventually he lifted his gaze to hers. 'You can't be right. There must be some mistake.'

'That's what Michael said, but I wouldn't be here if I had any doubt in my mind. I wouldn't do that to you.'

'Think rationally, how can it be? Connie's dead. She wouldn't have left me otherwise. We were going to get married.'

'I know,' Viv whispered, 'I can't explain it.'

'If it was Connie, why wouldn't she know you?'

Viv shrugged. 'I realise it doesn't make sense, but it was her, I'm certain.'

Charlie stared across the garden, his mind turning over possibilities. 'You said she had a boy with her?'

'Yes, did you and Connie . . . ?'

He nodded.

'The kid was the spit of you, dark curls, dimples . . .'

Charlie stood again. 'I can't wrap my head around it. How can she be alive?'

'I only know what I saw.'

James's eyes pinged open. He stared at Charlie from his blanket before his tiny face grimaced and he began to wail.

'Someone's hungry.' Viv jiggled her son. 'Do you mind if I feed him?'

Dazed, Charlie shook his head, averting his eyes.

'Did I do the wrong thing, telling you?' Her voice tremored.

Charlie couldn't meet Viv's eye, but he shook his head.

'What will you do?'

'What can I do? Look for her? Exeter's a big place.'

'Maybe we should go to the police.'

Charlie knew then, Viv meant business. 'You're certain?'

'Like I said, I wouldn't be here if I wasn't.'

He nodded.

'What about Jane?' There was a tentative note in Viv's voice.

Charlie buried his face in his hands. He glanced up at Viv through tears. 'I can't marry her. Not if there's a chance Con is alive. I've never loved anyone like I love Connie Harris.'

CHAPTER 54

The alarm rang shrill through Grace's head as she fought off the fog of sleep. At the sight of their suitcase, packed and ready for an early departure, her eyes filled with tears. She'd waited up until past midnight, but Bea hadn't materialised. Removing Eddie's arm, heavy with sleep from her torso, Grace climbed out of bed and tiptoed to the sitting room. Bea's bedroom door remained firmly shut, but discarded heels outside told her Bea was home.

Taking a sheet of paper and a pen from the bureau, Grace returned to the bedroom, sat on the edge of the bed, and wrote a note to her friend putting into action the plan she'd concocted during her broken sleep.

Dearest Bea,

As sad as things have turned out between us, I wanted to thank you from the bottom of my heart for taking in Eddie and me. I will never forget your kindness.

I realise you're upset, but in case you wanted to say goodbye, we'll be catching the 10.18 to Plymouth. I think it's time for a fresh start.

Please take care of yourself. We'll miss you more than you can imagine.

Your friends Grace and Eddie xx

Folding the paper in two, Grace wrote Bea's name on the front and returned to the sitting room, where she left it on the coffee table along with her keys.

Back in the bedroom, Grace dressed as Eddie stirred. She helped him into his clothes, his body still warm and sleepy. Pulling back the curtains, the weather sat in direct contrast to her mood. Cloudless cerulean skies stretched as far as the eye could see. A day for a new adventure, she reassured herself.

Not wishing to delay their departure, Grace picked up the case, took Eddie's hand and let them out of the flat.

'Where are we going, Mummy?' Eddie rubbed his face.

'We're going to have breakfast at Tinley's, then we're going to catch a train.'

Eddie grew wide eyed. 'A train?'

'That's right. We're off on an adventure.'

He grinned. Grace ruffled his hair, wishing she could share her son's enthusiasm.

* * *

Eddie pulled at her arm, impatient for their adventure to begin as they made their way into the city. Grace had to stop twice to rest under the weight of their luggage. The café was quiet, and they had their pick of the tables. Although her stomach was in no mood for it, she ordered a cooked breakfast for them both, unsure when or where they would get their next meal. She watched Eddie scoop up the food and enjoyed it vicariously through him. Glancing across the pristine lawn to the cathedral, Grace hoped one day they would return. After a few tough years, Exeter had been good to them.

Fortified, they set out for St David's station. The grand facade had Eddie in a state of rapture on their approach. Grace stopped at a phone booth before they went in.

'Mummy needs to make a phone call.' She pulled open the heavy door and they squeezed with their luggage inside. The booth stank of cigarettes, one had been left smoking in the ashtray. It reminded her of Mrs Blythe and how far she'd come. Retrieving her purse, Grace fished out a few coins and dialled the number for the Plymouth Gaumont. She took a deep breath and asked to speak to Alec Jenkins.

'Shh, Eddie,' she admonished as he tugged at her sleeve asking when they could go.

Grace recognised Jenkins's kindly voice as it came on the line.

'Mr Jenkins, you might not remember me. My name is Grace and we met at the Odeon in Exeter. I was working in the projection room.'

'Grace, I do remember. I was impressed with your work.'

She exhaled. 'Thank you, you're too kind. I'm calling because circumstances mean I'm moving to Plymouth, and I saw you had a job advertised . . .'

The line went quiet, making Grace aware of her own heartbeat.

'That's right. Are you interested?'

'Very interested.'

'Can you be here tomorrow at 11 a.m.?'

Grace didn't know where they were going to sleep or what she'd do with Eddie, but nothing would stop her missing this opportunity. 'I can.'

'We're interviewing for the position all afternoon, but I can fit you in first and see how you get on.'

'Thank you, Mr Jenkins.'

Hanging up the phone, Grace grinned at Eddie. 'Right, let's catch that train.'

She purchased two one-way tickets to Plymouth and for the first time found a flutter of excitement in her stomach. The prospect of a job interview and Eddie's fascination was rubbing off on her. He whooped when a freight train rattled through and raced up the stairs to their platform, his slight frame engulfed in a billow of steam.

'We've got five minutes to wait,' Grace said, setting their luggage down with relief.

As the London train pulled in on the opposite platform, the drone of the announcer listed the stations. *Tiverton.* Why did that sound familiar? The fire, Fred told her there was a fire at the cinema. A long whistle stole her focus. 'Mummy, look.' Eddie leaped off the ground as their train puffed into view.

'Grace.' She spun around at the familiar voice, shocked to see Bea running towards them, a station porter pulling a large trunk in her wake. 'I'm sorry I was an absolute beast. Can you forgive me?'

Grace hugged her friend. 'Of course you're forgiven, but what are you doing here?'

Bea directed the porter to a carriage door as the train ground to a halt. 'Isn't that obvious, darling? I'm coming with you.'

* * *

Grace smiled at Eddie as the train swayed out of Dawlish, his nose pressed to the window, astonished at their proximity to the sea.

Bea returned from the bathroom, where she'd been since they left Exeter, and took a seat opposite. 'Sorry, I'm feeling a bit under the weather.' She retrieved a make-up compact from her bag and set about reapplying her crimson lipstick.

'What made you believe me, Bea?'

Glancing over the mirror, Bea smiled. 'Oh, I believed you, darling. I knew you wouldn't betray me, but I'd had something of a shock the previous evening. It caused me to act out of character.'

'What kind of shock?'

'I'm pregnant.'

Grace gaped. 'Sanders?'

'Who else?'

'I'm sorry, I mean—'

'No, sorry about covers it. When I told him, he asked me how much I needed to get rid of it. Bastard.'

Grace covered Eddie's ears.

Bea winced. 'Anyway, I threw out a wildly extravagant sum, having no intention of going to some grubby little back street establishment, and to my surprise he agreed. He couldn't write the cheque fast enough.' Bea pulled a piece of paper from her handbag and passed it to Grace.

Grace stared at the sum, more money than she could imagine having. 'What will you do?'

'I was all for finding someone to put an end to matters, but when I woke up this morning filled with remorse for the awful way I'd treated you and saw your note, I thought, no, I'm going to have this child, to spite him. That cheque will more than cover our deposit on a flat.'

Grace couldn't take it all in. 'Are you certain?'

'I just threw up, so yes, fairly certain.'

'I meant about us getting a flat. I'm not sure having a child to spite someone is quite the right way to go about it.'

Bea applied blush to her cheeks. 'You don't think I want to do this alone, do you? Who better than you to guide me into motherhood?'

'I don't know about that.'

Bea reached over and took her hand, threading her fingers through hers. 'I do. You're a goddess, the strongest woman I know. Far tougher than me. You brought Eddie into the world alone and you survived. I couldn't have done it.'

'I only did what I had to do.' Grace glanced at her son, swelling with pride.

Bea peered along the carriage. 'Is there a dining car on this thing? I'm famished.'

Grace gestured behind. 'Down that way, I think.'

Lurching along the narrow gangway, they located the buffet and settled themselves in a booth.

'What would you like?' Grace asked.

'Anything that involves bacon. I seem to have developed a taste for it.'

Grace smiled. 'With me it was kippers.'

Bea grimaced. 'Here.' She proffered a note.

Grace went to the bar to place their order. A waiter materialised minutes later with a bacon sandwich for Bea along with coffee and a glass of orange squash for Eddie.

'Splendid,' Bea said, tucking in. 'Tonight, we'll stay at a hotel, my treat. Tomorrow, we look for a flat.'

Grace grinned, excited by the prospect of this new beginning. 'I have a job interview tomorrow at the Gaumont.'

'For an usherette?'

'Projectionist.'

Bea looked impressed. 'Good for you. I'll take Eddie flat hunting, in that case.'

Picking up her coffee, Grace raised her cup. 'To friends.'

Bea laughed and lifted hers. 'And new beginnings without stupid men.'

Grace glanced at Eddie, who was staring at them with a bemused expression.

'Oh, all right,' Bea conceded. 'Boys are allowed.'

CHAPTER 55

'Viv said the police weren't interested.' Michael leaned against the open bonnet of the Ford he was working on.

Charlie sighed. 'It's not enough evidence to reopen the case but they'll make general enquiries.' In truth, he was gutted.

'Sorry.'

'I knew it was a long shot.'

Michael folded his arms. 'I told Viv to leave well alone.'

'Don't go blaming, Viv. She genuinely believes it was Connie. I'd have been more upset if she hadn't said anything. Please don't let it come between you.'

'We'll be all right. I want Con to be alive more than anything but . . .'

'You don't believe she is?'

Michael gave a small shake of his head. 'I don't see how she can be. It doesn't make sense, why would she disappear? Viv told me you two were like Romeo and Juliet and I'd like to think Connie cared about me too. Even though I didn't deserve it.' Michael studied his hands. 'I realise I've got a lot to answer for, leaving Con with our dad. I'll regret it for the rest of my life, but he wasn't always all bad — at least, not

272

before the war. He could be strict, but he wasn't violent. The drink saw to that. I had hoped there might be a bit of that man left inside.'

Charlie wasn't sure how to respond. As much as he'd blamed Michael at the time for leaving Connie, having got to know the man, he appreciated the many attributes he shared with his sister. His eyes, his smile, his gentle teasing of Viv.

'Anyway—' Michael scratched his stubble — 'knowing how happy you made Con, it does my heart good.'

Charlie nodded, at a loss for words.

Michael stooped and picked up his wrench. 'How's Jane?'

Shame burned Charlie's cheeks, unable to meet Michael's gaze. 'Not speaking to me, and who can blame her? I should never have proposed. I just wanted to move on with my life so badly.'

'She'll be all right, in time.'

'I hope so. Are you sure I won't be in the way staying here? I don't want to get under your feet.'

Michael disappeared under the bonnet. 'Stay as long as you need.'

'Thanks, I'm hoping Mum will get over it soon.'

'What's your plan now?'

'I've put up a few posters in Tiverton. I'll go to Exeter tomorrow and put some up there. I need to keep busy.'

* * *

The following afternoon, Charlie walked along Exeter High Street, a swathe of posters in his hand featuring the photo Connie gave him all those years before. He couldn't decide if he'd lost his mind, as his mum and Jane had said to him in the bitter recriminations which followed him breaking off the engagement, or if this was the clearest thinking he'd done in years. Michael was right, he needed to prepare himself for the harsh reality Connie wasn't alive, and these posters might yield nothing but the pain of loss all over again.

Either way it was the right thing to do. Jane deserved to find someone whose heart was free to love her. He'd tried but he'd never manage to bridge the gaping hole left by Connie. If that meant he would end up on his own, so be it.

Pausing at a telegraph pole, he pulled a couple of drawing pins from his pocket and fixed another poster in place. He had no idea if he was allowed, but so far, no one had stopped him. He repeated this at various points along the street until he paused outside the Savoy cinema, which was set back from the road. Curiosity led him inside. Of all the places Connie might be found, surely a cinema was a real possibility. Much like the Odeon, the foyer was plush, far grander than the Tivoli. He took a moment to admire the decorous plasterwork before approaching the box office.

'Excuse me, I wonder if I could put up a missing-person poster? She used to work at the cinema in Tiverton.'

The lady behind the box office raised an eyebrow as he proffered the picture of Connie. 'Pretty girl, never seen her before but give it here, I'll pop it on our noticeboard.'

'Thanks.'

Outside, Charlie continued to Sidwell Street with one remaining poster. Encouraged by his success at the Savoy he thought perhaps the Odeon would be willing to help too. He just hoped he could avoid Mr Sanders.

In the Odeon foyer, he was approaching the ticket office when Sanders appeared, striding across the sumptuous concourse, directly towards him. Before Charlie could hide, recognition flittered across Sanders' features.

'Mr Smith, was it?'

'That's right, sir.'

'If you've changed your mind about the job, you're too late, I've filled the position.'

Charlie coloured. 'I'm not here about the job. I came to ask if I could put up this poster?' He handed Sanders the sheet.

Sanders gave the photo a cursory glance, then his complexion paled, and his eyes narrowed.

Hope flickered inside. 'Do you recognise her?' Charlie asked.

Sanders dragged his gaze from the photo. 'Attractive girl, who's she to you?'

Charlie swallowed his disappointment. 'She was my fiancée, a long time ago.'

Sanders thrust the poster back into his hand. 'Never seen her before in my life. I don't like posters stuck up around my cinema, it's unsightly, but I can assure you, she hasn't been here.'

Charlie smoothed out the corner of the poster where Sanders crumpled it and bid him good day.

Outside, anthracite clouds had gathered, bringing with them a smattering of rain. Charlie pulled up his collar and looked at the poster as heavy droplets soaked the paper. Blotches bloomed over Connie's beautiful face. A gust of wind snatched the poster from his hand. Charlie lunged, missing it, then watched helpless as it was carried off down the street, knowing his quest had already failed.

Whoever Viv thought she saw, she'd got it wrong. Connie wasn't coming back.

PART SIX

August 1996

CHAPTER 56

'Did you mention beer?' Anna opened the fridge. Eddie was still staring at the newspaper article. 'I think you need a drink. I think I need a drink.'

She pulled out two cans and opened them, offering one to him.

'This must be a shock. I'm sorry, did I do the right thing?'

Eddie placed the newspaper article back on the table and rubbed his face. 'I can't believe it.' He reached for the beer and took a sip. 'Mum told me she had amnesia when she was pregnant with me.'

Anna returned to her seat. 'Really?'

'Mum woke up one morning at this farm on Exmoor. She reckons she must have been about eighteen or nineteen at the time. Anyway, she didn't know who she was, or how she'd got there. The farmer said they'd found her passed out in a ditch. She'd been badly beaten around the head and her face was bruised and scarred.' Eddie stood and paced back and forth across the small kitchen. 'The people who found her were kind and nursed her back to health, but they said there was nothing in the papers about her disappearance and no one came to claim her. She got involved with the son but discovered she was already pregnant with me.'

'What happened then?'

'She left, came to Exeter, had me, survived — just. Mum doesn't like to talk about it, but I know it was tough.'

'Do you think it was this Frank Harris, her father, who beat her up?'

Eddie looked stricken. 'Which would make him my grandfather. This is so messed up. If he drove over the cliff and they believed she was with him, how did Mum end up at that farm?'

'It's lucky she did.' Anna reached for the newspaper article. 'Could this Charlie Smith be your dad?'

Eddie sat down again and took another swig from his can. 'Maybe.' He looked so despondent.

Anna placed her arm around his shoulder. She could feel the warmth of his skin through his T-shirt. 'What are you going to do?' she asked to distract herself.

'Talk to Mum, I guess. It's not going to be easy.' He checked the clock on the wall above his telephone and stood.

Alarmed, Anna stood too. 'You're not thinking of telling her now?'

'I could call and arrange to see her tomorrow but Mum's like a master sleuth, she can detect when something's wrong before I've barely said hello.'

Anna smiled. 'Motherly instinct. Mine has none of that.'

'Maybe it's better if I see her in the morning. I could take some time off.'

'Good idea. If you need any support, you know where I am.'

He offered up his dimpled half-smile. 'Thanks, Anna, I appreciate it.'

Anna held up her can. 'I should go. I've only had a few sips, so I'll be fine to drive home. Do you want the rest?'

Eddie appeared a little taken aback. 'You don't want to stay for food? Seems a shame to come all this way and not hang out for a bit.'

'I thought you might want to be on your own.'

'That's actually the last thing I want right now.'

Anna found herself at the mercy of his sad eyes, which, she had to admit, were pretty deadly. 'Okay, but judging by the contents of your fridge, we need to go out.'

The heat hit them like a wall as they stepped outside. Anna regretted wearing her denim jacket, but she'd flung on the dress as she'd rushed to get out the door, and didn't like the way it emphasised her broad shoulders. She glanced at Eddie, walking at her side, hands shoved in his jean pockets despite the heat, face clouded in thought. She wasn't sure why she was thinking about her shoulders in this moment.

'Is Chinese okay?' Eddie interrupted her thoughts.

'Sure, do you know somewhere?'

'Yeah, I'm a bit too well versed on the local takeaway options. Curse of living alone and working long hours. I should take better care of myself.'

'I can relate.'

They stopped outside a Chinese conveniently located on the corner of his street. No wonder Eddie ate so much takeaway. He fished out his wallet and insisted on paying. They waited outside, leaning against the wall where an awning provided shade, until their order was ready.

'Do you fancy eating this by the river? I don't feel like being stuck inside my flat.'

'Fine by me.' Anna feared if she didn't remove her jacket soon, the sweat blooming at her armpits would soak through.

The river offered a welcome light breeze but little shade. Finding a bench, Eddie unpacked the food. Anna thought she'd been quite restrained with a spring roll and a serving of noodles but as usual the portions were enormous and not easy to eat al fresco with gulls loitering. For a while they lapsed into silence and focused on eating. Anna enviously watched the way Eddie wielded his chopsticks while she struggled to get a single noodle in her mouth with hers. Her thoughts cartwheeled to their kiss. It had been a good kiss, not that she'd allowed herself to dwell on it, but it had. She'd do it again if the opportunity arose. Not tonight though. Eddie was too messed up.

She gave up her battle with the noodles and picked up the spring roll with her fingers, glancing at Eddie, who returned her gaze.

'It's kind of amazing that you found that newspaper article. Just think if you hadn't, I'd have carried on never knowing.'

'Do you wish I hadn't?'

Eddie shrugged. 'I'm actually kind of pleased but freaked out too, mostly about how Mum is going to react.'

'It's a lot.'

He nodded, his expression brooding. 'Do I look like him, in the picture — Charlie, I mean?'

'You have the same hair, but to be honest, it was your mom I was staring at, not Charlie. Sorry.'

'It's fine, I'm not going to know until I speak to Mum, and she might not even know either.'

'What do you think she'll want to do?'

Another shrug. Eddie balled up his carton and stared at the river. Ducks bobbed past, sending ripples across the still water. Anna studied him in the fading sunshine. He did look a little like Charlie now she considered it. In the photo, Charlie had dimples. Eddie did too. She thought about mentioning it, but he suddenly stood up.

'I think I need to see Mum tonight. I can't wait until morning.'

Anna folded away her food. 'Are you sure that's a good idea? Wouldn't sleeping on it give you time to . . . I don't know, find the right words?'

Eddie shook his head. 'I won't sleep, and Mum stays up pretty late.'

Seeing his mind was made up, Anna stood too. 'Do you want me to drive? You drank more than me and I think you might be a little too wired to focus.'

'Maybe you're right. Thanks, Anna. Sorry, I'm a bit all over the place this evening.'

'Don't sweat it. I think you're doing pretty great.'

They walked back to his flat in an anticipatory silence.

He nipped inside to grab the newspaper cutting before joining her as she unlocked her car. 'Nice wheels.'

Anna grinned. 'My pride and joy.'

Eddie folded his tall frame into her bright-red VW Beetle. She climbed in, feeling a little self-conscious about driving in front of him. She wasn't used to having a passenger. But she cranked the old car into gear and eased away from the kerb.

The mellow evening sun had a softness that bathed the roads in a sulphurous glow. It was a nice drive back to Exeter, surrounded by fields and hedgerows heavy with summer growth. Anna left Eddie to his thoughts, instead focusing on the scenery and the fact she couldn't stop thinking about that kiss, or the way he filled her car with his clean washed smell.

'Where does your mom live?' she asked as fields gave way to suburbs on the edge of the city.

'Heavitree.'

'Nice.' She headed into Exeter passing the university, which made her think briefly of Graham. But from there, her focus was absorbed by Eddie's directions. They pulled up on a leafy street of impressive Victorian terraces. Anna glanced at Eddie. He was staring up at one of the houses.

'Mums at the top.' He pointed to a tidy-looking house.

'Seems like a nice street.'

'Yeah, it is.'

'So . . . are you going in?'

Eddie nodded. 'Of course.' He undid his seatbelt. 'Thanks for the lift, Anna, you've been great.'

He leaned across and gave her a peck on the cheek. She couldn't help breathing him in.

'You're welcome.'

He climbed out of the car and stepped away, staring up at the building.

'It's going to be fine, Eddie,' she said through the open window. 'Call me tomorrow, let me know how things are.'

'Yeah, I'll do that.'

'Bye then.' She pulled away. When she checked the rear-view mirror, he was still standing on the pavement. It took all her strength not to turn back and take his hand.

CHAPTER 57

Eddie took a deep breath and walked up to the familiar front door. Since it was late, instead of using his key, he rang the buzzer. Minutes passed and he checked his watch: 9.48 p.m. *Perhaps it's too late?* He was contemplating what to do when his mum's voice came through the intercom.

'Hey, Mum, it's me.'

'Eddie, are you okay?'

'Yeah, sorry, I need to speak to you.' He hesitated. 'It's important.'

'I've got someone here, but look, take a quick walk around the block, would you? Then you can come straight up.'

The intercom cut out. Eddie stood back, momentarily blindsided. He knew his mum dated but this was the first time he sensed he'd interrupted something. He felt slightly weird as he set off down the street, trying to focus on the impressive terraces and not the fact that if he'd used his key, he might have caught his mum . . . well . . .

As he returned ten minutes later, a red Audi pulled away from the kerb on the opposite side of the street. His mum was waiting at the front door dressed in jeans and a T-shirt as if she was about to go to the shops.

'Is everything okay?'

'Let's go inside.'

Her light footsteps followed him up the stairs. She gestured to the kitchen. 'Do you want a drink?'

'No, I'm good.' Eddie noted the two wine glasses in the sink. Atticus regarded them from the window ledge. 'Did I interrupt something?' He inclined his head to the glasses.

A guarded smile spread across her lips. 'It doesn't matter.'

'Is it serious?'

'It has potential.'

Eddie swallowed his curiosity, returning to the matter in hand. 'Can we go through to the lounge?'

'Eddie, you're worrying me,' she said as she settled in her favourite chair.

He sat opposite on the sofa, lost for a way to begin, and pulled the newspaper cutting from his pocket. 'Anna found this.' He passed the article to her.

His mum's features worked through a series of emotions. Curiosity quickly gave way to shock. She read it several times before lifting her watery gaze to his. 'It's me,' she whispered.

'I thought so.'

'But how did Anna find—'

'Wrapped around some glass negatives she was sorting through.'

Her gaze returned to the article. 'He told me it wasn't in the papers, that no one was looking for me.'

'Who?'

'Joe.'

'The farmer?'

She nodded and stared at the article again. After a few moments she stood and walked out of the room.

'Mum?' Eddie followed.

She was in the kitchen filling a glass with water from the tap. She took it down in long gulps. 'I needed that.'

'I'm surprised you don't need something stronger.'

She set down her glass and leaned against the counter. 'Wow, this is . . . I don't know what to do with myself.'

'Do you remember anything about Charlie? Could he be my father? What about Frank Harris? He must have been the one who beat you up.'

She shrank from his question as if she were deflating before his eyes. He realised he was throwing too much her way at once. 'Sorry, Mum, I didn't mean to overwhelm you.'

'It's fine.' Reaching for a tissue from a box on the counter, she blew her nose. 'Are you staying tonight?' There was a tremor in her voice.

'Yeah. In fact, I need a lift back to Tiverton tomorrow, if you don't mind. There's no rush. I can hang out for a bit.'

She nodded. 'Good. There's lots we need to talk about, Ed.'

CHAPTER 58

Grace sat on the edge of her bed and pulled on her yoga leggings. She liked to practise in the early morning with the sunrise. Eddie would tease her, but yoga kept her centred in a way nothing else could. It gave her space to clear her mind, and on this particular morning her mind was very overcrowded.

Reaching for her glass of water from the bedside table, she noticed Dom had left his wristwatch behind. She winced, remembering the confusion on his face when the doorbell chimed just as they'd made it to the bed. He was even more aghast when she'd ushered him out because her son was at the front door. Eddie's voice always gave him away; she could tell something serious was wrong even through the intercom.

In the kitchen, she emptied her glass in the sink and refilled the kettle, setting it to boil. While she waited, she put out two mugs, spooned coffee grounds into a cafetière and stared out of the kitchen window, mesmerised by the birds coming and going to the numerous feeders she'd hung on the narrow balcony which ran across the back of her flat.

The flat wasn't far from the one she and Bea had shared all those years ago. Bea, her guardian angel, despite the fact she'd left Plymouth on the arm of an American businessman, her bump — baby Anna — swelling under her expensive clothes. Grace hadn't set eyes on her since, but they'd kept in touch by letter, the occasional transatlantic phone call at Christmas. She must tell Bea how wonderful it was to have Anna as part of their lives. How delighted she was at the burgeoning friendship between Anna and Ed, how she hoped it might develop into more . . .

The kettle clicked off, dragging her back to the present. Grace filled the cafetière.

In the sitting room, she opened the curtains and took a steadying breath before laying out her mat and beginning her warmup routine.

Connie Harris and Charlie Smith. Their faces bounced around her head all night as if they were strangers she'd read about in the paper and nothing to do with her. She was certain Charlie was Eddie's father. Although Eddie resembled her more closely in the face, those dimples and that hair . . .

The shock was still sinking in. She'd done her best to hide her disquiet from Eddie, but the revelation had come at a time in her life when she was relatively content. Was she ready to face the realities of her past and all it could bring? Taking another breath deep, she moved through cat-cow.

What about Charlie? Maybe this would be an unwelcome disruption to his life too. Surely he'd moved on. And Dominic . . . things were starting to get interesting with him.

But the possibility of meeting her son's father, of filling in her past. How could she walk away from that?

Restacking her spine into tree pose, she balanced on one leg, facing the rising sun. The article also briefly mentioned a brother, Michael. It was a revelation, to think she might have other family. What had become of him?

'Morning, Mum.' Eddie's muffled voice through the door almost caused her to lose her balance. 'I'm going to take a shower.'

'There's coffee in the kitchen.'

'Thanks.'

He sounded himself after their long discussion the previous evening, in which she'd tried her best to fill him in on the scant details of her history. The knot in her stomach eased as Grace dropped into child's pose, stretching her long back, enjoying the sensation at the base of her spine. She rose from the mat and lifted her arms skywards in a satisfying back extension, before bringing her hands to prayer across her chest. Grace rolled up the mat, then curled up on her chair.

Eddie walked into the room minutes later, hair damp from the shower, two mugs of coffee in his large hands. *Her son.* Just hers, but for how much longer? He offered her a mug and sat on the sofa, stretching his long legs in front of him. 'How did you sleep?'

'Not particularly well,' Grace replied.

Eddie yawned. 'Me neither.'

Grace forced her eyes to meet his. 'If you want to know the truth, I'm a little scared, Ed.'

He reached across and took her hand. 'Me too.'

His hand was comforting, warm, and it gave her courage to share her innermost mysteries. 'Charlie, he's the one I see sometimes.'

Eddie frowned. 'What do you mean?'

'It's hard to explain. I've had these sort of apparitions or flashbacks for years, ever since . . . but it's always him.' She shook her head. 'And the Tivoli? I can't believe I worked there. It says in the article they found my usherette hat in the sea. No wonder I felt odd in the projection room.'

Eddie squeezed her hand. 'I'll need to do some digging but I'm sure Charlie was still the projectionist at the Tivoli just before I started. Remember I told you about the *Casablanca* reel? Who else would have left it behind?'

She dropped his hand in shock. 'You know him?'

'No, but I might know someone who does . . . Do you think you'd like to meet him?'

Grace looked out of the window trying to work out how she felt. On the one hand she wanted to, very much; on the other . . . 'He might be married with children and grandchildren.' She dragged her gaze back to Eddie.

He shrugged. 'There's only one way to find out.'

The vulnerability in her son's eyes took her back to his childhood. This wasn't about her feelings. Eddie had every right to meet his father. Her truth was also his. 'Can we wait a few days while I get used to the idea before you try to contact him?'

Eddie nodded.

They sipped their drinks in silence.

Grace stared out of the window, wondering whether she was ready to face her unknown past.

CHAPTER 59

Eddie sat in the Tivoli office the following morning trying to compile a list of final jobs that needed completing before the cinema could open. But it failed to hold his focus. Linda had to know something about Charlie. He needed to find a way to approach the topic without causing another flurry of defensive arm folding.

He peered into the foyer. Linda sat behind the kiosk working on a piece of gum like a cow chewing on a lump of grass. Not that Linda was a cow. He blinked the image away — this wasn't a good start.

'Linda,' he called from the open office door.

She looked up from her magazine, then returned her gaze to the latest celebrity gossip.

Eddie pressed on. 'The projectionist who retired before I took over . . . what was his name?'

Linda set down the magazine and folded her arms, her expression guarded, defences engaged. 'Why do you want to know?'

Eddie shrugged. 'Asking after him, that's all.'

To his surprise, she dropped her arms and moved out from behind the kiosk. 'Charlie Smith. The loveliest man you're ever likely to meet.'

Hearing his father's name, Eddie felt a fluttering sensation in his stomach as Linda joined him in the office.

'Do you know why he left the reel of film in the projection room, with the note?' He gestured to the pinboard, where the note remained the only item.

Linda pulled out the chair opposite and sat down. She studied him for a moment as if she were weighing something up before leaning back in her chair and resting her platform boots on the edge of the desk. 'It was Charlie's dream to lease this place, but the owners wouldn't budge. When the chance finally came up, he put in a bid, but they went with yours. "Young blood" as they put it. Charlie was gutted but he took it with good grace. Said it was for the best, that it was time he stopped living in the past.' She looked at him pointedly. 'I don't know anything about the film reel or why he left it, but Charlie loved the Tivoli. He was part of the fabric. As important as the screen or the seats.' Linda shrugged. 'It's not the same without him.'

Everything fell into place. He'd inadvertently stolen his own father's dreams and Linda held him responsible for usurping a beloved friend. He couldn't feel worse. 'Do you know where Charlie lives?'

Linda's eyes narrowed. 'Why are you so interested in Charlie all of a sudden? Guilty conscience?'

Eddie shook his head. 'Never mind.' He returned to his list.

'Have you been through the paperwork?' She pointed to the filing cabinet in the corner of the room.

Eddie frowned. It was on his radar, but he hadn't had time. 'Not yet.'

'It's all in there, third drawer down, Charlie's personnel file.' She dropped her feet to the floor with a thud and left.

Eddie moved to the filing cabinet as her footsteps died away. Why hadn't he thought of it? The information had been at his disposal the whole time. He pulled open the third drawer and quickly found Charlie's file, just as Linda said. It was all there, Charlie's address and phone number. Eddie raised his eyebrows — the house was in one of the fanciest parts of town. Maybe he'd take a wander that way in his lunch hour. *Is that a weird thing to do?* He returned to the desk and sat down. Despite his curiosity, he knew he mustn't push it. It was up to his mum now.

At the ringing of the phone, he snatched it up, half hoping it was her telling him she was ready.

'Hey, Eddie.'

Eddie smiled at Anna's voice. 'Hi.'

'Just checking in. How did it go with your mom?'

'Okay.' He leaned back in his chair, glad to have someone to talk to openly. 'She was pretty shocked but took it quite well.'

'Have you tracked down Charlie yet?'

'I've found out where he lives but Mum asked me to wait a few days while she gets used to the idea.'

'Fair enough.'

'How's things with you?' he rushed on, wanting to keep her on the phone.

'Yeah, okay.' Her voice held a hint of emotion. 'Are things any better with the staff?'

Eddie sighed. 'I don't know.'

'Get that opening night sorted. You all need to get behind something.'

He knew she was right. Anna sniffed as if she'd been crying. 'Is everything okay?'

'Ignore me. I've just been dwelling on Mom's impending visit with her new partner.'

'Maybe you'll like this one.'

'It's not about liking them. No one is ever permanent in her life. There's never any point getting to know them because they never stick long enough. She's like Teflon.'

Eddie hesitated, unsure how to respond.

'Anyway,' Anna rushed on, 'let me know how it goes with Charlie.'

She hung up before Eddie could say goodbye. He set down the receiver, annoyed with himself for not finding the right words to comfort her. She'd been so supportive over the situation with his mum, he wanted to return the favour, but there was this weird tension which still hung between them. Maybe she needed some space.

Heeding Anna's advice about uniting his staff, he ventured into the foyer, where Linda was back behind the kiosk in her world of celebrities. Eddie cleared his throat. 'Linda, staff meeting tomorrow morning. We need to make a plan for opening night. I'll call Ben and Hayley.'

Linda looked up, a hint of surprise in her expression, then threw him a nod and returned to her magazine.

* * *

An hour later he was sweltering in the projection room running a test reel through the new projector. The clatter dulled the all-consuming guilt about destroying Charlie's dreams. He was so caught up in his thoughts, he didn't hear his mum enter the room.

'Linda said I'd find you up here,' she shouted over the projector.

Eddie stopped the machine. 'What would I do without her?'

'Still not friends?'

'I'm working on it.' Eddie didn't want to burden his mum with the disquieting discussion he'd had with Linda about Charlie. He didn't want to think about it himself.

'The new projectors look good. If you'd like me to give them a test run . . .'

'Any excuse, eh, Mum?'

'Am I that transparent?' She smiled, but it faded as she cast around the room. 'I think I remember being here. When I came to see you a few weeks ago I got this strange sense I'd been here before. Now I guess I know why. It must have been a special place for Charlie and me.'

'Maybe.'

His mum brought her gaze back to his, her eyes were shining. 'I know I said I wanted a few days, but I think I'm ready.'

'Are you sure?' The fluttering sensation returned to his stomach.

She nodded. 'Contact him. If he's willing, arrange for us to meet here. I want to know the truth about Connie Harris. I want to know the truth about me.'

CHAPTER 60

Eddie stood on the kerb, trying to pluck up the courage to cross the road. He wasn't sure he'd fully absorbed the magnitude of what he was about to do. Charlie Smith was completely unaware that in the next however many minutes a middle-aged man would knock on his door and tell him the fiancée who he'd believed to be dead for the last forty-five years was in fact alive and well. That she'd borne him a son and that the son was standing before him now. It was like something out of a film or an episode of *Oprah*. What if Charlie had a heart condition? A second peek at his personnel file informed Eddie he'd never married. That didn't necessarily mean he was single, or that he didn't have other children. Repercussions exploded like bombs in his mind, their ripples stretching back decades.

And what did *he*, Eddie Humphries, want from this?

There had been times in his childhood when he'd missed having a father, mainly to feel like he fitted in at school, although his friends seemed to accept the absence pretty quickly. He supposed he occasionally thought it might be nice in an abstract way, but he couldn't say he'd ever felt a gaping hole. His mum had always been enough for him, and he accepted things as they were in the way children do.

Sarah hadn't wanted kids. He'd accepted that too — but now he wondered, *What do I want?* It was odd at the age of forty-four to be asking himself that question.

He filed that thought away, too big to examine in this moment, and took in the house before him. It was a substantial double-fronted Victorian building with a walled garden and enviable proportions. Bay windows bulged out on either side of a front door concealed by a porch. The garden was laid to lawn with well-tended flowerbeds bursting with colour. Eddie tried not to gawp as he checked his shirt pocket, feeling the crinkle of the newspaper article between his fingers, the grenade he was about to drop.

Taking a fortifying breath, he crossed the road, opened the gate and approached the front door.

A man answered almost straight away, which startled Eddie. Deep brown eyes met his, questioning. Charlie looked well, trim, his salt-and-pepper hair neatly cut. He was dressed in jeans and a dark blue polo shirt. As silence stretched out between them, his expression slowly faded into a puzzled frown.

Eddie tried to assemble the words he'd rehearsed on the walk over, but they scattered like a dandelion clock caught by a gust of wind. Aware he needed to say something, he forced himself to speak. 'Hello, Mr Smith.' He offered his hand. 'You don't know me. I'm Eddie Humphries, I leased the Tivoli. Linda gave me your address.' It was almost true.

Charlie returned his handshake, his features relaxing into a bemused smile. 'What disaster has befallen the Tivoli to bring you to my door?'

'Nothing like that.' Eddie scratched his head and cast around, lost as to how he should begin. 'Sorry, do you mind if we sit down?'

'Of course, where are my manners? We can sit in the back garden since it's such a beautiful day.'

Eddie followed Charlie through a gate at the side of the property to a patio with a round table and four chairs. The garden beyond was equally well tended with a substantial shed

in one corner and a greenhouse bursting with ripening toma-
toes. He let his gaze meander to the back of the house. There
was no sign of another life, no one to enquire who it was at
the door.

Charlie gestured for him to sit. A large parasol umbrella
provided shade. 'Can I get you anything?'

'I'm fine.' Eddie pulled out a seat, now eager to get on
with it.

'How are the gang at the Tivoli?' Charlie asked, settling
in the chair opposite. 'Not giving you a hard time, I hope?'
There was a twinkle in his eyes.

'They're fine,' Eddie lied. 'I've been focused on the
renovations.'

Charlie leaned forwards, face animated. 'How's that
going? The place needed a good deal of work. The last owners
lost interest, they were blind to the potential. It was a battle
to stay open.'

'It's coming together,' Eddie replied, wondering if Charlie
would approve of the upgrades he'd made. 'I've put in xenon
projectors, a new sound system and given the auditorium a
facelift.'

Charlie smiled. Eddie noticed his dimples, more pro-
nounced than his own. 'Good, I'm pleased to hear it. Those
old Kalees did an excellent service, but you can't rely on carbon arcs these days, they're so inefficient and expensive to
run.'

Eddie nodded, a hint of pride causing his eyes to water.
It was wonderful to discuss the Tivoli with a man who shared
his passion, but they were getting away from the purpose of
his visit. An awkward silence stretched out. Charlie rested his
left hand on the table, and Eddie noticed there was no ring
— perhaps he really wasn't married. Why this pleased him so
much, he couldn't explain. He gathered himself and reached
for the newspaper cutting. 'This is very difficult but I'm here
on another matter.' He lay it out before Charlie. 'I'm not sure
where to begin.'

Charlie's face fell. 'What's the meaning of this?' His tone was sharp, his eyes wary. 'Why are you showing me that?'

Eddie met Charlie's raw gaze. There was a wound there, open and vulnerable. 'I'm showing you this, Charlie, because Connie Harris is my mother.'

'Connie Harris is dead,' Charlie snapped.

Eddie pulled a couple of photos of his mum from his pocket, one taken recently, the other in Plymouth from when Eddie was about seven. He passed them to Charlie. 'My mum is called Grace Humphries. When she was about nineteen, she woke up at a farm in Simonsbath on Exmoor with extensive head injuries. She had no memory of how she'd got there or what her life was before. The farmer told her he found her in a ditch, badly beaten around the head.'

Charlie took a moment to gather himself but studied the photos. He put his hand to his mouth, muttering under his breath, then looked up, his eyes liquid with unspent tears. 'It's her, it's really her.' He shook his head, a tremor in his voice. 'Simonsbath? How can that be? Frank Harris drove off the cliff at Countisbury.'

'They found her near the road. He must have dumped her there believing she was already dead.'

Charlie set the photos on the table and stared into the distance at something past Eddie's shoulder. Eddie waited, unsure how to comfort him.

Eventually Charlie's gaze returned to the photos; he studied them again. 'What happened to her after that?'

Eddie hesitated, fearing the consequences of another shock. He swallowed and pressed on. 'She discovered she was pregnant.' He paused, letting those words sink in.

Charlie's brow furrowed before understanding spread across his features. 'Pregnant?'

'She believes you might be my father. That you and she might have . . .'

'The night I proposed,' Charlie whispered.

'I found the film.'

299

'Sorry, I didn't know what to do with it. I shouldn't have kept nitrate in the building, but I could never bring myself to get rid of it.'

'If you hadn't left the film, I might never have discovered any of this.'

Charlie sat back, regarding him. 'Are you — I mean, all this — is it real? You're not, I don't know, some con artist? I can't work out what the con is, but . . .'

Eddie placed his palms on the table as if displaying he had nothing to hide. 'It's real, Charlie, as real as we are now.'

CHAPTER 61

Charlie studied the two photographs, searching for a reason to doubt what this man was saying, but there was no denying it. The woman in these photos was Connie Harris. His Connie, who in his mind was forever frozen at nineteen. In the image taken in Plymouth at the Hoe, she looked the same, apart from a slight scar across her eye — that smile, that face, a little strained, the auburn hair. In the recent photo she appeared a bright-eyed older woman, very beautiful, the same bobbed curls now shimmering silver. He wanted solitude so he might absorb every detail without appearing strange. Instead, he returned his gaze to the man sitting opposite him — *his son* — an expression of intense concern written across his features.

'Are you okay, Charlie? I know this is a huge shock. Mum's in shock too.'

Mum, the word hit home. Connie was a mum. 'How is she?' Charlie asked. He could hear the splinter in his voice, but he wouldn't lose his composure, not now, not until he was alone with only the walls of his house to bear witness.

Eddie's face broke into a smile and Charlie noticed his dimples. He really could be his son. 'Mum's great, a force to be reckoned with. She's a doctor of film at the university.'

301

Charlie's eyes widened. How far Connie had travelled without him. 'A PhD?' he repeated dumbly, his mind still unable to adjust to the fact they were talking about Connie Harris.

'She spent many years as a cinema projectionist before taking redundancy and going to uni to study film. Now she's quite the academic.' Eddie's face shone with pride.

Charlie startled. 'A projectionist?'

'Yeah, the first female projectionist in Exeter back in the day.'

He cast his mind back to his interview at the Odeon. Charlie couldn't remember the chap's name now, but he recalled his snide demeaner and how he mentioned his female projectionist quit. 'Where did she work?' he asked, knowing the answer.

'The Odeon on Sidwell Street for a while, then we moved to Plymouth, where she worked at the Gaumont. We came back to Exeter after a few years, and she got a job at the Savoy.'

All this time, Connie was in Exeter. The Odeon man had lied to him. Viv saw Connie and that man lied to his face. He shook his head. 'I can't believe how close she's been all these years, how ridiculously close.' His eyes welled up, his emotions hanging by a thread.

'Can I get you anything?' Eddie's tone was gentle. Connie had raised an empathetic man.

Charlie shook his head. More than anything, he wanted to be alone.

'Look, there's no pressure here, Charlie. I know this is a lot to take in and we're all getting used to the idea, but if you'd like to see Mum, she'd like that too.'

A surge of excitement mixed with panic cut through his emotions. 'I'd like that.' His voice tremored again, but this time the tremor contained hope.

Eddie smiled. Those dimples — unfathomable. 'Great.'

'When did you have in mind?'

'How about the Tivoli tomorrow morning? Shall we say 10 a.m.?'

Charlie nodded. 'Is she . . . I mean, is Connie married? Are there more children?'

'No, just me. She's dating, I think. To be honest, Mum's pretty guarded about her private life.'

Charlie felt a flush of warmth flood his face. 'Just curious.'

'I'm sure you'll both have lots of questions, but Mum goes by Grace now. It's the name she's been using since I was born.'

'Grace,' Charlie repeated, attempting to wrap his head around this change. 'I'll try to remember.'

Eddie pushed back his chair. 'I'll leave you in peace.' He picked up the newspaper article and put it in his pocket.

Charlie offered the photos.

'You can keep those, if you like.'

'Thanks.' He laid them back on the table, an immeasurable gift. 'I'll see you tomorrow.'

'We'll be there. I can see myself out.'

He watched Eddie make his way back across the lawn. Charlie sat for a long while, staring after him, until his gaze returned to the photos. Scooping them up, he walked inside the house. His hand shook as he picked up the kitchen telephone.

The line rang on until the click of connection, a short delay then a muffled voice answered.

'Viv?'

'Who is this? Do you know it's . . .' There was a pause. 'Gone one in the morning?'

'It's Charlie.'

'Charlie?' Her voice more alert. 'Is everything okay?'

'Are you sitting down?'

'I'm in bed, it's the middle of the night here in Melbourne.'

'Sorry. This is too important to wait. Is Michael with you?' He could feel the thrum of his heart knocking against his chest.

'Hang on, I'm putting you on speakerphone so Michael can hear.'

'What's going on?' Michael's voice, thick with sleep, came on the line.

'I've had a visit from a man called Eddie. He says he's mine and Connie's son. He showed me photos of Connie, recent ones. It's her, it's really her. She had amnesia and didn't remember anything before the night she disappeared, but she's alive, Viv, she's alive.' Charlie stopped, his voice overcome with emotion.

The line went quiet before Michael spoke. 'Are you certain, Charlie?'

'As sure as I can be. I'm meeting her tomorrow.'

Another pause, then Viv's voice, as choked up as his. 'Phone us once you've seen her. We'll be on the first flight home.'

304

CHAPTER 62

Grace peered through the glass doors at the front of the Tivoli. All was quiet. She stood back, capturing her reflection. She'd chosen a casual floral summer dress with cap sleeves and her white tennis shoes. *Too casual?* She was never normally this insecure. It had taken her a ridiculous amount of time to get ready that morning. This man had been her first love. She couldn't help wanting to look her best.

Hearing footsteps from behind, Grace turned to see Eddie walking down the alleyway in his jeans and T-shirt, a little unkempt but tall and, to her eyes, handsome. *What had Charlie made of their son?*

'Hey, Mum, have you been waiting long?' He kissed her cheek.

'Not long.'

'How are you feeling?' Eddie pulled out his keys and unlocked the doors.

'A little apprehensive. Okay, a lot.'

'Me too, and I'm sure Charlie is feeling the same way.' He held open the door, gesturing for her to go through.

'What if he doesn't show up?' Grace stood in the foyer, casting around for something familiar from her past.

'He will.'

'You sound very confident.'

Eddie shrugged. 'What man isn't going to show up to meet the woman he wanted to marry.'

Grace grimaced. 'What if I don't measure up?'

'Mum.' Eddie squeezed her shoulder.

'I'm being ridiculous, I know. Can I go up to the projection room, Ed?'

'Sure. Is that where you want to meet him?'

Grace approached the door and nodded. 'I think so. Is there something useful I can do while I wait?'

'Not really.'

'I'll tidy something.' She threw him a bright smile she couldn't feel.

Grace stood for a moment in the dark stairwell. Taking a deep breath, she climbed the stairs and pushed open the projection room door.

Sunlight flooded in at the window. Dropping her tote by the winding bench, she leaned against it, her gaze gliding over the space, lingering at the old leather armchair.

Grace stopped in the middle of the room and closed her eyes, allowing her other senses to engage. There was nothing. No memory, no flashback, no apparition. She was just a woman standing in a projection room. Opening her eyes, she crossed to the chair and sank into its worn cushion. Again, she closed her eyes and admitted to herself she was afraid. Afraid to fill the gaping hole of her past, afraid to discover the life she'd missed. Afraid to meet Connie Harris. Before she could plunge too deeply into her melancholy, the sound of Eddie opening the front doors snatched her attention. Charlie was here.

Standing, Grace searched desperately for something to occupy her shaking hands. Muffled voices from below drifted into the room. 'Not yet,' she whispered. 'I'm not ready.'

Grace stilled her fingers as footsteps echoed on the stairs. A pause so heavy, she could hear it and then a gentle tap.

She opened her mouth to answer, but nothing emerged. Her limbs were liquid. All she could do was stand, resolute, with her back to the door, staring at the chair.

The door swished open, and his presence filled the room. Grace forced herself to turn around.

It was him. The man who haunted her kisses. Older and greyer, but unmistakably him.

CHAPTER 63

She was caught in shadow, the glare from the window obscuring her face, but Charlie knew it was Connie from her silhouette and the way she held herself.

'Hello.' His voice didn't sound like his own. He became aware of his skin, his hair, the way the air particles touched his body.

She stepped forwards, revealing herself in the beam of light. Charlie sucked in a breath, shocked by recognition. Connie was stunning. She lifted a hand to tuck a stray curl behind her ear, the gesture so familiar he watched the years fall away.

'Grace.' She offered her hand. 'But I think you knew me as Connie.'

Charlie approached, mechanical as he lifted his hand to meet hers. 'Grace,' he whispered. 'It's incredible to meet you.'

She smiled, that same smile, but it didn't reach her eyes. She was still wary.

Extracting her hand from his, she stepped away to the winding bench. Charlie cast around the room.

'Has it changed much?' she asked, studying him.

'From when we were . . . ?'

She nodded.

He noticed the new projectors, impressed with the changes Eddie had made. *His son.* 'The projectors are different, of course, but otherwise, no, not really. This chair was even here then.'

Her eyes lit up. 'How funny.'

Charlie thrust his hands in his pockets, shy. Now was not the time to tell her they'd made love on it.

'Did we spend time together, up here?'

'Yes.' The answer caught in his throat. 'Up here and in the auditorium.'

He watched her process this information. Her eyes dimmed a little as if she was disappointed by her inability to recall.

'You don't remember me?'

'It's hard to explain. I didn't have a name to put to your face, or a location. Only a sense of you. I feel that sense now.'

'Is it a good sense?'

Her brow furrowed. 'It's complicated, this agony of what might have been.'

Charlie nodded. 'I've lived with that agony for forty-five years.'

'I'm sorry, Charlie.' Her voice splintered.

'It's not your fault.'

She studied her hands. 'No, but I'm sorry for us both all the same.'

A moment of silence stretched out.

He watched her regain her composure, put herself back together. She'd grown so sophisticated, but Connie remained in the way she moved, in her eyes and smile.

'You must have so many questions.'

She lifted her gaze to his. 'The article mentioned I have a brother?'

Charlie smiled. 'Michael. I'm in touch with him. He married Viv, she was your best friend. The pair of you used to run rings around Reynolds.' She looked aghast; he realised he was sharing too much, too fast. 'Michael lives in Melbourne now. He and Viv fancied retiring in the sun.'

'Melbourne?' That frown, so familiar, the line between her eyes, deeper but still enchanting. 'Does he know?'

'I told him. I hope you don't mind.'

She shook her head. 'Is he older, younger?'

'Two years older.'

Her brow furrowed again. 'I tried to find the truth of my life, but my efforts always ended in pain. All I knew was someone from my past beat me up. It wasn't an encouraging place to start.' She met his gaze. 'I had Eddie to think about, to keep safe. I couldn't go on waiting, I had to live.'

His arms twitched to hold her. He masked his dismay, realising the sacrifices she'd been forced to make. 'It must have been hard, raising Eddie alone.' Charlie hesitated over his next words. 'Is he really our son?'

'I believe so. I assume we . . .'

'Here, the night I proposed.'

She cast around the room as if she were trying to imagine it. Her gaze settled on the chair. 'Here?' Mischief replaced anguish in her eyes.

Charlie couldn't stop the smile that spread across his lips. Unable to trust himself to speak, he nodded.

She laughed. How he'd missed that laugh. It was the happiest sound, the best sound. Unexpectedly, his eyes filled with tears.

Noticing his changed expression, Grace's laughter died. She moved to take his hand. Her touch like a bolt, the elixir of life. 'You didn't marry?'

Charlie took back his hand and walked to the window, standing with his back to her so she couldn't see his emotion. 'I came close, but I couldn't get over you.'

Her footsteps suggested she was just behind.

'What about you?'

'Eddie was my priority, and I suppose I could never fully give myself to someone until I knew the truth about his father, but the years slid by, and that truth never revealed itself until now.'

Charlie turned around, finding her inches from him. She didn't move. Long-buried stirrings resurfaced. A mixture of loss and elation crashed in his heart. He still loved her. How could that be after all this time? He wouldn't say it, she'd recoil, and he'd lose her all over again. Instead, he took a deep breath and forced his eyes to meet hers. 'I want you to know I'm so glad you're alive in this world. That knowledge alone makes me happy. I say this without expectation, but do you think, when the dust settles, we might get to know each other?'

She smiled, eyes blazing. 'I'd like that, Charlie. I'd like that very much.'

CHAPTER 64

'Morning, Eddie,' Linda said in a tone that almost constituted friendly. 'Why are you staring at the projection room door?'

Eddie glanced briefly in her direction. The heat of summer did nothing to deter her from her regulation black outfit. 'No reason.'

'Okay.' She rolled her eyes and disappeared into the staff cloakroom.

Next, Ben sloped through the door. Eddie did a double-take. He'd shaved off his dreads. 'All right, boss?'

'Morning, Ben. No Hayley?'

Ben shrugged, then Hayley appeared, red-rimmed eyes settling on Ben. Head down, she stormed to the cloakroom. Eddie threw Ben a questioning look. He shrugged again and disappeared into the gents.

Eddie's gaze returned to the projection room door. They'd been about half an hour. Was that a good sign?

'A watched door never opens.' Linda smirked and took her seat at the kiosk. 'Are we having this staff meeting or not?'

Eddie grimaced, he'd almost forgotten. 'Yes,' he said, trying to sound convincing. He was about to join Linda when the projection room door opened and Charlie emerged, his expression inscrutable.

'Charlie.' Linda grinned, barrelling up to him and giving him a hug.

'Hello, Linda, how are you?'

'You didn't tell us Charlie was here.' Linda directed her reproach at Eddie.

'I was seeing an old friend,' Charlie explained. He glanced at Eddie too and smiled. *Were those tears in his eyes?*

Before Eddie could ask if things were okay, Hayley returned from the cloakroom, her glum face also lighting up at the sight of Charlie. Ben was next to emerge, the presence of Charlie causing whatever had arisen between him and Hayley to recede. Eddie watched the happy reunion, wishing he knew Charlie's secret. Feeling like a spare part, he decided to check on his mum.

She was sitting on the old leather chair he still hadn't got rid of, staring at the wall. Her face was serene, but he could tell she'd been crying.

'Is everything okay?'

She smiled; it was a little wistful. 'I think so. It was lovely to meet him.'

'And . . .'

'We'll see each other again, as friends.'

Eddie's expression gave him away.

'What did you think was going to happen? That we'd run into each other's arms to a soundtrack of Whitney Houston? We need to get to know each other again.'

'Sure, I know that.' Eddie studied the floor to hide his embarrassment. His mum pretty much described the scenario he'd entertained. 'Charlie's downstairs with the staff, it's quite the reunion. I was thinking about the opening night. Would you mind if I invited him?'

'Of course not.'

'He's good at bringing them together.'

His mum set her hand on his arm. 'Don't give up, Ed.'

* * *

When Eddie and his mum returned to the foyer, only Linda remained at her kiosk, engrossed in *Hello* magazine. She looked up.

'Blimey, you're Connie Harris?' Linda was on her feet, her face so animated Eddie worried she'd pull a muscle.

His mum laughed. 'So it would seem.' She turned to Eddie. 'I'll be off. Don't forget what I said. Bye, Linda.' She kissed his cheek and made a hasty retreat.

Linda stared after her, shaking her head. Eventually she set her gaze on Eddie, a softness in her eyes. 'Charlie said you reunited him with his lost love. I can't believe it's your mum.'

Eddie raised his eyebrows, surprised Charlie confided in Linda. 'Yeah, well, there's a bit more to it than that.'

Linda nodded. 'Sorry I've given you a rough ride.'

Speechless, Eddie nodded too. 'Thanks.'

'Ben and Hayley are in the auditorium. Do you want to fetch them while I put on a brew? It's about time we got this opening night sorted.'

Eddie flicked on the auditorium lights and cast around, finally spotting the hunched pair in the back row. A smile tugged at his lips. He cleared his throat twice before they noticed him. They disentangled themselves sheepishly and trailed back to the foyer, fingers entwined.

Linda was waiting with a tray and four mugs of tea when they returned to the kiosk. 'I wasn't sure how you took yours, so I guessed.'

Eddie accepted the proffered mug.

'So, opening night film ideas.' From her perch, Linda had clearly decided she was running the meeting. Eddie was happy for her to take the lead if it helped bring the team together. 'Ben, Hayley, what are your thoughts?'

Ben ran his hand over his freshly shaved head. 'How about *Seven*?'

Linda gave a dismissive wave. 'Too gory for opening night.'

Eddie agreed. They needed something with wide appeal.

She turned her kohled gaze on Hayley. 'What do you think?'

Hayley shifted from side to side, then went bright pink and said, '*The Truth About Cats and Dogs*.'

Linda frowned. 'Too sappy.'

Again, Eddie agreed, although he did have a crush on Janeane Garofalo. She reminded him of Anna. *I really should call her*. He blew on his tea and took a sip. Linda had got it spot on: milk, one sugar.

Next it was Eddie's turn to come under Linda's scrutiny. He shrugged. 'You know my idea, *Cinema Paradiso*.'

Linda nodded. 'I agree.'

Eddie almost spat out his tea.

'I borrowed the VHS from Blockbuster the other night. It's got it all: lovable characters, romance, nostalgia. A perfect opening-night film. All those in favour?'

Eddie's hand shot up and Linda's did too. Ben and Hayley looked at each other and followed. Linda gave a satisfied nod. 'Excellent, motion carried. Now let's set a date and get this cinema ready.'

CHAPTER 65

A week later, Anna hesitated outside Grace's office. Once the location of stolen moments with Graham, now she'd find her new supervisor behind that door. It left her with a confusing mix of melancholy and excitement.

'Morning, Anna.' Pip threw her a smile from behind her desk. She gave the spider plant Anna was carrying a quizzical look. 'Grace is expecting you. It's lovely to have her back.'

Anna returned her smile and glanced at the spider plant in her hand. Eddie once mentioned his mom liked plants and she thought it would replace the ones which had died under Graham's care, not to mention expunging his ghost. Maybe she'd bought the plant for herself.

With Pip still eyeing her, Anna knocked on the door.

Grace was standing on a chair reorganising her book-shelves. She'd thrown the window open, letting in the buzz of campus activity. Her silver curls were artfully dishevelled, and she wore a pair of wide-leg jeans, her signature tennis shoes and a loose-fitting blouse. Anna tried not to stare as she cast around the rest of the room. There were potted plants vying for space on every surface, and three vases of flowers adorned the desk, filing cabinet and window ledge. It wasn't far off resembling a florist's. Nosferatu had been replaced with a poster from *Casablanca*. The room had already been purged of all signs of Graham, it seemed.

With an elegant sweep, Grace stepped down and smiled. She pointed at the plant. 'Is that for me?'

Heat spread into Anna's cheeks. 'A welcome-back gift, but I can see you already have plenty of those.'

'You can never have too many and spider plants are wonderful, you literally can't kill them.' Grace took the plant from Anna's reluctant hands. 'Thank you. Make yourself at home.'

Anna perched on a plastic chair and watched Grace rearrange the window ledge to make room for her gift. 'What beautiful flowers.'

'I've been spoiled. Those are from Pip, these are from Ed.' She gestured to the vase on her desk and sniffed the mimosa. 'He knows all my favourites.' She turned to the vase of wildflowers on the window ledge. 'And these are from a mystery admirer.' Grace's eyes twinkled. 'It's so lovely out, shall we grab a coffee before we get started?'

'Sure.' Anna stood, too abruptly sending her rucksack crashing to the floor. She wished she could stop behaving like a thirteen-year-old fangirl.

Grace picked up her tote. 'Great.'

They set out across campus. Although the students wouldn't return for a couple of weeks, everywhere she looked there was a hive of activity. Lawns were being cut, rooms cleaned, a sense of anticipation fizzed in the air.

Anna tried to relax. She couldn't work out if her nerves related to her admiration for Grace, or because since the evening she'd showed Eddie the article, she hadn't been able to stop thinking about him.

'I wanted to thank you, Anna, for finding that article and sharing it with Ed.' Grace met her gaze. 'It meant a lot.'

'Really, it was no problem.'

'It's opened quite the can of worms, but in a good way.'

'I can't imagine what you must be feeling.'

Grace glanced at her hands. 'My main concern is Eddie. Finding his father after all these years . . . It will take some adjustment to our dynamic.'

'I'm sure Eddie is taking it in his stride.'

Grace touched her arm. 'I'm so glad he has you to talk to. It's important he doesn't bottle this up.'

Gratified, Anna smiled. In truth, she hadn't heard from Eddie since he'd met his father, although an invitation to the Tivoli opening had arrived in the post the previous day. She'd hoped he'd confide in her. 'He's one of the good ones,' she said in response to Grace's expectant gaze.

Grace smiled with pride. 'Are you coming to the opening tonight?'

Anna hesitated. 'I'm not sure . . .'

Grace stopped walking. 'Please come. If my dunder-headed son hasn't been in touch, it's not because he doesn't want you there, it's because he's scared.'

Scared of what? Anna was about to ask, when a taxi pulled up next to them and a woman flew out in a flurry of silk scarves and strong perfume, calling her name. She did a double-take. 'Mom? What are you doing here?'

Her mother grinned, her eyes focused on Grace.

Grace stepped forwards. 'Bea? Is it really you?'

CHAPTER 66

The coffee tasted a little bitter as Grace sipped from her cup and studied Bea across the cafeteria table. First Charlie and now her old friend. It was as if her past were a ghost train set to derail the carriage she was riding. Who would turn up next — Joe? She hadn't thought about him for decades. Sanders? God, that man, what a creep. Mercifully, Anna inherited Bea's thick brown hair and warm eyes, but there was some-thing of Sanders in her sharp Roman nose. It occurred to her again how much Anna had in common with Ed. Raised by determined mothers in the absence of a father. Although in Charlie's case the absence was unintentional. She recalled his face at their reunion, his features at once so happy and yet so mired in grief.

'It's wonderful to see you.' Bea broke into her thoughts. 'You haven't changed a bit. What's your secret?'

Grace laughed. 'You flatter me.'

Bea winked. 'Well, I always had a soft spot where you're concerned.' Her features lapsed into a frown. 'I know I've said it before, but I'll always be sorry I left you the way I did.'

'It's all water under the bridge now.'

'Maybe, but I want you to understand it had nothing to do with you. I was scared of being a mother, so I ran off

319

with the first man who showed any interest because I believed I needed a man to be a father for my child. I might have sounded full of bravado, but I don't think I've ever been more petrified in my life.'

Grace reached for her friend's hand. 'Why didn't you tell me?'

'I was ashamed. I'm not like you, Grace. You're such a fighter and a wonderful mother. You and Eddie had this incredible bond, and I knew I'd never feel that for my child. I wasn't capable.'

'You're being too hard on yourself.'

Bea shook her head emphatically. 'I'm really not, ask poor Anna. And you, gosh, you were someone to be admired. The way you got on with life in Plymouth. You had a job, Eddie in school, you made a home.'

'It was our home, thanks to you.'

Bea waved her bejewelled hand. 'Money was always easy to come by, that was one skill I had. Did you know I was in love with you?'

Grace felt a flush of warmth hit her cheeks. She'd always suspected, but hearing those words out loud, Grace realised the pain she must have unintentionally put Bea through. 'Why didn't you say something?'

'You didn't feel the same way, and I hated the thought of making things weird between us.' Bea glanced out of the window before bringing her gaze back to Grace. 'I've spent most of my life running away from my true self, and now when I've finally found a relationship that's honest, my daughter won't have a bar of it. I can't blame her.'

'Have you told Anna about Miranda?'

'Not yet. I was planning to today but then, well . . . Then I saw you.'

'Tell her. Anna thinks—'

'Anna thinks I'm a harlot and a useless mother. Is it any surprise when I've done such a convincing job of pretending that's who I am? Anyway . . .' Bea leaned forward with one of her determined looks, communicating the subject was closed. 'I want to hear more about you and this mystery man. I can't believe you finally found out the truth. You must be overwhelmed.'

'It's been quite a week.'

Bea squeezed Grace's hand. 'I can't tell you how good it is to see you and know you're part of Anna's life. And Anna and Eddie are friends. It's incredible.'

'I think Ed would like them to be more than friends, but you didn't hear that from me.'

Bea grinned. 'Tell me more.'

* * *

An hour later, Grace returned to her office to find Anna sitting outside, gaze focused on a book.

Anna removed her glasses. Her eyes were a little bloodshot. 'Where's Mom?'

'She's gone to her hotel to freshen up. Honestly, I didn't expect you to wait. If you want to go and see her now, we can reschedule. I feel guilty for whisking her away.'

Anna shrugged. 'You didn't do the whisking. Anyway, I'll see her later. I wanted to apologise: I may have seemed a little childish when Mom turned up. It's never been easy with us.'

Grace beckoned her into the office. 'What parent–child relationship is ever easy?'

Anna smiled. 'Yours. I envy what you and Eddie have. He adores you.'

'I don't know about that.'

'He does. You're there for each other, he knows you've got his back and he enjoys your company. My mom is useless. She's about to announce her engagement to her fourth husband. She's nothing but a raging cliché.'

It was hard to hear the pain in Anna's voice. Grace gestured for her to sit and pulled up her desk chair opposite, meeting Anna's gaze. 'Your mum saved my life.'

Anna's brow furrowed.

'It was tough after Eddie was born. I struggled to find enough work to keep a roof over our heads. Your mother plucked me from the gutter and gave me a home when I needed it most. She may not always have made the best choices, but she is a good person, and she loves you.'

Anna picked at a loose thread on her sleeve. 'I didn't know.'

'How about we ditch this meeting? Go and spend some time with your mum and I'll see you at the grand opening later. Don't forget, seven o'clock.'

Anna looked a little crestfallen. Grace watched as she gathered up her bag and headed to the door.

'Anna,' Grace called before she disappeared, 'keep an open mind when you meet your mum's new partner. You might be surprised.'

CHAPTER 67

Charlie hovered outside the Tivoli, marvelling at how little it had changed over the years. The same row of glass-fronted doors, their frames now freshly painted. It once held all his dreams and now it was about to deliver again. Inside was his son and this evening, he'd see her again. He'd see Connie.

Unable to conjure an excuse for calling, he was about to leave when Linda pushed open the doors. 'Hasn't anyone told you about loitering down alleyways?'

Charlie smiled. 'Morning, Linda. I thought I'd see how the plans for the grand opening were coming along.'

'It's all hands on deck. Are you going to stand out here all day gawping or come in and help? I've got a list of jobs that need the Charlie touch.'

Inside, Ben and Hayley were hanging bunting. The kiosk was fully stocked, and the foyer gleamed with fresh polish. Charlie's gaze drifted to the open projection room door.

'He's up there checking the film is ready for the hundredth time.' Linda rolled her eyes but there was a smile behind her sarcastic exterior. 'Is he really your son? I mean, I can see it now, those dimples.'

'He is.' Charlie was surprised by the hint of pride he felt.

'You dark horse, Charlie Smith. Go on, you go up. He'll be pleased to see you.'

* * *

Charlie paused at the bottom of the steep stairs. In all the years he'd climbed them since Connie's disappearance, he never could have dreamed he'd find their son at the top. It baffled him, what he'd now gained out of so much loss. If he dwelled on the injustice too long, pain would engulf him. There'd been nothing terrible about his life. He'd worked in a job he truly loved, had friends who felt like family, travelled, had brief love affairs and inherited enough from his family home to buy the house where nothing bad could ever happen. *Yes, for her.* But he'd also been stuck.

'Linda, is that you?' His son's voice from the projection room pulled him from his reverie.

'No, it's . . .' Charlie didn't know what to call himself.

Eddie appeared at the top of the stairs; his lips broke into a smile that sparked his eyes. 'Charlie.'

'I thought I'd see how you're getting along.'

Eddie beckoned to him. 'Come up.'

The scene in the projection room was achingly familiar. The clank of running projectors, the open window for much-needed air. Eddie had done an exceptional job of making the most of the room's mean proportions. Charlie noticed the new shelves and useful hooks for spools. Everything was well organised. He was a little ashamed at the way he'd left things, but his despondency about retirement had allowed him to slack off. Perhaps it was a blessing the owners chose Eddie and not him to carry the cinema forwards.

'I'm checking the reels for tonight.'

He could detect a hint of anxiety in Eddie's raised voice.

'It's going to be a great success.'

Eddie threw him a smile, but it was a little uncertain.

'Can I help at all?' Charlie offered.

'You could get the other machine warmed up.'

Grateful for the distraction, Charlie let the mechanics of film claim his focus. For the next hour, they worked side by side. Father and son.

* * *

At 6 p.m. Charlie stood before his bedroom mirror unsure which shirt he should wear. It was ridiculous to be in this state over seeing a woman, but this wasn't just any woman. What he wanted from this evening, he had no idea, to get to know her again, to understand the person she'd become. He and Eddie had studiously avoided talking about Connie, even though Charlie was desperate to grill him about every aspect of her life. It was Connie's story and he'd have to wait until she wanted to share it.

Opting for the blue, he checked his watch. Viv and Michael must be nearly here.

His attention was called by the chime of the doorbell. Descending the stairs, a smile spread across his lips as he anticipated seeing them. It had been over a year. He opened the door and there they were. Before he had time to drink them in, Viv flung herself into his arms. The years and five children had filled Viv out, but her smile was as radiant as ever.

'Charlie, it's so good to see you.' She stepped into the hallway to allow Michael, his same willowy self, to drag their suitcase through. 'Don't you look smart?' Viv commented as Charlie led them to the kitchen.

'I'm attending the opening of the newly restored Tivoli this evening.'

Viv gripped his arm. 'That's tonight? Can we come? I'm dying to see her.' He'd run up a fortune speaking with Viv on the phone over the last week.

'I thought you'd want to rest this evening. Aren't you tired from your flight?'

'We're not tired, are we, Michael? Come on, Charlie, do you really think we'd want to wait?'

Charlie checked his watch again. 'We need to leave in ten minutes.'

'Ten minutes! Oh, lord, I look a fright. Where's the bathroom? I can't meet Connie looking like this.' Viv headed to the stairs.

'It's Grace now,' he called after her.

Michael pulled out a kitchen chair. 'How did she look, Charlie?'

He took a seat too. 'Wonderful.' He hesitated, unsure if he was ready to share the depth of his feelings, but then the words tumbled out. 'I'm still in love with her. I couldn't tell her, of course, but it's true.'

'I can't wrap my head around it. I never thought this day would come. What about the boy? My nephew. Your son.'

'Eddie. He's great and he's hardly a boy. He must be in his forties.'

Michael nodded. 'You missed a lot.'

'I did. We all did.'

'Do you think it's wise, us coming tonight? If truth be told, I'm a little anxious. I don't know how Con's going to react to me. Viv's so excited I'm worried she'll overwhelm Connie too.'

Charlie met his friend's gaze. 'I share your concerns. All we can do is let Connie — I mean Grace — decide.' He was getting used to it, the name change, perhaps because it suited her so well. He'd always said Connie moved with grace. It somehow captured her essence.

Five minutes later, Viv returned with her signature slick of lipstick in pillar box red.

The three of them emerged from the house to keep a date with the woman who'd brought them together, dug the foundations of their friendship and left a gaping hole in her wake.

CHAPTER 68

Grace took a moment outside the Tivoli before alerting her son to her presence. The old cinema was festooned with bunting billowing in the gentle breeze. The alleyway leading to Fore Street would always be a little drab, but someone had swept away the usual dropped cigarette butts and discarded litter. The neon sign at the top was lit up, ready to welcome in this new era.

Eddie appeared on the other side of the double doors and let her in. 'You look great.' She glanced down at the dark green dress she'd chosen.

'Thanks, Ed. You don't scrub up too bad yourself.' Grace was amused by how much effort her son had gone to. He'd had a haircut and his usual five o'clock shadow was nowhere to be seen.

'Are you nervous?' she asked as they stepped into the foyer, where more bunting and balloons adorned the walls.

Eddie shrugged but his eyes gave him away. 'Yeah, I guess I am.'

She took his arm. 'It looks amazing.'

'Thanks. How are you holding up?'

'I'm nervous too.'

'Charlie?'

He'd invaded her thoughts too often over the last few days. She didn't want to let on to Eddie, but seeing Charlie sent her equilibrium into freefall. Enough that she'd broken things off with Dom. It didn't seem fair to carry on when she couldn't say she was entirely available. How ridiculous though. Eddie was studying her with his warm eyes. 'It will be nice to see him again.'

He nodded.

'What can I do to help? Where are Linda and the others?'

'They'll be here in a minute. Linda popped home to change.' He shrugged. 'I think everything is under control.'

'Then don't let me keep you. I'll have a look around while I'm waiting.'

'Thanks. I'll be in the projection room if you need me.'

Alone in the foyer, Grace let the air settle around her. She wandered into the auditorium and down the aisle, easing herself into a seat at the front. The magical hush took her back to her usherette days at the Odeon. That tranquillity before the crowds piled in.

Grace took a deep breath to quell her nerves. She didn't know why she was so anxious about seeing Charlie again. It felt like too much pressure, even though she wasn't sure where the pressure was coming from.

The low hum of voices took her back to the foyer. Linda was dressed in a black-velvet tube dress and platform heels, and her hair bore her trademark streak of pink. She was talking to Anna, who looked lovely in a pair of black wide-leg trousers and a red floaty top which brought out the copper in her hair. They turned in her direction. 'Wow, look at you two.'

Just then Eddie emerged from the projection room. 'Anna, hi.' Grace watched her son and knew he had it bad. She suppressed a smile.

'We'd better get the drinks ready.' Linda made for the cloakroom.

'I'll help.' Anna disappeared after her.

'Grace.' Bea emerged through the double doors, gliding down the steps, a huge smile lighting up her face.

Grace turned to Eddie, who was looking at them, bemused. 'You probably don't remember my friend Bea. We lived with her in Exeter and briefly in Plymouth when you were little. She's Anna's mum.'

Eddie shook his head and offered up a distracted smile.

Bea took his arm. 'So, this is Eddie all grown up. Don't you look like your mother? Delicious. Come with me, I want to talk to you about my daughter.'

Eddie threw Grace an alarmed look as Bea dragged him away. Smiling after them, she glanced to the door. Charlie walked in with a woman. Grace couldn't help but frown. *Had he brought a date?* As she tried to work out how she felt, the woman rushed in her direction, a look of pure elation on her face. She pulled up short. Charlie hastened to her side.

'This is Viv. You were very good friends when we all worked here together.'

Grace studied the woman who stood before her. Red lips, golden hair — although perhaps now it was out of a bottle. 'The bus,' Grace whispered. 'You were the woman on the bus.'

'You remember me?' Viv looked earnest. 'I screamed at the driver to let me off, but by the time he did, you'd gone.' Her face fell.

Grace didn't know what to say. The memory of that day was still potent even though the bus had only played a small part. Another missed opportunity to find her true life.

Viv recovered and pointed to the kiosk. 'We used to load up our trays over there.'

Grace followed her gaze as if she expected to see the shadow of her young self, this woman she couldn't remember.

'Michael will be here in a minute,' Viv continued. 'He's outside having a smoke.'

Understanding slowly dawned. No one had mentioned her brother was in the country, but if Viv was here, of course he would be too.

Charlie's brow furrowed. 'I hope we're not bombarding you. Michael and Viv just arrived. We thought—'

'It's fine.' Grace forced a smile to mask her inner turmoil. Before she could stop them, tears filled her eyes.

'Please don't be annoyed with Charlie,' Viv cut in. 'We couldn't wait to see you.'

'I'm not annoyed.' Grace tried to recover. 'I wasn't expecting . . .' Her sentence died as a tall man appeared at their side, a head full of silver curls, exactly like her own.

'Here he is.' Viv took Michael's hand.

He was nervous, a frown line etched between his eyes. 'It's incredible to see you, Con.'

Grace gazed at him. There were no words to express how she was feeling. She took a step backwards and then another until she bumped into the kiosk. 'I'm sorry,' she whispered and rushed to the exit.

Outside, she steadied herself against the wall, searching for memories that wouldn't come.

Patrons were arriving thick and fast now — including, she noticed, a man from the local press with a camera slung over his shoulder. Grace tried to remain inconspicuous, but the pressure building in her head was incredible. She massaged her temples and steadied her breath.

Eddie drew up at her side. 'Mum, are you okay? I spoke to Charlie and met my uncle.'

Grace gave her son a tremulous smile. 'I didn't know Michael would be here.'

He wrapped his arms around her. She looked up at him through watery eyes. 'They're all so excited to see me and I don't know how to be the person they remember.'

'Maybe you don't need to be that person,' he whispered. 'Maybe you need to let them get to know you now.'

'What if I can't meet their expectations? I'm not Connie Harris anymore, I don't know her.'

'You're Grace Humphries and she's pretty great.'

Grace squeezed his arm. 'I'm so proud of you.' Drying her eyes, she stepped back and smiled. 'Who'd have thought after all these years of being just us two, we'd suddenly find ourselves surrounded?'

Eddie returned her smile. 'It's kind of nice.'

She took his arm, and they walked back to the cinema.

As they crossed the threshold, Grace spied Anna in the corner of the foyer, clutching a glass of wine. She stopped to look at her son. 'Do you love her?'

Eddie frowned. 'Who?'

Grace inclined her head in Anna's direction. 'Because if you do, for pity's sake tell her. Life's too short.'

Her son winced. 'It's complicated and right now, I've got a speech to make, Mum.'

CHAPTER 69

In their brief absence, the foyer filled with guests. Eddie disappeared to prepare for his speech. Grace noticed a ribbon had been tied across the auditorium doors ready to be cut by the local mayor. She searched out Charlie, who was chatting to Linda. There was no sign of Michael or Viv, and Anna had vanished too.

Bea's arm threaded through hers. 'Have you got a moment?' she whispered.

'Only one, I don't want to miss Eddie's speech.'

They stepped outside again, where an elegant woman with thick hair plaited and coiled into a high bun was finishing a cigarette.

'Grace,' Bea said, beaming. 'This is Miranda.'

'So, you're the famous Grace.' Miranda dropped her cigarette and offered her hand. 'Bea has barely stopped talking about you in the last twenty-four hours.' Her drawl was southern and warm. She threw Bea a wink.

Grace took her hand. 'It's been lovely to see Bea again after all this time and to know she's happy.' She turned to Bea. 'Have you introduced Miranda to Anna?'

Bea grimaced. 'Not yet.'

'You should, and soon.'

The tinkle of a glass caught her attention. Grace beckoned for them to follow and they returned to the foyer, where Eddie was launching into his speech. She beamed with pride. For a moment his eyes settled on hers then moved on. She knew who's face he was searching for. Anna was at the back of the crowd, beaming too, her gaze locked with Eddie's.

Applause followed, then it was the mayor's turn. Grace sensed a presence at her side. She glanced up. Michael, those eyes a mirror of her own. *Her brother.* It didn't seem possible. They stayed side by side for the remainder of the speeches, Grace stealing shy looks at this man who'd shared her childhood.

Gradually guests filed into the auditorium.

'Can we talk, Con?'

Grace cast around for Eddie. He was heading up to the projection room, Charlie in his wake. 'Where's Viv?'

Michael pointed to his wife, who'd joined Hayley at the doors, taking ticket stubs and ushering guests through. 'Old habits.' He grinned. Grace felt she should know that smile. It was rather charming, but it was the smile of a stranger.

They made their way to the exit.

In the twilight, Grace leaned against the wall, waiting to hear what her brother wanted to say.

'I'm sorry. Sorry I left you with our dad, sorry I wasn't there when I should have been. I can't help feeling this tragedy is all my fault.'

She studied his earnest face, recognising something of herself in that furrowed brow. But his apology didn't resonate, how could it when she didn't know the details of his misdemeanour? 'I don't know what you think you did, Michael, but it's in the past. We can talk about it tomorrow. Tonight, let's just be us.'

They fell silent for a moment, relief in his eyes. The faint boom of the film vied with the hubbub of a Friday night on Fore Street. There were so many questions and yet she couldn't conjure a single one.

Michael met her gaze. 'I'm not trying to interfere, but he still loves you, you know — Charlie.' He shook his head. 'I've never seen a man so ripped apart by grief. When I think what he went through, if I'd lost Viv the way he lost you . . .'

Grace kept quiet, taking in his words and storing them up in her heart. 'I'm looking forward to getting to know him again, and you and Viv too.'

Michael smiled. 'We'd love that.'

She peeled herself from the wall. 'We'd better go in or we'll miss the film.'

Viv was waiting at the doors to the auditorium. She offered a nervous smile as Grace and Michael approached. Grace wanted to put her at ease, but no words came. Instead, she took her hand and gave it a squeeze.

Inside the auditorium, the trailers were underway. Michael and Viv found seats, but Grace chose to stand, leaning against the wall. Her gaze lifted to the projection room window, wondering at Ed and Charlie up there, and how they were getting along. A memory, gauzy and insubstantial, pierced her mind. She closed her eyes and let it come. Her younger self standing at the back of the auditorium, gaze persistently drifting to the projection room window, but this time it wasn't at the Odeon, it was here, she was certain. A small smile spread across her lips.

Grace swivelled her head at the slam of a door. A few patrons threw disgruntled glances, but most were mesmerised by the screen. Anna stormed down the aisle, followed by Bea. Grace pinned herself to the wall as they paused a few feet away.

'Geez, Mom, I don't want to meet another potential father. Are you that shallow you can't survive without a man? I've been on my own my whole life. I've never relied on a soul, least of all you.'

Grace watched her friend's face crumple in the face of her daughter's fury. 'Anna, please . . .' Bea pursued her down the aisle as she picked her way to a seat in the centre. Her raised voice was audible over the film. 'It's not a man I want to introduce you to, it's a woman. Anna, I'm a lesbian.'

Bea came out to her daughter so loud, half the audience refocused their attention. Some even let out a cheer.

Anna shot out of the row and back up the opposite aisle before disappearing through the double doors.

CHAPTER 70

Eddie tore his gaze from the projection room window. Whatever had taken place between Anna and her mother, she looked distraught. Charlie, having witnessed the scene too, came to his side.

'That's the girl, Anna, the one you like,' he shouted over the clatter of the projector.

Eddie glanced at him, curious about what his mother had said.

'She seems pretty upset,' Charlie observed. 'Looks like she could use a friendly ear right now.' He turned to face him. 'I'm not sure why you're still standing here since you've got me to run the film.' His eyes creased in amusement.

'Right.' Eddie backed away to the door.

In the foyer he almost collided with his mother, who was shepherding Bea to the kiosk.

'Where's Anna?' he asked.

'I don't know, but find her, Ed.'

He nodded and made for the glass-fronted doors.

'Who's running the film?' his mother called after him.

He spun around. 'Dad.'

A gust of wind hit his face as he stepped into the chill night. Anna was leaning against the wall, swigging from a bottle of rosé. She glanced in his direction.

'Hey.'

'Hi.' He thrust his hands in his pockets.

'Sorry Mom and I fucked up your screening. What a way to come out to the world.' She took another swig and offered him the bottle. 'I'm drowning my sorrows, but you probably worked that out. I stole this from the cloakroom. Sorry about that too.'

Eddie took the bottle and leaned against the wall next to her. 'It's been quite an evening.'

'Why didn't you call me?' There was reproach in her voice.

'Did you want me to call you?'

'Answer the question, Eddie.'

'There was this weird tension. I thought maybe you were a bit confused. I didn't want to add to that confusion.' Eddie took a drink. He could hear her breathing next to him, her face in shadow against the lights from the foyer. 'I've just spent the best part of an hour with my dad.'

'Oh yeah? How was it?'

He shrugged. 'I like him.'

'How's your mom feel?'

'Your guess is as good as mine. I had this ridiculous notion they were going to run into each other's arms like in a movie.'

'The night is young.'

He smiled. 'I keep thinking what a waste, all those years we could have been a family. I can't help feeling sad about that.'

'They might have ended up hating each other and splitting up in a bitter divorce.'

Eddie laughed. 'You're not in the mood for fairy tales this evening.'

Anna moved to face him. 'In my experience they don't happen often.' She grabbed the bottle back. 'Look at my fucked-up mom.'

'She's not so bad. I had an interesting conversation with her earlier.'

'Easy for you to say. You have the best mother in the world. She might even be the reason I've fallen for you.'

Eddie felt his heart contract. 'What did you say?'

'I said,' Anna took another swig, 'your mother might be the reason I've fallen for you.'

Eddie grabbed the bottle and took a fortifying drink. 'That's the un-sexiest thing I've ever heard.'

Anna grinned. 'I know, right?'

'Is it true?'

'Which bit?'

'The fallen-for-me bit.'

'Give me the bottle. I can't answer without a drink in my hand.'

Eddie set the bottle on the ground out of her reach. 'Nope, how drunk are you?'

'Drunk enough I don't care that I humiliated myself in front of the entire audience. Sober enough I might regret this conversation if you don't do something about it in the next five seconds.'

Eddie counted down to three, savouring the anticipation before pressing his lips against hers.

At that moment the cinema door swung open.

'Sorry to interrupt,' Bea said as he and Anna sprang apart.

'Mom, you have impeccable timing.'

Bea's eyes were red. It was obvious she'd been crying. 'Can we talk?'

Eddie squeezed Anna's hand. 'I'd better get back inside.'

A grin was still stuck to his face as he made for the projection room door.

Linda intercepted him. She looked a bit like one of those Spice Girls. 'Don't go up there.'

Eddie frowned. 'Why not? Charlie's on his own.'

'He has a helper. I saw your mum go up five minutes ago.'

'Right, well, okay then.' He followed Linda into the auditorium and leaned against the wall, surveying his packed cinema.

He couldn't quite believe he'd pulled it off. Restored the Tivoli and brought his staff together. He'd be paying for the renovations for months but hopefully it would be worth it in the end. After a few minutes, Anna appeared at his side.

'Everything okay with your mum?' he whispered.

'Yeah, we're all having brunch tomorrow — Mom, Miranda, you and me.' She leaned her head against his shoulder. 'If you don't have other plans?'

He didn't.

CHAPTER 71

Grace took the reel from Charlie and slotted the spool onto the winding bench. She wound the film back with the hand crank while Charlie loaded the final reel onto the second projector ready to make the switch that would be indiscernible to the audience downstairs in the auditorium. They worked in rhythm, their concentration claimed by the task at hand.

She placed the reel back in its can, added it to the pile and joined him at the projector. He threw her a smile and positioned himself ready to make the switch. She waited and watched, drinking in the face that had haunted her dreams and invaded her kisses for over forty years. Dust motes frolicked in the beam of the projection light, then she heard the clunk and the first projector ground to a halt. Grace ran the reel off, glad to have something to occupy her hands.

With the final reel running, Charlie joined her at the winding bench.

She glanced up, finding herself the subject of his steady gaze.

'It was you, wasn't it, who taught me to use a projector?' she asked, too aware of her actions under his scrutiny.

Charlie looked a little sheepish. 'You were a natural.'

'I'm grateful. It opened the door to a career I loved and allowed me to build a life for me and Ed.'

'You remembered things like that?' His expression was open, interested.

Grace nodded. 'Skills came to me, almost as muscle memory. It was people and the details of my life I couldn't remember.'

His gaze flickered to the projector then back to her face. 'I wanted to apologise for springing Viv and Michael on you earlier. They were so excited. I should have—'

'It's fine,' Grace cut him off. 'I'm sorry for the way I reacted. It never occurred to me I might see Michael tonight. It was a shock.'

'Have you had a chance to speak to him?'

'I have.' She lowered her focus to the film she was winding and kept it there. 'He told me how hard it was for you, when you believed I was dead. I wish I'd been brave enough to search harder for the answers. I hate to think of your suffering.'

Charlie busied himself readying the can.

'You don't have to talk about it if you don't want to, Charlie.'

He turned back to face her. 'It's not that. I feel a little foolish.'

'Why foolish?' She placed the reel in the can he held open.

'It broke me in ways it's taken me years to understand.'

Grace didn't know how to comfort him, but she longed to.

He added the can to the pile and leaned against the winding bench. 'I thought grief was something you eventually got over or repackaged into a more manageable size, but as life went on, I realised grief has its own force, its own agenda, and you're never done with it. Even now, with you standing before me, the grief of what we lost is as potent as ever.' He held her gaze for a moment then looked away. 'I sometimes wonder what I've done with my life.'

'Your life has meaning, Charlie. You've touched Michael, Viv, Linda, Ben and Hayley's lives, now mine and Ed's.'

341

He smiled, those dimples. 'Anyway, your brother has a big mouth.'

Your brother, she still struggled to get used to the idea. It was incredible to think of this other person who shared her blood. Who could fill in the gaps of her past. 'I'm sorry I haven't had a chance to speak to Viv.'

'You will. Michael and Viv are jet-lagged, and in any case, this was Eddie's evening. There'll be plenty of time to get to know them.'

Grace moved to the projection window, a little over-whelmed. 'And I'll get to know you too.'

Charlie's eyes twinkled. 'How about we start with my favourite film? It was a question you asked me the first time I brought you up here and I never answered.'

'Did I tell you my favourite film?'

He looked pleased with himself. '*Casablanca*, of course.'

'Ah yes, the proposal, but it's not my favourite film anymore.'

He raised an eyebrow. 'Interesting . . . what is?'

'I want to know yours first.'

Charlie joined her at the projection window. 'Back then, I have no idea, but now . . . the film playing out on screen.'

'*Cinema Paradiso?*'

He shrugged. 'It's about a projectionist. What's not to like?'

Grace laughed, and something inexplicable happened in her stomach. She could see why Connie had fallen in love with him. Perhaps she was in danger of falling herself. Only time would tell.

Her gaze returned to the window. In the auditorium below, she could just make out Anna leaning against Ed. She beckoned to Charlie and he glanced down at them too. His smile was as wide as hers.

The final scene of the film started. The hairs on the back of her neck stood on end. Funny how the denouement of a good film could make that happen. Grace turned to Charlie.

His eyes met hers and she realised she wanted to experience what it was like to kiss Charlie Smith, not just as fragmented memory, but for real. Grace pressed her lips briefly against his. For a second, he looked startled, then gently cupped her face in his hands. 'I think we can do better than that,' he whispered.

The credits rolled behind them, and downstairs people were vacating seats and shuffling to the auditorium doors. In the projection room, Grace kissed a man she hadn't kissed for forty-five years. She didn't know if this was the start of something or an opportunity to indulge in a vague nostalgia. In that moment, Grace thought about all the lives she'd lived and knew, beyond all doubt, her favourite was the one she was living right now.

THE END

343

ACKNOWLEDGEMENTS

Thank you to my editor, Emma Grundy Haigh, and the Choc-Lit team for believing in this novel and making my publication dreams come true. It's been a joy working with you. Thanks to my wonderful agent, Saskia Leach at Kate Nash Literary Agency, for taking a chance on me and my writing. I'm excited for what's ahead.

Thanks to Jenny Kane — your cheerleading, wise counsel and encouragement gave me the confidence to pursue this path. Thanks to Sara Cox for brilliant writing advice and support. Both the Cheshire Novel Prize and Summer School took my writing craft to a new level.

Thank you to my talented writing friends for their insightful feedback. Lottie McKnight, friend, walking buddy and sounding board. Members of the Half-baked manuscript club: Inge Van de Plas, Nick Paul, Hugh Ryan, Eliza Aiken, Mark Dudley and Steph Pomfrett. I can't overstate the value of this community.

In the research of this novel, my thanks to the Bill Douglas Cinema Museum for access to their collection of books and cinema ephemera. The Museum of Mid-Devon Life, where I trawled through newspaper archives to discover what films were shown at the Tivoli and the details of the fire which helped shape my story. Merlin Cinemas for allowing me access to the Tivoli so I could glimpse behind the scenes. The Exeter Memories website and Facebook community, both of which were invaluable to my research into the Odeon cinema and the city during the time the book is set. Lawrence Sutcliffe, friend and film enthusiast, for advice on films, projectors and books. Julian Del Giudice, fellow film archivist, for help with nitrate film research. Author Morwenna Blackwood for giving me insight into what Tiverton was like in the 1990s.

A huge thank you to my family. My sister, Hilary Geilinger, for steadfast belief, encouragement and feedback. My husband Darren and son John for giving me the time and support to write and accepting my hermit-like existence. My cat Ditsy, the perfect writing companion. My dad, who taught me to pursue my dreams with tenacity. I wish you were still with us to see those dreams come true.

THE CHOC LIT STORY

Established in 2009, Choc Lit is an independent, award-winning publisher dedicated to creating a delicious selection of quality women's fiction.

We have won 18 awards, including Publisher of the Year and the Romantic Novel of the Year, and have been shortlisted for countless others. In 2023, we were shortlisted for Publisher of the Year by the Romantic Novelists' Association.

All our novels are selected by genuine readers. We are proud to publish talented first-time authors, as well as established writers whose books we love introducing to a new generation of readers.

In 2023, we became a Joffe Books company. Best known for publishing a wide range of commercial fiction, Joffe Books has its roots in women's fiction. Today it is one of the largest independent publishers in the UK.

We love to hear from you, so please email us about absolutely anything bookish at choc-lit@joffebooks.com

If you want to hear about all our bargain new releases, join our mailing list: www.choc-lit.com/contact